Fascist Rock: Stories of Rebellion first published in 1990 by Times Editions Pte Ltd; *Saving the Rainforest and Other Stories* first published in 1993 by Times Editions Pte Ltd; *The Gunpowder Trail and Other Stories* first published in 2003 by Times Media Pte Ltd, with support from the National Arts Council of Singapore.

Cover design: Steven Tan

Published by Marshall Cavendish Editions
An imprint of Marshall Cavendish International
1 New Industrial Road, Singapore 536196

Other Marshall Cavendish Offices:
Marshall Cavendish International. PO Box 65829 London EC1P 1NY, UK • Marshall Cavendish Corporation. 99 White Plains Road, Tarrytown NY 10591-9001, USA • Marshall Cavendish International (Thailand) Co Ltd. 253 Asoke, 12th Flr, Sukhumvit 21 Road, Klongtoey Nua, Wattana, Bangkok 10110, Thailand • Marshall Cavendish (Malaysia) Sdn Bhd, Times Subang, Lot 46, Subang Hi-Tech Industrial Park, Batu Tiga, 40000 Shah Alam, Selangor Darul Ehsan, Malaysia.

Marshall Cavendish is a trademark of Times Publishing Limited

National Library Board Singapore Cataloguing in Publication Data
Tham, Claire, 1967-
The Claire Tham collection. – Singapore : Marshall Cavendish Editions, c2010.
p. cm.
ISBN-13 : 978-981-4302-83-8

I. Title.

PR9570.S53
S823 – dc22   OCN630007837

Printed in Singapore by Times Printers Pte Ltd

the CLAIRE THAM COLLECTION

Marshall Cavendish
Editions

CONTENTS

THE GUNPOWDER TRAIL AND OTHER STORIES

ABOUT THE AUTHOR

FASCIST ROCK: STORIES OF REBELLION

Baby, You Can Drive My Car

The only reason I went out with James in the beginning was because of his car.

I was sixteen, he was twenty, and he drove a BMW that rode smooth as velvet. (On such bases do the world's great romantic partnerships begin.) I loved cars, speed, things fast, the sensation of being wind-borne. I also had a tacky tinsel imagination: when I was older I was going to get myself a Parisian page-boy haircut, black shades and long golden droplets for earrings and cruise around in an open-top car making all the boys on the street corner go, *Waah!* This was the most complete antithesis I could think of to living with my mother in a crumbling post-war flat earmarked for demolition, where the corridors were so pitch-dark I imagined molesters to be lurking in the shadows. Small weedy men with hollow chests and nervous tics. Then again my mother belonged to the sterner school of Confucian morals, where school, studying and success were the ruling triumvirate. I escaped with a vengeance into a fake magazine existence— white villa and the sound of the sea in the morning. Which brings me to James and his car.

Then, he was just emerging from the NS cocoon. His father had been ambassador to some West European country, his mother was a lawyer, he was entered for medicine; the world, as far as I could see, was handed to him on a platter, but all he did was to look at it with detachment through the black blindman's glasses he used to wear. With his shaved head, the glasses made him look like a Chinese Mafioso. "Eyes tell lies," he said; he liked to kid me in a dry, ironical way which I didn't think funny. Five years of being bounced around the globe had made him impervious to the things which excited the rest of us; in addition he seemed to have read almost everything and he had a habit of correcting me in a mechanical way that drove me mad.

"You're a bloody condescending know-all!" I'd yell.

He would consider this dispassionately. "Yeah, I suppose that makes me sound pretty gruesome, doesn't it?"

"You don't even bother to deny it! What are you, God?"

He never raised his voice in an argument, which was what impressed me most in the beginning, coming fresh from all-night shouting sessions with my mother. His self-control was pitched to perfection, partly because, I think, he didn't care about anything too much. He was also given to saying things like, "Frankly, I don't think the political situation in Warsaw will warrant a resumption of the Cold War mentality," which to me was plain showing off; in those days I suspected everyone of trying to be superior.

We went to parties where I was the youngest and didn't know anybody and guys with gelled rainforest hair and beaded sweaters would ask me whose kid sister I was. Every hairdresser in town would be there, frantically ululating in his clothes like a giraffe in the wind; models resembling Eiffel Towers wrapped in layers of Versace would come jellyfish-wobbling in; deejays with bracelets would darling everyone in annoying transatlantic accents interspersed with bizarre *lah*'s. The menagerie was completed by every Bright Young Thing, would-be popstar and magazine journalist; the constituents of the so-called avant-garde scene. I don't know what James found in their natural idiocy and charming narcissism—some unthinking release, perhaps. He never confided in me. As for me—man, I was dazzled. I thought this was the secret to life, the universe and everything: the secret was hedonism and talking about the emptiness of modern life with casual references to Kierkegaard—which was not exactly the best training for someone who still had to go to school every day to listen to searing excoriations on the subject of pink socks.

I remember a party where a girl in a diamante dress standing in the middle of the room suddenly burst out crying; the glass she was holding slipped through her long chopstick fingers to the floor, while the tears, coursing down her face, dissolved rouge, lipstick and eyeshadow in long colourful streamers. I never found out why she was crying; people I asked later simply looked blank. When Joo Kwan disappeared after June 4th— he simply failed to show up anywhere—I ran into the same complicity of silence, as though they were all trying collectively to blank out some distasteful memory. You could fall through a trapdoor at their feet, and they wouldn't blink. In those days I seldom read the papers—and never the obituaries.

Joo Kwan was James's friend, a six-foot string-bean with hair like thatch and a wild, lopsided grin that showed one tooth; an exuberant madman obsessed with his own fantastical world. He took nothing seriously, found everything funny, even the army. I used to wonder how he and James got along: James was nothing like him; James also disliked the army. The dislike, according to Joo Kwan, was cordially reciprocated: James's C.O. thought he was an arrogant son of a five-letter word, the reason being that James had shown a marked lack of enthusiasm for confirming his masculinity by singing a dirty song on the way to Pulau Tekong.

"Oh, James can't pretend," Joo Kwan said. "If he thinks something's stupid, by his standards anyway, he shows it. A very uncomfortable person to live with. Actually," he added dreamily, "the only reason we get along is mutual stinking wealth. There's nothing that quite binds souls together like money."

He liked to think he was jaded ("I'm *so* jaded, for God's sake") but he was one of the few people I knew who got high on life itself and especially the movies. He tramped after every horror flick, every Kurosawa and Truffaut screened here: "I love French films, man. No, no, I *adore* them, darling. One never knows what's happening. People walk in a garden and talk and there's a wonderful Freudian moment when a little girl's uncle taps her on the knee with a mallet. Perhaps he was a doctor, but the exact significance of the action, my dear, escapes me for the moment, *lah*."

His other fascination was America; America for some reason was dreamscape to him, an extended fantasy sequence from a movie musical; it was Chandler's L.A. and Martin Scorsese's New York, a place where things could happen around the corner without any particular wonder. It started with Kerouac's beat visions. Up till then he'd read nothing but Graham Greene and the post-war British novelists; after Kerouac he went on a literary rampage: "You know what I think of, when I think of Britain? Stodgy food. Vaguely left-wing soggy liberals who've been refined and civilised to a point where they don't know how to get a kick out of life any longer. America, man, America's a figment of the romantic imagination...

"'So in America when the sun goes down and I sit on the old broken-down pier watching the long long skies over New Jersey and sense all that raw land that rolls in one unbelievable bulge over to the West Coast...'"; those lines from the last paragraph *of On The Road* for some reason would make him laugh and cry and bang on the table: "That's poetry, man, that's poetry, what d'you need stanzaic forms for? Poetry oh boy is feeling!"

"Hark at the great soul-boy," James said sarcastically.

"James always reads me like a book, don't you? I'm Chinese but I've got rhythm in my soul and nothing to work it out on, so help me, brother—"

James looked at him with his quizzical, half-twisted smile. "You're nuts," he said kindly. "You're not black, white, or native American. You live here. You probably have to live here for the rest of your life."

Joo Kwan howled. "Well, for God's sake, that's it, don't you see?"

I knew what he meant. Ways of Escape. James hadn't a clue because nothing touched James, or so I thought.

"Tell me what you want to be," Joo Kwan said abruptly.

"A doctor," James said, to humour him.

"Not what you are going to be. What you want to be."

"Can we cease this puerile conversation, huh?"

"I'll tell you," Joo Kwan said. "You want to be a religious mendicant. You're nothing but a sad-eyed, ascetic truth-seeker with no truth left to seek. You were born in the wrong century, James." He said to me, "D'you know what happened when James was twelve?"

"Shut up," James said.

"He went through a solemn little apostasy of his own. We were both Catholics and he tried to practise a bit of Nietzschean philosophy on me, only we didn't know what it was. 'God is dead.' So we went to this brother who taught us and he absolutely disgusted James by saying he was one of those who can never stray very far from God, whether he likes it or not. He's tied, hand and foot, while we sinners have to pray like mad to keep within sight of land. 'Snot fair, man. So what d'you think?"

"Being Christian here is just a middle-class phenomenon," James said matter-of-factly. He was tapping his fingers, his eyes narrowed and looking into the distance as if he saw some indefinable object we didn't. "Why the hell are we talking about this anyway?"

"I'm drunk," Joo Kwan said. "When I'm drunk I sober up."

He asked me to dance. His dancing was peculiar, like a road-runner's energetic walk.

"Do you always talk about stuff like that?" I had to shout to make myself heard.

"Stuff like what?"

"God and stuff."

"God and stuff," Joo Kwan repeated thoughtfully. "Hey, what a great title for a book ... No, not always. But James—he's a very peculiar guy. I used to think, drop any of us on an island in the middle of the ocean and we'd go raving mad from the isolation in a week, but not James. Indestructible sanity. Frightening, man." He said, "Music's giving me a headache."

"So why do you come to parties like this?"

"Me?" He laughed. "I hate being alone. It's as simple as that. I'm a very uncomplicated homo sapien. I crave human warmth. In return I exude my fascinating charm. It works both ways."

I kicked him in the leg. "Ouch," he said politely. "So why do *you*?"

Why *did* I? "I want to have a good time. I'm sick of being like everybody else. I hate school. I want to die young. That's about all." I must have been drunk. My mother would've died.

"You like to think you're tough, don't you?"

"It's a good defence," I said airily.

"Poor James."

That was the last thing he said to me. About a month later I overheard a guy on a phone say in exasperated tones, "I keep telling you, Joo Kwan's dead." Finally I got someone to tell me the truth. Apparently a grenade had blown up in his face in the army.

I didn't fully take it in until some days later, when my mother and I were having dinner and the wailing banshee sounds of the neighbours' Cantonese opera were renting the air. I burst out suddenly; my mother put down her chopsticks, stared at me judicially and waited for me to stop.

"So—you don't like the food, is that it?" she said drily.

"No; a friend died."

She looked at me doubtfully. She had a long Modigliani face, cheekbones high and protruding, her mouth small, closed and tight; her hair was pulled back into a bun. "So— was it cancer?"

"No—he was in NS—killed by a grenade."

"You know I don't like you mixing with all kinds of riff-raff from NS," my mother said automatically, "but you never listen to me, do you?" I had to get out; the food was choking in my throat. My mother wanted to know where I was going. Out. Out where? Out, out damn spot—out where Joo Kwan's death meant something more than the crockery on the table.

"Sit down," my mother said peremptorily. "Term is going to start and I want you to study." I said the thought of studying made me physically sick and she got into her I Carried You For Nine Months routine, a routine not even the Marx brothers could salvage after the hundredth replay. "Look, look, I'd've been premature if I'd known how!"

In her special, quiet voice that's supposed to tear at my heartstrings, she said, "How can you speak such a thing to me?" but I was sick of the sad old lie that won't drop dead: you owe that devouring monster, your family, your mother, you owe us, you owe us! I don't owe anybody a damn thing.

Somehow whenever I looked at my mother I seemed to see two thousand years of Chinese mothers' sufferings etched in her face; she always had this guilt-ridden effect on people. Perhaps she had it on my father too—he left when I was five and never returned. My mother's face goes grey when the black sheep is mentioned. My mother, you have to understand, is one of those people whose suffocating intensity of moral purpose could blight you with more devastating effect than a nuclear holocaust.

By then I was out of the flat and down the midnight-ridden stairs. I knew what she'd do after I'd left: she'd sit for a while composing herself, then she'd clear the table and light the joss-sticks for my father and me. If there's one thing I hate, it's being prayed over. It makes me feel like the sacrificial lamb. I knew I was being unfair, but I was past caring. I walked along, kicking stones, not thinking.

On a sudden impulse, I went to a call-box and called James up. His mother answered the phone: "James, did you say? James is rather busy at the moment—" Then I heard James: "For goodness' sake, Mum." "She sounds," his mother said with finality, "rather young." James himself sounded surprised to hear me; I'd never bothered to ring him before.

I waited for him by the call-box, watching the light fade. People our age didn't die, at least not within my immediate experience; those who did were always friends of friends of friends; somehow you always felt safe yourself, within a circle of good luck and immunity; and the worst of it was, while I was standing there, still seeing Joo Kwan's face before me, my mind kept playing, as though a record needle had got stuck in a groove: *The sun is up, The sky is blue, It's beautiful and so are you, Dear Prudence, won't you open up your mind?* over and over again, maddeningly.

James came after fifteen minutes; I got in and he drove off without a word.

"Why didn't you say he was dead?" I said at last when he didn't volunteer a remark.

"What's the point of talking about it?"

What was the— "I liked him. A lot."

"I liked him too. He was my best friend."

"You might show a little more emotion," I said nastily.

"I can't break down to order."

"You never break down." I kicked the dashboard, I flung myself back in the seat, I did everything bad method actors do to simulate Grief, Rage and Unadulterated Despair. "You're just a f__king ice-machine!" He didn't even bother to be shocked.

"Listen," he said, "I was going to meet some friends tonight. You might as well come. That is, if you want to." I shrugged. James, the King of the Easter Island effigies.

I don't remember which hotel it was. There were three of them, two boys, Tien and Alphonsus, and a girl. I didn't listen to their conversation, which was all about someone going to the States to study journalism: "He'll probably settle there, what the hell, can you imagine him coming back with the political atmosphere here?" They depressed me; I could imagine whole groups of them, all over the island, rabbitting on in their pale, pseudo-angst-ridden tones, being collectively world-weary. I was tired of pretension that night. I sat pulling a serviette to bits; James gave me a slightly appraising glance, smiled quickly and looked away again. He sat for the most quiet without saying anything, one arm flung across the back of the seat.

Finally someone said, "Hey, James, why so silent, huh?"

He shrugged. "You're saying it all." Halfway through he and Alphonsus went off to the men's; and a leaden silence enveloped the rest of us. Tien and the girl exchanged expressive glances over the top of my head; I guess I knew what they were thinking: that James's last steady but one had been a first-year at Harvard. How the gods had descended from Mount Olympus, etc ... the mind boggled. Man, I didn't care—I was in it for the fun and the drink and if he was going through a regressive phase of liking uncultured gamins in jeans who didn't know who Nietzsche was, that was his own problem. I didn't like or dislike him; neutrality was the essential keyword.

Ten minutes ticked past. A waiter hovered in the background like a large spider. "Gosh, they've been gone long enough for five spontaneous cases of diarrhoea to erupt," Tien said.

"Erk." (Erk, my God.) "Do you have to be so crude?"

When they did come back, James had his glasses on. Alphonsus walked several paces behind him, giving him quick apprehensive glances. He touched James solicitously on the shoulder; James jerked his whole arm away. The other boy's face flamed. "Sorry," James said at last. "I think we'd better leave."

"You all right?" Tien said curiously.

"Sure," James said irritably. The fingers of his right hand kept flicking over, caressing, an odd dark-coloured spot on the back of his left. "Listen, I have to make a call first." We watched him go out again.

Alphonsus flopped into a chair in relief. "You'll never believe what happened," he announced. He leant forward, arms on the table. Apparently, James had had a dizzy spell in the rest-room, but he'd recovered after a while and asked for a cigarette; having lit it, however, he'd seemed to be mesmerised by the red glow creeping up the fag, "like a disease," he'd remarked. Then, with unerring precision, he'd stubbed it out on the back of his hand, slowly, giving off a stench of burnt flesh.

"I grabbed it away," Alphonsus said. "There was no one else inside and I was terrified. I asked him what the hell he thought he was doing. I was shouting, man. James just said, Look, what sort of difference would it make if I simply stubbed out the rest of myself? I went near-crazy. Danced up and down. Carried on like my own father would about university and life and getting married and having great children and he stood there against the sink, not listening, staring at nothing in particular."

They were all three silent. "God, he needs help," Tien said at last.

I slid out of my seat and went out to look for James; he'd finished his call but was standing there absently flicking the dial with his finger. He saw me, his finger arrested in the dial, then came over and we went out to the car-park.

Now it was my turn to be quiet. I was trying to take it in that James had actually used himself as the equivalent of a human ashtray. It was, categorically, not sane. One up to James, Joo Kwan ... The car squealed out to the main road; Orchard Road was lighted up like some vast pathway in the night. James picked up speed when we left the area; now the wind was tearing through the car like a crazy banshee, shearing our hair and making it fly out perpendicular to the ears.

"Where're we going?" He said he wanted to drive up the PIE to calm himself down. I leant both arms out of the window, wished we weren't bipeds, what a rotten slow way of getting around. Who was it who said man's first instinct is to eat, the second to fly?

"Do you want your arms chopped off or what?" James said patiently.

"I didn't stub a cigarette out on myself," I pointed out.

He was silent for a while. "I don't know why I did that."

He flicked radio channels restlessly, but this wasn't Joo Kwan's America; there were only Radios One and Five and the BBC. Six pips sounded, the signal for the news.

"Let's not listen to the news, huh?"

"*Ssh*," he said. There was the usual recital, Lebanon, the Middle East, Vietnam; I switched off.

I was staring at, without seeing, the rows of flats we passed, grey monolithic structures with the white fluorescent lights coming off like a luminous unearthly glow. Within six months my mother and I were supposed to move to a new flat of our own—

Then it said on the news that John Lennon was dead, killed by a gunman outside his New York apartment; and in the wind I imagined a gunshot, a crack that was so realistic that I nearly jumped. James said, very softly, "Oh, my God," and switched off the radio.

"Hey," I said, but when I turned it on again the skiing results were being read out. I was always baffled by the pre-ponderance of skiing news, which surely had less relevance to us than Morris dancing. Why not polo or snooker or racquet-ball?—but I was digressing; I didn't want to think about what I'd heard.

I glanced across at James and got a shock. He was crying, without a sound. A single tear was making its way down his face; it dribbled into the corner of his mouth and he licked at it. I sat there, curled up, embarrassed, all the fury earlier in the evening damped out like dying embers. I tried to think back to the last major rock star's death that I remembered. Marc Bolan, with his green eye shadow—Elvis, of course. The Day The King Died, the papers screamed, but I was twelve then and Elvis' death meant nothing: he was the hero of jocks and men with sideburns who sat around with beer glasses in their hands waxing nostalgic and the awful Elvis impersonators who gyrated across our screens on variety show night. But John Lennon—man, he was different, he was the thin scarecrow with the prim round glasses and the long nose quivering in amusement at himself, the confused idealist who said, *I Am The Walrus*...

"I heard it earlier this evening," James said; "I couldn't believe it. I mean, why him, why not some fat-assed politician ordering another round of missiles—"

He was crying so bad by then he had to pull over by the side of the road; he leant against the door, his hand shielding, no, crawling over, his face, all the while making these hiccupping, coughing noises which he was trying to stifle; and it wasn't only the murder by then, it was some other grief, his whole life perhaps, Lennon's death being the wholly unexpected catalyst. I didn't know what to do. "Hey, James—" I took his hand and he gripped mine so hard I thought the bones would break ... So anyway there we were stuck in the middle of nowhere keeping our own messy vigil for a snuffed-out rock icon ... Finally the crying died away altogether; he ran his hands through his hair, slowly at first, then frantically, then slammed his fist against the window. It didn't shatter. He sat, head on hand, staring out at the road.

"So was he a personal friend of yours or what?"

He gave a tired half-grin. "C'mon—But I mean, when you've grown up with someone's music—Joo Kwan and me—it's like—losing—I don't know——a part of you—" He spoke slowly, with difficulty, almost as though every word was a wrench. "We bought every single Lennon release. There wasn't anybody else—" Elvis was a white rhinestone has-been hiding behind an electric fence in Memphis; Bob Dylan was drifting; no one took Bowie seriously yet—"and he was the Thinking Beatle, right, the one who had a response to everything; we were regular little intellectual snobs ... Sometimes you tend to remember whole bits of your life by the music coming out then—1970, it was Instant Karma, yeah, gonna get you; '75, Shaved Fish—Shaved Fish, I loved that album title, man ... just snatches of songs, y'know, defining certain times for you."

He was talking about the old Elvis-when-I-was-young syndrome. I didn't want to interrupt—I mean, I admired John Lennon, okay, but it was nothing like the intense mystical experience it seemed to have been for James.

He said nothing for a while. "Joo Kwan—" he stopped, he tried to laugh. "He had this smuggled copy of the *Two Virgins* LP when it was the next worst thing after communism, nature as nature meant it to be. It was an investment. He said it was going to be worth, what, $200 in the year 2000."

I knew about the *Two Virgins* LP. He'd shown it to me.

James tried again. "He was my best friend, man."

"You said that before. Like it didn't mean a thing."

"It's a fallacy," he said, "to assume every death must have a meaning. God, I hate it when people say, He didn't die in vain. Death's meaningless, an end-stop, and any amount of window-dressing isn't going to change it." He was angry now, biting his lower lip.

"That's what I kept thinking. At his funeral. He hadn't any face left to speak of, from the grenade, I mean. His mother was having hysterics and his grandfather, ninety and gaga, was going, Whose funeral is it? Why doesn't someone tell me? and I was blank, man, I couldn't feel a thing, I couldn't get up at the memorial service and make all those I-knew-him-when-he-had-a-face remarks, couldn't even react to the phony In-the-midst-of-life-we-are-in-death platitudes. I just kept thinking, so what? What difference does it make? I thought there was something wrong with me."

His hand was knocking, absently, against the window. "Even now—I can't feel it except through someone else's death. Someone I never even knew. It makes you wonder about yourself, I'll tell you.

"Maybe it's because I've read and listened myself blind," he said. "I see everything second-hand, in terms of, 'what category of impact would it make?' Maybe it's all those years of retreats and sharing sessions at the Catholic schools I've gone to, disliking the psycho-therapy jargon, shutting my self off, being deliberately pig-headed. Maybe it's just me."

I didn't understand him. I didn't understand this looking at yourself from the outside, fly-on-the-wall technique, seeing yet not seeing yourself. I wanted to smash something, anything as recompense; I didn't want to sit, and critically analyse my emotions. Talk about clinical detachment—but then he'd cried. James Had Cried. It was like Garbo talking, no less.

"Oh God," he said, "I wish I were dead."

He looked at me. "Anyway, that's why I didn't want to talk about it." He released my hand and I flexed my fingers, covertly.

"So what're you going to do?" I said, idiotically.

"I don't know. Let's run away together."

"Shut up."

"Where the hell would we run to anyway?" James said. "Ama Keng? Christ, I wish we could get away. Somewhere where you aren't expected to make something of yourself. I'm sick of-expectations ... Sick of staying on an island no longer than a peanut. Problem is you have to share that peanut too with about two million others—" His mouth was compressed, eyes narrowed, the closed look on his face again.

"You said we were all doomed to staying here. Joo Kwan was the one who wanted to break loose."

"I'm tired," he said.

Lights from the passing cars played over us. I don't know how long we sat there but the night air was cool and I was thinking, all you ever see of anybody is one-sixth of the iceberg and the rest is submerged wonder—which is something new to me. It felt like we were in limbo, nowhere definable, like the feeling you get when you've passed beyond the stage of mere sleepiness to some ultra-refined, ultra-alert state of consciousness and everything's weirdly clear which wasn't so before...

"Do you want to go home?" James said abruptly.

"No. Not really."

"All right." He let in the clutch, calm now. "I thought perhaps you wanted to."

"Hey, it's the night John Lennon died. We can't go home."

"Yeah?" He smiled suddenly, and I felt an awful compulsion to tell him about the lurid magazine fantasies and why I'd gone out with him in the first place. But I didn't.

He was talking again. I think it was a relief to him to talk, to spin words when they couldn't possibly mean a thing now. About how, as a kid, he used to go down to the Esplanade to watch the Indian boys scrabbling for worms in the mud at low tide, "—and once I saw this guy, some tourist, one of those knocking around on a shoestring budget, old pyjama pants, torn top, bearded, straight out of *On The Road*, and he sat on a bench eating cold baked beans out of a tin with a plastic spoon, oblivious to people staring. He was sitting and looking out to sea, just looking. I don't know what he saw, but I wish I saw it too. I told Joo Kwan later about it and he went crazy, said, yes, YES, that's what he'd meant all along and he said, how, whenever he went down there, he wanted to kick the railing in frustration because he couldn't bear to think that was the limit to where he could run."

"He was a madman," James said.

All of a sudden, he stuck his head out of the window and yelled, "You're a madman, you know that? Wherever you are!"

"What'd you do that for?"

"I don't know—" and the people across the street at the bus-stop jumped perceptibly and stared after us as if we were a cavalcade of lunatics; and it all seemed extremely hilarious somehow as we sped off; but it was a night of release and on the radio they were playing Imagine. For days after you couldn't turn it on without hearing his music.

A few weeks later it said in the papers a plot of land in New York's Central Park was to be called Strawberry Fields in memory of John Lennon. Joo Kwan would've loved that. Poetry oh boy is feeling.

Homecoming

There was a tap at the window; a pair of glasses was visible between the panes. He got up and went to the window. The man who stood outside was about forty, with a smooth clear skin and a slight paunch—it slopped out like a deflated punching bag over the low-slung belt around his waist.

"What do you want?" he said calmly: there was a hint of an accent in his voice and the man outside began to look faintly antagonistic.

"The owner of the flat died—about a week and a half ago and the HDB has taken the flat back. Strangers are not supposed to be walking in and out—"

"I'm his son," he said. "I've just returned from England and I'm sorting out my father's things."

The man said, "Really, ah? I didn't know he had a son. In fact, didn't even know he was married. He was so quiet, you know—"

"Yes, I know," the son said softly, and closed the window-panes, but so gently that it hardly seemed like a snub. There was a tentative tap at the window again; he ignored it and the tap was not repeated. Far below, he could hear someone's radio blaring out the American Top 40, while a piano was being thumped on in the flat above. He could even hear the raised voice of a mother furiously and nasally scolding her child in Hokkien. He had forgotten about the noise, all those years away, and he thought for a while about how noise even sounded different in a cold climate—it seemed to echo more, to have a quality of being suspended in air like fragile crystal-ware, giving a sense of breathless anticipation, of not knowing what to expect as you rounded a corner. Or so he thought. Here, noise seemed to come from the gut of some monster in the earth.

He roused himself. His father had slit his wrists and bled to death in his bed and he wanted to find a reason for it, if he could. The police had said, in a shocked way, Murder? Not this time, and they had stared accusingly at him, as though he had driven his father to suicide himself, and was now trying to cover up for it. Loneliness, they said glibly. The man had lived utterly alone for five years—no relatives to speak of, no wife (ran off with a foreigner, hadn't she?—bad lot), only son studying in the wilderness of Britain. No friends to speak of either—he was terribly reclusive, the neighbours said. Withdrawn. Retired, moreover, three years ago. Did nothing but stay in his flat all day, re-reading the papers and waiting for the day his son would come home. Well, then. Motives, reasons galore. He had wanted to shoot the whole police station to bits.

He stood in the middle of the sitting room and stared round—but it was no use, he could get up no feelings of regret, even recognition, for the home he'd once lived in. He thought the two-room flat looked terrible, with its mottled, aquamarine walls, mottled, aquamarine furniture, and the glaring starkness of those same walls and furniture.

He thought he remembered a faded Van Gogh print and three Chinese scrolls—they were gone. The closet in his father's room contained a week's change of clothes, all grey, all unironed, the artifacts of a man who did his own washing and had ceased to care what he wore. Under the bed he'd discovered a pile of magazines about China, dust-ridden. His father, he knew, had been born in Shanghai, had fled as a boy of eight on a boat to Hong Kong during the Second World War, then Singapore, all the while taking care of a younger brother who had eventually died of cholera. It was a spectacular immigrant's story—the stuff of tear-jerkers in the Chinese press. As a child, he had always enjoyed his father's narration:

He (prompting): Then what did you do, Dad, when you got to Hong Kong?

His father (sighing): *Aaia*, I was just eight, but what a resourceful eight! I sold newspapers, I shone shoes ... I undercharged the street price once by a cent and they pulled a knife on me—I ran incredible risks for that lousy cent! I held car doors open for the women at the Jockey Club, while dodging the commissionaire. Do you know, I would have held those car doors open for nothing. I just liked looking at a world I had no part of ... they wore the most marvellous dresses, I thought, particularly the Chinese women. They felt they had to keep their end up, I suppose...

His father had been a romantic, an unabashed sucker for sentiment and nostalgia. Even as an adult, he would take his only son with him in the evenings to a small hill-rise to watch the sun set and quote half-remembered snatches of poetry. His wife thought he was a right nutter; she said so, too. She made it clear that one had the prerogative to enjoy sunsets only after one had shown one could provide for the family—which he was rather inept in doing. It wasn't his father's fault, the boy thought loyally; even then he'd disliked his mother's no-nonsense realism, her work ethic, her battle-cry of, The Chinese are not like the others—we Chinese, we work.

(Thinking about it now, the man was reminded of the Indians and Pakistanis he'd met in England who said scornfully of the English that the only reason for unemployment was because the Anglo whites were afraid of getting their hands dirty.) Finally, though, his mother had relieved herself of her two burdens—there one day, gone the next—and she had never come back. The child had rather hoped she would; after all, she was still his mother and the only one of them who could cook properly—but she never had. He had given up hoping after a year.

Those magazines on China bothered him. Had his father been planning a trip with his CPF savings? He had distant cousins there, no more. Perhaps life in Singapore had become increasingly remote to him, as he lived alone, and only his childhood, in the so-called motherland, had been real to him. His father had given no inkling of the kind in his letters.

Those dry-as-dust, factual little letters that were each a replica of the ones before. He had always read them after his day at the university, standing by the window of the bed-sit he had rented to cut down on living expenses and which wasn't large enough to swing a cat in. He, too, had lived alone, and within the confines of the Asian community at the university. Read the letters while the Jamaicans next door played their reggae and got high on ganja and dreamed of the Rasta man free in his own land. The letters were like whispers through the crack in his mind which was the only admission he gave of the existence of his country. He had, for a while, gone through a violent phase of apostasy regarding the political and social systems he'd been brought up in; the other Singapore students, as a result, had cut him dead.

> *Dear son (the letters ran, in small, beautifully formed Chinese script), How are you? I read the London temperature in the papers today—ten degrees Celsius. It seems to me extremely cold. You had better keep warm. Thank you for your letter, but I don't want you to feel you are obliged to write regularly. Your studies are far more important, believe me. A scholarship student like you has far more to live up to than the ordinary paper chaser. I am well, myself. As you know, I have been following* The Father's House *on Channel 8; it is exciting stuff...*

They told nothing and gave nothing away and their tone remained the same even when the son was furiously scribbling out his spleen at the government who had sent him overseas and allowed his father to finally purchase his flat only in middle age. It was as though his father spoke his whimsy to some cardboard offspring he had stuck on a wall in his room, ignoring the real one. But that was his father, of course; he had realised that, when the exasperation had died down. His father's life's work had been to escape reality, all along.

He could not find any of his letters to his father, except for the last one, which had been found by his bedside. He was piqued at not finding any, and even hurt, for a moment—but his father had kept remarkably few things. No superfluous pieces of paper—no lists, no bills, no diaries, no books—only his most important documents, tied up with a rubber-band.

As though to be able to account for his existence if ever any mythical Secret Police broke in. No photographs, the son realised. No badly taken shots of him as a child, smirking horribly in various places of interest, no wedding snaps with everybody standing around trying to look as if they were enjoying themselves. No record of a life anywhere. He thought his father must have been trying to whittle himself out of memory and mind. Paring himself down to nothing.

He knew, now, why the police were so certain his father had committed suicide, despite the absence of a suicide note. How could you cry for a man who wanted so desperately to be forgotten?

He had never known his father. That sounded trite—after all, very few people did; their fathers were figures in the background, sources of funds, reproaches and unwanted advice. But his father hadn't even been that. He had always been shadowy and towards the end of his life he had stepped into the dark altogether and there was no spotlight strong enough to reclaim him.

For a moment, he was angry. He had *liked* those photographs, dammit, they were a part of the life he had left. He hated coming back to find a robbed and empty mausoleum. His father had had no *right*—

Going into his old room, he flung himself on his bed, staring at the ceiling. His father had left his things alone at least—the book prizes he'd won at school and never read, his track medals, other schoolboy bits and pieces. They revolted him now; everything in the flat revolted him and when he thought of the packet of sugar and tin of beans he'd found in the kitchen, nothing else, he wanted to throw up. War rations! What did his father do with the sugar? Lick it? Feed it to ants? Crunch it with his toes? And again the senselessness of his father's life and suicide struck him. Okay, so his father hadn't wanted to live, had nothing to live for. A son whom he hadn't seen for five years—the scholarship money didn't cover vacations—was nothing to live for and so he had left this life as quietly as he had lived it.

He wanted to shout, Murderer, and, What have you left *me* to live for now? He had wanted to come back, triumphant, with a First, and take care of his father in his old age, the old tale beloved of Chinese moralists, the tale of filial piety. Well, Dad, you had to take *that* away with you as well, didn't you, when you took everything else. Then he began to blame himself. He should have sensed that his father was slowly going under: anyone would, with nothing but four mottled aquamarine walls to talk to. He should have known. He should have brought his father out. He should have—

—slit his father's wrists for him. He lay for nearly an hour, fuming, battling his anger. Above him the piano-player crashed out the opening chords of Beethoven's *Fifth Symphony*, every chord with a note wrong. He winced, and sprang to his feet. "Shut up!" he yelled. The piano-playing stopped for an indignant moment, then resumed, louder, more defiant than ever. Instantly, he was ashamed of himself, and the shame made him snap back into the level-headed, even-handed, slightly aloof persona he carried about like a wallet. These things happen, he told himself. Of course they do. The world was going mad, that was all.

He wondered, with fleeting morbid fascination, what his father had looked like with his wrists slit. Like a victim, a martyr, slain on the bed of an indifferent society? Poetic, but unrealistic; fascinating, but unedifying. He had missed the funeral due to a mix-up of letters at the Post Office, which delayed the news, a strike at Heathrow, which delayed the flight. At the airport he had wrangled with a blonde-haired, halibut-faced man at the airline desk, who had said, "Really, these things are beyond our control," as if it were clear to the meanest intelligence. He had been sick in the men's room through fury and anxiety. He hadn't cried, but he had been sick, and he thought, wryly, someone should write a book about the different ways in which emotion grips people.

After five years, his country looked pretty much as it did. Greyer, higher, hotter, more sophisticated, perhaps. Hordes of Westernised, gaudy youths with spiky hair gleefully apeing street fashions culled from glossy magazines and videos crossed his path. He was taken aback. The bare bones of the street style were there, but the pissed-off contempt, the shock-for-the-hell-of-it, was not. There was no anger in their dressing. These kids *were* kids— let loose, riotously, in a fashion shop. More than ever, he felt disembodied, a ghost let off his chain to wander in increasing frustration.

He found that a couple of his father's old colleagues had paid and arranged for the funeral, in the son's absence. He visited each of these men in turn, to thank them; they avoided looking him in the eye, as though suicide were infectious. "Had to do it," they muttered. "Couldn't allow him to go unburied. Wouldn't have been decent. Nice man, your father—too quiet. Kept himself to himself—never really knew him." It could have been his father's epitaph.

He heaved himself off the bed, locked the flat up, emerged into the open. Sunlight glinted off the back of cars in the car-park and burnt the back of his neck. Children ran screaming between the cars. A couple of policemen were warning a boy not to cycle in the void deck, and he listened sullenly.

"You go and die!" a girl was screaming at her boyfriend—he glowered and marched off. He might just do that, kid.

Scraps of charred paper flew about; cans of melted wax with joss-sticks aslant in them stood on the grass. The Feast of the Hungry Ghosts, wasn't it? It sounded like the title of a slapstick movie.

When the letter came, he saw with surprise it was from the Singapore police. All sorts of impossible misdemeanours ran through his mind, all except the truth. He read the letter twice and turned off the radio, which had been playing *Afrika Bambaata*—he remembered that quirky detail because of the group's name. One of the Jamaicans banged on his door, crying: "You got a cigarette there, man?" though they knew he didn't smoke.

He made an airline reservation by phone, with no idea of the strike to come, astonished at the circumstances which had led to his homecoming. Whatever he had envisioned, it had not been this. He walked for two solid hours around the city, thinking of nothing in particular, and finally bought a bag of cherries for dinner.

There was a Singaporean family at the same fruit stall, trying to bargain—that, and their accents, had told him they were fellow countrymen.

They gave him The Look, which he had seen every member of a minority group give to another member of the same minority group on the streets of a foreign country. It was a look of furtive complicity, among other things, and it suddenly made him feel violently, identifiably, Singaporean—as though a mark had been burnt on his forehead.

But now that he was back, he felt nothing. Grief came and went in spasms. Most of the time he just felt a dull sense of loss. Like a missing tooth. Something taken for granted inexplicably wrenched away, and he was too tired to search for it again. Father, family, feeling, country. No more, man, no more. He would never come back again.

A Question of Song

Here we are! Here we are! In the Hall of Fame ... The putrescent little ditty rattled through Patsy's mind and refused to be dislodged by her valiant efforts to call up the sound of African Burundi drums. How much more of this? she thought, gazing at the seniors energetically conducting the frenzied chanting. Song-fights and mandatory cheering, it had been explained, were good for the soul—they fostered community spirit by making everyone participate, which was simply another way of saying that if you kept enough people in a state of stupefaction from mindless mass singing long enough you had a wonderful weapon of crowd manipulation.

"Patsy Lui!"

Irwin Goh was in third-year engineering, an aerobics freak who exuded a powerful smell of perspiration at all times. Patsy loathed him from his Adidas head-band to the dayglo socks he wore.

"You did not open your mouth to sing!"

There was mass silence while sixty pairs of freshman eyes rounded on Patsy and sixty throats took a well-deserved breather.

"You're mistaken," she said mildly.

"Don't answer back to a senior!"

Sod you, Patsy thought.

"Don't you have any fundamental sense of courtesy?"

"Is it called for in the circumstances?"

"We can't allow this to pass until you've made a full apology and promised to correct your attitude." Irwin was benevolent, even paternal, Il Duce leisurely exercising his power over an erring member in the throng. It was odd how even in the mildest, most flabby personality there was some power instinct lurking, merely waiting for the opportunity to be released; and how it disguised itself behind some catchall label of The Cause or The Spirit. No one would admit it was the sheer headiness of power, plain and simple, the sight of people snapping to attention, on edge, before you.

Patsy was boiling; she'd had enough of five-kilometre early morning runs ("Physical exercise is a very important tool in all-round conditioning"), being hauled out of bed at midnight to howl sinfully bad songs at an invading hostel group, folk-dancing hideous formations that couldn't possibly be claimed by any indigenous population with any respectability, going around reverentially intoning, Greetings, Senior Lady or Senior Gentleman as the case may be, and generally being pounded to an infinitesimal speck of dust. She was tired of the worn-out philosophy that it was a sign of moral courage to be able to take all kinds of crap and emerge unscathed, to inflict the same kind of crap on the next generation. Where was it written that the mark of civilisation is the ability to endure and perpetuate specified barbarities?

"My attitude's fine; it's your ego that needs checking."

The five seniors looked at one another; four of them, led by Irwin, hurriedly broke into *Here we are! Here we are!* while the fifth, a large girl called Janet who was Irwin's general factotum, hustled Patsy off and harangued her in a corner. Did she know, Janet said, how lucky she was to get into a university hostel that had a fine long tradition of Cabinet ministers and wonderful food? The least she could do was sing.

A red spark exploded in Patsy's brain. She would not sing. That was it. She simply would not sing. And by that infantile act of defiance she was going to express her wholesale contempt for the institutionalised fascism that was at work.

The Master of the Hall had made a moving after-dinner speech. He had cited Nzietsche, Spinoza and Woody Allen; as to the general substance, the audience, nodding off after Topnotch Telematch, was unclear. There was a two-hour break between dinner and mass dancing at eleven—"I'm not going," Patsy said, lying on her bed in her room, the Grateful Dead blasting away beside her ear.

"I don't know what's the matter with you," Lee Siu, her room-mate, was neat, invariably polite to her seniors and totally quiescent. She found Patsy inexplicable. "Why are you deliberately making trouble for yourself?"

"Because I can't stand it, that's why. I thought I'd come to university—definition: an institution of higher education—instead it's back to kindergarten, folks, with Ring A Ring O' Roses."

"It's not that bad," Lee Siu objected, with suppressed irritation. "If you can't take this now, how are you going to take anything later on?"

Patsy sat up in bed. "I'm tired of hearing this. Who's going to threaten you with physical jerks in an office?"

"It's not that," Lee Siu said. "You can't take criticism. You can't take orders. It's a negative attitude. All you English-educated are like that."

The way she enunciated 'English-educated', with ringing finality, seemed to put them on either side of a yawning divide. Patsy felt an obscure regret—she rather liked Lee Siu—also exasperation.

"Oh for God's sake, what's it got to do with what language stream we're in? Irwin speaks like a BBC twit and he's the worst of that little military junta. It's being treated like a—like a salad, tossed and turned and pulled in all directions, not being left alone, not even considered to exist outside their awareness of you."

Lee Siu looked at her with a peculiar expression. "I don't know what you mean. Orientation is for our benefit, and the seniors went to a lot of trouble to try to make us feel part of the place. I think you're just—" She bit off the word.

"Spoilt," Patsy said. "Go on, say it."

But Lee Siu never did, because at that moment a group from another hall poured into their garden and the banshee shriek that was Irwin's call to action brought the freshmen to their balconies in expectation of a song-fight. "Come on!" Lee Siu said, flinging down her brush.

Patsy flopped back and turned up the Grateful Dead. Outside the calls zinged back and forth: *Here we are! Here we are ... We're riding tall! We're riding tall...*

The general rumour was that Janet was in love with Irwin, who felt no answering pang but found it useful to have her around. Janet had the plans and the organisational ability, but Irwin had the charisma, the personality to put them across. Or so it was generally acknowledged. Patsy, who found Irwin as congenial as congealed bacon, sat opposite him in the hall's lounge and thought otherwise.

"I hear you didn't join in the song-fight," Irwin said without preamble.

"No." Patsy couldn't be bothered to deny it.

"You're being extremely silly, you know." Irwin never seemed to wear conventional attire; he was in shorts as usual, and a Live Aid T-shirt, with a towel slung round his neck. "If you continue like this, you may be forced to give up your room. If that happens, the Master will have to put a black mark against your name and it won't go down well with the university. I'm putting it to you as one intelligent person to another."

"Look," Patsy said, "there is no rule that says I have to be commandeered into doing things against my will in return for a hostel room, is there?"

"No," Irwin said carefully. "We can't force you to do anything, that's true. We prefer voluntary cooperation. We want a genuine spirit of community. Most freshmen seem able to come to grips with that simple requirement. Why can't you?"

"Because it's an emotion that can't be manufactured. It's there or it isn't." Why couldn't he see it? Or perhaps he did—Irwin was no fool—but the rules of the power game prevented his saying so.

"That's true," Irwin said, smiling benignly. "But it's also true that if no attempt is made to breed it, we might end up a collection of strangers coming together just to eat and study. It sounds a cliché but we can't all go our own way. Society is about interaction. Only connect. E.M. Forster said that in a different context—" ("I know what E.M. Forster said—") "—and it applies more than ever in a motley institution like this. You're a literate, articulate person, Patsy. I'm sure you know about the feelings of alienation and isolation and the subsequent breakdown of the social fabric that's been observed in so many inner-city housing projects in the West. Even in our own backyard we've got our own problems of killer litter, etc. It's the absence of community, of civic responsibility, of—" he shrugged "—I don't know—friendliness—that's contributed to it. You're mature enough to understand that everyone's got a social responsibility, I'm sure."

For the first time Patsy understood what was meant by Irwin's much-feted charisma. It lay in the simple technique of his gazing levelly at you, straight into your eye, and holding that gaze while he spoke in a reasonable voice into your ear. It was a mellifluous voice, with the rhetorical highs and lows pitched with unerring accuracy, neither too strident nor too soporific. That, combined with the gaze, had a slightly mesmerising effect so that you were apt to forget your own line of argument in the contemplation of the sheer artistry of Irwin's performance. For no one else could possibly link the post-industrial decline of Western societies to Patsy's refusal to sing.

Patsy, filled with unwilling admiration, took some time to collect her thoughts. "No one appointed you the guardian of social responsibility."

"There are two kinds of people in the world," Irwin said cosily. "Those who act of their own accord when they see the need and those who act only when told to. It would be nice of course if human beings were perfectly ordered, self-regulating creatures who behave and interact as they should, but since they aren't, I think you've got to admit someone has to step in to do it for them." (Hobbes? Locke? At any rate it was a devastating admission of the lust to rule.) "All right, perhaps we've got to resort to crude methods sometimes—and I know you think this whole orientation programme is silly—but surely it's the aim that's important." He was a vastly different Irwin now from the Irwin who'd shouted at her in the gym yesterday: yesterday's Irwin had been a stock authority figure playing to the gallery, today's Irwin was a calm, logical, sane Mephistopheles.

"So you don't believe in the whole farce you're enacting; you're using it as an instrument for social manipulation, that's all. You're scaring everybody into toeing the line."

"Don't you think you're exaggerating? Orientation only lasts four weeks. After that you're free to walk in and out, no problem, no coercion. It'll be all over." Over for us, Patsy thought, while you trot off to another waiting set of lambs. He dismissed her with a dazzling smile and got up, absently flicking his back with his towel. "Think about it."

As he passed the mirror, he gave an unconscious arch of the head and a quick, sidelong glance; and this narcissistic gesture reduced him again to manageable human proportions. He was nothing but an aerobicised Juan Peron.

Janet bounced in after Irwin had left, trailing a collection of scotch-tape, thumb-tacks and vanguard. She was the sort of person who never went anywhere without five pins in her mouth to signify hard industry; at the moment she was organising a build-the-fastest-teepee-from-canvas-shoes hoopla.

"Well!" she said. "I hope Irwin made you see sense," and she launched into her own tirade. Patsy was able to conjure up the African Burundi drums without much difficulty and watched Janet's moving mouth with interest. After Irwin, Janet was a limp rag. She lacked finesse.

The ragging was slight at first—a tape of hers disappeared, to be discovered at the bottom of the fishpond—then built up inexorably. Notes started appearing on her pillow, cheerful little missives about Song: *Song Sung Blue, If Music Be The Food Of Love*, etc.—then progressed to insulting, variously, her family and her mental health. One night she returned to find a group assembling a mock-corpse on her bed, an artistically arranged bolster with a knife through it, the whole topped with a Japanese face-mask. She told them in no uncertain terms to go to hell.

"What—can't take a joke, is it?" someone said.

"I don't see the punch-line, do you?" She was sick of grotesque pranks performed in the name of some demented humour, and of the code that demanded that you stood, laughed and took it in the name of sportsmanship and the toughening of moral fibre. It was a code that demanded to be debunked.

"You think you're so grand. Just because you stand outside and sneer."

They were four boys, grouped around her bed, and there was undisguised dislike in their faces; one of them was flipping the knife in a speculative manner. For a moment Patsy felt a twinge of real horror, and bizarre, absurd headlines flashed through her mind—Girl In Hostel Murdered For Refusing To Sing. At that moment Irwin entered.

"What's going on?" he enquired.

Patsy rounded on him. "I bet you put them up to it, you ___"

Irwin gave her a deprecating look.

"Honestly, *lah*—" (when Irwin used 'lah' he was, paradoxically, at his most affected) "there's no need to be obscene." He nodded to the boys. "Come on, get out."

Before Patsy's unbelieving eyes, they meekly dispersed, leaving herself and Irwin in a now strangely empty room, Irwin exuding his usual reassuring horsey smell.

"Where d'you train them? In some stable?"

"Boys will be boys," Irwin said gravely.

Irwin had manifestly never been a boy. He had obviously been born, prematurely old and disillusioned, in jogging gear and head-band.

"I think you're obscene," Patsy told him. "I think you're fat and obscene and I'm going to expose you for the potential little tyrant that you are." It sounded hysterical and, unintentionally, amusing.

"You're flattering me," Irwin said absently. He was the most unruffled person Patsy had met. He picked his way about the room, managing, despite his bulk, to give the impression of something insubstantial flitting about. Patsy watched him gaze with interest at the posters on the wall, one depicting Cleopatra, the other a whirling Kandinski, then drift over to her cassette collection.

"Put those down!" Patsy said.

"Kandinski, huh? Grateful Dead, Velvet Underground, pretty electric—"

"Cut out that crap."

"I don't suppose Lee Siu's even heard of them." He leant against the wall, arms folded. "You know, you're quite an unusual person." Was this a new attempt to suborn her? "Nobody else here has heard of the Velvet Underground. Late sixties, early seventies avant-garde New York band, fronted by Lou Reed, offbeat black-fingernailed, tortured songwriter." He reeled off the facts mechanically, beaming.

"Clever!" said Patsy sarcastically.

"I'm trying to show you that I'm not a—" he wrinkled his brow— "dumbkorpf, that we speak the same kind of language basically, you and I. We use the same sort of clichés; we're aware of the derivative nature of those clichés. Don't get me wrong. Most of those who come to this university are here for one reason only—to get a degree. Everything else is secondary. Even the fun activities they get into, the games, whatever, are on a frankly prepubescent level. Let's face it—this place is a cultural wasteland. No one's into ideas or enthusiasms or artistic discoveries— most can't even articulate themselves. Unlike you. Unlike me. As you've probably noticed, I've got a pretty wide vocabulary—"

Patsy stared.

"—which half the time I can't exercise because no one would understand me. Take Janet for instance. She's studious, she's a terrific organiser, she knows her stuff, but she's boring. You know why she's boring? She doesn't understand anything beyond the Singaporean milieu of work and pragmatism. She doesn't know anything internationally. Not about politics, books, art, music. Most of them are like that. You see what I'm saying?"

Patsy said nothing for a while, stood there with her hands jammed into her pockets.

"Why're you smiling?" Irwin wanted to know.

"You're trying to persuade me we're the last two defenders of civilisation in a barbaric world and that we've got to band together as some sort of intellectual elite to control the hordes."

"Terribly well put," Irwin observed.

"You're still not getting me to join you, even if it's from the top."

"Why not?" Irwin demanded, eyes narrowed.

"I'm not interested in power."

"Fool," Irwin remarked benevolently, and strolled out. She kicked the door shut after him.

"Sing," Irwin said genially. The boy in front of him was a freshman, just out from the army, eyeing him mutinously.

"I did," the boy said through gritted teeth.

"Well then, let's hear it. Prove to us you've got lungs."

There was a ripple of laughter, which died down as the boy and Irwin continued to lock gazes. Irwin was jogging very slightly on the spot— he stingeth like a bee, he floateth like a butterfly. There was a distinct similarity between him and Muhammed Ali: they both had an all-enveloping, self-sustaining grandiosity. The boy's gaze flickered; his neck turned red. Glazed eyes fixed on some indefinable point in the distance, he began to sing in an exaggerated roar.

"You're whispering," Irwin said coolly. He suddenly began to clown around, cupping his ears, beaming idiotically, putting his ear to the floor. Laughter rose again as Irwin improvised on his Lovable Russian Bear routine: it was cruel, and yet funny.

"It's the loudest I can manage," the boy said angrily. His anger, beside Irwin's tomfoolery, made him look ungracious, uncouth, and he was aware of it. One of the quietest freshmen, he had taken extreme care the whole month never to draw attention to himself, to blend unobtrusively into the background; with the spotlight suddenly swinging on him, his control and his wits were fleeing, visibly, one by one.

"Oh come on," said Irwin. "Who was with him in the army? Did he sing? Could he? Does he have a voice, guys?"

"No, no," shrieked the freshmen in an ecstasy of mirth.

The boy tried to speak.

"What?" Irwin said. "Please preface all remarks to me by saying, Senior Gentleman SIR!" He was at his most deliberately wilful, lazily dancing the crowd before him on a string, selecting what could not have been a better victim—through boredom? Patsy speculated, wishing she could escape. Perhaps for once the chanting had failed to grip and Irwin wanted something spicier.

"Senior Gentleman SIR," the boy said wearily.

"Proceed," Irwin said gravely. The shrieks redoubled. Irwin, probably realising in infancy that someone like him—intelligent and overgrown, a fatal combination—would always be the perennial Butt, had developed an irresistible drollery over time, goofing to disarm and conquer.

"Look. Can't we just continue as usual?"

"We're not going to deprive any of the guys here of a chance to stretch their throat muscles and yodel. But first we want to hear you sing—"

"No," the boy said. He was white now. "I took all that for two years okay? I don't have to take it from you. Not you. You're nothing but a large blimp anyway."

A solitary cheer rose from the back, to be quickly subdued. Irwin had stopped jogging and he and the boy were regarding each other with the concentrated intensity of two polecats. Then Irwin relaxed and grinned. "Do you know, I agree with you entirely?" Shrieks again, but the boy was still white and heaving; some last restraint had snapped—they could see the thin coiled fury in him. He turned and walked out a little blindly, stumbling over the step at the exit.

"Oh come on, Wing Mun!" someone shouted. Janet, eyes raised to heaven at this insubordination, started after him, but a slight shake of the head from Irwin stopped her.

"Patsy Lui," said Irwin, "was that you in transsexual disguise?" His tone was as light as ever; no one would ever know if he had been taken aback. He cultivated inscrutability assiduously. But you lost, Patsy thought, and knew with a sudden giddy lightheadedness that the witch-hunt was over.

"Anybody else want to walk out?"

Nobody stirred. "All right," Janet said peremptorily, "let's see Miss Patsy Lui do her part for once. I think we've had enough defiance for one day." Her brisk NCC shout dispelled the lingering uneasiness from the walk-out; faces lit up; attention focused on the true scapegoat. Janet was annoyed with Irwin's little games; brute force, one could see her thinking, was the answer.

It was immaterial now if she sang or not. With infinite scorn, Patsy leapt to her feet and howled out the revolting little cheer. She hoped the rafters shook; she hoped the hall rang; perhaps then the building would collapse and bury them all in thankful ignominy. She managed somehow to make the words sound like the most lewdly pornographic literature penned in history, and, simultaneously, like a call to full-scale, joyful revolt in favour of individualism—me, myself, mine, I. There was a silence after this truly awful rendition. Patsy Lui had sung, but no one seemed to feel it was a capitulation. No one seemed particularly inclined to press for an encore.

Irwin was eyeing her quizzically; again there was the uncanny suggestion that they were co-conspirators in some pact. She resisted his gaze. What would he make of her singing?

Irwin, however, she had to admit, was sterling—the very stuff presidents and talk-show hosts were made of. He put his hand up in the middle of a renewed chant; it stopped. He had the dreamy look of a man possessed by a vision.

"What we had over this past month," he said conversationally, "was an interesting exercise in power. Look at it this way. We had no weapons of coercion to force any of you to do the things we organised. You were under no real compulsion to obey. We were five against sixty. Yet fifty-nine of you chose to participate. Some of you found it enjoyable, I don't doubt. You're either sado-masochists or incredibly well adjusted. Some of you disliked certain aspects but went along because of, I don't know, the pressure to conform, timidity, the principle of 'suffer now, gain later'. You're probably the majority. And you're the kind, dare I say it, that would let a dubious authority sneak into power and, once in power, be far too scared or indifferent to agitate against it even if it were to prove fascist or dictatorial. We all have a fundamental instinct to be dominated. As to who dominates, it's simple: he who cracks the whip loudest does."

Patsy could feel an upwelling of indignation around her. It was intellectual showiness they resented, not arbitrary domination. "Hey, Irwin, who appointed you lecturer in political science?"

Why was he shifting the onus onto them? Making them feel small for moving when he cracked his whip?—and suddenly Patsy understood. It was his way of turning her non-compliance and Wing Mun's walk-out (Irwin's failures) into his moral victory, by representing the others' compliance as a weakness. There was something sneakily admirable in this calm rationalisation, in his refusal to be wrong-footed; he was definitely an incipient monster.

"You're—um—leaving?" the master said. He was a gentle, self-effacing academic in his middle thirties who had been born, clearly, sixty years of age. He blinked at Patsy a little doubtfully through the square black-rimmed glasses he wore. "You don't like it here?"

"I think I'd be happier elsewhere, sir," Patsy said.

The Master groped. "You've been through orientation?"

"Yes."

"Well then," he said, bewildered, "I can understand if you were unhappy because you hadn't been through orientation."

"Well sir, I think there's an unnecessarily paramilitary atmosphere about the place."

"But of course," the Master said happily. "That's the general idea. To make student days and student life such a tough stretch that what follows will be comparative paradise. It's beautiful training for the real world. The British have practised it for hundreds of years through their public school system and it produced a wonderful empire." To be lapidary was not his style. He meandered through centuries of history and philosophy and it was late when Patsy finally escaped, reeling from the cerebral stimulation.

Picking up her bag, she began to walk down the hill to the bus-stop in the lurid gaze of the evening sun. The university, concrete-white and sprawling, looked like a travestied modernist version of an acropolis from where she stood, with small scrambling student-figures dotted here and there. *Et in Arcadia ego*, she thought sardonically. The bus trundled over the crest of the hill and screeched to a stop; Patsy ran for it.

Fascist Rock

"How was the G.P. test?" "How?" "How?"

Howl! thought Chris. She swung her bag on her shoulder and scrambled over the desks, determined to be out of class before they conscripted her into another of their interminable class activities—the cross-country run, the teachers' day party, the national knees-up competition, the use your elbows campaign, the inter-CT flip-yer-noses contest. She had had enough of it, up to the eel's eyebrows. "Christina!" somebody shouted despairingly after her. "*Aah*—forget about her!" she heard somebody else exclaim. She had sunk like a stone in their estimation after she had been seen actually smoking a cigarette outside a well-known shopping centre. 'Havoc', was she? Labels didn't worry her. Sticks and stones may break my bones, but words—can be erased.

Someone did manage to corner her, as she was running down the stairs. It was a girl called Suet Ling from her old convent, a sentimental sophisticate, if there were ever such a thing. Chris listened with half an ear to the familiar recital: Miss Mah, their chemistry teacher at their old school, was going to the States to further her studies and a farewell present from her old pupils would certainly be in order.

"I can't stand the old cow," Chris said frankly; she watched in amusement as Suet Ling elegantly pretended she hadn't heard and said, the tap of charm still flowing, that, yes, of course she understood the, er, nature of

Chris's feelings, but this was rather an exception. "I'll think about it," Chris said.

Didn't any of these girls understand that there were some bestial ones among their lot who didn't go weak at the knees at the mention of their old school? The sight of the interminable present-giving, flower-giving, tears in the corner of one's eyes, corsages, pin-cushions, fond little cards, Snoopy mascots and Wordsworth poetry ... the paraphernalia of unadulterated femininity ... made Chris want to puke. She thought of getting down on her knees right there and then and doing so at Suet Ling's feet. She grinned. Suet Ling looked at her enquiringly. "Nothing," Chris said hastily.

Oh, she had a demon in her all right. Her mother said so often enough, with gesticulations to boot, when Chris went out and dyed the back of her hair red against her express wishes; when Chris refused to go to church with her, saying that she liked Jesus right enough, but she couldn't stand most of the rah-rah boys who claimed to represent him on earth or the pseudo-psychoanalytical, group-therapy jargon they used, either; when Chris failed five tests in a row and won the first prize for G.P. at the end of the year; when Chris stayed out past midnight at parties at which the police were frequent raiders. Her mother said grimly it was a wonder that Chris wasn't in jail.

"Why don't you ever give me some credit for common sense?" Chris once asked her curiously. She knew just how far to go. She really did.

"You shouldn't be going anywhere at all," her mother said with finality.

"Oh shit," Chris said in exasperation and deftly evaded a slap. She wanted to shout, this country's boring enough as it is, our only indigenous culture is a shopping-centre culture, kicks are few and far between, when you're dead it's as though you never existed, so why the hell shouldn't one ... but she didn't expect anyone to understand. She accepted that. After all, there were a lot of things in this country she had difficulty in comprehending too.

Like Patriotism, National fervour, College spirit, a trio that rang in her mind with the clangour of rusty metal. Government leaders who gave interviews, ministry officials who came to college to give talks would say, Now think about this. Be glad thou art not living in Jamaica where the natives sleep all day in the sun of a sluggish economy. Be glad thou art not living in New York, where the homicide figures are higher than maggot reproduction rates, or in China where they have no water-closets. Comparison was a pretty listless and smug way of inspiring thrills in the national breast. All right, so she was glad, she supposed, though she thought it would be rather fun to sit on a back porch and watch the sun go down and hear reggae riding the air-waves ... her own flat looked out on a car-park and a rubbish dump and her mother had the radio tuned to Chinese Rediffusion permanently. What really irritated her was the whole issue of college spirit, however. People seemed to think it was a magic word to galvanise a tardy college into action, and pupils sat around in groups earnestly discussing how they could chalk up the college spirit index. Suggested solutions: cheering sessions, false enthusiasm and a lot of talks on the subject by the school principal, who bore a striking resemblance to W.C. Fields. It was all play-acting, a big con-game designed to give a seething mass of pupildom some sense of legitimacy. Perhaps that was necessary. But she did wish somebody else besides the cynical, affluent blase prats of the humanities classes would point out the fragility and essentially synthetic quality of the college spirit ruse.

She was thinking about this as she ran up another flight of stairs to the library to return an overdue book. The girl at the counter had some difficulty in finding her card and Chris watched in resignation the entrance of Mr William Ng, tutor in charge of the school library, the school pederast and a fine exponent of sanguinary language.

Stories abounded in college of how he had coyly invited several youths up to his office and of how, when these callow lads cravenly refused, they had been subsequently marked down in their papers. True or not, these tales kept the rumour-mill grinding. Meanwhile, the man worked off any excess libido by running the library like a concentration camp. He was in the habit of creeping up on pupils who wore T-shirts in the library—an unforgiveable crime, that—and shouting in their ear, "You, get the bloody hell out!" He would accompany this by dramatically sweeping the pupil's things off the desk and watch him or her pick and scramble after them one by one, all the while heaving like a pitching ship. He was always noticeably more cheerful after each outburst.

He saw Chris immediately. "I thought I said no T-shirts in the library." He had a flat, very nasal voice which always made Chris conjure up a mental picture of someone twisting his nose like a screw.

"I'm just going, sir," Smarminess before retaliation.

He told her she should go that very minute, card or no card, and slammed shut the book on the librarian's finger. She winced. "I don't make these rules up for my own bloody amusement, you know!" He thrust the book at Chris. She stood and stared at him and the whole library sat up and stared at her. By rights, she should have crawled out in a pitiable condition by now. Chris was fighting a fit of compulsion—one of those that made her lean over a railing, dangerously, half-intoxicated by the idea of a fall. The impulse to call Mr Ng a four-letter word that would adequately describe him for all posterity was choking her.

"I said, 'get out'." His voice was rising ominously.

She threw the book on the counter and left. It was childish, puerile, she knew, but she was still at the stage where she fought instinctively, maniacally, on a self-sustaining anger born of inability to really change anything. On Monday the skies would rain bolts of lightning and sundry Acts of God, but meanwhile it was Saturday morning and her motto was, never think too much about anything you didn't have to...

...Took the bus downtown, got off outside the shopping centre with all the other posh trendies, their glances sliding off one another, casually flipping their long fringes back, cool as ice under all the perspiration. The gaudiness amused her. It was stupid, of course—another form of play-acting—but it had the added attraction of being termed corrupt. Decadent. Aimless. You even had editorials written about you, for goodness' sake. All that spiky gelled hair, dayglo socks, rouge—fond, too-late imaginings of what punks looked like. Chris had never seen a punk before, but she was willing to bet a real one would be apoplectic at the sight of his imitators.

Did she think she was a rebel? She'd once been asked by a reporter, nosing around and trying, sadly, to write a hip article on hip youth for the Sunday paper.

No, she wasn't a rebel.

No? Then why the dressing-up? Why the (critical glance) all-black gear? To get up people's noses. To intimidate. People were intimidated by black lipstick.

Wasn't it the same thing? How could she say—

No, it wasn't the same, because her dressing-up was strictly outside school hours. The aggressiveness, the attitude, was ersatz. Let's not get away from that. She was still a fully-paid-up member of the school chain-gang. She was no rebel.

Funnily enough, the reporter's article the following Sunday had omitted all mention of her interview.

It was a funny thing about dress. In her sister-of-Dracula outfit—black gloves, stockings, torn top, hideous make-up—she was totally at ease, knowing that in her clothes what mattered was not how she appeared to people but how they reacted to her. A debasement of femininity, she'd once heard someone say; it always amused her that passers-by saw her as something threatening, or even savage—after all, the reasoning went, what sort of person went to the opposite extreme of vanity and mutilated herself sartorially—and shied away violently if she came too near. Then there were the people who thought her appearance gave them a certain God-given right to make lewd remarks—she waded into them with a promptness that, whatever else it accomplished, certainly didn't turn them on. She didn't want to attract. She wanted to show exactly how pissed off she was and the clothes were a handy emblem for signifying a careless, rip-it-up attitude. A rock and roll attitude, really.

She was in school uniform as she got off the bus and already she was fidgeting in it, hating the way it stamped her and conditioned her behaviour, in spite of herself. Of course that was why they made you wear uniforms; it was a psychological form of restraint. She dashed into a lavatory in one of the fast food restaurants to do a quick change of clothes. Roll on, liberation day.

Chris ran a comb through her hair at the sink, under the raised arms of two girls who were primping their hair into place and mourning a barren love-life. Chris wished they would pat their fringes less and had fewer pimples—and waited for a plague to strike her for her scurrilous thoughts. Nothing happened. She washed her hands and left, her ears ringing with the plaintive cry of, "Should I ring him?" Should I not? Doo-wah, doo-wah...

The plain fact of the matter was, she didn't like her own sex too much. They could be divided into earnest paper-chasers who were pragmatic, clever, unsentimental and rather dull, sophisticates who were impossibly sweet, cracklingly artificial, adult and upper middle class, boy-crazy fiends who were the silliest of the lot and usually the kindest, the tomboys who struck Chris as cases of arrested development—So she walked alone and cultivated the oddballs and they called her 'Havoc' resoundingly behind her back.

She stopped to read the headlines of the afternoon paper. VANDALS ARRESTED FOR DEFACING SUBWAY WALLS. By twisting her head, she could make out the fine print: "... it is thought the accused may have been influenced by the recent spate of films depicting the hip-hop 'breakdance' culture of the South Bronx ..." and there were blow-ups of the graffiti in colour. Chris studied them for a while. "You want to buy or not?" the news vendor said, glaring.

Chris shook her head and moved off. Oh boy. She could see her next G.P. lesson looming like a black cloud over the horizon. Juvenile delinquency and working mothers! Civic responsibility and the environment! Something edifying like that. They had just spent a whole term on test-tube babies and artificial insemination, which had been instructive insofar as the whole class had been led to discuss Sex voraciously amongst themselves, then furiously photostating the sheets handed out by their tutor to make up for their inattention. Before they had discussed Abortion, Education, Population, Pollution and Sport/Politics. Someone had suggested Sexual Deviancy, in a hopeful way, and that had gone under Moral Education, which quite took the titillation out of it. Religion for a while had been mooted, despite their tutor's feeble protest that "it hardly ever appears on the G.P. paper," but it had been hastily shelved when a Protestant fundamentalist in the class said, good idea, what about the papal infallibility rubbish, and the Catholics had woken out of their stupor and rediscovered their faith on the spot in bristling indignation and the freethinkers who of course, as everybody knew, thought nothing at all, looked helpfully blank. So they switched to the Arms Race instead and dutifully cut out articles which described peace marches by thousands of young people in Europe as "actions instigated by Soviet propagandists playing on the ivory-tower leanings of youth as a whole." Apart from the indestructible blandness which G.P. lessons could bestow on even the most controversial topics, Chris was also irritated by the way the class wrote down every statistic that fell from their tutor's lips when a test was round the corner. It may have been human nature, but it was hypocrisy all the same.

"Why do you worry about things like that?" she could hear her mother's voice in her head. "Your duty now is to study and learn. Not to criticise. The problem with you is—you think you know everything. You don't like anything."

The problem was—both assertions were true.

The graffiti headline stayed in her mind. She thought of a story she'd once read, about a boy in L.A.'s East Side who had chalked his name all over town in a pathetic, rather funny attempt to leave his mark on a world bent on ignoring his existence. She could understand that—it was like dressing-up in a way. You liked the flash, the attention, the secret knowledge; you felt like a star. A psychopathic star, perhaps, but still, a star. You even liked the bitterness underlying it all, the bitterness of crashing face-up against a wall, a dead-end. It was your weapon against the world.

She was the second to arrive. Only Kai was there, leaning against one of the white-painted metal chairs, smoking. There were five of them who went around in a group; they went to parties together, shopped for clothes together, were collectively bored, laughed collectively like hyenas in public to show insouciance, were each and every one of them known as the one who "gave their former school a bad name." And yet they did nothing particularly heinous beyond being collectively crude and attention-seeking. Chris had no illusions about their cosmic importance, their place in society or their motives. She just enjoyed having a group to hang out with.

Kai offered her a cigarette, which she refused.

"Sandra can't make it and the other two are coming late," he said, then, having discharged a disagreeable duty, he switched on the ghetto blaster he'd brought with him. Chris sat in a chair, hands clasped behind her head, hair glowing with a red-dyed lantern effect in the sun and suddenly she laughed, hilariously glad to be out of school and free from the shackles of lessons, if only for two days. Kai looked at her, smiling, rather puzzled; he wore an earring and it seemed to give a sharp focus to a face that was all bones and hollows. He wore jeans, a checkered shirt and tennis shoes— hardly outrageous, but then he didn't go in for the sartorial splendour of the others. His deviance was entirely of the mind; he was entirely screwed-up inside; for one thing he didn't seem to mind solitude the way the others did. They had banded together out of mutual defensive-ness or superiority to the common herd and nothing could be more nefarious than being left alone.

"You know what I'd like to do?" Chris said abstractedly, thinking aloud. "Get a spray can and spray 'Fascist' on every wall in school." He regarded her seriously. "Why?" Chris unclasped her hands. "Teachers are fascists, that's why. I mean, they have almost unlimited power to palm their opinions onto us and be petty tyrants if they want to. Who's to stop them? Certainly not us. They can smoke and swear their heads off in front of us if they want to, but God help us if we light up. They have a class of twenty-eight human beings under them who're legally under-age, have no income, no real rights, no power to vote, strike or hand in their resignations. It's a megalomaniac's dream. It really is. And you want to tell me that's not fascism?" She began to laugh, eyes narrowed in amusement.

"You're an anarchist," Kai said succinctly.

"What, the spray paint? Of course I won't do it. No guts. Under all this drag, I'm just a nun, you know. I'm just an Asian young lady."

Kai laughed in spite of himself. "What's that supposed to mean, huh?"

"Oh, we had a talk about that from our principal yesterday. We were a disgrace to Our Culture, he said. The Asian Young Lady is becoming extinct. I loved that. I'm extinct! He can say all these weird and wonderful platitudes without blinking an eyelid. Things like, Think of what your forefathers have done for you and be grateful. Things that invite destructive forces beyond his control. He's no comic relief, I can tell you."

"Like I said, you're an anarchist."

"Only a verbal one. All hot air and temperature rising."

She glanced at the next table, where a Eurasian boy sat, seemingly embalmed in a trance, yellow-orange-dyed hair flopping in a smooth arc over one eye. She had seen him at parties but didn't know his name. Kai followed her line of gaze. "He looks as though he's high on something," she said.

"They say he sniffs glue," he said matter-of-factly. No shock or contempt, devoid of judgement, old in vice. They'd all lost something, Chris thought, not really putting her thoughts into words. A defensive mechanism that screeched, Stop! when things became too hot.

"Listen, you're going to like this one," Kai said. His elder brother was studying in England; in his latest letter he mentioned how, one evening, he had seen a car-load of youths drive up to a couple of policemen waiting to cross the street. One of the youths had stuck his head out of the window and yelled, "Fascists!" before the car drove off with a lurch and a bump. The policemen had looked at each other, shrugged and crossed the street.

"Anarchy in the U.K.," Chris said thoughtfully, quoting the title of a Sex Pistols song. She slitted her eyes, looking into the sun; the roar of traffic was like the sullen growl of a monstrous dog straining at the leash. "Imagine that happening here. Could it? It couldn't. We're not politicised, and I don't know if that's good or bad—anyway, 'fascist' isn't in the usual vocabulary of our *Ah Bengs*."

"They could yell other words. The violence would be the same. And what a bloody superior attitude—"

"I've nothing else to be superior about," Chris said in agony.

"You don't take anything seriously, do you?"

"No. Should I? What for? The ability to laugh at everything and believe in nothing is the secret to a happy life—" She tilted her chair back, and she was cracking up again.

"David Bowie said all rock stars are fascist and Adolf Hitler was the first rock star. He staged a country, Bowie said." Kai dragged on his cigarette, smiling.

"David Bowie? He dressed up in drag, didn't he?" Chris said, to annoy Kai; Bowie was one of his heroes and he applied an intelligence to the music which he rarely showered on his studies. School bored him. It was his misfortune to have a father who was a university professor and whose love for the written word was matched only by his distaste for the one-line articulation of the rock culture.

"So what if he dressed up in drag? Ronald Reagan's an actor, isn't he? Chiang Ching was an actress. Why sneer at their backgrounds? Politics is about manipulation after all, isn't it, and the greatest manipulators are those who appear on screen and the rock stars on stage. Charisma is fascism of the spirit allied to the fascism of the media." He opened his eyes in mock awe, impressed by his own diatribe.

"Cynicism bores me," Chris said. "Even my own."

"Don't you think for a moment they may be right?" Kai said abruptly. "People like your principal, I mean, when they say the younger generation knows nothing about hardships, war or building a nation from scratch and slags everything off in ignorance."

"Of course they're right," Chris said. "They don't have to say it all the time, that's all. It's a bloody syndrome, that's what it is. Things will never be the same again. Listen, I'm not going to sit under a weight of guilt for not having been born in a war I never saw and five thousand years of Chinese civilisation which we hang on to by a slender thread. I'm sick of it, I tell you. All those ghosts from the past."

Kai didn't laugh or concur. "Maybe," he said. "But they're—" He stopped for a moment to think. "They're like *our* ghosts, you know. It's a legacy nobody else in the world has. Other countries have their own versions but we have ours."

Chris looked at him curiously. She liked him better than she did the others—but she didn't understand him. "You're an idealist," she said. "Do you realise I've just cursed you, saying that?"

The ghetto blaster was now playing a sepulchral song by the self-same David Bowie and Chris tried to remember what the title was. She thought it odd that Kai, with an earring in his ear, should be feeling any pull of responsibility at all towards a cultural ethos he was so busily rejecting. "Ashes to Ashes," she said suddenly; that was the song-title. "Play something new, huh?"

"I listen to what I like." He threw his cigarette away and lit another, turning it over restlessly between his fingers. "Life is really boring, you know? You wait to grow up and when you've grown up you wait to die. In between you're happy for about one-sixth of your life."

"One-sixth is ample," Chris said flippantly.

"Listen," Kai said suddenly. "You hear that?" He turned the volume way up and the voice rose in mock agony: *I've never done good things, I've never done bad things, I never did anything out of the blue.* Chris folded her arms on the table and studied her nails, each one painted a lurid colour. The sun cut a swathe of heat across the back of her neck.

"That seems to me the worst thing anybody could say about himself, man. 'I did nothing,' that's what it's saying. It's like a slogan for obscurity."

He broke off and grinned briefly. "I did it again. Taking rock music seriously, I mean. I once asked our Lit. teacher why we couldn't analyse Bob Dylan's lyrics the way they do in America. 'That's because, dear boy, we are here to study the literary and not the commercial use of the English language.' What a load of crap. Don't authors and poets want to sell their works either? Listen, don't ever argue with an academic." His father was an academic. "Local or foreign. I mean, with our Chinese teachers, you know they hate all the Western pop culture which they think is eroding our roots or whatever. It's a cultural and moral hostility. But with these other guys, it's just sheer intellectual snobbery—why am I running on like that?"

"I don't know," Chris said.

"It's so stupid. A single lyric from a song of no literary merit says more to me than reams of D.H. Lawrence and all the other literary hotshots. It says more about the lives most people lead than most books. Do you know what I'm talking about? When I'm dead I don't want that to be something that can be said about me, Chris—"

"Turn it down," Chris said. He did so and sat, frowning and smoking, not looking at her. The song faded out. She ran a hand through her hair and propped her head on her arm. Kai's intensity, his odd way of looking at things, always made her feel awkward, but she thought she knew the source of his frustration. She was thought by her class to lead some crazy, unruly, magazine existence, unfettered by parents or a conscience, and they looked askance at her hair, the things she said, her nonchalance. All this, while she sat outside a fast food restaurant, listening to someone talk about human insignificance. *I've never done good things, I've never done bad things, I never did anything out of the blue.*

Okay, so you dressed up, went to a few parties. Appeared in a young adults magazine, surrounded with glamour in the eyes of your peers. But where do you go from here? A line from a thousand love songs. All that was left to do was to screw off the earring and climb back down onto level ground and take your allotted place in the line. The only thing left being a countdown to reality. The lights turned off, the auditorium empty.

"Hey, imagine us twenty-five years from now, looking back on us sitting here," she said, looking up. "What d'you think we'll be saying, huh?"

"'What's on TV tonight?'"

The others appeared suddenly, all togged-up. Cigarettes waved, earrings flashed, laughter tinkled out, faces turned away coyly, self-consciously, packets of fries spilt generously down the legs of chairs. Chris could see that in a few months' time, she would be as bored with the whole circus as she had been previously with school and home, but meanwhile the idea of trekking back to a quiet afternoon in her room was curiously repellent.

Pawns

They have cleaned up everything, everything down to the last smidgeon of blood. The Great Square of the People gapes at the wide, encircling sky. It will be some time of course before the tour buses ease back, decanting their loads, before the tidal wave of bicycles that engulf the Square return; but they will, and who then will believe that the tanks rolled in one night to crush the bodies of the protesters asleep in their tents?

If we had made a mistake, it was in being naïve, but there is no bigger crime in politics than naïveté. We thought we held the senile old men running our country in the palms of our hands, we thought we could close our fists and squeeze, forcing them to capitulate. We were drunk, giddy with exhilaration; in truth it was youth itself we were celebrating, in a society where to be young was held against you and humourlessness was a positive virtue. Exultant, we laughed in their faces.

Yes, I admit I started running the moment I heard the army—the real army—was coming in to mop up the Square. I was running for dear life when the first shots cracked and the whole bloody mess began in earnest. I heard later that some of the students occupying the Square linked arms, forming a human chain before the advancing tanks. "Don't shoot," they pleaded. "We'll leave quietly," and they began to step backwards. Did they have time to feel amazed before they fell like dominoes before the gunfire?

Self-preservation, the basest of human instincts, took me unerringly to the station, where I intended to take the first train out. In the mayhem, I calculated that the authorities would probably have forgotten to stop the trains—as it turned out, I was right. Rationality may have dictated flight, survival; but why was I not in that chain with my friends? It's not a question I can answer.

Along the way to the station, I came upon a soldier the enraged populace had strung up from a lamp-post. He swayed slightly in the breeze, a disembowelled puppet whose stuffing hung loose for all to see. How could any of us know that this shot would be replayed time and time again on state television by the senile old men to an unsuspecting countryside, as evidence of the 'counter-revolution' the army, regrettably, had to suppress? In my dreams he swings again and again, poor dead soldier, for eternity.

"Oh God," my sister, Su-Mei, said when she saw me. She grasped the entire situation at once, and her face wore a glazed look, as of a rabbit hypnotised by fear.

Someone brushed against me in the narrow corridor outside the flat; stumbling, I was dragged in precipitately by my sister. She was frightened and furious. "How could you come? Someone might have seen you. How could you? I have a *baby*—"

As if on cue, an infant's howl arose from the back room, and she dashed off like a demented hare. The noise reverberated round the flat, which was nothing more than a cramped hovel, with a curtain separating the sleeping area from the kitchen. From behind the curtain, Su-Mei emerged, cradling the baby and repelling my feeble attempts to cheer it up with a cold stare.

"You can't stay here," she said flatly. "It's unthinkable. Don't you realise his position? He's a Party cadre, for goodness' sake. We'll all go to jail. He'll kill me." *He* was her husband, a Party stalwart and the last of the Neanderthals.

"I have nowhere else to go."

"He'll kill me," she repeated monotonously.

Rage was growing in me as well. "Where *is* the Neanderthal anyway?"

Su-Mei flew into a quivering passion. "Go *away*," she shrieked. "Go away, you blithering idiot. Yes, you are an idiot, despite all your brains and fine qualifications." Her voice shook with scorn. "Why, you haven't learnt the first thing about life, have you? I saw you on television, little brother. In the middle of the Square, waving—what was it?—a pro-democracy flag. Captured for posterity! They'll never stop looking for you now. And then to attack the soldiers, so that they had to open fire—"

"That's a revolting lie."

"What of it? Ultimately you and your friends are responsible. You dared those in power to change their ways. Did you honestly think the leaders would let themselves be humiliated by a bunch of silly, irresponsible children capering in front of their offices?" She took a deep breath and said, very controlled, "And now you expect me to shelter you?"

I felt dizzy, ravenous and depressed, the still-rollicking motion of the long train journey passing over me in waves. I thought, this is a terrible mistake, how could I have forgotten what my sister was like?

The baby had stopped crying and was now sitting up looking at me enquiringly. It was an exceptionally homely baby. "It's only for a couple of days," I said. "I know someone here—who can get me out of the country. Then I'll be off, I promise. I don't want to burden you either."

"Why couldn't you stay out of it?" she repeated. "Why couldn't you mind your own business?"

"You don't," I said furiously, "understand anything."

She started crying, silently. The tears dropped onto the baby's face; it blinked, alarmed and began to grizzle in unison. Ashamed, I tried to hug her, clumsily; she pushed me away. From next door, the sounds of mahjong percolated through paper-thin walls; the entire building was a fragile, flimsy beehive, humming incessantly to a muted symphony of quarrels, laughter, a dozen chattering television sets. Tiredness was building a glass bubble around me, through which noises came distantly, and my sister appeared far away, though she was right beside me. I told her I would go.

"No, don't," she said. "Sit down." She pushed me into a chair.

For the first time, I noticed how careworn she looked. She had always had a certain delicate porcelain beauty, the kind that fragments easily; remnants of it clung to her but she had aged considerably, while on the left side of her face were traces of what looked like a subsiding black eye.

"I'll talk to *him*," she promised. Why did she always speak of him with that peculiar lilted emphasis? "Are you hungry?" Without waiting for a reply, she went to the stove.

It was the first time in two days that I could relax my guard. Petrified that I would say something incriminating in my sleep or be caught unawares, I had stayed rigidly awake on the train, gazing fixedly at the toothless gums in the snoring mouth opposite me. I must have passed out or something, because the next thing I remember is Su-Mei shaking me awake frantically, and my brother-in-law regarding me with intense loathing across the kitchen table.

• • •

Su-Mei had a pathological obsession with security. Every night she got up twice to check the locks on the doors, which were reinforced with steel bars. She maintained she was afraid of burglars—which, now that the concept of property had been abolished, must be an ideological joke of sorts.

On a June day in 1969, then four years old, Su-Mei was refusing to practise her writing. The day was sultry, an effulgent sun creating large slanting rhomboids of light on the floor; a fly harried her continually, while, most cruelly, she could hear the sounds of other children playing in the street. Folding her arms, she wore a mutinous expression. Her mother, a history lecturer at the local university, was vexed. Stern-faced, she got up to fetch a ruler: she was a strong believer in the efficacy of corporal punishment.

The sound of children's laughter became intermingled with an odd buzzing, then, abruptly, ceased altogether. The buzzing coalesced into the high-pitched rant of chanted slogans, which were meaningless to the little girl—what on earth was a 'bourgeois counter-revolutionary'? A loud hammering on the front door was her opportunity for escape; sliding off her high chair, she stood, gleeful, poised for flight.

The next moment the wooden door shattered; long splinters of wood flew across the room under the blow of an axe. Su-Mei, amazed, opened her mouth to scream. Her mother seized her; she was pale but calm. "Get under the table," she ordered. "Now!" Her magnificent cheekbones, her greatest asset, looked more prominent than ever, the skin drawn fine and taut over them.

An inch of daylight showed between the edge of the frilly tablecloth and the floor, an inch flooded totally by the shiny boots of the Red Guards, which made a tremendous clatter on the wooden floorboards. At one point an enormous boot intruded under the table, almost trapping Su-Mei's fingers; for days after, they would throb, unaccountably.

Her mother's voice said, "You have no right to be here."

Peals of laughter. A merry voice told her she was no longer their teacher—school was out, didn't she know? Enemies of the state had to pay their dues.

"I have never," my mother stated, clearly, categorically, "been an enemy of the state."

Another mirthless laugh from the Red Guards, followed by a slap. Su-Mei's skin tingled, felt flayed, as though *she* had been smacked. They walked round Mother musingly. Wasn't she a divorced woman? Wasn't she ashamed of being morally lax, promiscuous?

Mother said her personal life was none of their business.

They seemed to tire of conversation after this; someone barked an order and she was dragged out, into the courtyard.

All Su-Mei heard now were muffled blows and the resumption of chanting, growing more and more frenzied. Much later, she would think of it as having the characteristics of a kind of ritualised cabal, a political exorcism of spirits. Meanwhile, she crouched, motionless, quiet as a mouse, under the table for hours thereafter, waiting for Mother to tell her that it was safe to emerge, but Mother said nothing.

Days after the beating, her aunt found her wandering around the home, singing little childish songs to herself and living off a diet of bread and water. With much tongue clicking and clucking, her aunt took her home to stay with her. For a whole year, Su-Mei refused to speak; at six, she suddenly recovered her voice and her aunt thought, thank goodness, she'll be a normal child hereafter.

• • •

Mother was left for dead but against all the odds she recovered and was packed off to the countryside. She stayed there for a decade, during which time she met my father and gave birth to me. We moved back to the city following the general amnesty granted after the death of the One and Only Supreme Leader, and I saw my sister for the first time. She was at that time an extraordinarily pretty girl; even then, however, there was the nervous laugh, the panic that would engulf her at the slightest indication of any trouble. In joy bordering on delirium, she kept touching my mother's face and hands. "Mother, mother," she kept saying, "what have they done to you?"

I was surprised. In my childish stupidity, I had assumed that she had been born with her curiously misshapen nose, the scar across her left cheek, the pronounced limp, the iron-grey hair; I had always been vaguely ashamed of her appearance. Only when I was older did I make the connection. The greatest change, however, was not in the way she looked. The assault, the years in the country had produced a permanent, frozen calm, a perpetual reverie from which she could not be stirred. She lived, thought, spoke in a time-frame a beat slower than all of us, as though she had made a ferocious vow never to let anything affect her profoundly again. Huddled on a remote planet of her own, I never saw her agitated or emotional about anything.

As for my father, he was a peasant, kind, uncomplaining, but bewildered by the city and already an old man. My parents died when I was ten.

My sister has never really got over what happened. A Freudian, I suppose, would say she was terrified of being abandoned again, of anything that could remotely be construed as disorder. Never get involved, is her motto. Politics is anathema to her. Consequently, or paradoxically, she married an arch-Party man, the kind who, whatever his other limitations, would at least guarantee her a roof over her head and stability for the rest of her life; at least, this is the only way I can account for the Neanderthal.

• • •

"He can't stay," my brother-in-law said through gritted teeth. I got up to go.

"No!" my sister said peremptorily. "It's only for a day. Besides—you know—there might be worse trouble if he got caught and they knew he was related to you. It's better for all of us if he tries to escape overseas."

My brother-in-law's face coloured deeply. He was not overly popular at work, I knew, thanks to a consuming zealousness and a certain flip arrogance which kept thwarting the comrades' desire for an easy life. Was there a possibility that they would not be above baying for his blood if they discovered he was related by marriage to a political undesirable? He had, after all, been exhaustively questioned about my mother, a woman he hadn't even met.

He turned to my sister; she flinched and took a step back. The flat side of his hand hit me a glancing blow on the side of my head instead.

"Don't pick him up," his voice floated above me.

"And don't ever describe him as being related to me. He is *your* brother." He swore at her; the baby shrieked.

"He'll let you stay," my sister whispered after he had stalked out. "I'm so sorry."

To her eternal credit, she never reproached me again. Why, why didn't she shame me into slinking away? For I had lost all volition to depart of my own accord. Fear of capture, fear of death, a great, hulking, demonic presence, drove all other emotions away. Instead, I let her feed me; together, we shared a bowl of soup. Occasionally, she would look up and give me a half-smile; once, she said, "He's not always like that, you know." In the clear soup the pig's intestines bobbed jauntily, grey little tubular vessels; and the image of the soldier flooded back, spinning from his post. An overwhelming wave of nausea swept over me and I retched.

The necessary papers would take a couple of days, I was told, while the ship would arrive only a week later. There was a strike, they said, in the nearest foreign post, which accounted for the delay. A week: I was in despair, it was eternal, it was a point in time which would never come.

My contact lived across town, in a crumbling modern apartment similar to my sister's. He was in only at night; the moment it was dark, I would slip out and thread my way there—the answer was always 'no news'. Four days of interminable languor, of days spent in the cramped flat and nights skulking in the street, passed in this fashion. I began to lose track of time, sleeping at odd hours and waking up abruptly from some nightmare. Once a neighbour wandered in without first knocking and I barely had time to dive behind the curtain.

My brother-in-law failed to come home at night, as a sign of grim non-complicity in the whole affair. Where he stayed, my sister had no idea. He came back twice to collect a change of clothing. Twice, in response to my sister's entreaties to let her know where he was, he boxed her ears. I understood. My sister was his hostage. The longer I stayed, the more she would suffer. He steadfastly ignored my presence. I didn't like him, but I found it hard to hate him, for myself, that is. This was none of his making, after all, the system, the demonstrations, my sister's relatives. Like my sister, he was passionately meticulous, in love with order—it was their way of coping. At the first sign of unravelling, his response was to lash out.

It was easy to hate him for my sister's sake, though.

"He's hit you before, hasn't he?" When she wouldn't answer, I followed her around the kitchen. "How often? Once, twice a week?"

"You're such a child," she said.

"Why don't you leave him?"

She held the baby and looked at me numbly. "He'll come back."

On the fifth day, I woke with a start. I couldn't imagine where I was, but a certain staring intensity from the window told me there was an eye pressed to a crack in the drawn curtains. I flew to the window, but the eye had withdrawn.

The fights, the unaccustomed noise of the past four days had apparently not gone unnoticed by the neighbours; only the night before, one of the women had come to the door and sweetly asked Su-Mei if anything was conceivably wrong: there was such a racket, the curtains were always drawn, and her husband—where *was* he because she needed to see him urgently about some committee matter. My sister, listless and uncaring, had shut the door in her face.

This fifth day, she sat, rocking the baby, not speaking to me. She fed the baby, but ate nothing herself and in the afternoon lay face down on the bed. I shook her gently; she flung my hand away. There was nothing to do but to wait for nightfall, with that tense anticipation that draws every second out to infinity. As a matter of fact the events in the Square seemed wholly remote; when I thought of it at all, it was with a touch of amazement at our overwhelming youthful egotism; no, the here and now was bound up in this tiny darkened room, with its ineradicable smell of stale cabbage and baby's diapers.

The news that night was good, so good I could scarcely believe it. A ship would be arriving the next day: I would simply have to show up at the appointed hour with my false, shinily new papers. The rush of relief that engulfed me was so great that I astonished the contact by starting to sob. This state of near-hysteria accompanied me all the way back to the flat; I imagined getting my sister off the bed, unmade for days, watching her smile her slow reflective smile.

Instead, the Neanderthal was back and they were both having dinner. Or rather, he was tucking in. My sister was turning a vegetable leaf doggedly between her chopsticks; she avoided my eyes.

"Did anyone see you?" the Neanderthal enquired.

"No, I don't think so."

"Good, good."

His weird geniality confused me.

"Any luck?"

"I'm leaving tomorrow."

I expected my sister to look up, but she didn't.

"Aren't you glad, Sis?"

"Yes, of course," she mumbled.

"Come and have dinner," the Neanderthal said hospitably.

This magical volte-face left me nonplussed. Perhaps they had made up? Perhaps whatever it was that drew this grotesquely mismatched couple together had reasserted itself. I said, no, I would just go to bed.

At that moment, there was a knocking at the door. My sister's head came up sharply; her face looked white with despair. Something clicked in my mind—how could I have been so stupid? I made a mad rush for the back window.

Somehow, I had imagined a grand set-piece: a succession of gunshots, the locks smashed, a shower of wooden splinters raining in all directions. The reality, of course, was infinitely more prosaic. Within the cramped confines of the flat, my brother-in-law had the door unlocked in half a second. How could I have gone out of the back window anyway? It was a sheer drop to the ground. I went, as they say, quietly.

The fresh-faced young policemen, pleased as children at their capture, assured me later the Neanderthal had done his patriotic duty. Two days after the crackdown, word had gone out that the government was prepared to reward any sane and upright individual who informed on the fugitives. A crisp roll of posters advertising the reward had arrived at the local police station and my brother-in-law, as a Party man with connections, had been one of the first to know.

My sister had refused to cooperate, initially. He had told her that if she tried to warn me in any way, he would leave her and take the baby.

For days after my capture, they said, my sister took no food and spoke to nobody. Then, quite suddenly, she began screaming and smashing the crockery; once she started there was no stopping her. With innocent relish, they recounted how the police had to be called in to overpower her; what a struggle she had put up, for such a tiny woman. Fortunately, they managed to wrestle her to the ground, strapping her arms behind her back. Heavily sedated, trussed and tied up ignominiously, they had borne her off, proudly, to the mental institution in the next district.

I've read somewhere that recovery for the survivor of a disaster is frequently psychological, rather than physical. Many are attacked by a crushing sense of guilt at having the wit, or the level-headedness, or the cowardice to escape; the guilt rests, like an evil little spirit in the pit of your stomach, dispensing poison. In the days that followed, the poison worked its way through my system; it left me indifferent to my interrogators, to the assaults, the beatings, the white lights, white heat. In the end I signed the confession. It seemed silly, churlish, not to since they were so determined to have it and declared themselves ready to forge my signature in any case. As I signed, it seemed to me I was expiating in some small way the nagging fact of my having survived mother, father, friends, sister.

They hang me tomorrow. Or the day after. The days here tend to merge into one another. I wish they would do it quickly. I am tired of waiting.

Lee

At first, he couldn't pick his daughter out from the crowd at the airport when he went to meet her, and he panicked, imagining all sorts of things. All he had was a rather smudged photograph to go by, showing a girl with long Janis Joplin hair framing her face, her smile wide and lopsided. He saw her finally, by the soft-drinks machine, inserting coins; no drink emerged and she kicked the machine, once, twice, three times. He should have recognised the flowing hair, but her clothes—a black man's jacket and tight red jeans—had led him to suppose it was someone older. She looked up, her forehead furrowing in doubt, when he came up.

"Are you my dad?" she asked in a pronounced American accent.

"Li Wen?"

"Yeah. But everyone calls me Lee."

Clumsily he hugged her and she accepted it with a sort of grudging nonchalance. She kept looking at him with a certain measured surprise— they hadn't met in eight years, he remembered, not since his ex-wife, having won custody of their eight-year-old child, had taken the first plane out to California and never come back. He'd heard that she'd got a job at a refugee centre, helping displaced Asians settle in their new country. Three weeks ago she had drowned accidentally in a friend's swimming pool in L.A. hence Li Wen's return. To be with her kith and kin, as his mother had sonorously put it. He had had great difficulty persuading his mother to stay away that night; he'd needed, he said, to be alone when he met Li Wen. "Is that a new-fangled Western concept or what?" his mother had demanded. She had never understood that one sometimes needed a modicum of privacy, a moment to take stock; everything had to be done As Family.

He picked up Li Wen's luggage, all three small pieces of it—"Oh, just my favourite shirts and a couple of records"—while she swung her own tennis racket carelessly and walked ahead of him. Her step was jaunty, light-footed; it was almost like cat-walking. She was as tall as he and he was five foot nine. She was sixteen.

"Hey," Lee said, when he caught up with her, "it's kind of hot here, isn't it?"

"Don't you remember anything about your country?"

He dumped the luggage in the back of the car.

"My country?" Lee said, as if not sure what he meant. "Oh. Yeah. Some. Not much. Not the humidity."

"You won't need that jacket here."

She looked down at it, flicking an infinitesimal speck of dust off the lapel, and an odd reflective look came over her face; he was to recognise it well; it was the look which signified she was back in L.A. in her mind.

"I guess not," she said.

In the car, she made straight for the radio, her hair swashing over the gears. Backing out, he didn't pay attention to her restless flicking of channels, her sarcastic exclamations of, "Oh my God" and "Can this be real?"

"Man, is that all the radio there is? M.O.R. and Bach?" She sounded flabbergasted.

"We don't believe in being swamped by the media here," he said in amusement.

"Hey—stop," she commanded. Her tone was imperative.

"Why?" They were near the exit of the car-park.

"I gotta get my Walkman out from the back. I can't listen to this junk. Kenny Rogers—" She rolled her eyes.

"Do you have to listen to anything right now?"

Lee said intensely, "I need the music, man."

He was about to say, No, annoyed, then relented. So he stopped the car and she was out and back in a flash; now she sat contentedly, legs tucked under her, swivelling her head round in curiosity at things which caught her attention along the road. She played the music loud and he could hear it above the noise of the traffic; in a way, it was a relief not to have to talk and he was almost apprehensive when she finally turned the thing off.

"So what do you do?" she said, prepared to be amused again. He told her he was a deejay.

"Gross out, man," she said; her tone was midway between being tickled and patronising.

"What?"

"Forget it," she said soothingly.

It was a long way back to the apartment; his instinct when he was nervous was to talk and he gabbled on in the inconsequential deejay manner about all her cousins and how glad they'd be to see her—she listened, half-impatiently, without saying a word, and that merely increased his awkwardness.

"Do you live with anybody?" she said suddenly.

"Live with—?"

"Like in 'cohabit'. You know." She was looking at him with a straightforward directness that disconcerted him.

"No," he said at last.

"They don't approve of it here, is that it? I seem to remember Mom telling me." She spoke of her mother coolly, without hesitation.

"Well, you have to remember this is an Asian society."

"Yeah? A catchall for everything from being conformist to looking back at the past all the time. That's what Mom used to say." She was challenging him; he refused to rise to the bait. "So do I call you Dad or what?" she said finally.

He shrugged. "Whatever you like."

She stretched her legs. "Man, it'll really be funny calling someone Dad again. The guy Mom lived with—Alan Piscopo—he didn't like me calling him Dad; he said the future of the nuclear family unit was doomed and parents were just another symbol of repression. But for years, y'know, that's how I thought of him, though he was white, of course, whiter than they come, even. He had this pale maggot skin that wouldn't tan, no matter what he did. In California, can you imagine, my God." She laughed.

He gripped the wheel, feeling a wholly unexpected jealousy directed at the faceless Piscopo, whom he visualised, for some reason, as a small weedy man with a brush moustache who walked around swimming pools in boxer shorts with a highball in his lily-white hand. He had never seen his ex-wife's lover and he'd resented it, fiercely, when Piscopo had broken through the protective wire-mesh netting around his world by writing to him after the death, asking him to reclaim Lee; she was a 'great girl' but he didn't feel up to the responsibilities of fatherhood. Piscopo's writing had been tiny, neat, regular—disciplined yet feminine—perhaps that had explained his mental image of him.

"What was he like?" he said cautiously.

His daughter said, "Alan? He's six foot one and he dresses like a trucker. You know what a trucker is?" He assented, gloomily. "Yeah. Right. Well. And he teaches at this Baptist college for girls. He was some kind of activist in the sixties, either for Goldwater or the whale, I don't remember, long hair, kaftan and all. He showed me a picture once. That's when he got into the Asian ethnic thing. He used to get at Mom and me for not being able to speak Mandarin; he could himself, after a fashion. Of course he could be a bit of a pretentious creep, but he was fun at times too."

And he knew, from the deliberately insouciant way she said it, that she'd been puzzled and hurt by this guy Piscopo's sending her away. Perhaps she'd even stormed—but he couldn't imagine Lee storming. He wanted to hug her, again, but he had to drive; it was, he thought, going to be equally hilarious being a father again. When Piscopo's letter had arrived, he'd felt at first as though some conjuror had pulled an entirely unwelcome rabbit from a hat and presented it to him. It was his mother who'd been excited; he had had to adjust himself to the fact, a little every day.

Lee said, "You think I'm a bastard, don't you, talking on about Alan?"

He found her arrow-straight questions embarrassing in the extreme; he hedged, though he did wonder why she didn't talk about her mother instead. At the same time he tried to convey to her that the set-up she'd lived in for years was not precisely conventional in a local sense.

"Hey—they didn't f__k in front of me, if that's what you mean," she said, generously exonerating them.

He sustained a shock, but managed to keep the car on the road. By this time, they were driving through Orchard Road, and she hung out of the window, watching the crowds outside the shopping centres—it was still only eight at night—with frank curiosity. Her hair streamed back in the wind and someone whistled at her. Quick as lightning, she shot whoever it was the finger. "Hey, Mac's," she said, head swivelling at the gaudy yellow sign. She leant her chin on her hands, folded on the window-edge.

"I thought it was going to be like Indonesia," she remarked. "This looks like parts of downtown L.A. Glitzy."

"When were you in Indonesia?"

"Last year. I asked Mom if we could stop over here, but she didn't want to. Third World countries are really sad; I suppose that's a bit of a cliché, but—anyway—what's saddest is the way you get these big concrete office blocks owned by ITT or something standing next to this zinc hut where you see a guy in the doorway selling a tent. I don't know." The lights from the hotels drew strips across her face.

"Hey," she said suddenly. "How come you never wrote?"

He'd asked himself the same question many times, overcome by an utter paralysis whenever he'd taken out a pen and a blue air-letter to write to his child.

"I thought it was pointless. Much better to put it all behind."

"Yeah. Guess I can understand that." She looked at him. "Mom hated this place. I couldn't get her to talk about it. What made you marry and split up?"

"That's impertinent," he said wryly.

"Hey, I'm on hiatus from conventions."

"All the wrong reasons," he said firmly.

"God," she said delightedly, "that sounds like a line from a movie."

"I don't eat meat," Lee told him the next day at lunch. She hadn't had breakfast either, he remembered, had stayed in her room all morning with the door shut. Now he looked at her in annoyance and at the chicken rice he'd prepared.

"I suppose you do eat," he said.

"Oh yeah, I'm interested in health foods and stuff. Yogurt. Celery sticks. Do they sell that around here?" She talked about food as if it were a hobby she occasionally indulged in, he thought.

"Celery sticks," he repeated.

Then she'd gone out to explore the condominium complex, wearing a pair of extremely short shorts and a Hawaiian shirt tucked in. Her records were stacked next to his own extensive collection: they included everything by the Grateful Dead (a formative Piscopo taste, she'd explained) and critically acclaimed L.A. bands, some of which he hadn't been able to obtain himself.

Through the doorway of Lee's room something caught his eye. Going in, he found the walls plastered with pictures from head to foot; they were mostly photographs and photographic stills, with a smattering of art posters. They swirled before him and he found it difficult to locate individual images. He started scrutinising from the left. His eye took in old tramps, bag ladies, shady hoods peddling at street corners, little girls sitting in a swing, all seven of them—no, on closer inspection they turned out to be seven dwarfs in dresses—shots of people dancing frenetically. 'New York: 1977' was a leafless tree viewed from a window which he judged to be on the second floor. There was a picture of two girls in the back of what he took to be a London cab; they were dressed for some reason in the clothes of a Jewish sect, the elder one turning her fine-boned troubled Slavic face to the ceiling while the younger girl whispered gleefully in her ear; through the glass behind them were the smoky Coke neon signs in the night. 'Say Cheese' was a man with a maniacal expression standing over a Stilton and wielding an axe. 'Blind' showed a man on a rooftop, his jacket flung over one shoulder, looking across the street at a single lighted window in the night, where a girl was sewing bright red cloth under a naked bulb. The square of brilliant yellow took up nearly a quarter of the space near the top. The man's face was lit up from the street below, not only from the lamps but from the flickering red of—he guessed—police sirens. He stared at the photograph a long time, wondering why it had been given such an enigmatic title.

Without his realising it, Lee had come in and was sitting on the bed beside him.

"I like that best, too," she said, pointing. "I think—he's this guy all crazed with wanting to know what life's all about. He sits up nights drinking black coffee and arguing and when he goes up to cool his head, he's struck by this girl, just sewing. She's illuminated and he's in the shadows; he still can't see what he wants desperately to see."

He looked at her in some amazement.

She flung herself back on the bed. "Sounds like a load of crap, doesn't it?"

He learnt to get used to the fact that people mistook Lee to be much older than she really was. It wasn't so much what she said—which veered between childish imperative exclamations and surprisingly adult conversation—as her whole demeanour, her air of taking people as they came and her lack of surprise.

He observed her daily, as he would have a new pet or a stranger in the neighbourhood. She resembled neither of her parents, not only being much darker, but her features too were sharper and more defined than the bland Southern Chinese faces he was used to, her cheekbones forming a high perceptible ridge under her eyes. Her face terminated in a semi-aggressive pointed chin; everything about her reminded him of a long-boned Modigliani woman.

It constantly amazed him to see her coming out of a room, calling him Dad. In a fit of fatherly reminiscence one day, he got out all the old albums and showed her the photographs of herself as a kid; and he remembered, wryly, the studied politeness with which she'd looked at them. Like her mother, she had little use for the past. He had been afraid, in the beginning, that she would mope for her previous home, and she had, he thought, come perilously near to it when a letter from Piscopo arrived, describing his latest intention to trek to India to seek enlightenment, "the last trip in '68, dear Lee, being clouded by its being a trip in more senses than one and certainly in the chemical sense." However—"The phoney bastard," Lee said succinctly; and while he winced at the language, he had to agree with the sentiment. He was glad when she threw the letter away, not bothering to reply.

She stocked up on yogurt, carrots, celery, cream cheese and HVA Health-Fi All-Vitamin Tonic. "Meat is poison, Dad," she told him. "Thousands of poisons. It's been scientifically proven. Fact." She was, he thought, the embodiment of a Californian cliché, as he watched her, dumbly, go through her aerobics-calisthenics routine on the sitting room floor.

If she was too diplomatic to fret openly in front of him, she showed it in other ways. Her second night at home, she had flicked television channels impatiently, staring half-mesmerised at some Quran All-night reading competition. "So what do you do around here, nights?" In those early days, he had taken leave from his night stints at the station to be with Lee, but he found the companionship distinctly awkward after a while, and himself racking his brain for things to say. He envied those fathers whose long-standing familiarity with their children had enabled them to evolve a comfortable shorthand code of grunts, pauses and secret family words intelligible only to themselves. Being an overnight father, almost, he had to start from scratch; and, ignobly, he copped out. That night, they went to a lounge where Lee, because of her appearance, ordered and downed two Martinis in succession and was peacefully asleep after an hour. These outings to night-spots he thought of with shame later, but he could not bear to see her wandering fitfully around. She needed, he realised, to be constantly entertained; the restless jigging jitteriness that she sometimes betrayed was the cold turkey of someone used to media stimulus from all directions. "People say L.A.'s uncultured," she said in scorn. "All freeways and smog. But this, my God, this is Dullsville." She spent hours listening to music over her headphones, lying on her bed and staring at the photos on the wall.

"Don't you read?" he said at last.

"Recommend somebody then," she said ironically. She always fended off his attempts at parenting with detached amusement.

"Dickens," he said vaguely, "Eliot, Austen—"

"I had to do a book review of *Mansfield Park* once," Lee said. "I nearly died." It turned out she read, spasmodically, Scott Fitzgerald, Norman Mailer, Ann Beattie, which, he supposed, not knowing much about it, was a respectable enough list of authors. But Lee, 'on hiatus' as she put it, was sorting out her perceptions and given, for the moment, to not doing anything.

The first few weeks, they went around the island, sightseeing. She liked the Esplanade, though she said the Merlion was 'tacky' which he gathered meant anything vaguely gauche or down-market. The other places, however, proved to be unmitigated disasters. Lee lagged behind him, dragging her feet and kicking stones along the ground, watching the people instead with frank curiosity and the remoteness of someone who felt herself uninvolved in their lives.

In particular he remembered a woman at the Chinese Gardens. She wore enormous tinted glasses and sported a beehive hair-do of tight permed curls; with her was a child, whom she was wrestling with and slapping, and shrilly vilifying in dialect. A self-assigned protector of the vulnerable, including all animals and children, Lee's first instinct had been to kick the woman in the shins; he stopped her.

"Man, you could always tell a Singaporean woman in L.A.," Lee said. "She'd look just like her. Way-out sunglasses and big bouffant hair-dos. Wearing *batik* prints and taking photographs of everything."

He disliked her tone. "They're your people too," he said to her, at the same time feeling ridiculous at his rush of patriotic emotion.

Lee said, "What's with this loyalty stuff?"

The woman looked the way he saw thousands of women look around the estates, not bothering about her appearance, her stomach slack, slopping around in fake Scholl slippers; and he wanted to tell Lee that he saw something fundamental, even noble, certainly lovable, in the woman now hugging the child to her and alternating threats with wet kisses, but he was hampered as always by his embarrassment at anything to do with emotion, and he forced it down again.

Then too there was the time they went down to Chinatown with a couple who were friends of his and fervent members of a fundamentalist church; that, so far, had not stood in the way of their friendship with him, an easy-going non-believer. Indiscreetly, they tackled Lee on the subject of her religious beliefs. "I don't believe in organised religion," Lee said politely. "I don't believe in God."

They turned on him vociferously. "I didn't have anything to do with it," he protested.

As they got out of the car, he heard Lee say under her breath, "Alan would have a fit if he knew there's a patch of the Bible Belt right here in the East. A real slice of the God-fearing Mid-west."

He sighed. "Look," he said to her, "you have to stop criticising—and start accepting—sooner or later things as they are here."

He realised that this might be harder than he'd foreseen as he saw Lee, wandering ahead, being accosted by a stall-holder, who was gesturing at a table frantically, smiling hopefully; his fingers were hooked in Lee's arm. He ran up to extricate her. "She's local—Singaporean," he repeated in Mandarin. "Leave her alone, will you? And no, we're not accepting your inflated prices either."

"He thought you were a tourist," he told her. She shrugged. She didn't really, he thought, look Chinese; Hawaiian perhaps or native American even. Part of it was the odd, casually scrappy way in which she dressed; that night she was wearing jeans of an extremely faded blue and a moth-eaten T-shirt with the seams ripped at the shoulder, the outfit of a thousand neo-hippies bumming around the East on a shoestring budget. It made her look more war-orphan emaciated and wirier than ever.

With a flash of irritation, he said, "Do you have to dress like that?"

He had never seen her lose her temper before. Now she gave him her twisted, half-sneer, James Dean scorching look, heavily nasty.

"So what the hell do you suggest I dress like? Those wimps in the shopping centres?"

"Well, why not?" he demanded. "They're neat at least."

"Because I think it's tacky, that's why."

"I am sick and tired of hearing you use that word," he said.

"Then you can shove it!"

And in repudiating him she seemed also to be repudiating her origins and all that around her. They wavered dangerously on the brink of recriminations. People were staring; he hated to be the centre of a scene.

"Oh hell," Lee said, passing swiftly from fury to remorse. "I'm sorry," and he had found her apology much harder to take than her recalcitrance; he wasn't used to people apologising to him.

Once he asked her, "Those pictures on your walls. Where did you get them?"

"Neat, huh?" she said, grinning. "I tore some out from library books. Others I got from Mom's *LIFE* magazines."

"What's their attraction?"

"They're—cool," she said, and she'd laughed. "Hey, I know I've got a rotten vocabulary. What I mean is they're detached—from you—but even the most artificial of them, even the most deliberately constructed and deliberately aligned, you know they've got an echo. In life. Some of them can be really weird too."

He didn't know what she was talking about.

"Do you miss your mother?" he said abruptly.

"I—guess so," she said off-handedly. "The really strange thing was—" she stopped. Have you seen those David Hockney prints? Cool glassy pictures of swimming pools in L.A. with some woman sitting in a deckchair or floating in the water, looking perfectly flat and one-dimensional in a striped bathing suit. And in a corner there's a sun with five rays and the thing's called Sunglasses or something like that."

She twisted her hair in her fingers, absently. "When I found Mom—in the pool—that's what I thought. A David Hockney print come to life."

There was a family reunion at his mother's flat the Saturday after Lee's arrival. His mother was a small indomitable woman who had raised a family of six by herself after her husband had decamped. She was staunchly Buddhist, Confucian and pro-PAP and her home bore testimonies to her three loyalties in the form of an altar, a porcelain sage and a framed picture of the Prime Minister. Privately, he thought his mother probably made as many obeisances to the PM as to *Kuan Yin.*

Lee was a head taller than her grandmother and she hunched involuntarily; it struck him they were like two wild birds meeting in their posture, crooked over. Lee's Cantonese being abysmal, he had to act as an interpreter.

Grandma: Ask her if she's glad to be home.

Lee: Tell her not to push the home-motif too much, okay?

"She's glad," he told his mother. He frowned at Lee, who shrugged. She was looking at the altar, tucked in a corner of the room, glowing redly. "Hey, that's cute," Lee said, going down on her knees. "I saw one in California. At the home of a Professor in Oriental Studies."

He shook his head, marvelling at her mother's capacity for burying her culture.

His mother said, "Goodness, look at her gawking at it as if she didn't know what it was."

She tapped Lee on the shoulder and beckoned. They went to the kitchen, where his mother fed Lee from a variety of local snacks.

"Hey, this is great," Lee said, grinning. "Tell her it's great."

"Ma, you're going to make her sick."

"Look at her. What's she been eating, air?"

He thought of the celery sticks and left Lee to her repast. From the kitchen he heard her speaking in her atrocious Cantonese, "Over there— we seldom ate—Chinese food. Just hamburgers—like this—"

Lee's cousins treated her with circumspection and respect, as though she were a giant freak on a visit. Used to the company of adults, she couldn't understand the hearty, artificial tones her uncles and aunts adopted towards her or the silly, inane questions they asked. "You don't understand," she would say, explaining some point about the States to them, but then she saw they hadn't really been interested in the first place; and she sat, uncharacteristically silent, in a corner after that.

His sister said, "I still think you should have made her stay at the convent. There's nothing like a good Catholic education."

Lee was at the American School now. He remembered her coming back after her first day at the convent, rather sarcastic about some girls who had cried at a test-mark of sixty-four out of a hundred. Then there had been a 'think-in' which he gathered was a sort of spiritually glorified group therapy session, whereby the girls were invited to share something significant in their lives (preferably the sort of thing one wouldn't reveal in a million years) to help the others understand them better. The ball had started rolling when a girl whispered that she cried at night for her father, who was an atheist, "then they all started crying and told the most gross-out things. It was fascinating, like a very bad movie you can't stop watching." Lee repeated, "Gross, man, gross." The crunch had come in her Chinese classes: her Mandarin was practically nil and her casual, heavily ironic attitude mildly infuriated the Chinese teacher, who had spoken wittily of Westernised corrupted cultural illiterates (meaning Lee in particular). Lee, sensing the drift rather than the actual meaning, called her an unprintable word in English intelligible even to the Mandarin teacher. The result was that Lee had finally been enrolled at the American School, much against his will, for he did not want her to have dual loyalties.

"Well," he said now, deprecatingly.

"Obviously," his sister said disapprovingly, "you've been giving in to her right, left and centre." She gazed at Lee. "She knows a lot for her age, doesn't she?"

"All the wrong things," he said gloomily, meaning, her weirdly in-depth knowledge about Jewish history, Watergate and the sex lives of American Presidents.

"I agree," his sister said. What she meant, he realised, was that Lee was too sophisticated for her age. 'Havoc', wasn't that the word? He felt intensely irritated with these moral labels.

His sister was saying, "Hasn't she been baptised?" She carried on a running battle with her mother about religion, the old lady adamantly refusing to forsake heathenism for the path to heaven.

"She doesn't believe in God," he said drily.

"Arrogant, isn't she?"

He looked at his sister with amused affection. "All intellectual arguments against the existence of God you'd put down to a question of attitude and upbringing, wouldn't you, Lily? To not eating one's vegetables when young. That's why people go around saying such terrible, terrible things—"

"Oh, you can make fun now," his sister said ominously. "You—the agnostic and the deejay."

He laughed delightedly.

On the way home, Lee sat with her head propped against her hand. "I like Grandma," she said thoughtfully. "She's got character." She yawned. "The rest of them—gosh, people here are pretty spineless, aren't they?"

Lee was moving with an entirely American crowd now. It was what he'd feared, but he didn't know how to rectify it. He began to find groups of them lounging in his sitting-room, breaking off their conversations when he walked in.

"I wish you'd make some Chinese friends," he told her.

"Dad, don't be so parochial."

He tried to interest her in her culture, but she seemed to shy away from it, treating it with a sort of fascinated repulsion. He left books on Chinese history lying around the house, purposefully; at dinner, he'd say, "*Shih Huang Ti* was the Chinese Fidel Castro."

"Dad," Lee said, "I don't want to hear about the Bay of Pigs in a Chinese context."

In particular a youth called Holden Mankiewicz from Algonquin, Illinois, began hanging around their flat, haunting it like a ghost. He was lean and lanky, with red hair and a galaxy of freckles stretching from ear to ear, a heavy metal freak who blasted Iron Maiden in the early hours of the morning.

"I don't like him," he told Lee, when he found Mankiewicz's head in the lower recesses of the refrigerator, apparently scrambling for spuds.

Then, one night, he found them in his bedroom; his head thundered, and he stormed out, slamming the door behind him, cursing parental burdens. He walked around the car park, grimly; he hoped, very much, they hadn't gone the whole way, but he had his doubts. He groaned.

"That was disgusting," he yelled at her later. Mankiewicz had bolted; Lee stood in the doorway of her room, buffing her nails.

"It's a matter of opinion," she said.

"Don't answer me back!"

"We didn't do anything. It was just fun. What d'you want, an affidavit?" She shook her head. "Jesus Christ."

"And stop swearing, if you don't mind!"

It was, he thought, all her mother's fault; but the moment he mentioned Lee's mother, his daughter straightened up and shot him her James Dean vile look. "That's sick," she said, and marched out. They didn't talk to each other for two weeks, except in tones of exaggerated politeness; all in all, he was convinced, he must have suffered more than her during the silence.

As always, it was Lee who broached a reconciliation; somehow he always hung back, hoping cowardly it would all blow over. She asked him if she could go with him to the studio one night; relieved, he agreed. It was strange seeing her there in the cold studio in her black jacket, flipping through the record selection, wearing gold dangling earrings as large as saucers. He kept thinking he ought to mention The Night—his sister, if she had known, would have insisted—but he knew he didn't have it in him to deliver moral strictures, once he'd spent the initial rage.

"So what made you become a deejay?" she said curiously.

"Oh, I don't know. I wasn't very good at work. Scraped through A-levels. I spent more time listening to the radio than studying."

"So who did you like?"

"The Beatles, of course. Jefferson Starship. Marc Bolan. David Bowie—but that was much later—"

"Hey, I like him too." She raised her eyebrows expressively. "I think he's cool. Besides," she added thoughtfully, "you're not stupid."

"Why—thank you—" but she had to wait, as the record playing had come to an end. He spoke deejay patter into the mike and spun his next record.

"—about my not being stupid," he said encouragingly, grinning.

"Well," she said. "What's a crummy mark anyway? It just shows you did well in a test at a certain date at some point in your life. But no one here buys that. The other Asians in my school in L.A., they were all crammers too. Some crazy tomfool idea of success. It's their parents' fault. Look, maybe you and I can't study. So what? It's just one facet of learning. I don't see why a guy who can memorise facts is necessarily smarter than a guy who can surf really well. It's just—" she frowned—"different centres of the brain being sharper than the rest."

"But don't you think the guy who can memorise facts is going to be more useful to the economy?"

"With the computer around? Can a computer surf?"

"Lee, you're a philosopher," he said solemnly.

"Don't kid me," she warned.

She sat on the console, swinging her legs, an air of portentous gestation about her; he wondered what it was.

"I don't think—" she'd cocked her head on one side and was regarding him with a certain shame-faced defiance—"I like being Asian. Or Chinese." "Why not?"

"God, it's so claustrophobic. It's a neurotic culture. All that jazz about saving face, losing face—it's hysterical. Then the 'respect your elders' bit. You have to keep repeating that because you strip away all dignity from the old. Don't you see? Keeping the grandparents in the extended family as babysitters—that's really great. Oh sure you talk a lot about the wisdom of the old, but you don't really believe that, it's just a camouflage because anyone over sixty here has had it—always barring one exception—and who says anyway the old are necessarily wiser or mellower than they were at forty? It's mostly a myth. And when they talk about the West here—'Look how they treat the old; they actually live alone without a hooked-up life-support system to their children—'"

"You, you, you," he said. "What about you?" She sighed. "Yeah. Right. I keep forgetting."

"Look, Li Wen," he said. "I'm going to tie myself up in knots but I want you to listen anyway. For hundreds, no, thousands of years (this isn't a dinosaur story though it may sound like it) we—Chinese, Indians, whatever—had a magnificent culture while the Caucasians were still scrabbling in the dust. Then in the last couple of hundred years the West just overtook us—snap—and we were left looking like reactionary fools from a backwater. It makes you look silly, I'll tell you. That's why you get this paranoia, this phobia of the West and the mad clinging to so-called Eastern values. It's the protective shell of a people trying desperately to catch up at the same time. That's what I think anyway. And for those of us who were lucky or unlucky enough to leave the motherland, who're immigrants, living in proximity to the West just gives a hysterical edge to the whole business. That's why you get the frantic studying, the emphasis on material success. Because it's been so recent. And when you do have it, like Japan, the soul-searching still doesn't stop either—the rot's set in too far."

He stopped and grinned, not realising he'd gone on so long, but he had become impassioned for the first time in years.

She sat with her hands wedged between her knees, looking at him, her gold earrings glittering under the lights.

"And they wrote you off in school, didn't they?" she said. He shrugged. "Sure," she said at last. "Maybe. But it's still not easy."

But he was satisfied.

The next day she took down the 'Blind' photograph from the wall of her room and gave it to him. He tacked it up in the studio, alongside the peeling Mick Jagger posters and Cream record covers. Sometimes, at night, before he went to sleep, he could still see the lighted window hovering in a corner of his mind.

Jeanne

"I hate to leave you," he said. He took her hand in his and played with it.

"Don't," she said, sharply. "We're in a restaurant."

"So?"

"A public place."

"You never cared before."

Ruth withdrew her hand.

She was being difficult today, unlike her usual effervescent self; even the bright red of the two-piece suit she wore looked limp, like a last, pathetic gesture of defiance. He drummed his fingers on the table, irritation filling the silence between them.

"Don't you want to go on this trip with Jeanne?" Stupid question, that. Jeanne was his wife.

"No," John said warmly. "I've read somewhere that a holiday together is the surest way to break up an unsatisfactory marriage. Away from work with only each other for company, husband and wife find that they can't bear each other's conversation, personal habits—and end up having terrific fights—"

"And you don't want to break up your marriage, of course," Ruth said, ironically.

He hesitated.

Seeing this, she interrupted him. "No, no. Don't tell me." She stood up, abruptly, collecting her things. "John, I have to go."

He had been far too engrossed in his own affairs to think, properly, of her, and he felt a pang of compunction. Seizing her hand again, he promised, "I'll call you as soon as I get back."

People at the next table, wedged against theirs, were looking at them covertly. Ruth, flushing, nodded and was gone.

As he stood up, he caught sight of himself in the full-length wall mirror and was momentarily startled by the tall, suited figure that looked back at him, indistinguishable from the others in the room. Every inch the banker: him. He took a perverse pride in conformity, in looking the part. The crafted facade, the blandness—he revelled in it, knowing, as he did, that it was mere papering over the teeming, victorious secret life he carried within him. Realising he had been staring, unseeingly, at his own reflection, he felt a little foolish and began to thread his way out among the tables.

Florida steamed. Whatever else they had expected, it was not the blast of humidity that greeted them the moment they left the Orlando airport. "We should have stayed at home," John said in resignation. His reasons for coming, if any, now seemed to him terribly obscure. Jeanne, ignoring his bad temper, slipped on a pair of enormous sunshades and stepped forth to hail a taxi.

It was late by the time they arrived at the hotel but he insisted, in his usual methodical fashion, on obtaining all the details about the attractions from the front desk. Jeanne went upstairs—not to unpack, of course. When he returned she was reclining on the bed, absently flicking through TV channels. At one time her casual, drifting insouciance had charmed him; now he saw it as chronic laziness. He disliked her indifferent housekeeping, her haphazard ways. He said as much, over the synthetic voices of the newsreaders. She gave him a wide-eyed, noncommittal stare and said nothing. This holiday, he remembered now, had been planned to celebrate the arrival of the baby. But they had lost it. She had lost it, by miscarrying. Quite irrationally, he had started to blame her for most things.

In the flickering darkness of the room, another air-crash was announced. How many was it now—five, six, this month alone? He'd lost count and he felt ill. Lately, death, even in the abstract, had begun to chill him—more than usual, that is. He had taken to feeling twinges of his own mortality at the most inopportune moments—in bed with Ruth, at an office meeting where he had to concentrate hard on not letting the feeling get the better of him. In between these attacks, however, he forgot their intensity. Ruth, unsympathetic to his panic-stricken behaviour, thought he was using an imaginary fear of death to mask a more deep-rooted guilt. And he had laughed at her analysis, feeling more isolated than ever.

The peculiar vivid reality of a crash in particular always made his gorge rise. He imagined the passengers sitting forward, waiting for the impact. The game of roulette seemingly involved every time he got on a plane always left him slightly dizzy and he felt a bad sour taste in his mouth. Ashamed of his weakness, he made himself a drink from the tiny, expensively-stocked fridge.

Jeanne saw his expression and understood. "You are morbid," she said wryly. Like Ruth, she thought his fears grotesque. Unusually for her, she went over to him and began to rub his shoulders. Grateful, he kissed her.

In the beginning, her cool reserve had excited and challenged him; she seemed to him a cypher and he was determined to discover what it was she hid so sedulously. A former model, she had a capacity for stillness, a kind of stateliness which continued to fascinate him—it was as though she were posing to the instruction of some unseen cameraman. At first, he thought her reserve a way of concealing an inner anarchy—their first few months together, she had surprised him by leaving home and running to him (even now, he could recall her absurdly young, anxious, uplifted face)—but now he was less certain. Marriage for him had become a treadmill; he often thought that he and Jeanne moved on identical parallel courses through their house and their lives without really meeting.

And yet it was also true that in the beginning his passion had frightened him a little—it was not something he had thought himself capable of. Somehow she had managed to penetrate, all unwittingly, the defences he had erected so comfortably around himself, and it showed, the obsessive pride he took in her, the way he couldn't stop looking at her, couldn't get enough of her. His mother had remarked sourly that there was more to marriage than good looks and great sex; at the time he had rounded on her, furious at her unreasoning hostility to Jeanne. Now, he sometimes wished he had listened to her. Since then, there had been the frustrating attempts to have a child, the internecine sniping, the growing distant politeness, the miscarriage. He suspected that Jeanne, too, was disillusioned. Once, she had confided in him artlessly; now, he had little idea what she thought or felt about most things and, frankly, he cared little. He had thought countless times about separation—what with Ruth and all—but he did wonder if something in Jeanne had escaped him, something elusive which she deliberately held in check, doubting his worth. It made him think, every time, that it was impossible to leave without breaking that final reserve. It was an irrational feeling, no doubt, but there it was.

It seemed hard to believe, but Orlando was apparently the top tourist destination within the United States itself. With its strip shopping malls and leafy suburbs it was the classic American small town set in sub-tropical weather. It was neither picturesque nor scenic; the weather broiled; tourists came for one reason only, to flood the theme parks galore. Along with the other hordes, they wandered through dutifully, some eighty dollars poorer. Despite everything—the heat, the queues, the unwanted company of his wife—John had expected to enjoy himself. He loved amusement grounds; ever since he was a child he had wanted to go to the quintessential theme park, and he discounted as snobs all those who said Disneyland was infantile. Now that he was here, however, the magic refused to do its work. The adult inhibitions refused to shed themselves and give way to unbridled hedonism: the prices of everything rattled him and he wondered, with a jaundiced eye, why every other American seemed to be of a serene whale-like obesity. His enthusiasm became perfunctory.

"Did you see?" Jeanne said, while they were in some queue or other. "The little girl in front of you just keeled right over in the sun."

"You mean she fainted?"

"Well, of course."

Her huge shades hid her face, but he knew she was dispirited. So was he. The small army of children warring underfoot reminded him too painfully of his own—his invisible children, whose voices he sometimes thought he could hear, if they didn't happen to be just out of earshot. The child, it seemed to him, stood between them now, reproachful at their having come without him. But we tried to bring you, he appealed, in the absurd conversation that ran through his head. We tried—with a minor fortune spent on consulting gynaecologists, specialists and even a *bomoh*, at John's mother's insistence. (Jeanne had refused to see the last.) Jeanne's pregnancy, so unexpected, had seemed at first an anchor in their rudderless marriage, but that, like so much else, had come to nothing. He was glad, in a way, when she said she had a splitting headache and wanted to go back.

The bus back to the hotel was crowded and they sat lodged next to an American couple, a pleasant, sun-baked, middle-aged pair, who asked them how they liked Orlando. "And have you been to the theme parks? We think they're wonderful."

"So do we," said John.

"They're incredibly polite, aren't they?" Jeanne remarked.

"Who?"

"The Disney employees. Everything's so mechanical. I don't mean that badly, but every time I see them smiling so hard my own jaws ache. Didn't someone say it was benignly totalitarian?"

"Well, it's kind of a cliché to say that ... but the Disney ethos is to put the customers first."

The man was looking at Jeanne in frank admiration; she did, John thought, look good in a loose green shirt and black pants.

Later, he asked her, "How could you?"

"What?" she wanted to know, unpinning her hair.

"Be so critical in front of them."

"People don't mind as much as you seem to think." It was one of his pet axioms that people hate at all costs to lose face and one of her principles that she didn't care if they did.

"Incidentally," he said, "would you mind telling me why you have to flirt with every other man you meet?"

"Don't be ridiculous. I don't flirt, as you call it. We've had this conversation before." She pulled her blouse over her head and sailed into the bathroom. He leant in the doorway.

"Oh no? You were all over him. His wife was wishing we were somewhere else."

He was being ridiculous, he knew. Jeanne, with her poise, her striking good looks, would sail into a party like a ship coming into port; around her the wives and girlfriends would create a politely-frozen, dead lake of silence, anticipating, wrongly, that she would try to upstage them. It was not surprising that she preferred the company of men, that she had developed an easy, confiding air with them that made John, even now, querulously jealous, even though he knew it was all perfectly innocent. (It also had something to do with a remark he'd heard once which he had not meant to overhear, to the effect that no one knew what had made her marry a jerk like him.)

"And don't you? Wish you were somewhere else?" His mocking-eyed wife flashed him a look in the bathroom mirror.

He ignored this. "I don't understand you," he said. "Opening up just like that in front of a complete stranger and telling him the weirdest things."

"Dear John, I only come alive for you in someone else's eyes, don't I?"

What makes you such a frigging Madonna? he wanted to ask, goaded, but did not. The rest of the holiday stretched before him, for an eternity.

They spent long days at the pool. The mornings were the best time, the shrieking children hauled off to Disney World. John, who had swum for his university, would be in like a fish, covering forty, fifty lengths of the small pool furiously; occasionally he had these wild bursts of energy and would have to work out for an hour or more. Jeanne, never a great exerciser, would bob by the side, then rise out of the water to tan. She looked marvellous, his wife, in a swimsuit, tall, with all of a model's supple grace, shaking the water out of her hair; he felt inordinately proud of her, the pride of a collector, he had to admit, in a particularly fine object. He loved her at moments like these, when she was so inexorably, indubitably, his possession. These brief, glorious moments came and went too soon, however, like the flashes of gems embedded in rock; the rest of the time, they were locked in a pattern of tedium, irritation, non-communication, which neither could break.

Ruth was tiny. Small hands, small feet, a neck which his palm could encircle. In his mind she was always the bright lodestar; just thinking of her filled him with a pleasant, erotic warmth and he turned on his back and floated, light as ether, in the sun.

How much did Jeanne know, he often wondered. It seemed to him incredible that she suspected nothing; her wilful ignorance (he presumed it must be that) by turns soothed him, by turns enraged him. It was all part, he felt, of her closing herself off from him. Whenever Ruth slunk into his thoughts, as she was wont to do at the oddest times, he became seized with an irrational panic that it would show on his face and that bystanders would look at him in amazement. At other times he was so full of her, so positively bursting with illicit love that the secret bubbled on the surface, threatening to break. It seemed too much that it should be muffled—he wanted, often, to take poor, ignorant (his epithets) Jeanne by the shoulders and shout, Look at me, Listen to me.

What a tangled web we weave. The phrase came at him out of nowhere; he racked his brain, trying to remember, but it eluded him. He had a brief vision of the web tearing, unravelling, the spider on a precipitous slide. Settling himself beside Jeanne on a deckchair, he smiled at her.

The immenseness of America filled his cramped island soul with a certain scared awe. Who built these endless highways through fields that galloped off into the distance, who ordained the rolling sky, alive with a temperamental presence of its own, the thick, rolling clouds pressing down heavily? The speedometer showed seventy, eighty miles, way over the speed limit: he slowed down, and the Cadillac tailing him for the last mile overtook in a blur of chrome hugeness, the rear-fins cocked insouciantly at him. It was a game you played on the highway, making good time while trying not to exceed the speed limit by too much, and keeping a lookout for the cartoonish state troopers lying in wait in the grass verges.

And this was just Florida.

The thought of hundreds, thousands of miles looping their way across the continent, racing to catch up with the sky, dazzled him. He was reminded of a certain maths teacher he'd once had, a young man, fresh, enthusiastic, not yet jaded by the system. Think of a big number, he'd urged, so big you can't possibly imagine it. He had got them from millions to tens of millions, to hundreds of millions, to weird, gleeful things called googols; for John, however, the numbers remained as words; for some reason, try as he might, he could never make the transition from mouthing the figures to grasping the giddy feeling of near-infinity and he had concluded that those children who said they could must have been lying. Now he drove on, with a rekindled sense of wonder.

Northern Miami finally loomed, an urban sprawl criss-crossed by highways, skyscrapers sparkling in the sun. Crossing the Tuttle Causeway, they bumped slowly into Miami Beach, that eccentric strip of land just off the coast, dominated by the mile-long row of Art Deco hotels. The hotel they finally chose was pale lime green, dwarfed by the birthday-pink of the Delano. The proprietor, a lugubrious elderly retiree with quivering nostrils from which hair sprouted luxuriously, showed them to their room.

From their window, they could see the beach and the ocean, a bandage of white fringed by clear subterranean blue.

"Gosh, isn't it lovely?" Jeanne said. "Come on, I must go for a swim."

He was unpacking. "Couldn't we at least wait—" But she was already gone. Sighing, he followed her down, to an empty deckchair on the beach next to two stout, middle-aged women. Flinging her towel down, she walked, tall and tranquil, to the water. The two women, breaking off their Spanish chatter, watched her dive into the ocean, and turned to John. "Where you from, honey?"

He told them. They nodded in satisfaction. "Don't tell me, it's in China, right? My sister went there last year. Beautiful, she said it was." It was his turn to nod, not bothering to correct them.

He saw Jeanne's head bob in the water; she was facing out to sea. Slowly, she began to swim out against the tide. To the right of her, a young couple was embracing in the water, heads interlocked. Their daughter, a long-haired, five-year-old doll in whom one could see, even at that age, the seeds of the stunning beauty she would later become, stood, furious and neglected, stamping her feet in the sand. His worried eye returned to Jeanne; surely she was going too far out for an indifferent swimmer. John hesitated, then began to strike out towards his wife.

"Are you mad?" he said, treading water some ten feet away from her. "Come back."

Her chin grazing the surface of the water, she was contemplating him, he felt, with a hint of contempt. And the horrible thought came to him that it would be so easy for her to drown—easy for him, that is, released in a flash from this marriage. He pictured himself, the grieving widower, discreetly marrying Ruth after a suitably decent interval.

As if sensing his thoughts, she said, coolly, "Don't worry, I'm indestructible."

He turned and began to swim back.

The little girl was gouging sand out in a rage. As her parents emerged from the ocean, hand in hand, a watery primordial Adam and Eve, she burst into tears and a fierce Spanish altercation ensued. How emotional they were, John thought, one minute all flashing tumult, the next proceeding happily up the sand, the child being swung along between her parents.

The two women also gathered up their belongings and left. "Be careful," one of them called out to him. Careful of what? He waved.

The ferocious heat of the day had lifted, the glare melting away, the ocean receding into the shadow of a pinkish sky. The backs of the cream stucco hotels appeared suddenly drabber; you could see the paint flaking off, the windows that had not been washed for ages. Even the palm trees looked draggled and unkempt, away from the brilliant camouflage of the sun. The unaccountable melancholy which frequently attacked him at home at this time of day touched him here as well. It was the transitional twilight, the dissolution, which unsettled.

Jeanne was walking across the sand towards him. He handed her her towel.

"Happy?" he said sarcastically.

"Very," she assured him.

He couldn't tell whether she was serious. Sorry, now, for his speculations about her convenient demise, he asked her, hesitantly, "Do you remember the first time we went away to the beach together?"

"Yes," she said, in a tone discouraging further reminiscences. He thought her hard and knew he was responsible for this new, unaccustomed flintiness.

"What got into you?" he said, meaning the swim.

"I love it," Jeanne said. "I love the space, the openness of everything. You can breathe here. I wish we lived by the sea."

To his surprise, there were traces of tears in her eyes. Unable to imagine what had brought on this flower-like burst of emotion, he looked away and she continued up the beach towards the hotel, by herself.

Miami recalled for him a Jackson Pollock painting, seen long ago between the pages of a book—great wide slashes of colour intersecting, fading, looming, their vividness compounded by the hard brilliance of the light. A monorail system wound its way, tiny, serpentine, perched on air, around downtown's glass city. Dotted around Miami, cheerfully incongruous, were pastel-coloured, upbeat funeral parlours, cordial invitations to, rather than portents of, mortality.

"Why would anyone want to die here?" Jeanne said, abruptly.

"Retire here, you mean." Miami, retirement capital of America.

"No, die here. Death doesn't seem real in this place. All this light, this vibrance—"

He hit the wheel of their rented car in irritation. "Oh God, do we need to have another of those conversations? Do we need to delve into everything? Can't we be just a normal couple on holiday?"

She seemed amused. "I'd forgotten," she said presently.

"What?"

"Your fear of death."

"And you think I'm just morbid? Overdoing it?"

"It does seem a bit irrational," she admitted.

"And you're not? Afraid?"

"Not the way you are."

"That's because," he said, through gritted teeth, "you're killing me."

She looked out of the car window. At moments like these she had developed a knack for excluding him.

He could not forgive the matter-of-fact way in which she spoke. If love was merely a way of staving off death, of keeping the nightmare beast from the door, then he was drained of it, to judge by the nights he had stayed awake staring into the dark, fighting off the thing that sat on his chest, suffocating him. Jeanne's sleeping presence did nothing to alleviate the panic: indeed he wondered how she could sleep so heartlessly through it all, deaf and blind to his predicament, his nightly demons.

He had dreamt of Ruth the night before. She stood, far off, on the shore, in her red suit, watching the waters enclose him, doing nothing. In the second half of his dream, she had no idea that he had drowned and was trying to reach him at his hotel, growing more frantic by the minute. It was so real that he woke with a start, sweat-drenched. He lay for a few minutes, collecting himself, listening to the comforting roar of traffic down Collins Avenue. Jeanne slumbered on, oblivious, while he padded to the bathroom.

His wife seemed to him that day lumpen, crude and tactless, jarring on his nerves with a cruel accuracy. Her tone, voice, attitude irritated him; her navigation, so-called, infuriated him. He longed for Ruth, her quickness, her flashing intelligence, the way she could make him laugh. She would have made sense of the map, for example, in a few seconds. If Jeanne noticed his barely suppressed annoyance, she gave no sign. Her obtuseness inflamed him further.

They were going to the Vizcaya, at Jeanne's insistence. It turned out to be a mock Italian Renaissance palace, set in sub-tropical splendour. This costly incongruity had been the work of a turn-of-the-century industrialist called James Deering, in the days when industrialists wielded unimaginable clout and thought, in their boundless optimism, that culture was something which could be imported and transplanted wholesale. A mousy guide intoned her litany in flat monotony, gesturing at the many genuine artifacts taken with cheerful profligacy from churches and palazzos. John had a mental vision of tight-lipped nobles declining to sell the family heirlooms then crumbling, helplessly, before the proverbial American offer that one couldn't refuse.

"Who did the guy think he was?" he said to Jeanne in some indignation. At the same time he was impressed. It wasn't so much the wealth; it was the breathtakingly grandiose folly of it all. What was it like, he wondered, to feel that there were no limits to what one could accomplish? It was so intensely American. And it was an undeniably lovely house.

"God, to think what you can do with money," he said, on the say back. It was his constant refrain. "Without it, you're nothing."

Jeanne was driving. Her lower lip stuck out slightly, like a child's, in concentration. "We have enough," she said absently.

Her middle-class contentment irked him, as it always did. She was genuinely uninterested, he knew, in the arcane mysteries of being rich: where the money came from, where it was going, and who was on his way up (or down). Her lack of envy seemed to him an intellectual deficiency; the fact that she could not share his excitement about such things made him resent her sharing his rise in the world. She held him back.

"We have enough because I make enough. Would you mind bearing that in mind? Money doesn't grow on trees, though you probably think it does." He had never quite got over the fact that she grew up wanting nothing and he everything.

"Look, you were the one who didn't want me to work," she said evenly.

It was true, he remembered guiltily. He had made her give up her job as a model. It may have been atavistic, but he didn't want his wife to work. It was as simple as that.

"All right," he said hastily.

"Incidentally, I've been thinking that I do want a job."

He saw the web unravelling.

"Why? Don't you have a fantastic house to look after?"

"You're so chauvinistic." She seemed amused, more than anything else. He said nothing.

"You didn't buy me from a shop, you know," she said. "You can't just wind me up like a doll and make me talk or whatever it is—when you want it." Still, he said nothing.

He had met Ruth at a business lunch, at which she had appeared in what looked like a frivolous cocktail party confection, and had talked nineteen to the dozen, ignoring him. His estimation of her, already low, hit rock-bottom when she accidentally broke the heel of her ridiculous stiletto shoes in a pavement grating and had to hobble, screaming with laughter, to her car.

He had to see her again, however, to discuss a deal. This time round, she seemed supremely businesslike, all the raucous jollity tucked away. She also had a nice smile. His dislike lessened. She could talk agreeably on a range of topics of which Jeanne knew nothing, and he found he enjoyed listening to her. Over the next few months, they met regularly, on a professional basis. His antipathy towards career women remained, but in his fretful restlessness, Ruth attracted him irresistibly. Jeanne, pregnant and inaccessible, seemed to him then like a ship becalmed after a storm, trapped in her isolation. Everything about Ruth at that moment, from her smallness to her vividness, was the antithesis of Jeanne.

Ruth was divorced and living alone with her two-year-old son. She talked about her ex-husband, now living in Australia, with a casual biting nonchalance that slightly shocked him; about her situation ("there's such an old-fashioned stigma against divorced women here; it's so mediaeval.") There was so much about her, like him, that was self-wrought, from her name, which she had given to herself, to her accent and her determination to climb the ladder, socially and professionally. They shared the same hunger for the good things in life, the same capacity for intense selfishness: these traits, which he occasionally had the grace to dislike in himself, somehow appeared endearing in Ruth, a fellow creature under the same skin.

Two months later he asked her out for dinner. She went rather pink, but said yes. Neither had any illusion but that this would be the prelude, long and gracefully played out, to an affair, and this tacit understanding formed a comfortable undercurrent to their conversation, all surface innocuousness. To his surprise, she displayed an insatiable curiosity about Jeanne, whom she had met once, pronouncing her 'absolutely gorgeous'. Flattered, he gave Ruth to understand that his marriage was not all that it should be. That Jeanne was there, but not really there for him. That perhaps all marriages are attempts to get away from the importuning demands of other people and end up as struggles to get away from the importuning demands of each other. That Jeanne's pregnancy had walled her off from him. He was charmed by Ruth's spirited feminine defence of Jeanne: "Yes, but are *you* there for *her*?" It was like chess: all the preparatory moves had been made, a casual, tender, bantering intimacy established. Only the final step remained.

He had assumed implicitly, for some reason, that he would have a son. Instead he was informed over the phone one evening at work by his mother-in-law that Jeanne had miscarried. He flew to the hospital; there were complications, they said, and initially refused to let him see her. Summoning up all the overbearing aggression of which he was capable, he created a scene, until they relented. In any case, she was heavily sedated, lying in bed in a sort of untidy helplessness, mouth slightly agape, which both pierced and repelled him. Oddly, he had little thought left over for the baby: it had never really been anything more to him than a hypothetical, a might-have-been. It was the disruption in the smooth flow of his life which shook him. Assured that Jeanne would be awake in the morning, he went home, but found the ticking silence of the house unbearable. His mind both feverish and blank, he drove over to Ruth's house, wanting, and expecting, nothing more than coffee and to talk.

Clad in a red dressing-gown, she received him with a solicitous gravity that touched him. Humbled—he felt that the gods were patting him back and forth that night in an inscrutable game of their own—and grateful, he made love to Ruth. It had a sad finality about it, as if it were the last, rather than the first, time, and though he was to lie, cheat and indulge in elaborate subterfuge in the coming weeks to spend time with Ruth, it never felt the same again.

Jeanne made a quick recovery, but nevertheless chose to stay over at her parents' house for a while, to recuperate, she said. His parents-in-law—who represented relatively old money in the jarringly new island state—treated him with an even more marked reserve, he noticed. Jeanne, he knew, would say nothing, but in the too correct coolness between husband and wife, they must have been confirmed in their initial opinion of him as a jumped-up opportunist marrying the family name rather than the daughter. He loathed them, remembering the days when his passion for Jeanne had come up against their suspicion like an immovable brick wall. Eventually, Jeanne returned, slightly thinner, moving through the house with her usual Garbo languor, taking up again the activities—macramé, French, celebrity modelling at society functions—which filled her time. Though he refused to admit it, her return made him calmer, happier, as if the still centre of his life had steadied. But he had no thought of giving up Ruth.

Ruth, wearying of being the Earth Mother, also had her black moments. He knew she had had other affairs before and that she was afraid this would end as the others had, in messy squalor. Then she would tell him to go, before it reached that stage. He took these oscillations of mood as a woman's prerogative: indulgently giving her a few days to brood, he would then call back. Her voice, subdued at first, would regain its rapid, animated singsong and the whole dance would begin again. He could not leave her but neither could he go to her. The perfect solution, he thought, was for the two women to merge. The ideal Ruth-Jeanne combination dream-woman.

"Men are so poorly equipped to deal with reality," Ruth would say to him in the same brisk tone she used with clients. "Why do you always want us to be other than we are?" The solidarity she implied with Jeanne nettled him.

They were his two worlds, and he was falling in the abyss between them.

"Are you really going to get a job then?" he asked Jeanne that night in their motel room.

"I think I am." She was sitting by the edge of the bed, writing postcards. He sprawled across and stroked her hair, her back.

"It might be a good idea," he said thoughtfully. If it ever came to a divorce, it would be far better for Jeanne to have some employment to fall back on. He muzzled her neck.

She spun round. "Oh, stop it," she said. "You make me sick."

Now that the moment had arrived, he felt both calm and exhilarated. The tension of the past few months had been killing.

"I had a life before you and I'll have a life after you." Her breath came quickly; she was angry.

"After me?"

She asked, point-blank, "Are you seeing another woman?"

He studied her watchfully. "Yes," he admitted. There, it was out. The relief was immense.

He waited for a reaction, a flailed fist or a scream. Instead she stood by the window, looking out, carved in perfect stillness. She was rising to the occasion, he felt, quite marvellously.

"Do you want a divorce?" she said at last.

"I don't know."

"What do you want?"

"I want you. I want our child."

It was the wrong thing to say. Inflamed, the flush he knew so well rose to her face.

"Stop lying to me. Just stop. You've never wanted me, just some image of me that you have." He opened his mouth to protest, but she swept on. "And what do you want with children anyway? As further ornaments to set off your house, your wife, your car?"

He winced. This was an injustice of a particularly wounding kind, and he said so.

"Your feelings don't matter very much to me at the moment," she said. He wished she would shout, scratch, anything other than inflict on him the tone of measured reasonableness she was using. She was robbing him of his weapons. "Let me guess. You started this—thing—after we lost the baby, is that right?"

He sighed. "Yes." It slipped out before he could stop it; now he wished he could recall it. Jeanne went white. He felt criminal, remembering her helplessness in that terrible period. "You asked," he said feebly.

She ignored this and began to walk up and down.

"Look, I don't care who she is and I don't want to know. To tell you the truth, I've suspected it for months and I don't even mind very much. What I do mind is your thinking you can run circles around me and manipulate poor little Jeanne. Don't ever pity me and don't look so smug."

He was not aware of looking smug. Somewhere, far off, a siren wailed. He had waited for ages to utter Ruth's name in front of his wife, to savour the strange sound of it on his tongue. He had assumed that Jeanne would want to know everything, to calibrate, like all women, the power and the weapon of their hurt. Her refusal to demand details for some reason diminished Ruth—their affair seemed distant and echoey, in another life altogether, although he had dreamed of her only the night before. Instead he found he could only concentrate on Jeanne's pacing, the way she hugged her thin arms to herself.

"What are we going to do?" he wanted to know.

"Oh, we'll all survive," she said callously, flippantly.

"That's you all over, isn't it?" he said. He found he was angry, the anger feeding into self-pity. "The martyr, the victim, the wronged one. Your favourite role. I'm so sick of it. I don't ask for much, just for you to act as if I'm there once in a while. I don't think you hear me or see me any more. I lie awake nights and I want to turn to you, but I can't. There's only so much I can take and so much waiting I can do. Life's too short for me to wait and see whether you'll give your queenly consideration to the matter—"

She listened to this attempted justification scornfully. "Oh, of course," she said with terrible sarcasm. "I'm killing you. I quite forgot."

A flash of his bad temper showed again. "Yes, you are, you bitch." She averted her face and he shrugged. "Okay, okay, I'm sorry. That was an exaggeration. But tell me, why did we get married? At least, I did. You stayed on on the sidelines, reserving judgment, isn't that so? I don't know what you think, what you feel. Or do you?"

"I don't know why you think I don't. Perhaps you don't want to know."
And then: "You demand so much attention, John. All the time. You've
swallowed me up, you know. I don't even have an identity of my own any
more. I'm sorry, but I have nothing left to give."

"Hey," he said, trying to smile. "It's not that bad." Fight for me, he was
trying to say, selfish to the last, but the words stuck in his throat.

"I'm tired," she said. "I want to sleep. We'll both think more clearly in
the morning."

She huddled, as she always did when they had a quarrel, by the side of
the bed. Something in the curve of her body made him unutterably sad.

"I love you," he said. He thought it was true. Above all, he refused to
believe that his fate was being decided in this shabby motel room.

She made an impatient movement and shook her head, but at least she
made no resistance as he slid over and put his arm around her. They both
seemed to be waiting for something: at last he drew his arm closer and she
felt him sigh and relax, his weight on her growing heavier as he drifted off
to sleep, while she lay, wide-eyed, in the dark.

Faces

David still remembered that last day of school. He was sitting at the top of the flight of steps that led to his flat, and he could see, framed by the doorway at the bottom, a bright rectangle of hard, jaunty, afternoon sunlight, hammer-like in its pounding insistence. By contrast the stairs and the interiors were dark and murky, filled with bilious half-light that alighted perversely on the flaking strips of paint hanging like forlorn streamers from the walls. David contemplated the squalidness without rancour; this was one of his more philosophical days, when he reflected calmly that at least, living at rock-bottom, he couldn't possibly sink any lower and according to the laws of probability things should be picking up for him soon. Usually, he longed with fervour for the day when these government flats would be demolished and flattened to nothingness.

David was smoking a cigarette; it was a compulsive habit with him, even though he was only fifteen and had already been hauled up twice before the principal of his school. It wasn't that he really enjoyed it—it was a refuge, a defiant act of release from frustration. A clattering of steps broke the silence and the lady from upstairs whisked by him, disapproval emanating from her broad back. With exaggerated indignation, she brushed away the thin coils of smoke that hovered, tentacle-like, in the air.

David watched her descending; he was thinking, with a horrid fascination, of a painting he had seen at the national museum earlier that day. An art exhibition by German abstract painters was on and David's teacher, with some vague idea of instilling culture in the pupils, had brought David's class to view it. The paintings were severely geometric, and David, who had seen his father's attempts at the same thing, was bored. He might have missed the painting, for it was hung in a sort of recess, except for the fact that he had gone in there to smoke a fag in peace. He confronted it unprepared, with a sudden shock—of recognition, he realised later.

His first impression was of a vast, unrelenting muddiness; seemingly a crude daub at first sight, he became aware that out of the thick stripes of paint, what seemed a million, barely visible faces were glimmering through: ordinary faces, but all wearing the same foolish, self-satisfied expression in their eyes, mere masks hiding hulking, reverberating hollows in which everything had perished. These faces saw nothing except what they wanted to see; they were sightless and blind to all that had no immediate claim on them. The painting was called, simply, 'Faces'. It was horrible and slimy, it suggested a terrifying, living death or death-like life, and it exerted a peculiar fascination over him. It repelled him and yet made him feel unreasonably, tearfully sad; he caught himself praying, over and over again, that this would never happen to him, and he thought of all the people it had already happened to. They didn't really live, the people he knew, toiling and grinding away to no discernible end, submissive cogs in a wheel and accepting it; worst of all the crowds in the streets, teeming, teeming humanity, not living, just kept in a state of existence, surviving and multiplying like ineradicable weeds. He hated their facelessness. He felt rooted to the spot, unable to tear himself away and knowing he was being ridiculous; he was glad when a classmate came up and, viewing the picture dispassionately, gave his considered opinion, that it stank.

Snuffing out his cigarette, he went down the stairs and emerged onto the pavement, blinking in the glare. He wandered in the direction of the coffee-shop at the street corner, passing the taxi stand where the drivers sat, comatose and squat-legged, like shrivelled old gnomes. The coffee-shop was always crowded, resounding with the roar of conversation and interminable frying, a constant hive of sound, surmounted by the throbbing, rhythmic grind of the ceiling fans that whirled in dizzy circles full-blast.

A short rotund man stood by the coffee-shop, his hands behind his back, smiling affably at all who passed. He was dressed in spotless white, innocently virginal, his hair a dyed jet-black. David had seen him at his afternoon post for as long as he could remember, and he called him in his mind by his sister's definition, Mr Lau, slightly weak in the head.

"Ah, David!" said Mr Lau, with an ear-splitting beam. "How is your grandfather today?" He never failed to courteously inquire after the gentleman in question, even though he had been dead for years.

"Very poorly," said David politely.

"I'm sorry to hear that."

"Yes, he's got entero-subjunctivitis. It attacks the parts of the brain that store poetry and bad puns and he's been singing rude comic songs for hours. Did you ever get entero-subjunctivitis?"

"No, I can't say I ever did," said Mr Lau, with a look of strained effort on his face, as he tried to understand. "What was it again?"

"It doesn't matter. He'll get well in a day or two. See you, Mr Lau." David walked on hurriedly, just to stop himself from lying; he could go on effortlessly for hours in this make-believe vein. His gift for fantasy was more often a curse than otherwise, and he teetered along the border between the real and the imaginary, afraid of falling into either.

Two figures were toiling up the road, two shadows trailing mutinously in their wake. One of them was a girl, of a restless disposition, who was never still: her hands flashed, her head tossed and she moved with a constant, exhausting gyration. "You're so slow!" she cried with annoyed emphasis to her brother, for such it was, walking stolidly on. Suddenly, with a cry of delight, she dived into the interior of a pet shop, from which issued strange sounds and the intermittent lapping of water, rather like a jungle one could hear, but not see. Seng Chooi, her brother, saw David and ran lightly up to him.

"We had an end-of-term party," he said, "and I had to follow my sister to some shopping complex. That's why I'm late home." He was in David's standard at school, one of the few prefects who managed to be popular, as he possessed a breezy, attacking charm to which everyone succumbed. He and David had been neighbours for years, as they lived near each other, and their friendship was amicable, if superficial. Seng Chooi was sometimes hectoring, and monopolised the conversation far too much, but David, who was shy, didn't know many people, was grateful for his friendship.

Seng Chooi said with assumed diffidence, "You did well in the exams, didn't you."

"Not really," said David, uncomfortably; he could not prevent a wry twist to his mouth. He knew that Seng Chooi was fiercely competitive and was determined to be rich, respectable and middle-class when he grew up; he knew, too, that part of Seng Chooi's liking for him had to do with a half-formulated hope that he could somehow imbibe knowledge from David, whom he and everyone else believed to be unfairly intelligent without even trying. "It was just a fluke," he hastened to add, dissociating himself from the whole thing. "What are you looking so gloomy about? Your results are great too."

"No, they're not," said Seng Chooi, mechanically and pessimistically. "They're just lousy paper qualifications anyway."

"Don't give me that. You know you can't be a success in life without them."

"What's so important about being a success anyway? I'm serious. All people mean by being a success is having enough money to buy things they don't really need and becoming a slave to the god of consumer goods. And then they spend their lives being pressured by advertisements and never thinking or talking about anything else. Or else they go on expensive holidays and come back not even remembering what they've seen, for goodness' sake. Or start reading bestsellers, never any decent books, and be boring as hell—"

"Ah, go and die," said Seng Chooi, not unkindly. "What do you know about being successful, anyway? You and I haven't lived outside this dump at all. Look, idiot, people have a right to a certain standard of living, don't they? We're not animals, you know."

"Well, why shouldn't there be a fixed standard of living, you know, and instead of having a lot of people grubbing for themselves only, they'd all be working for the collective good—"

"You're not being practical at all. Look here, in our society it's not possible at all. It is a rat-race, but you don't see the positive side; it's competition that will ever really bring about progress. People who work hard and decently, they don't just do it for their own egos, for goodness' sake, it benefits society as a whole too. Society."

Seng Chooi looked flushed and warm, evidently seeing himself in the light of a bastion of civilisation, defending society single-handedly.

"You mean a society of people plasmolysed by self-satisfaction. They might as well be the living dead!"

"You're just generalising, and being insulting to anybody who's got a decent job. I haven't seen zombies walking about, good grief. And the words you use: plasmolysed!"

"Sorry," said David. "It's because of this painting—" It was luridly clear in his mind.

Just then, Seng Chooi's sister appeared in their midst, glowing with triumph.

"I've bought a terrapin," she announced, opening her palm, on which reposed the terrapin, small and humped. Gently, she turned it over, and they saw a neat, square pattern of yellows and greens on the underside. "Naughty boy!" she cooed, stroking it with her forefinger. "Isn't it lovely!"

"That makes four," said Seng Chooi. "My sister now has four terrapins, six white mice and a stuffed turtle. Where will it all end?"

She gave him a calmly superior look, fringed with contempt. "Oh, shut up," she said, and stalked off. She had not even noticed David, who thought to himself that she was an odd creature, sharp as needles and disconcertingly, pouncingly alert; she had a mystical affinity for all animals, about which she talked in a strangely intimate way, rather as if they were kindred spirits, and lavishing on them all the smiles and courtesies she gave no one else. She was the rudest person David knew.

"Yes," said Seng Chooi, sensing David's thoughts, "she's a holy terror. Hey, d'you want an ice-*kachang* or something? This is a sweltering day."

"No money."

"You can watch me then," and they laughed, idiotically, with the beginning of high spirits. They kicked a pebble all the way to the market, pretending it was a football and vociferously discussing strategies. David, mechanically, unthinkingly, foraged for a cigarette and lit it.

"You smoke like a chimney, David," said Seng Chooi, wrinkling his nose. "I'd love to see the state of your lungs. What do your parents say about your filthy habit?"

David flushed, and said the first thing that came into his head, "I wish it was snowing."

He was as slippery as an eel when it came to evasions. His family was a secret, which he carried about with him like an indelible scar; most of the time, he managed to shelve them in some corner of his mind marked 'obliterated' but he could not mentally will them away all the time.

There was his father, a retired civil servant, fallen from the starched impeccability of officialdom, who spent all his time painting with a furious, concentrated energy that was painful to watch. He was a slob, sullen and morose, who slopped about in undershirts and slippers, with a perpetual cold in the head, so that he was always sneezing like a grampus. He drank heavily, and the colour of his skin was permanently lobster-red; when he was drunk, he appeared the height of sobriety, but when he was cold-sober and saw the world clearly, he invariably collapsed into a state of helpless self-pity, babbling about Gauguin and the artistic temperament. He hated his periods of lucidity, when he was apt to wreck the furniture freely.

David's mother had long ceased caring about him; she was sunk in apathy, trailing around the flat like a deaf-mute, hearing, seeing nothing, praying to her gods of wood and metal, and making innumerable trips to the temple to burn joss sticks. Religious fervour and bargains were her two chief passions; the only sparks of life she showed were when expatiating on the insupportable, gross thievery of hawkers. She was perfectly indifferent to everyone; sometimes she would dart sudden, murderous glances at the wall or ceiling that rather alarmed David.

His sister Daphne or Li Ying was seventeen and temperamental; she seldom came home and wished desperately to be married, so that she could get out of the hell-hole, as she called it; she went about in an armoury of bracelets, flounces and necklaces and read love stories voraciously. David's father, in a moment of clarity, had estimated her mind to be the size of a pea and reduced her to tears.

David stayed out of their way as much as possible, especially his father, whom he would watch, sniffing and swilling beer, until ejected from the flat, with kitchen missiles thrown at him for good measure.

He wished he was independent, then he would be free of them all. He read, drew, did his homework, filled in CPF and tax forms in the kitchen on a rickety old table, amidst a sea of bowls, vegetables, half-sliced carrots and spilt milk, while his mother moved slowly in the confined space, keeping up a thin, monotonous trickle of abuse, which she seldom broke except to ask David to pass some knife or other. Above the table was a single, naked bulb, illuminating the black walls and showing cracks filled with streaks of green slime. This blob of light glowed with furious intensity in his mind now, transmuting itself into a burning gob of bitterness that worked with such force in him that he felt suddenly sick, and he threw away his cigarette. He glanced sidelong at Seng Chooi, talking innocently, and took a long, silent breath to steady himself.

To get to the hawkers' centre, they had to pass through the market, a dimly lit cavern, the ceiling so high that it was shrouded in darkness, while underfoot was a network of rivulets and puddles of opaque, sloshing water. The old market was deserted in the afternoons, filled with an eerie silence that reminded David strangely of the atmosphere of a church, after the worshippers had left. Near the entrance of the market were a cluster of wooden tables, stalls selling drystuffs, mostly empty now as their proprietors slowly cleared away the goods to store in cupboards and boxes. A thin young man was sitting cross-legged on one of the wooden tables, contemplating the sunny road outside reflectively. In his arms he cradled—David opened his eyes wide in surprise—a saxophone, cursorily wrapped in brown paper so that most of it was visible.

"Isn't that Danny Lee?" he half-whispered.

"Yeah, it is."

"I didn't know he had a sax."

Danny Lee was a well-known figure in the neighbourhood. He was tall and almost wraith-like in his thinness; his cheekbones stood out prominently in a face that was very pale, so that his eyes by comparison appeared uncharacteristically large and dark, sunk deeper into their hollows. He looked hardly more than twenty-two. He was considered an oddity; everyone knew a little of his life history or claimed they did, but it was all contradictory and inconclusive. Opinion was divided as to whether he was mentally ill or merely incapacitated by secret drinking. There had been rumours of an accident and brain damage. As for himself, he spoke with a convulsed stammer that precluded the possibility of finding out anything from him. David had seen him walking about, an awkward, gaunt figure, but with a certain aloofness that fobbed off potential jibers. He didn't look to David like someone who had brain damage, sitting calmly there on the wooden table. A fall of hair hovered on his forehead, threatening to swing down and curtain his eyes.

"I s'pose he's been evicted. His mother died some weeks ago and of course he doesn't really work, so there's no money to pay the rent or anything. Poor idiot."

Seng Chooi spoke with an authoritative, prefect-orial air; his mother was an inveterate gossip, who took a keen, ecstatic joy in ferreting out news, and, with great ingenuity, she had wormed out from Danny's mother all there was to know about him.

Danny's mother was pale and anaemic; she had the defeated look of someone sinking under a load of drudgery and her eyes were large and dark like Danny's, with a wariness in them that spoke of her dislike of intruders. She was an abnormally reticent woman, building around herself an impregnable, sometimes immensely terrifying wall of silence. She kept herself to herself, preserving her independence with stubborn pride, barely managing to eke out a living by taking in washing. Danny's father had been a wastrel, improvident, ineffectual, notorious for his helplessness; his chief passion had been birds and he had liked nothing better than to spend a day at the bird-lovers' den, talking with gentle enthusiasm about the creatures over cups of tea and listening, lulled, drowsy and contented, to the bird cries that assailed him from every corner.

When he died of a heart attack, no one except Danny, who was ten at the time, regretted his absence much. Danny had loved his father, unreservedly and unquestioningly, because he had been the only one who had cared much about gaining Danny's affection, and for months people glimpsed Danny with a face haunted and stricken with grief. There was not much sympathy for him, however; his looks inclined towards the theatrical, with their meagre hollows, and people instinctively recoiled with the distaste of the practical from anything that smacked of feyness. They thought Danny and his mother peculiar and melodramatic. For a while he immersed himself in school work, regularly winning prizes and absorbing knowledge like an insatiable sponge; then came the accident and he was laid up for half a year while doctors battled over his illness and his mother watched in resignation all her savings going towards medical fees. He recovered—barely. He looked a physical wreck. The doctors had warned of the possibility of brain damage and shook their heads over the speech impediment he had developed that made him stammer uncontrollably. He developed a habit of silence now, as he was acutely sensitive of his stammer. He withdrew into himself and lived an internal, fermenting life; he felt helpless and pinioned, driven half-crazy by an overwhelming suspicion that everyone was waiting to see whether he was really brain-diseased. Sometimes he wondered if he hadn't already succumbed and the world he thought he saw around him was nothing but a figment of a disordered imagination. It scared the hell out of him.

The doctors had advised his returning to school as soon as possible, the better to readjust, but he found he had been away too long; during his illness, he had had a lot of time for a long examination of everything around him and it was as if he had come to the conclusion that none of it really mattered. Badly troubled, he tried to concentrate on his work, but the pretence was exhausting. He felt like some conspicuous deformity in a sea of normality, and soon he drifted gently out of school, dew evaporated from a leaf with nothing left behind. Then only sixteen, he started making strenuous efforts to leave home. Jobs were hard to get at his age and with his stammer, and finally he simply left home of his own accord, driven by a desperate wish to escape the invisible prisons he felt were fencing him in. His mother, reputedly a cold, bloodless woman, went into surprising hysterics; she harried the police and they brought her son home, a protesting, bitter minor. They had found him in the precincts of Bugis Street in the company of a down-and-out musician, a sore irritation to tourists, his victims. When asked what they did together, Danny replied insolently they were lovers. Danny's mother had roused herself into a passion; it was the only time in her life she had done so and at the end of it she was white and nearly gasping for breath. She reviled Danny, told him he was an ungrateful wretch, a lazy good-for-nothing, a totally unfilial son. Danny tried to explain about the illusion of freedom which had him in its grasp, but she told him he was talking nonsense. Apparently, she threatened to have him certified if he ever ran away from home again and she brought up the brain damage slur which Danny had been trying unsuccessfully to erase from his mind. Danny went white at her words; he felt as though someone were hacking him to pieces, tearing gobbets out of his soul and leaving an empty husk. He remained at home, outwardly docile; only he knew what angry, unending screams thrashed in him, if any. The flickering resentment he harboured against his mother soon died down into resignation, and his mother sank back into her former moroseness.

Danny now spent all his time being an accomplished loafer, lying in bed for hours at a stretch staring at the ceiling or reading interminably. Sometimes he went for long, meandering walks, during which passersby would dart glances sidelong at him and murmur, "Poor beast" under their breath, as Seng Chooi had done. He had no friends or companions, living entirely in his own world, speaking to nobody and no one had the faintest idea what wild, fantastical, madman's thoughts coursed through his mind or—and this was the general consensus—whether it was a more probable, utter blank. He was like a person locked in a room, completely solitary. Sometimes, he worked sporadically as a ticket collector, window cleaner or odd-job man; once, a teacher from his former school saw him lounging about and was horrified. He sought out Danny and told him he was wasting his life: he had always done brilliantly at school and ought not to let his brains idle. Danny listened with an expression of irony on his face; he said drily that it was a moot question with his mother and a lot of people whether he had any intelligence at all, let alone brains. He refused to go back to school; academia hadn't done him much good. But his former teacher was determined not to let him slip through his fingers, and he made Danny have tea occasionally with him, during which he purposefully discussed all sorts of topics with the boy to make him sit up, as he put it. It did Danny a world of good, but his relations with his mother were still strained.

They were suddenly exacerbated by her returning from market one day to find a young man outside her door; Danny was out on one of his walks and the stranger had the utmost difficulty persuading her he was not a criminal type. He called himself Danny's companion in adversity and her face darkened, as she realised that he must be the musician the police had spoken of. He looked weatherbeaten and downtrodden, his face unnaturally lined for someone who could not be more than thirty, and he had a curious habit of constantly drawing his finger across his nose and dodging his head as if to avoid his interlocutor's eyes.

To Danny's mother he appeared completely unprepossessing. He had a package for Danny, he said, a bulky object wrapped in newspaper, which she regarded with suspicion. It was a saxophone, his stock-in-trade, which he had taught Danny to play during those weeks together. He spoke of Danny's escapade deprecatingly, and seemed a little shy of mentioning it; the gist of it was, Danny played the sax a great deal better than he ever did or would, and since he was leaving the country to make a fresh start abroad—he mentioned this with a child-like sense of adventure—he thought he would give it to Danny, the poor fatherless boy. He had an unexpected sense of humour and there was a gay element of nonsense in all he said which saved him from being altogether raffish, and he related lightheartedly how he was going to stow away on a boat to China and reverse the route of his ancestors, but he failed to pierce her armour; she listened with poker-faced rigidity and got rid of him unceremoniously. She hid the saxophone, meaning to sell it for some money, but Danny discovered it and clung on to his possession with the will and tenacity of a limpet. He refused to have it sold, preferring to turn over his meagre savings to her; he put up a silent, immovable struggle, under which she sank weakly. She revenged herself by cuttingly deriding his choice of acquaintances and was very witty on the subject. The saxophone became the symbol of the mental battle they waged against each other; Danny's mother grew positively to detest the instrument and since she could not sell it, she locked it away. She did not love her son, she loved no one, but Danny was her only tangible possession and her instinctive reaction was to keep him at hand. She saw him as a commodity she had been hoarding and she was determined to squeeze her dividends out of him.

Seng Chooi's mother had caught her at a weak moment, when she was flu-stricken and confined to her bed; with delight, Seng Chooi's mother visited her with herbs and medicine, and went away only when she had the whole story, newly minted for circulation. Seng Chooi's mother said that the poor woman seemed positively relieved to unburden herself of the story.

"What d'you think of it?" said Seng Chooi with something like complacency.

David said nothing, except, "Why's he just sitting there? What's he going to do now?"

Danny's gaze shifted, wavered and broke; he noticed the two boys and smiled a tremulous half-smile at them. His fingers, long and lean, were caressing his instrument, which gleamed with a muted sheen.

Very slowly, he lifted the mouthpiece to his lips and in an effort of concentration, his brow contracted and his hair fell, screening his eyes. He made no attempt to push it back; David could see he was taking a breath, then gently releasing it, while like a wound-up mechanical toy slowly getting into action, his fingers moved down the row of knobs. David felt suddenly, horribly embarrassed for him; the whole scene was ludicrous and Danny was going to be a consummate fool blowing away at an instrument from which nothing issued. He dragged his eyes away from the calm figure, who seemed embalmed in some sort of extraordinary stillness and peace, a temporary Nirvana, and wanted to walk away quickly.

Seng Chooi grabbed his arm. "No, let's stay," he said in an undertone. "You aren't squeamish, are you?" He evidently considered Danny in the light of a monstrosity, and ascribed David's wish to leave to timidity.

David stood and listened against his will, his eyes on the ground, staring wth enraged concentration at a squashed cabbage leaf near his left foot. He thought they were taking unfair advantage of Danny, scrutinising him as if at some grotesque exhibit at a fair, and he was filled with self-contempt.

Danny played with complete self-absorption; he was oblivious to his surroundings and when David stole a glance at him, he thought in surprise that it wasn't so much that he was producing the music as that it seemed an integral part of him, over-spilling in pure, easeful sound. It was a slow, light tune Danny was playing, each note separate, lingering and clear, following one another in leisurely procession, going into sudden mischievous dips and dives and slowly surfacing with a hint of regret and sadness. David supposed it was slow jazz or something; it was entrancing, uncluttered by any meaning, lazily elegant, with a disarming simplicity of heart. David was unaware of exactly how long he had been watching that limpid ghost of a dancer in his mind's eye; who slid with carefree, unstudied insouciance over the dance floor, carrying an inviolable circle of spotlight with him. Very faintly, the dancer's body glistened with barely visible flashes of light from the sequins, the only hint of glamour. All else was stripped of trimmings down to the bare essentials; nothing but the music mattered or existed, and it was gently insistent and clarion-clear. Every note of it was a release from the tortuous inarticulation, physical or otherwise, that lay trapped in Danny; it was a paean to the freedom he knew lay in the palm of his hand. David found that an extraordinary thing was happening to him; the music seemed to be churning up his emotions and coalescing them into a burning conviction that he was on Danny's side, whatever it was.

"He plays quite well," said Seng Chooi, impressed in spite of himself, and David, suddenly hearing the traffic outside, became conscious the music had stopped by the sudden silence in his head.

"He plays great," said David with emphasis.

The few vendors still in the market had ceased all activity and were watching Danny with affable puzzlement. When he stopped playing, they shrugged their shoulders good-humouredly, and began discussing him in muted tones. Scraps of their conversation wafted over to David and Seng Chooi: "All alone in the world, no ties, no money," "It's not right, someone in his state wandering about the streets homeless..."

Danny apparently heard snatches of their conversation, for he smiled wryly. He continued sitting, resting his cheek against the saxophone, thinking his own thoughts. There was a loose-limbed grace about him now and he looked the picture of serenity, in a way that David had never seen in anyone else. He seemed waiting, with relaxed patience born of all the time in the world, for invisible energy to seep back into him, totally unconcerned about his fate or destination. Perhaps, David thought, he wanted things this way, he wanted to be a solitary island, timeless, sprung out of nowhere, accountable to himself only. The two boys began to move off; with the end of the music, they felt it was impolite to stare, unasked, at Danny. Looking back, they saw Danny unfurl his long legs and pick up his belongings; he moved in the direction of the bus stop.

"Who was he playing for?" asked Seng Chooi. "There's no getting away from it. Even if he's not raving mad, he's still all twisted up inside. My mother knew of this man once. He appeared very normal on the outside and all, but everyone knew he gobbled up newspapers in secret. I wonder where the poor idiot's going. Woodbridge, perhaps."

David longed to hit Seng Chooi; the constant harping on Danny's unknown sanity infuriated him.

"Someone who plays like that can't be mad," he said slowly and evenly.

"I should have thought it proved it," said Seng Chooi obscurely. People didn't expose their soul in public, which he felt dimly and with a recoil of distaste, that Danny had been doing; he thought it pointed to some strange, twisted wantonness in him.

Danny was still standing at the bus stop, an object of curiosity to all passers-by, who swivelled their heads back to glance at him. He held the saxophone loosely under one arm.

"I'd hate to be him," said Seng Chooi with commiseration.

"I think he's happy," said David.

SAVING THE RAINFOREST AND OTHER STORIES

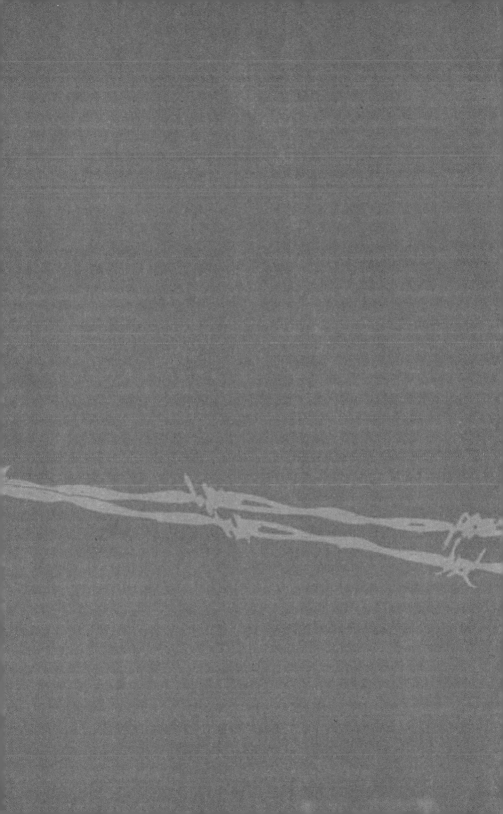

Saving the Rainforest

I have known Ethel Png for twenty-five years now, ever since, at the age
of fourteen, we were caned for wearing pink socks to school. It was 1966,
the Western world was in turmoil, the Beatles were in the ascendant, and
we were still in an environment where wearing pink socks was a major
transgression. "I'm *dying* here," Ethel wailed to me more than once.

Not long after, her family, then one of the richest in Singapore, sent
her to the United States to study. It was never clear *what* exactly she was
studying, but she wound up in California, in the company of millions
of assorted freaks, and began to "go wild," as her distraught mother put
it to my mother. Ethel showed me photographs of herself back then, a
small, even tiny figure, buried under an avalanche of hair that stopped
somewhere around her kneecaps, and clad in exaggerated bell-bottoms
a mile wide. She looked like Yoko Ono on a very bad day. Other
photographs showed her sitting in a ring of similarly garbed people, all
smoking joints. You could tell they were joints, because everybody had
this fogged-out, loopy and yet perfectly ecstatic look on their faces. These
pictures, which she stupidly sent back, threw her family into a tailspin
and, in a fit of moralistic frenzy, they cut off her funds in an attempt to
make her return. Instead, she started cultivating marijuana in her back
yard in order to make a living, got busted, and languished in custody for a
month, until her arresting officer, who was smitten with her, posted bail,

after which they took off to Woodstock for the festival, of which she didn't remember a single thing. She did Woodstock, she did the lot: pot, junk, LSD, transcendental meditation, yoga, Zen, yoghurt, etc...

In 1972 her father was declared a bankrupt, the family money petered out, and Ethel was back in Singapore with a Eurasian baby christened Rainforest Peace Png, whom she called Rain. She said the father (her arresting officer) was a louse and a fascist who supported Nixon and she never wanted to see him again. Ethel's mother took one look at Rain, checked for signs of a wedding ring on her daughter's finger, found none, and promptly had hysterics. Ethel's father committed suicide, consumed with shame at the collapse of his business. Her mother eventually retired to a small house in Katong with the faithful family retainer, leaving Ethel with a mountain of debts and relatives who treated her like a pariah.

Meanwhile, my life continued its slow and enervating course. I read law at the local university, I had one or two boyfriends, nothing serious—earnest, steady boys who wore glasses. My parents went on being respectable, refusing to go mad or spectacularly bankrupt. Even though Ethel's life was clearly a mess, I could never see her without feeling a pang of envy: how could one person monopolise all the excitement rationed out on this island?

Ethel took a look at her situation and decided it was serious: she had an illegitimate son and no money. So she decided to put her Californian experience to some use: she started a health food shop. At that time, everybody thought she was making a mistake. They told her meat-guzzling, oil-slurping Singaporeans would stay away in droves, and they did, at first, but Ethel refused to admit defeat. A committed vegetarian herself, she wrote articles, pamphlets, appeared on TV, gave talks; at one time, it was impossible to avoid Ethel's face or voice, expounding on the benefits of lentils to the digestive system. Ethel's *Healthy Living* stopped being a mere curiosity shop as she began to see some return on her investment.

The only problem was that for years she never abandoned her uncompromising hippie lifestyle: she never stopped smoking pot, for example, which, in the antidrugs hysteria then prevailing, led to her arrest (again), but the charges were dropped for lack of evidence. Magnanimously, she invited the investigating officers around for a vegetarian cook-out at her place; several of them, seduced by the great chilli stringbean recipe, no doubt, later became her lovers.

I thought she was completely mad and told her so.

"Darling, I've given up worrying what people think of me," she said. "You should try it—it gives you a marvellous sense of release."

But I knew I never would.

• • •

Rain was a large, solemn baby who never cried. He grew into a plump, stolid child with the unnerving habit of standing silently by your elbow while you talked on, unaware of his presence. He was watchful, unchildlike. Eurasian children are often said to be gorgeous, but there were no traces of it in Rain, who was ordinary, even homely. As far as I knew, he never asked after his father. When I asked him why, much later, he said, in a matter-of-fact way, "Because I thought Ethel *was* my father *and* mother." (He called her Ethel.)

Ethel and I kept in touch regularly, though by the time we hit our thirties we had become totally different people. At university, I had had visions of myself being gloriously martyred at the stake of legal aid, dispensing good in my best lady-of-the-manor fashion. After six years of unremitting drudgery, however, I had switched to corporate law, turning my back forever on the Causes, and was ready to do battle with anybody (but especially Ethel) on the question of selling out and joining the rat race. I worked long hours in the office and then worked out furiously in the gym, I kept my figure, and I shed the gawkiness that had so painfully accompanied me through my late teens and early twenties. After an early bad incident, when I had burst into tears before a senior partner after he had ticked me off, I made a vow never to parade my feelings before the world again. I put effort into mastering a cool, detached exterior; I learned that to say little except that which was pertinent could be an intimidating weapon. Behind my back, I knew, I was described as cold; I counted it a victory. It had taken me years to reach this outwardly calm, emotionless pinnacle; I had no intention of ever climbing down again.

Ethel, true to her philosophy of doing precisely what she wanted and cocking a snook at the world's opinion, decided at age thirty-five she was going to let it *all hang out*, "including wrinkles and saddlebags on the thighs," she added cheerfully. She stopped wearing make-up and worrying about her weight, and she chopped off her tresses. Overnight she evolved from a flamboyantly dressy woman battling futilely with her figure to a crop-haired, kindly, chunky, mid-life person ("There is no such thing as middle age," said Ethel. "Middle age is a state of mind.") whose main concerns were saving the environment and her son, who was running around with a manic skateboarding crowd. Yet she was as attractive to men as ever, though some unkind persons were heard to say it wasn't possible, given the way Ethel clumped around. "It's my devastating earth mother quality," she would say, rolling her eyes, "I'm a terrific cook, I never interrupt those tiresome monologues men are so keen on—what more could they want?" But she had momentary regrets; once, scrutinising me carefully, she sighed. "You know, I could pass for your mother," she said wistfully. But at some deeper level she was at peace with herself now; tolerance for the world and its foibles oozed from her, thick as honey, comforting, and soon she was kidding me about my hair: "If I hit it with a hammer, what do you bet the hammer will break?"

• • •

You know it's downhill all the way when the children of your friends start to marry and you're still single. You start to feel unaccountably old—an imaginary pain starts up in your knee, you take out Procol Harum, *A Lighter Shade of Pale*, and play it to a nostalgic death on your turntable.

I was in no mood to go to the wedding of Lee Su Ting's daughter, the second in a month to which I had been invited. Su Ting's daughter Deanna (Deanna! for God's sake) at the ripe old age of twenty-two was walking down the aisle with the son of a timber merchant from Sarawak, and the ninny was delighted that she would be safely married before she was washed-up at twenty-three.

The wedding was being held in Deanna's grandfather's house, an old colonial bungalow set in, as the real estate brochures say, spacious grounds. I thought I would show myself, present the *ang-pow* and melt away before the service started; that way, I would avoid being inflicted with the unctuous "Till Death Do Us Part" rigmarole.

The young couple had been educated in England and had certain ideas as to how the whole thing should be conducted. They wanted to be married in the garden, under bowers and in the light of the setting sun, an idea which, in this climate sounded like sheer folly; luckily, it had rained in the afternoon and was considerably cooler. Deanna hugged me impulsively: "It's a shame, you're looking wonderful, when is your turn coming?" No less than four people asked me this question (her fiance, her parents, and her grandfather, whom I remembered from my youth as a keen lecher constantly inviting young girls into corners with him), at the end of which I was ready to stagger out and drown myself in the punch bowl.

I wandered off aimlessly into the garden. Someone waylaid me, wanting to know about a legal matter; I looked about desperately for an escape route, and it was then I saw a peculiar young man, hovering by the buffet table, eyes closed, lips moving silently. He was dressed entirely in black, black T-shirt, black jeans, black loafers. More than one person was looking at him in deep suspicion. He opened his eyes, saw me glancing at him, and came straight over, purposefully. "How are you?" he cried effusively, and bore me off on his arm.

"Wait," I said, struggling to free myself, "what are you doing?"

"Didn't you want to be rescued?"

"Yes, but I'm perfectly capable of doing it myself."

He released my arm. "OK," he said amiably. "You just looked terribly bored."

"Do you always rescue people who are bored?"

"Always," he said, gravely. "Life's too short to be bored. You should do something about it." Then he started to laugh, and couldn't stop. When he finally sobered down, he asked, politely, "So what do you do?"

"I'm a professional wedding gate-crasher." I amended this to, "Also a lawyer. And how old are you anyway?"

He looked at me as if I'd asked him something indecent. "Nineteen."

"For your information, I'm thirty-nine."

He shrugged. "So?"

"So I don't need someone who's practically a child rumbling in and oozing self-possession all over me."

He said nothing, except that his eyes narrowed and a rather tight look came over his face. I began to be sorry for what I'd said. "I didn't mean that exactly."

"Yes, you did," he said. "Why say things you don't mean?"

"Because a certain amount of hypocrisy is essential to a civilised life."

"Yeah?" he said, with a glint. "Well, screw civility."

I could have left, but some instinct of curiosity made me ask him what he had been doing by the table.

"That? Oh. Well ... praying for the souls of all the dead animals slaughtered for the occasion." He gave me a challenging stare.

"Oh, come on."

His eyes, a very light grey, bored into mine suddenly, illuminated by a stern joy. "That's just the lawyer in you speaking. Eternally sceptical. Only money, power, the things money can buy, are your verities, right? Hey, I'm not only a vegetarian—I've been one ever since I was born—but I know all of us living things are meshed together in this giant, interlocking organic whatchamacallit. You can't dislodge one piece without fucking the whole thing up. That's why I can't stand this century, man, it's a systematic attempt to de-harmonise the whole universe and deny the natural order of things..."

He went on in this vein for a full fifteen minutes, his eyes flashing, and his delicate, slender nose quivering, the whole complicated system of bones and muscles moving, shading fluidly in that narrow, angular face of his, his thin body held taut, whip-like, in his intensity. Periodically, he would flick the straggling, honey-coloured hair out of his eyes, then his hand would slide back into the back pocket of his jeans, his hands were always in those back pockets; even when he was standing still there was the indefinable hint of a light footed, cat-like wariness. He would never live from day to day, you could see that, he would always be hurling himself against some imaginary obstacle, carving his way furiously through the very air he breathed. He wound up with the air of having settled life, the universe and everything, with the arrogance of extreme youth, but he was smiling at his own seriousness, a lopsided smile stretching to his left ear.

"Your name's Rain, isn't it?" I said, when he'd finished.

"How did you know?"

"Oh, I know."

• • •

It was with some relief that I located Ethel in the sitting room, eating her way through a large slice of cake. "I've met your son."

"Oh, good," she said, vaguely.

"He's changed, hasn't he? I haven't seen him for years. He used to be such a fat child—"

"My genes," Ethel said, nodding.

"He's really rather—beautiful now."

Ethel gave me a sharp look. "Hmm." Meditatively, she crumbled her cake. "I don't know what to do."

"What about?"

"He's due to be called up for National Service soon. I'm not sure whether he should do it—you know he's still got American citizenship and he's got to make a choice soon between that and remaining here. It's not so much the dangers of army life I'm worried about. You know he's always been at one or other of the international schools here all along. I'm not saying it isn't my fault, but I just don't know how he's going to take to army discipline and all. You may have noticed he's rather strange."

Ethel, draped in a parti-coloured paisley smock and decked out in five-inch miniature Eiffel Towers for earrings, might have been described as being rather strange herself, but I forbore pointing this out.

The band in the garden struck up the wedding march. Ethel winced. "I suppose we should trot out for the nuptials. What a bore. Do you realise," she said thoughtfully, "I've never been married?"

"Neither have I."

"That makes two of us."

Ethel drifted out to the garden and I went to the back of the house to escape. But it was a large, rambling construction with odd corners and turnings, and I found myself instead in a long, high room, with a table piled high with wedding presents—or I suppose they were wedding presents, since they were unwrapped. It looked as if someone had raided the hardware and crockery departments of a store and dumped the contents, higgledy-piggledy; there was enough stuff there to equip five households at least and still have extra to spare. In spite of my determination to leave, I found myself drawn towards this unabashed display of materialism—not least because I had spotted a charming Royal Doulton figurine standing in the middle of the clutter.

I have a confession to make. I am an inveterate porcelain collector. I am also mildly kleptomaniac. These two tendencies sometimes mesh, with unfortunate results (to the owners of the porcelain, that is), though I usually confine my thieving instincts to filching stationery from the office. I was single-handedly responsible for a memo circulated earlier this year, calling for frantic economies in office stationery. In case you think I'm being unduly facetious, I know I have a little—uh—problem, but I relish too much the irony of someone who's involved with the finer interpretations of the law being actively involved in transgressing it to give it up. I do it for the kicks, in other words.

It took barely half a second for the figurine to disappear into my bag. Turning to go, I saw Rain standing in the doorway, and froze. We were both extremely still for what seemed like a very long time; then he broke into a slow grin, and began to whistle. Slowly, I replaced the figurine and made my way past him, his black-clad body flattening itself against the door frame to let me through. I felt, rather than saw, the amused, benevolent look on his face, the same irritating tolerance which Ethel brought to bear on the menagerie of freaks and downbeats she collected around her. I ran for the road.

As I was reversing my car, I glimpsed Rain, a tiny, black speck in the side mirror. Squinting, I could just make out that he was standing by an Alfa Romeo, eyes closed again, lips moving in benediction. What was he praying for now, salvation from the oil crisis, staving off global warming? That ludicrous, sanctimonious little brat. Then, as I watched, he picked the lock, jumped in and roared off with great verve, in a flurry of squealing brakes and screeching tyres. A thin echo of the Wedding March floated through the air.

• • •

Two days later Rain called me at the office to ask whether I would go with him to watch a Hungarian movie being screened by the Film Society. I said I never watched anything that had been mutilated by censorship, and, with this thoroughly pompous reply, hung up.

A few days after this, he woke me from my sleep at midnight to invite me to dinner with him. I said no. He said, why not? I lay awake for hours, staring into the dark.

I have one other vice. I watch movies alone. I need the luminous darkness of the auditorium, the plunge into another perfectly circumscribed universe.

As I recount all this, I'm aware I sound like a progressively dotty—what is it? Oh yes—*old maid*. Someone who spends time and effort cultivating her eccentricities like rare plants, rather than rearing a child. Ethel, for example, is fairly bizarre, a walker on the wild side, but because she's fathered—sorry, mothered—a son, she is somehow exonerated in the eyes of this society which sometimes sees women as nothing more than fertility symbols. Whenever I see one of those advertisements promoting happy graduate mothers and their babies, I feel so angry I have to restrain myself physically from smashing the television. To paraphrase the song, they're my genes and I'll squander them if I want to.

Anyway, I was talking about solitary moviegoing. In *The Moviegoer* by Walker Percy, the hero, who is searching for a meaning beyond his everyday existence, goes to movie after movie alone, a symptom of his disconnection from the modern world. It is a good book, but have you noticed it is always men who get to make these grand, angst-filled gestures? I don't pretend to be grasping after the meaning of life in a celluloid fantasy; I go alone because I'm old enough to enjoy my own company.

Sometimes I manage to stumble on an unexpectedly good movie as well. Or, in the case of *The Pope of Greenwich Village*, a good bad one, starring Mickey Rourke and Eric Roberts as a pair of Italian-Irish cousins who tangle with the mafia. Much of it was basically contrived, but I've always liked buddy-buddy themes, what with all that inarticulate emotion and sentimentality disguised as toughness. A kind of licensed homo-eroticism, if you know what I mean. Also, the cinema was almost completely empty, apart from someone snoring in the front row and a couple of people at the back—blissfully peaceful.

My only fear at these times is that I'll meet someone I know. It hasn't happened often but I hate finding myself in position where I have to explain why a thirty-nine-year-old woman is doing something as adolescent as sneaking into a cinema alone. Why don't I pair up with a VCR, if I can't find a man, I can feel them thinking—or perhaps it's just incipient paranoia on my part?

So you can imagine why my heart sank when I saw Rain outside. He *would* go alone, of course. He spotted me and came up, his eyes full of that lively, ironical curiosity I remembered so well from the day of the wedding. He suggested going for a drink and I found myself agreeing, guiltily caught in the second unsocial habit of my life. It struck me, not for the first time, that he was always catching me at a disadvantage—my God, it was enough to put anyone into a really foul humour.

Except that now his head had been shaved to an unbecoming stubble, and he was several shades darker, with a constellation of spots sprayed over his nose, taking a little of the bloom off that unnerving beauty of his. He was again all in black, a lupine, theatrical figure, and yet innocently natural within that theatricality. He touched each lamppost he passed—absent-mindedly or for luck? I asked him how he liked the army; he shrugged and said, "It's OK."

We went to a coffee-house, where I ordered an orange juice and he ordered soup and salad. "You don't mind if I eat, do you? I'm starving."

"Salad's not going to fill you up, is it?"

Again that shrug. "It's the only vegetarian thing on the menu."

"Don't you want," I said, struck by an idea, "to pray for the souls of all the dead carcasses in the kitchen?"

"Not if you don't want me to."

"Are you always this intense?" I was baiting the kid, but I couldn't help it. "Do tell me what you want to be when you grow up—no, let me guess, a missionary, yes, that must be it, a visionary missionary, you have this desire to convert unbelievers—your only problem, as far as I can see, is finding a theology, unless Green politics fills the gap—"

"Hey," he said, breaking in, "I thought you liked me a *little*."

"What made you think that? You're Ethel's son, certainly, but I haven't seen you for ages. You were a very unfriendly child. Just as *intense*."

He wasn't listening. "It's this *age* thing, isn't it? It doesn't bother me, so why should it bother you? You know, this society, this world, just places too much goddamned emphasis on one's age. It's ridiculous. Age has nothing to do with it, unless you're a middle-aged guy, right, and you're sporting this little itsy-bitsy *doll* on your arm and everyone says, hey, you lucky dog, wish I could trade in *my* wife. (See, I've got impeccable feminist credentials—wow, three words with three syllables each at least.) You could be a hundred years old and I could be ten and I'd still like you. You're different."

"You know, you talk far too much, Rain. And you don't know what you're talking about. Believe me, I know, and I draw the line at younger men, especially very young men still living at home with their mothers."

"OK. I'm nineteen and you're thirty-something. So what? It's only a negligible difference."

"Only? Are you *completely naïve*? The gap is interstellar. *Intergalactic.* It's unhealthy. What you need is a cold shower. That will sober you up."

"Oh, come on," he said. "You talk about me as if I'm a sex-pervert-alcoholic-dope-fiend who's murdered his grandmother. I'm not. I'm a very nice guy. I love animals, I'm remarkably broad-minded for my age. I'm a bit pompous, but that can be cured." He grinned, taking the sting out of his words, and added, handsomely, "Besides, you're stunning to look at and everything. I bet lots of people must have told you that."

"No, actually they haven't."

"Besides, we were *born under the same star*."

"I *beg* your pardon."

He grabbed my hand suddenly. "Look, this is the lifeline ... it says you were born with a fatal weakness for expensive china and though you can afford to pay for it ten times over, it's more fun to relieve their owners of them ... anyway, they don't *care*, right...? And we could go to the movies together. We'll be together but we can pretend we went there alone."

I dragged my hand away. I was afraid of enjoying this too much and giving in to a crazy impulse to say yes. "No," I said. "Just eat up and let's go."

"OK," he said, throwing the napkin on the table. "Let's go." This little gesture relieved me a little; it gave me a concrete flaw to focus on.

He steamed to the cashier's. We paid our shares, and the cashier gave Rain a three-page receipt, each the size of his hand. Rain looked at the receipt and looked at the cashier. "What the *hell* is this? Why the *hell* is this place using three pieces of paper for one stupid receipt? Why *not*? I'll tell you why not. Because trees are a diminishing resource, that's why not. The rainforest is disappearing and no one gives a damn. We'll all go down in this sinking ship, gagged by waste-paper, smothered in dust."

His metaphors were becoming wildly mixed; I practically had to drag him out. "What is the *matter* with you?"

He sneaked a look at me, calm now. "I don't know. I'm a basket-case."

"Then get some help! Grow up!"

"I'm sorry," he said. "Really, I am."

I'm not sure why I didn't simply walk away from him then. Some nagging sense of responsibility, perhaps, or his gravely penitent air, which I didn't trust. "Come on, I'll give you a lift home."

He fell in step beside me. "Hey, I've thought of another argument."

"What?"

"In no time we'll all be dust and ashes."

"That's very comforting."

"Hurl yourself into the breach. No regrets."

We had reached my car by then. "I'll leave you here," he said. "I'm meeting some friends later."

"You didn't have to walk a geriatric to her car."

"I like walking geriatrics to their cars."

Oh, the corniness of it. Someone had catapulted me into a movie—that was it—a thrilling one, of mythic proportions, with my very own starring role, but which was rapidly hurtling towards a close; at any moment I expected the projector to shatter, the reel to fly out in whirling streamers. Experimentally, I placed my arms around him; it was like hugging a shadow, hard and yet somehow flickering and elusive. He tried to kiss me, but I wouldn't let him. Not yet, anyway. And yet I didn't push him away. I foresaw a lot of trouble. And ridicule. And an unpleasant, crepuscular old age as punishment. Why, oh why, can't we grow younger as we grow older? I felt something cold against his neck, a thin chain, with the words *Save the Rainforest* in silver filigree.

"What is this, your mantra?"

"Yeah," he said. "Rescue me." And he looked ecstatic.

• • •

What do you do in a relationship like that? A lot of the time was spent eating, or rather, watching him eat, as he was constantly hungry. Sometimes we went to the cinema but he was always so tired from training that sitting down without the stimulus of food made him fall asleep instantly, head lolling against my shoulder. Once he dragged me into a bowling alley, a place I hadn't stepped into for years, where he practised obsessively until midnight, while a group of girls watched admiringly and I plotted his, and their, collective murders. But his curious mixture of sure-fire arrogance and infectious enthusiasm, so different from my own pallid teenage years, made me laugh, and I've never been able to resist anyone who made me laugh.

Some three weeks later came the telephone call I had been dreading; Ethel sounded cool and distant and aggrieved.

"I hear you've been going out with my son."

"Ethel. It was just for dinner."

"Really, I thought better of you."

"What has Rain been saying?"

"That he likes you."

"As a friend."

"Not *just* as a friend. In case you didn't know, he broke up with his girlfriend a month ago and he's rather restless and excitable."

"You talk about him as if he were a *puppy*. You know he's old enough to decide what he wants to do. Honestly, I thought you'd be wanting to protect *me*."

Long silence. "Ethel?"

"I'm too furious to speak to you now," she said coldly. "I called up hoping you'd deny everything, or that you'd act like a responsible adult. I'm going to make a tofu vegan meal—with lots of oyster sauce—and simmer down. Don't ask me for the recipe."

Now she was working me up as well. "Why this attack of conservatism all of a sudden? Gosh, when I think of all the times I could have told you you were making a fool of yourself ... I mean, you called him Rainforest, for goodness' sake! What kind of name is that?"

"That was then!" Ethel said. "This is now!" She hung up.

I was upset and the next time I saw Rain, I contrived to have a really big dust-up about Saving the Whale. I said it was all a load of virtuous hypocrisy on the part of the West while he turned white around the temples and I was thinking, why am I having this silly quarrel, I don't give a damn about whales, dead or alive.

"Ethel said she called you," he said at last. "That's what this fight is all about, isn't it?" (He and Ethel had one of those tiresome parent-child relationships where they thrashed everything out 'as adults', and in the weeks to come I began to feel I was going out with *both* of them, so indistinct did the line between Ethel/Rain and Rain/Ethel become. There's a lot to be said for the stiff upper lip, I feel.)

"All right." I said. "Partly. She's one of my best friends after all."

"Hey," he said, catching both my hands in his, "you don't think we're doing anything *wrong*, do you?"

Wrong? I had forgotten the meaning of the word. I continued to feel an intermittent guilt towards Ethel, but I also had the curious sensation of stepping outside myself at times and watching this woman, whom I thought I knew so well, acting, behaving in a totally uncharacteristic fashion—but knowing that she was perfectly happy. Yes, glad, in spite of everything.

Occasionally, he was confined for the weekend, and then I became acutely conscious of the serried ranks of shaven-headed NS boys milling about Orchard Road, each, it seemed, with a very young girl clinging onto his arm; dear God, was I really degenerating to the level of those girls, waiting for a nineteen-year-old to be released by his sadistic commander or whoever it was? At moments the situation struck me as being so insane it was all I could do not to burst out laughing at the most inappropriate times, such as office meetings.

"I'm glad you see the ridiculousness of it," Ethel said, grimly, when I went to visit her at her shop; I hated the growing rift between us.

"Ethel, there's nothing going on."

"Then why are you wearing one of his shirts?" I looked down at myself. It *was* his shirt, a striped blue and white one: I liked its preppie, collegiate look. I had thrown it on without thinking, and I could think of nothing suitable to say now, though I was able to come up with a list of impressively innocent reasons later—by that time, of course, Ethel refused to listen.

"Excuse me," Ethel said frigidly. "I'm extremely busy." She was taking stock, and she moved efficiently, purposefully, down the shelves of muesli, cans of curried beans, raisin snacks, not the sort of thing I would ever want to eat, but I loved the genuine wooden decor of her shop, the folksy atmosphere, and the good, clean smell of wholemeal wholesomeness. Normally she would insist that we sit down and have some camomile tea and carrot cake, but today, I could see, was not going to be one of those days. Ethel wasn't the type to rant: her method was to practise a kind of biting reasonableness, with the intention of making you feel absolutely criminal. She almost succeeded, but not quite.

• • •

Surreptitiously, I devoured articles and books on my predicament. The gist of it, which I could see for myself, was that all the men my age were either married, gay, or, if single, appeared to have undergone a lobotomy. My only alternatives were widowers my father's age, younger men and *very* young men (a category growing every day), or a heroic celibacy—and I was prepared for neither the first nor the last. Yet I knew, rationally, that this thing with Rain was temporary; it was a fairy tale interlude, a glitch in reality—the end was already incipient in the beginning, and this, paradoxically, made me calmer, fatalistic, able to drift along without too much agonising self-examination. The people at the office remarked (maliciously?) that I was growing a softer look—at the same time as George Bush outlined his vision of a kinder, gentler nation, and the Cold War continued to thaw. Under Rain's influence, I threw out the cans of hair spray et al—full of CFCs, after all—though I kept the rows of night cream, body lotion, etc. on my dressing table, despite Rain's dogged eulogy of the Natural Woman. For a woman, nature has nothing comforting about it: it's a guerilla assault on her attempts to halt the onslaught of time. Besides, he was being disingenuous—I had no illusion that our attraction was anything other than largely physical, no matter how much he talked about a meeting of minds and idiosyncrasies; and physical attraction for a woman doesn't usually come cheap or unaided. Even feminists and environmentalists have their blind spots.

• • •

"How come you never married?"

"I don't know."

"Was it because of X?" X was the married man I'd had an affair with for eight years. I finally saw he would never leave his wife and that her tenacity was greater than mine.

"It's none of your business. Ethel had no right telling you."

"I'm sorry."

"Don't be. I'm glad to be out of it."

He played jazz saxophone sometimes in a band on Saturday nights. He said he had saved for years, helping Ethel in her shop, to be able to afford the saxophone—ever since he had been fixated, as a kid, by a picture in a book of a black jazzman, swathed in a zoot suit and wreathed in clouds of smoke. The picture had stuck in his mind, as a symbol of freedom and how-to-be-hip; even then he had, like his mother, an instinct for the iconoclastic and the offbeat. It was an odd ambition for a child to have, here, anyway, and indeed his whole life, apart from this shaky desire to play tenor saxophone and to save the world from eco-disaster, seemed to be ambitionless, shot through with a studied aimlessness that I didn't understand.

"What are you going to do after the army? Have you applied to go to university?"

"What is this, the Spanish Inquisition? You sound just like Ethel."

"You've got to decide what you want to do sooner or later."

He quoted the part in the Bible about the lilies of the field and how they toil not, neither do they spin etc., etc. I pointed out the flaw in his argument viz, that he was not a lily of the field.

"Power structures," he groaned. "That's all you're ever interested in, *power structures.*"

"There's no scope for a Bohemian life here, in case you haven't noticed." He smiled, lazily.

So far I had avoided introducing him to any of my friends, and I had no inclination to meet any of his. "Are you ashamed of me?" he asked once, eyes glittering; of course I was. I also had the superstitious feeling, not easily explained, that if we met any third parties, the gossamer-thin basis of our relationship would simply disappear.

He kept asking me to watch him play, and it seemed churlish to refuse continually. So I went down one Saturday night, unknown to him, about midnight; they were playing Thelonius Monk. It was one of those niche-in-the-wall haven concepts, where you practically sat with your knees jammed up against the back of the person in front and the cigarette smoke became a thick fog. The whole thing was so cool everybody onstage wore shades; I wondered how they saw enough to keep from tumbling off the miniscule podium. Rain recognised me, however, and raised his shades just the necessary fraction to give me a wide grin. He had a couple of solos, and got through them flawlessly; there were cheers and catcalls. Evidently, he had fans. Around one A.M. they bowed out, to lively applause, and a Filipino band took over. After some hesitation, I went round to the stage door.

The dressing room was so tiny I had the impression people were standing one on top of the other. There were about six of them, all much older than Rain, complaining about the horrible influence of jazz fusion on modern audiences: "Nobody wants to listen to the traditional stuff any more—" Rain rushed over and hugged me. "Hey, I'm so glad you *came*." He introduced me, not saying who I was. There was a chorus of hi's and they looked expectantly at Rain. He looked at me and for the first time since I'd known him, I noticed a glimmer of self-doubt.

"Uh, this is my aunt," he said, and ducked.

"You've got a really talented nephew here, Miss Whang. He's wasted in this place, wasted."

"Absolutely," I said.

• • •

Rain danced frenziedly around me, doing a distracting jitterbug as we walked along.

"I'll explain everything to the guys later. I'm going to kill myself."

"Forget it."

"I just sort of—blanked out."

"Rain, I would have done the same thing. I'm not angry."

"Well, I wish you would. Get angry. I hate this reasonableness—it's like my mother's moods, it means you're going to do something drastic later. *Please* get angry," he begged.

"I can't get angry to order." And then the hysterical laughter that I'd suppressed and that had been building up inside me for weeks suddenly bubbled to the surface. I laughed so hard I had to stop and catch my breath; the few people still about gave me anxious looks and crossed to the other side of the street. I laughed and laughed a lifetime's worth of frustrations. Rain gazed at me in astonishment, then concern, then, when I didn't stop, he walked further down and leaned against a pavement railing, arms crossed, not looking at me.

"I'm not laughing at you," I said, explanatorily, when I could speak again.

"Oh yeah?" he said, frowning.

Finally, when we had both calmed down, we went back to my place and made love. He said he loved me.

"I'm very fond of you, Rain," I said, truthfully.

"What do you mean, *fond*? You can be fond of a dog—or a stuffed toy. Come on."

But he was too tired to argue. I watched him fall asleep; I felt maternal, paternal, avuncular, the adult in charge of the situation once again. Then I got up noiselessly from the bed, so as not to disturb him, and padded to the kitchen, where I ate all the ice cream in the refrigerator.

• • •

Ethel called me again a month later.

"Hi," she said.

"Hello," I said, cautiously, formally.

She heaved an enormous sigh down the telephone. "I can't stay furious at you any longer," she announced dramatically.

"Really?"

"Yes, I don't have so many friends that I can afford to dispose of them like banana peel. Incidentally, did you know banana peel's wholly edible? I've got a marvellous recipe for it. Remind me to give it to you."

"I have to consider my options."

"Will you relax?"

I did, I was so glad to hear from her. "I was going to call you myself."

"Well, talk about telepathy."

"Ethel," I said, "I'm sorry."

"Hmm," she said. Pause. Rain hovered in the air between us, a phantasm. "You know he's talking about going to California after the army, to look up his father, he says, heaven help him. The man probably supports Pinochet now. It'll give him a chance to decide whether he wants to stay on."

"Yes, I know. He says he'll probably enrol at a university there to do film studies and practise the saxophone."

"That layabout. Thank goodness the American government has to foot most of the bill." A little tartly, "And what will *you* be doing?" "Surviving, mostly," I said.

Sundrift

So many people had no idea how to dance, just stood around on the dance floor jerking inanely and self-consciously along to the rhythm. Clumping. Leena had no patience with them. Dance was a ritual, a ceremony; you had to learn the steps, patiently, or it was no good. With a tingle of malicious pleasure, she would fling herself into some complicated routine, knifing her small slender body through the throng; she loved it when a Latin-inflected song came on and the crowd thinned out, groaning, because the steps were too difficult, and she twirled into a flying patchwork of calypso, rumba, mambo, lambada—names that were wonderfully evocative and faintly absurd, while people would stop dancing to watch her, even to clap, and at the end of it she would give a deep, ironic curtsey.

• • •

She had noticed Steve the first night, leaning over the railing that separated the bar from the dance floor. She didn't think he was a guest at the hotel, of which the disco formed a part, or she would have noticed him sooner: she was the front desk receptionist. She knew he was watching her, and she liked the way he looked: tall, tennis-player lean and blonde, his hair just a tad too long and grazing the collar of his T-shirt.

She went dancing three nights in a row, and each time he was there, watching her. He knew she knew. She concentrated on him now, Salome-fashion, when she danced.

On the third night he moved towards her casually and asked if he might buy her a drink. She flicked her tangled hair out of her eyes.

"Why not," she said.

• • •

Of course, he had to be from California. Where else? California by way of Germany, where his parents were born.

"My parents were born in India," she said. "Kerala," she added, for his benefit, and of course it turned out that he had spent time in an ashram in India in the 1970s. It was too much. He reminded her of those assembly line actors in the American television series of her childhood: lanky in jeans, driving round in open-topped cars, vaulting fences, spouting cliches. Except that Steve never said much, letting her spin, like a whirlwind, from one topic to another. He was not as young as he'd first appeared to be; nearer forty than thirty, there were slight lines around his eyes and streaks of grey amidst the blonde. When he moved, his movements were like a cat's, slow and lithe and deliberate and sinewy. His low drawl was casual to the point of impenetrable.

He seemed to Leena inscrutable.

"Honey, I'm just an Oriental cowboy." She hit him, hard; she detected a lurking sardonicism.

• • •

"What are you doing out here?" She meant in Singapore.

"Business. Things."

He lived in an expensive condominium apartment and drove an expensive car. The apartment was in his name, starkly white and sparsely furnished, the austerity relieved by two gigantic abstract canvases in the sitting-room—curiously impersonal, and yet, curiously Steve. A Siamese cat called, improbably, Bhumipol, padded its way warily from one room to another, occasionally springing onto Steve's shoulder and nuzzling his ear, but leaping away with a diabolical yowl if Leena tried to approach it. She fully reciprocated its loathing.

"Such as?"

"Commodities. Raw materials. Import, export. I buy and sell stuff, set up deals, that sort of thing."

"Wheeling and dealing?"

"You could call it that."

"Ethical?" Leena said. "Or not?"

He grinned.

He had an office in one of the shopping centres to which he went at ten in the mornings and came back around three. Visiting the office once, she found it as spare as the apartment, with a single bored receptionist buffing her nails. She did not inquire further. In that respect, she feared, she had been culpable.

• • •

"Why is everything in your apartment white?"

"I'm a colourless person."

"White is a colour."

"No, it's not," he said. "It's an agglomeration of all colours. It's the negation of colour."

"Black is the negation of colour."

"Black is a kind of white and vice versa."

He was being deliberately wilful. She gave up.

• • •

Steve's friends were a wilder, ever changing crowd of expatriates, more rowdy and hard-drinking: oilriggers, seamen, jewellery dealers embroiled in litigation, various other people with ill-defined and probably dubious jobs. Leena suspected that one or two of them belonged in jail: the more charming they were, the more their criminality shone through, like a rash. They turned up on Saturday nights, uninvited, with crates of beer and stacks of country music records, great wholesome chunks of sentimentality to which they cried and stomped their feet along.

Like many expatriates Leena had met, they seemed oblivious to their actual surroundings, living, in their case, in a permanent mental American heartland frozen circa 1975. Vietnam was still an incendiary topic and opinions were evenly divided. One night, two men started a fight over the War, right in the middle of a Grateful Dead song; someone screamed, and Steve heaved a bucket of ice water all over the pugilists, who demanded, aggrieved, Wassa matter, man? And Steve said, Nobody interrupts the Grateful Dead. They claimed, all, to be flag-loving Americans "through and through," although none of them seemed particularly to want to go back: they were in hiding from ex-wives demanding arrears of alimony, governments demanding arrears of taxes; they were in the East because it was cheap and to "get their heads together." They talked, desultorily, about fleeing to Bali for good, they were caught up in the stream of their slow, rootless, restless drift around the world, a peregrination to nowhere. They believed, superstitiously and silently, that each new destination was another bead on a charmed necklace, the purpose of which, ultimately, was to stave off death: they were all, in the end, refugees.

Amidst all this unfocusedness, Steve moved through with the sharp, defined edges of a diamond; he was not in the drift, or so she thought.

• • •

They were married three months later.

• • •

Her parents were quietly horrified. Who was Steve? What was his history? What did he do? And where had she met him? Stiff with grief, as if someone had died.

They had never understood where her hoary streak of rebellion came from, her need to kick, mercilessly, at every perceived restraint. Changeling. Viper in the bosom. A tiny wisp of a girl in an otherwise ample family: any one of her brothers could have picked her up bodily with one hand. A mouth as wide and full-lipped as a jazz singer's, a pert, swinging walk seen at its best in short, flared skirts, a direct, challenging stare.

Her parents, nonplussed by all this sensuality, did their best to stamp it out. Leena was expected to be both a scholar and a traditional Indian woman, helping her mother with the chores while her brothers gambolled off. Chafing, Leena alternated between docility and outbreaks where she disappeared from home for days at a time. At eighteen, her truculent announcement that she was not going to university unleashed storms, her father (who ran his own law firm and believed firmly that life other than as a professional was not worth living) warning darkly that she was condemning herself to "a slide down the social ladder." Leena, unmoved, moved out: being the black sheep of the family was a draining activity.

But this was the decisive break—Leena and her parents both knew it. Leena had deprived her mother of the pleasures of matchmaking, of the noisy, triumphal excesses of a wedding; she had married a man who, in the orotund words of her father, had "the odour of too many scams about him." Again and again, her mother demanded to know: *why* this hole and corner business of popping into the Registry of Marriages one afternoon without informing anyone? Was she, heaven forbid, pregnant? Leena tried to explain: it seemed like a crazy, wonderful, impulsive thing to do! Her father said, swelling: crazy—wonderful—impulsive—we are not characters from a Victorian novel or a Hollywood romance!

Leena sat in the sitting-room of her parents' home, watching the clock on the wall. Two hoiirs of heated discussion: nothing achieved, except mutual feelings of irritation and ill-will.

"Wouldn't you like to *see* Steve at least?"

"We never want to see that man."

A shade of doubt crossed her father's face at these words: even he seemed to think they sounded faintly ridiculous. But it was too late to recall them, they had been spoken. Leena said, "I'm sorry," and flew out of the driveway to where Steve stood, waiting, leaning against his car parked in the shade of a roadside tree.

· · ·

The women of her family were fertile, if nothing else. Leena quickly found herself pregnant, and embarked on a voyage of unrelenting nausea, rollicking waves of it that made her feel as if she were at sea. She had to give up her job. Marooned in the apartment during the day, she was bombarded with calls from her family, entreating her to come home. But I want to be with him, she said, an unanswerable retort. She got the number of the apartment changed, twice, knowing that her family would be too proud to visit.

"There's no need to be so ruthless," Steve said.

"You don't understand," she said. Incapable of divided loyalties, she only understood partisanship.

Alone, she brooded, fitfully, on Steve. "I'm not an autobiographical kind of guy," he said once; at the time, she thought it a quaint phrase. She found that trying to glean information about his past life was somewhat like extracting teeth, a laborious, unyielding process. If she went too far, she could feel him recoiling, warily, and if they were in bed he would roll away from her and walk out to the balcony. There was always a final, inviolable territory to which he retreated and which no one could enter; she felt like an intruder for trying, even though she knew her questions were perfectly reasonable.

"Aren't they?" she said to Bhumipol the cat. "Isn't it reasonable to want to know a little?"

Strange thoughts occurred to her: perhaps Steve will be reincarnated as a green-eyed cat? And, I feel like a gangster's moll. Living in a zone of careful, studied ignorance.

She looked through his personal correspondence and his accounts when he was not there, but they were as unrevealing as Steve. When they kissed, it was as if they were sealing a pact of complicity—complicity in what, though, she couldn't say. And his unspoken resistance was wearing her down too; day by day she found it less and less unpalatable to accept him for what he was obviously determined to be, a fully sprung enigma.

• • •

She read in the paper one day that an American Vietnam War veteran, who had married a local Malay girl, had gone over the edge, kidnapping the children from his estranged wife and blowing his brains out in a messy suicide.

That night, troubled by a certain train of associations, she asked Steve whether he had ever been in the Vietnam War.

He laughed. Wouldn't stop laughing.

She grew annoyed. "Were you?" she persisted.

"Are you kidding? Come here." She settled, heavily, on the sofa beside him. Pregnant, she felt as large as an aeroplane hangar, ankles swollen and elephantine. "I feel ugly," she said disconsolately.

"Never," Steve said, his face buried in her tangled hair: barbed wire, she called it—she hated her hair. Taking hold of his wrist, she ran her fingers over the intricate bones, testing each knob; the pulse in his wrist throbbed, steadily, under the pressure of her thumb.

• • •

When the baby was born, they called him Ranjit. He was a tranquil baby who seldom cried, and seemed contained and self-sufficient in his cot, gurgling at invisible, friendly presences.

Leena cut off her hair and wore it close-cropped, penitential: she felt in need of a change after Ranjit's arrival. Depressed, intermittently tearful, she sat for hours beside the baby's cot, regarding him with the fascination she would have brought to the arrival of an extra-terrestial: he looked like a cat, she thought, a large, unblinking, hairless, skinned cat. (When she told Steve this, he said, worriedly, "Shall I call your mother?" And she snapped, "No!") She would start sewing clothes for the baby and, just as abruptly, would tear them up again. She remembered the French boyfriend, acquired at the age of eighteen, and how he had seemed to her so incomparably cultivated, until she had discovered he was seeing another girl. Then she had taken a pair of scissors to all his clothes. In moments of reverie, she could still hear the snip of metal tearing rents in cloth: a sweet, vindictive sound.

Steve said to her, "Are you going to be all right?"

She said, "Yes."

She wondered what she had got herself into.

• • •

In the beginning, she had liked the idea of it. Steve said he had business to do in various parts of Malaysia, that it involved a lot of travel over the next few months, and why didn't she come along? Leena was enthusiastic: she wanted, badly, to get away.

So they swathed the furniture in heavy covers, left Bhumipol with a friend, and piled, baby and all, into Steve's car one morning while the dew was still fresh on the grass. Wearing a red halter top and sun-glasses perched on top of her head, she looked so good that Steve insisted on taking a picture of her, which he did, and he stuck the Polaroid on the dashboard, for luck, he said; and when Steve rolled the top of the car down and the wind pinioned her to the seat and she could see the Causeway approaching in the distance like a flat, grey snake swimming across the surface of the water to connect the two land masses, she was glad, glad, glad. She slipped her hand round Steve's neck as they sped on, and though he smiled, he continued to look straight ahead and not at her.

• • •

So began that somnambulistic trip.

Her memories of it were disjointed, like a film made with a jerky, hand-held camera: images skittered on and off, isolated names resonated.

Everywhere women in the Islamic headdress and men staring at her and Steve; she imagined silent strictures where there were none, then she grew indifferent. Everywhere the same small, dusty towns where the new and the decrepit stood side by side and the shops sold the chunky sweets which she remembered from her childhood in the same transparent plastic bottles on which the flies clustered thickly.

They stayed in the ubiquitous international chains in the larger cities, and in small family establishments of dubious cleanliness in the more rural places. Was it her imagination or was there a night when dozens of cockroaches crawled out from under their bed in the ramshackled Hotel Labuan and did a sort of jig in the middle of the floor, while she flew about, swatting them in her horror, while Steve said, drowsily, from the bed, that even cockroaches had the right to live?

And the time that the baby caught the flu, and it turned blue in the face from the fever and when they finally located the doctor, he pursed his lips and said they were mad to go tramping about the country with a newborn baby, didn't they know any better? And that was the only time she had seen Steve lose his temper, shoving the doctor up against the wall, unnecessary violence masking his—their—guilt, and they had had to leave town in a hurry, since the doctor was threatening a police report. The baby was fine in a few days, though.

Memory was a slippery, skidding thing.

• • •

Steve's 'business' consisted mainly of looking up various numbers in his diary and arranging appointments in every town. In the beginning, she accompanied him to these meetings. The acquaintance was invariably some Chinese man hoisting a handphone to his ear while his eyes raked Leena up and down curiously, and she glared back, defensively. In the larger towns, he wore a polo T-shirt and loafers and was called Johnson or Freddie; in the small towns he sloped into the restaurant (Steve's business was usually conducted over lunch) wearing slippers. They all seemed to know Steve from a previous incarnation: names of mutual friends, people she had never heard of, would be swapped with an artificial zest, the conversational equivalent of two boxers circling each other in the ring before a fight. Then they would suddenly descend to the nitty-gritty, talking in a cryptic code which Leena didn't understand and didn't bother to understand. (Her father had always deplored her lack of interest in money matters. Money, he liked to say, was the only vernacular in Singapore.) Calculators would be produced, and filofaxes, and impressively large numerals bandied about: sometimes the advantage would be with Steve, sometimes with the other man; it seemed to ebb and flow according to a barely understood law, indicated either by a discreet lift of the eyebrows or a crude banging on the table. All the while the Chinese man would urge Leena to eat, eat, a new mother needed sustenance, and if she said, no, she wasn't really hungry, he would look at her, frowning, and reply that he had ordered the best dishes in the restaurant. When she got bored, she would start reading, openly; finally, the Chinese man, unable to bear the provocation, would ask her what she was reading and she would show him the cover, with a creditable show of indifference. "No Harold Robbins, huh?" he'd crack, and she'd smile daggers at him and say, no, not today.

Steve said to her, "Do you have to be so childish?" She thought she might say to him, "Do you have to sup with the devil?" But she didn't.

So she took to walking around the streets with Ranjit propped in a sling across her shoulders, while Steve was out. People were friendly, Ranjit being a useful conversational tool, and they grew even friendlier when she practised her kindergarten Malay on them, making them laugh. Drifting from stall to stall, she would buy armfuls of oranges, roasted corn on the cob, chestnuts, *kueh pinang*, and nibble her way through them with a furtive, guilty, sensuous pleasure. Coming back, Steve would find the hotel room strewn with half-empty bags and feign horror. He himself never seemed to eat, lived on a diet of salads, mineral water and bread, if that; he was getting ascetic in his old age, he said, only half-jokingly.

• • •

There was the time too that they woke up one morning to find a note slipped under their door saying, 'Get Out OR You'll Be Sorry', which she thought rather funny and clumsily melodramatic, but Steve had taken it seriously, going to the extent of questioning all the hotel staff about security: who was at the front desk the night before, didn't they see anyone coming in, what the hell, did they call this a hotel? By which time the staff were glowing with hostility and resentment, their faces closed in like so many fans snapped shut. And Leena standing in the background, pleading with him to drop it, it wasn't important, Steve, let's go. Seeing him as he must have appeared then: a crass, bullying American, a living justification for charges of neo-imperialism. Refusing to speak to him during the long ride to the next town, all four, dusty, bone-shaking hours of it, except to ask, Steve, do you have any enemies? And knowing then, knowing always, that he wasn't going to answer that.

It was best in the beach resorts, where she could lie on a towel on the sand all day, leaving the baby with the hotel baby-sitter, while Steve went off to town. Through half-closed lids she contemplated the shimmering bay, fringed by wooded hills, with a slight sense of misgiving that such unaccustomed physical beauty could exist, while all around her the mostly European guests baked themselves insensible, white maggot flesh metamorphosing into a blotchy lobster-red: her own skin ached for them in commiseration. When she could summon up the energy, she would take the launch out to go snorkelling (what a word, it sounded like a combination of snorting and snivelling). What did the fish see, she wondered, a gigantic behemoth with a face-mask goggling at them from the surface of the water? Letting her body go inert, limp, while they swarmed trustingly around her, and suddenly she would flail, faking a seizure, and watch them dart away in uncomprehending terror.

• • •

Once, he left at nine in the morning and failed to be back by four, as promised. She sat bolt upright in the hotel room, her eyes fastened with a painful concentration on the hands of the clock on the wall. She felt chained to it, every second ticking past a slow, corrosive drip on her patience; it snapped, finally, when Steve stepped into the room at midnight and she flung a book at his head and burst into wild sobbing. It took him a long while to calm her down, apologising all the while, rocking her back and forth, and gradually she stopped shaking and lay in his arms, docilely, while he stroked her hair, very gently, as though he were stroking some wounded animal. Later, she would think of that night as the night that he had unwittingly broken her in, like the horses he had broken in as a boy on his father's ranch; and she no longer remembered, not caring to remember, a life before Steve.

• • •

In Penang, she befriended an elderly German couple, peeling valiantly in the sun. Childless themselves, they made an extravagant fuss over the baby, who had developed a predilection for rolling his tongue. "Gr-r-r," he would say, menacingly, tiny fists clenched, and they would look at him in unbounded admiration.

"And how long have you been travelling, my dear?" the German woman asked Leena over lunch.

"Four months."

"With a baby? Oh, that is too remarkable. And how do you manage?"

It hadn't occurred to Leena that there was anything to manage. "I like change," she assured the other woman.

"And how old are you, my dear?"

"Twenty-three."

"Yes," the German woman said, musingly, looking at her with what Leena surmised, with some resentment, to be a look of pity.

When she told Steve about this conversation, he grew annoyed and said they had to leave; he didn't like people interfering.

"She wasn't interfering. And I like it here." But Steve was already packing. She maintained an ominous silence. Passive resistance.

"You know,' she said, "I'm beginning to have my doubts about you."

"Only now?" Steve said, drily. He glanced across at her. "Honey, you're watching too many of those TV movies. I promise you I'm not a psychotic killer or a Bluebeard or a guy who secretly likes little boys, OK? This is just how I make a living."

"So what is your living?" She lay back on the bed. "You're always so *mysterious*. What am I supposed to think?"

"I'm a very ordinary guy," Steve said, ironically or not, she couldn't tell.

• • •

Clichés, she thought. Stars, hundreds of them spangled with a lush carelessness on a black canopy, hundreds of hackneyed phrases and trite sentiments slewed across the night sky; she had never realised there were so many before. It's the reflection of the city lights that obscures them and makes them invisible back home, Steve said, and she replied, sleepily, oh yeah? as she settled back on the cool, night sand. The tide was coming in in the dark, the water's edge marked by phosphorescent pinpricks of light, a wavy, luminescent hem. Wrapping her arms around Steve, she imagined she was embracing some long, hairy, unknown animal, a whippet, perhaps; the thought amused her. A civet, Steve whispered in her ear. I've always wanted to be a civet.

• • •

Two weeks later, her nightmare began. Steve left for one of his interminable meetings and failed to return by nightfall. He had taken the car, or she would have driven out to look for him. She told herself not to panic: he would be back by midnight, like the last time, and she would kill him, then fling herself on him in exquisite relief. Sitting in the lobby in dark glasses, she ordered one daiquiri after another, losing all sense of time, until a waiter told her that the bar was closing. One A.M.

She went back to the room and lay down on the bed, fully dressed. Alcohol-numbed, she drifted off, dreaming fitfully of a splintering sun falling in a shower of ragged sparks to earth. A door banged in the corridor; asleep, she said aloud "Steve?" At dawn, dry-eyed, she watched the sky brighten, like a reddening weal, and made up her mind to go to the police.

The police failed to take her seriously at first. Yawned, unimpressed, in the middle of her recital. Called, impatiently, for coffee to erase the lingering traces of early morning inertia. Seemed to think that Steve, like many Caucasians in the town, had probably visited a local fleshpot and overstayed a little. Murderously, in the tone of voice meant for an idiot-child, she said, "But I'm trying to tell you Steve isn't like that."

Desperate to shake their apathy, she drew out some money from her purse and laid it on the table. Their faces rumpled with indignation. Was she trying to bribe them? She shrugged, and for a moment it looked as if this gaffe had thrown the fragile state of bilateral relations between their two countries into the breach, when one of the officers, relenting, wordlessly gave her a form to fill in.

It was a missing persons report. "Eyes," she read. "Hair." "Height." "Race." She checked it twice to make sure she had left nothing out, then settled down on the one hard bench in the station to wait. An officer suggested to her that she should wait at the hotel, but this elicited such a wild, swivelling glare that he retreated hastily.

· · ·

Six hours later, they fished Steve's body out of the river. He had been stabbed cleanly—if cleanly was the word—through the heart. The wound was barely visible. It was clear that he had died before being heaved into the water. Attempts had been made to tidy up the body before she was asked to identify it at the mortuary, but a discoloured strand of seaweed was still strung, like an incongruous tribal decoration, around his neck.

· · ·

"Suicide?" the police inspector hazarded, hopefully, pencil hovering above the stack of forms he had to fill in. Leena felt an impulse to scream, to smash something, rising up unbidden; only the thought that there was no one to hear her—no one who really mattered—constrained her. She was telepathically aware of an unspoken, insidious, floating suggestion that

Steve's death was more of an administrative nuisance to the police than anything else. If they could have closed the file on Steve Bauer, they would have done it with a smart click and an exhalation of relief.

"I want an autopsy," she insisted. "He was *murdered*. Do you hear me?"

Her vehemence was such that the inspector adroitly removed all sharp objects (mainly pencils) from her vicinity. Sighing paternally, he pointed out they had no leads. She had no idea what her husband did, whom he had gone to meet. His diary was missing. They would do their best, but really—he gave another shrug, wonderfully expressive of a resigned fatalism. "You should go home, Mrs Bauer."

Leena tried to call her mother in Singapore from the hotel, but no one was answering. Replacing the receiver, she was startled when the telephone burst into shrill, ringing life: it was the mortuary, wanting to know what her plans were.

"Plans?"

"For the disposition of the body."

"I'm sorry, I can't think right now," Leena said.

A pause. "Well, we *are* running out of space..."

She left the phone dangling, and, sweeping Ranjit up in her arms, fled to the beach. The afternoon sun had the intense white brilliance of a magnesium; she felt blinded, bludgeoned by the light. The fine powdery sand ran over her toes and burned the soles of her bare feet. Fully-dressed, Ranjit asleep against her shoulder, she walked into the sea, kept walking, until the water covered her waist, and stood, irresolute, looking towards the horizon.

Deep Sea Sloth

Jek has just turned seventeen. He has shot up in the last few months: that sudden spurt of growth has fined out his frame and wrought a subtle transformation. I am aware that he simply does not look like other boys his age, though it would be impossible for me to pinpoint exactly this niggling difference. Feature for feature, he is ordinary, surely: clear, questioning eyes that reproach me for my cynicism, shaggy hair that flops into his eyes and over his collar, despite his mother's entreaties that he get a haircut, nose, ears, chin, like everybody else's. Yet, not quite like everybody else: I see heads turning to look at him when he walks down the street, girls' especially, but he seems oblivious to the attention, or at least I hope he is.

I believe in the sanctity of the ordinariness of everyday life: beyond its charmed boundaries lies confusion. Confusion, a sense of being under siege, are what I remember from that restaurant dinner when a man came up to our table and insisted on giving us his card. He said he was a professional photographer who was always looking for interesting faces. "Those cheekbones," he said, euphorically, "those planes, is 'sculpted' the word I'm looking for? It's perfect." We looked at him as if he were mad. Jek turned bright red, and my wife's hand closed, instinctively, over his. "He's only a child," I said in anger, rising. The man backed away, hands flung up defensively before his face: "Hey, no offence, man." The other diners were staring, cutlery poised in mid-air. Jek turned on me, outraged: "Dad, I can take care of myself!" "Ssh," my wife said. We finished our meal in silence.

• • •

When I was Jek's age, I was acne-ridden, bad at games, awkward around girls. It took me years as an adult to stop feeling self-conscious about myself, to stop feeling that my body had been foisted on me in an experiment gone awry. I watched Jek with a certain envy; I watched his skill at games, his uncomplicated ease, his facility with girls, and I waited for some cautionary lesson, some adolescent trial to surface, but it never did. Jek steamed on, unruffled, unvanquished.

Life was too easy for him, I thought: he needed privation, deprivation, a spell of living on bread crusts and water, some long hard grappling with the soul in the depths of night.

My wife ridicules my notions; in fact she gets livid whenever I air these views. My wife is a psychologist who believes in the untrammelled development of the individual (i.e. let the kid run wild).

"You don't know how hard life was for your mother and me," I tell him. "We came from large families; we never had anything new; we knew the value of hard work."

Jek rolls his eyes, says, "Yeah, yeah, yeah, yeah," acting hugely bored. His new word for me is *fustian*: "It's sort of Old English for square."

His latest girlfriend is called Siew Ping. Her waterfall hair screens half her face and has to be flicked back, constantly; on her first visit she told us she wanted to be a merchant banker because it was a growth area in financial services and would I, as someone working in a merchant bank, give her a few useful tips? She seemed at least a decade older than Jek.

Jek admits he isn't too enamoured of Siew Ping himself; she is too energetic and ambitious for him. Lately, he has been overcome by bouts of inertia and has taken to lying on his bed, refusing to get up for dinner, refusing to take calls. "I'm having a withdrawal," he says, if we ask him what the matter is; and if we ask, withdrawal from what, he says, dreamily,

"Life." (His real withdrawal is from his mother and me; he has become—not secretive, but the days when he would burble on happily about his feelings—he was, if anything, a fledgling narcissist—are over.) This sort of behaviour drives me wild, and Jek knows it: he wants to see how far he can push me.

"You know what I want to be?" he says. "One of those deep sea creatures that never see the light and inch across the ocean floor. A sort of deep ocean sloth."

How can anyone fail to find him engaging? Nobody understands what I mean when I complain about his deliberate perversity, the delight he seems to take in thwarting me. By complaining, I appear like a mean spirited curmudgeon. I love my son, but I feel we are engaged in an hourly, unspoken tussle that can only end in complete victory for one of us; compromise is out of the question; yet if I were asked what the nature of that tussle is, I would be unable to give shape or word to it.

His best subject is English. My greatest fear is that one of these days he will come and tell us that he wants to be a writer, and I will be obliged to be, as he says, *fustian.*

• • •

Frank Ying was the colleague I knew least of all, a quiet, rather moody man who smoked heavily and was always the first to arrive in the office and the last to leave. We knew he was married, but he seldom mentioned his family, and that set him a little apart, in an office where we bragged, unashamedly, about our families. He told me once, casually, that he had seriously contemplated joining a religious commune in India; when I asked why, he replied, flippantly, "Oh, celibacy." Despite his obvious competence, he had been passed over, repeatedly, for promotion; the consensus among top management was that he was too much of the analytical intellectual, lacking in a certain basic ruthlessness. Yet Frank stayed on, though we often wondered how he felt about being undervalued.

Not being close to him, I was surprised when he came over one day and suggested that we go for lunch. "Sure," I said; I guessed it was to vent his frustration over work and to ask me about his future in the bank; I have had several of these lunches before.

We went to a Japanese restaurant where I discovered that Frank, among other virtues, could speak Japanese. He said he had spent a year in Japan in his youth.

I said that, with his myriad interests, he was wasted in the bank.

Frank never misses a nuance; he smiled, wryly. "I like working in the bank, you know," he said. "I like the work. Advancement doesn't mean that much to me."

"Well, as long as you and your family are comfortable."

"What?—Oh, yes." He fell silent, again retreating into his taciturnity.

Then, unexpectedly, he asked me whether I had ever been to a certain nightspot notorious for being an expensive pick-up joint. I said, no, and ordered some sake. If this was going to be one of those conversations, I needed ballast.

He had gone there to pick up someone, anyone. He said this matter-of-factly (as if I were privy to this sort of reckless desperation): his marriage had been over for some time, his wife and son had gone back to her parents in Malaysia.

"I'm sorry," I said.

He brushed this aside; it wasn't what he wanted to talk about.

• • •

I don't (he said) go to these places as a rule. I don't like the searching scrutiny, the intensity of which can make the back of your neck shrivel: men scrutinising women, women scrutinising men, under cover of their bright, senseless, machine gun patter, patter which they have used all day in the office and find it hard to discard at night, patter which becomes frozen in predictable channels over long, cool drinks with silly names.

I don't remember what I was thinking that night, something about my family, nothing I could articulate: all I knew was that I had this black dog of depression clamped, remorselessly, on my shoulder. I get these attacks sometimes and there's a physical texture to them, something grey, viscous, damming up my lungs and vision. Do you know some psychologists think that depression can be a creative force, that it was probably one of the sources of Churchill's genius? I've never believed that to be true, except of inherently creative people. If you're like me, just some office worker who sits in a refrigerated little box from eight to eight every day, there is nothing fruitful about depression.

I started observing the crowd; I like observing people, it gives me the illusion I'm outside of myself for once, free of the burden of self-consciousness. There was a party of teenagers in a corner, which was unusual, because it's not really a gathering place for them, the prices are too steep. They were trying to order alcohol, even though it was clear they were all under the age limit; they thought it uproariously funny to make the waitress repeat, over and over, "We don't serve alcohol to minors." And they would hoot, "*Minors!*" and fall about, laughing. They were making too much noise, their crass, unbridled effervescence a direct affront to all the brittle cheer that the adults around them were faking. They were middle-class kids, you could see that, the bright, articulate, prematurely sophisticated, terribly immature type, the type that got to use their parents' credit cards and were allowed to drive the old man's car on weekday nights. A few of the girls sat on the boys' knees and there was a lot of playful cuddling and squealing—kind of touching, really, they were so young and unknowing, despite their assumed adultness.

There was one boy who sat facing me directly, his head slumped on the shoulder of the girl next to him, a little distant from the general boisterousness around him. He was a good-looking kid. It wasn't some vacuous perfection; he had an interesting face, some quality that made you pause and look again, something of the hooded austerity of a monk and the canny knowingness of a street hustler, something intense, ascetic, wary. Do I sound crazy? I can't describe it, him, very well. All I knew was that I wanted to take that face between my hands and kiss its forehead, its eyelids; I wanted to run my fingers over its contours, as I would a sculpture.

I see now you want to ask me about my marriage, the question hovering on your lips, is that why—? I can't answer that. Possibly. I don't know. I've never admitted it to myself and it's not something that would occur to my wife, whose innocence would be touching if it weren't so lethal.

To be honest with you, I'm not particularly interested in sex with either sex. My wife was the only person I slept with in the first thirty-five years of my life; there were two others, both women, both one night stands in Thailand before the happy advent of Aids. Not that I haven't wondered what it would be like with a man, except that I have no idea how to go about it, how I would recognise another man like me if I met him. That, and the fear of being identified with the ultra-feminine boys in school who had always repelled me with their graceful, swaying walk and talk of lipsticks and eyeshadow. Of course I realise there is an element of self-hatred in all of this: that if I am what I am (which I do not yet admit), then I am no better, or worse, than what those boys are. Yet we persist in drawing ridiculous distinctions in the face of logic or decency, in claiming a monopoly of virtue, masculinity. I am no better, or worse, than anybody else when it comes to blind self-righteousness.

But that night I thought I saw a glimmer. Not sex, not physicality, I simply wanted some connection with that strange boy. I wanted, very intensely, to know what he was like. What games did he play, what school did he go to, what did he want to do in life, which books did he read? My main emotions were curiosity, and, yes, a very distinct excitement. The sort of excitement you would feel if you had been searching for something all your life and it dropped into your hand, suddenly, with a reproachful clatter at your lack of faith.

I had no idea how to approach him, though, in the middle of that crowd, and I thought I would surely go mad unless I spoke to him; I had this palpable need to *see*, to *hear* him.

And then, incredibly, he looked at me, saw, I suppose, this incredible, despairing need, took pity on me; or perhaps he was curious too, just like I was—I sensed he was probably used to people staring at him, appropriating him, seeing him as a commodity to be savoured, tasted. What is it about beauty that puts it in the public domain, that makes you and me feel freely entitled to it? He said something to his friends, and, unbelievably, he was walking towards the bar, where I sat, he was taking a seat next to me, his eyes never leaving mine.

With that same incredible self-possession, he said, "You could buy me a drink." He spoke simply, even seriously. I think he was testing me, to see whether his instincts had been right.

I said, stupidly, that he was a minor. He said I could pay for it and he could drink it, and so I did; I don't remember what it was, but he gulped it down in one shot and gave me this brilliant, watchful smile.

"You're scared," he said.

"Yes," I said.

"You want to go to bed with me, don't you?"

My mind went blank; his nearness, his audacity, seemed to be muffling my thoughts.

"Yes, I think so, probably," I said, idiotically.

He said, simply, "Well, then, let's go."

And I followed him out of the door. I expected his friends to call out to him, but they didn't, although there was one girl who was watching us like a hawk, the girl whose shoulder he had been leaning against, a girl with long hair falling over half her face and which she clawed back, distractedly, from time to time. I felt her gaze at my back, even as the boy and I left, I felt it all the way to the car park, even as I was watching the boy stride ahead of me. She knew, I don't know how, but she knew, and she would have willingly killed me out of that age-old, maternal protective instinct for the young. (He had a funny, loping walk, a sort of quicksilver cat burglar prowl, leaning slightly forward on the balls of his feet.) And then, as we drove off, and the unfamiliar, miasmic quality of the enterprise overwhelmed me, I forgot the girl and her furious, unblinking gaze.

In the car, he sat low in the seat, long legs bunched up against the dashboard; he said nothing, looking straight ahead with that unsmiling concentration, as if he were tracking his own distant star. His silence unsettled me. I've never been able to bear another person's silence, though God knows I've been accused of the same unnerving trait myself, and I started talking to plug in the silence, before it suffocated me.

I told him about Clara. The usual, and not so usual, story. We married young, in a curious coming together of fatalism on my part and a desire to escape home on hers. Fatalism because I knew I had to get married, it was one of the things you had to do. I wanted to get it over with, all because I had to prove to myself that I could want a woman, live with a woman. We went into it with the ruthless practicality we would have brought to a business transaction, except that neither of us knew that this passionless beginning would erupt into a passion of tears and recriminations that was like being edged nearer the brink of death every day. Clara with her demands for attention, her wanting a part of me which wasn't there, which I couldn't give...

And I watched myself falling deeper into the morass with every despicable thing I said about Clara, and for what? To propitiate this boy who didn't seem to be listening, and if he were listening was probably doing so with a youthful, weary contempt, vowing to make me pay for inflicting this utter, utter banality on him.

In the end, I stopped talking altogether, and he said, "Nice car. How much did you pay for it?" and he ran his fingers, appreciatively, over the fittings.

He wasn't intending to be cruel; by the lights of his sheltered world, he was being polite by doing me the favour of asking me about my car.

I told him. I had the sensation I was having one of those fabled out-of-body experiences; I had become a speck on the ceiling of the car, watching my physical self go through these contortions, asking ridiculous questions: "Do your parents allow you to be out so late?"

"My parents?" he said, slowly, as if he had never heard of this concept before. "No, I guess not."

"Won't they be worried?"

"Hey, if you did everything they wanted you to do—"

"You'd be a better person."

He looked at me, frowning. "What do you do for a living?"

"I work in a bank."

"So does my father. He's senior vice-president."

"So you're a nice, well brought up, upper-middle-class child."

"Are you trying to make fun of me?"

"Heaven forbid."

"Do you mind not calling me a child? My father does that all the time and I can't stand it."

In the house, he wandered about, touching objects with a wondering curiosity, refusing my offers of food and drink; he seemed completely at ease, except for that flickering, watchful quality in his gaze, which came and went from time to time. Anybody watching us might have concluded that he was the host and I the interloper, a blundering moth that had strayed in from the dark. My home looked different to me, distended, askew; and I was cold, unaccountably cold, hands numb, feet numb, shivering slightly.

He paused, finally, before a photograph of my family on the side-table. "Is that your son?"

I said, yes.

"How old is he?"

"Eighteen."

For the first time that night, he looked at me as if I had come alive, flickered into reality, for him.

"I'm seventeen," he said, fingers tracing, perhaps unconsciously, the face of my son in the photograph.

I wanted to die, I assure you, and yet I had never felt so keenly, glitteringly alive: every moment had a sharp, faceted, diamond clarity.

"I want you to understand—I don't normally do this sort of thing."

"Do what?" he said, very deliberately, wanting to pin me down, a wriggling insect, to watch me squirm. Then absolving me: "You don't have to explain anything to me."

He came and perched on the armrest of the sofa on which I was slumped; he was so near I could smell his young warmth, smell the freeze-dried, crackling, acrid smell of cigarette smoke in his clothes, his hair. I knew what he was thinking—you don't believe me? He was thinking that if he were to leave now, walk out of that door, I would be hugely relieved, would dismiss this whole episode as a reprehensible, but forgivable, lapse. And he was considering doing it, considering being kind; considering whether he had it in him to be kind, he was not an unkind person, no, it was just that it was still a novelty for him to discover that he could put people so completely in his thrall, hold them captive in the palm of his hand, just by their looking at him and wanting him, wanting him with a desperation that was alien and a little repellent and yet not unflattering to him—he was flexing, testing that power, in a pure spirit of experimentation. In ten years, five, he could be a monster of manipulation, but that night there was still something artless about his attempts at learning how to walk.

He touched my shoulder, lightly; I flinched, went still. His hand crept up to my neck, began a gentle, caressing motion. I closed my eyes; a sort of lassitude had taken hold of me; suddenly, I wanted, very badly, to sleep, to fall asleep with him next to me; and then his hand was sliding into my shirt, and I felt his lips on my neck.

And then I was pleading with him to stop, which he did; and with an effort I removed his hand, kissed it, let it go.

"What's the matter?" he said. "Why are you crying? Didn't you like it?"

I answered his first two questions. "I'm drunk." The embarrassing tears were trickling, salty, into the corners of my mouth.

"No, you're not," he contradicted.

"No, I'm not."

I tried to light a cigarette, but my fingers were trembling too much. Wordlessly, the boy leaned over and did it for me. He lit one for himself too, watching me all the while with that unceasing wariness, leavened, now, with genuine curiosity.

After a while, he said, "You're ashamed, aren't you? Or you think you ought to be."

"Why are you doing this?"

He didn't answer. I asked him again.

"I'm bored," he said. "Bored with life, bored with family, bored with girls, bored with everything."

"Your life must be too easy."

"That's what my father says."

"Your father and I probably have a lot in common."

"Look," he said, "I have to go."

I grabbed his hand. "Why are you doing this?"

"Look, I have to get back."

"I'm talking to you."

"Kicks," the boy said. "Can I have my hand back?"

"Kicks? You're too intelligent."

"My father has my life mapped out for me," he said. "'A' levels, medical school in America, specialisation in some field, probably gynaecology, because that's where the money is. I dream sometimes that my father's holding me down by the throat while the waters close over my head."

"Very dramatic," I said. "Very banal. I don't believe a word of it."

He sighed. He looked faintly disappointed, sulky, as if the evening had elided into the farcical and he wanted to call a quick halt to the proceedings; the sulkiness brought back the hint of the self-absorbed child that he must have been not too long ago. I seemed to be seeing him for the first time, and what was he? A moderately attractive teenager, with a face I now recognised—brazen, yes, but not dangerous, not extraordinary, not incandescent. No. That heightened sense of madness which had flooded me when I saw him was draining, ebbing; I was tired.

"Look," he said, "I have to get back."

"What do you want to do instead?"

He hesitated. "I want to write."

At that point I began to laugh.

"You won't write about this, will you?"

"I probably will," he said, coolly.

"You know, you should be more careful."

He smiled then. "What, serial killers and stuff?"

"Among other things."

"I can take care of myself."

"You're very strange, you know that?"

"Speak for yourself," he said, equably.

"Come on," I said, "I'll send you home."

And he followed me, obediently, to the car. He was asleep by the time I backed the car out of the driveway, waking up only when I deposited him, yawning, at his front gate. He slept the sound, impregnable sleep of the exhausted and the just, curled up like a baby in his seat, and there was in his sleeping figure that same trusting, reckless abandon with which he had walked up to me and asked me whether I wanted to go to bed with him. I no longer wanted to touch him; he had become as remote and obscure as one of those surreally beautiful people on screen, whose existence you fail to believe in even when you see them, tenuously real, in the flesh.

He never asked me how I knew where he lived.

• • •

"It's strange, isn't it," said Frank, "that the same genes can produce such different results in different people. He does look like you, you know. Yet—not like you."

"I've always thought it was less trouble to be ordinary," I said. I seemed to have difficulty swallowing my food.

"What's his name?" Frank said.

I told him.

"Of course, you'll accept my resignation."

"Please," I said, "let's not be melodramatic. You just said you liked your work."

He said he wanted to take a year out to travel and to think. I told him, as I felt bound to do, that this would be suicidal behaviour, no organisation would re-employ a man in his middle forties who did something so impulsive; and yet recognising that perhaps this was something he should have done long ago, Frank was not a corporate man or a team-player or interested in getting up the learning curve or indeed in jargon of any sort, and never would be. We argued back and forth, skirting the real issue that lay just beyond the parameters of our conversation, until I was reluctantly prevailed upon to accept (as we both knew I would) his resignation.

He paid for lunch and we shook hands, expressing mutual regrets, going through the rituals of civilised behaviour, rituals which you deride when young but learn to see the utility of as you grow older. Because, when all else fails, it is to the outer forms that we cling, with the desperation of a drowning man.

• • •

I left work early; it was impossible to work that afternoon. Knowing that Jek was playing in a football game after class, I drove to his school on impulse and went to watch the game, in the long, encroaching shadow of the late afternoon sun. A flight of steps swept down from the assembly podium to the field; I sat on the top step, self-conscious and sweaty in my office clothes, remembering the football games of my schooldays, the way we would prolong them for hours, while the building emptied and grew silent, and the sound of the evening traffic cranked up, audibly, outside the school walls and that fierce, mid-afternoon glare gradually receded, without our knowing it, because we were reluctant to leave—unwilling that those wind-billowed afternoons of field, grass, sky, skidding falls, rushing ground, should end, stopping only when we could no longer see the hands of the clock on the neo-Victorian tower and knew it was time to go home.

Jek came pounding up the steps breathlessly.

"Dad, what are you doing here?"

"I thought I'd drive you home."

He gave me an odd look and said that a group of them were going out after the game.

"Tomorrow's a school day, isn't it?"

"Dad, don't be so *fustian!*"

I let him go. We always want to protect our young, beyond the time when they need protecting. And as I saw Jek's figure loping off the field, a glory of mud from head to ankle, I believed that nothing wrong, nothing untoward, would ever befall my son.

The Perpetual Immigrant

I have always wanted a daughter. Strange desire, for a Chinese. My mother grew up with the knowledge that she should have been left to die of exposure on a hillside in China at birth. Her parents already had three daughters; my grandfather's wrath was terrible. She was saved through the intervention of the midwife, who hid the baby in her house until my grandfather had simmered down somewhat. Grudgingly, he let the baby back into the family.

As if in recompense, my mother had three sons and I have four. But the sense of a narrow escape has haunted my mother all her life. At eighty, she shows no sign of flagging; a tiny, shrivelled doll in her *samfu*, jade bracelets clashing on her wrists, she sits on the sofa day after day, watching her imported Hong Kong soap operas. Her air of fragility is deceptive: her will to live is like a sacred flame tended by an acolyte—its intensity may vary, but it will never die. She saw my father to his grave and I think she may see me to mine.

• • •

I have been in this country for twenty-three years—more than half my life—but I never cease to feel like a stranger. Even now, I think of England as a mere stopover on my journey, a blip on the perpetual immigrant's restless, shiftless trail for success. A country of narrow roads, narrow houses, narrow, grey vistas, and narrow, pursed lips saying, "Well, you should have thought of that sooner, shouldn't you?"—but of course I will never leave now. After all, for the perpetual immigrant, one place is very much like another. It is not an ideal country, but I am not a believer in Utopias. More importantly, I have my own restaurant—business concentrates the mind wonderfully—and whatever might be said about the English, they leave you alone if you leave them alone. In many ways the English and the Chinese are alike.

• • •

I forgot to mention that my two eldest sons are English. At least, their mother was English. The last time I saw her was five years ago, at a motorway restaurant of all places, on my way back to London from a business trip. She was in the company of a pale, red-haired, crumpled looking man. She hailed me across the length of the room: "Well, speak of the devil!" She wore a red leather jacket, white polyester pants, white sling-back high heels, pancake makeup—I noted all this, clinically—just like the hundreds, thousands, of women you see shopping at Sainsbury's or at the Co-op; I might have passed her without a second look in a crowded supermarket.

She seemed highly amused to see me. One of the things I had liked best and hated most about her was this cheerful, flippant irony, this refusal to fight. At the height of our worst quarrels, she had a habit of giving up; lighting up—she knew I hated the smell of cigarette smoke—she would blow smoke-rings and shrug, as if amazed that she had been induced to lose her temper. She thought I was terminally serious, woefully humourless and chronically bad-tempered. I expect she was right.

I thought of leaving the moment I saw her; only the thought that this would be unbearably rude and a sort of curiosity propelled me towards a table and fixed the neutral look on my face when she came over and insisted on sliding into the opposite seat. I had stopped hating her by then, but I still found it difficult to look directly at her.

She said she was glad we had met. I said I doubted that. "But I am," she said; she seemed hurt.

I told her I had my own restaurant now, and she smiled, absently. "Really? I always knew you would do all right."

I could see her reflection in the window pane. She had tried to keep her looks, what they call in the papers an English rose beauty, though the rose was turning a trifle brassy. Or perhaps I'm being uncharitable. The roots of her hair, as usual, were showing their natural dark brown; she had always been a little careless about keeping up the treatment. "I'll tell you a secret," I can still remember her saying, the first time we went out together; she looked at me, wickedly, checking to see whether I was breathless with anticipation, "I'm a *bottle blond.*"

I asked her about her lover, the one she had run off with after six years of marriage. She shrugged. "Oh, that soon blew over," she said, surprised that anyone could think it would last. "He was just an escape valve, nothing more." Yes, I imagine that the length and breadth of the country is littered with blown gaskets and shattered valves, relicts, reminders of her brief, tornado presence.

She seemed strangely nostalgic. "You're not still sore, are you?" she wanted to know. She meant, about her leaving. "It was all for the best, you know. It was an impossible marriage."

Before we had got married, she had warned me that she was impossible to live with. In fact, it was largely at my insistence that we shuffled down to the city registry one winter's day and became man and wife before a bored clerk, she grumbling all the while. Shacking-up had been out of the question: it would have prostrated my mother, who had visions of a grand wedding and a graceful, upward ascent into middle-class heaven. Actually, the whole rationale for my coming to England, in the first place, was to secure an education and I had wrecked my mother's shaky, but magnificent, edifice of dreams by falling for, as she inelegantly put it, the first floozy to walk down the street. Trust my mother to spot these nuances. She arrived from Hong Kong too late to stop the banns, as it were, and instead settled in, grimly, to keep the vigil of a deathwatch over my marriage. At least, that was what my wife said. As for my mother, she thought her daughter-in-law common. Years of living in a single-room flat in a decaying tenement in Kowloon had not altered her unshakable conviction one whit of her elevated station in life and the glory that was to come for me, her (hitherto) most promising son.

I am not sure what it means to be common. Perhaps it only means to be incapable of hypocrisy. My wife had told me, from the start, that she had had lovers and couldn't promise that she wouldn't have more. Two of her previous boyfriends had been black, a Jamaican and a Guyanese. She said she had a weakness for exotic men (including me). They say forewarned is forearmed, but in my experience that is almost never true.

I asked her whether she ever felt the need to see her children. She fiddled with the rings on her fingers.

"I always thought a clean break was better," she said, apologetically. Then she looked at me challengingly. "Anyway, I was never the maternal type. You knew that. It doesn't mean I don't think of them—what do they look like now?"

I said the younger one looked a lot like her. She laughed, pleased. "Well, let's hope they don't lead my life." Leaning forward, she touched my hand, lightly. I flinched, but she didn't notice. "What are you doing later?"

"Going back to London."

"If you like, we could meet later," she said, in all seriousness. "I know a hotel down the road..."

"What about your friend?"

"My friend?" She traced a circle on the table top and glanced back at him. He was drumming his fingers on the table, scowling.

"No thanks," I said. It would have hurt too much.

She studied me reflectively for a moment. "You always were a self-righteous Oriental bugger," she said without rancour. "How's my ex-mother-in-law? Still wrecking marriages for a living? I'm sorry, I shouldn't have said that, should I, I've broken about twenty codes of filial piety, haven't I? Oh dear. But seriously, look after the boys, will you? But of course you will." She gave her sudden, brilliant smile, tucked her hair back under her beret—a red one, which she wore cocked at an angle—and walked off, with that pert, jaunty step I had seen for the first time all those years ago in Liverpool. It was the mid-Sixties, I was barely a month off the plane, and the new city was throbbing with pop music, girls in incredibly short skirts and the heady infectiousness of being young. In the next few months people would be sporting metre-length hair and garish, primitive colours and designs. Ethnicity was in; Maoism was part of radical chic. I decided to cash in, who had never even looked at a girl before. "I've been told I'm a dead ringer for Marilyn," my future wife said to me, complacently. "Marilyn who?" "Why, Marilyn Monroe, of course, you big silly." I was twenty-three, she was twenty. I was homesick, bewildered and madly in love.

I never saw her again.

• • •

When they were young, the boys would ask me occasionally about Kay. James, the elder one, was six when she left, old enough to retain a tenacious memory of her. At dinner, he would make casual references to his mother: "Mum used to have a pair of dangling parrot earrings, didn't she? I saw a pair just like them in the shop today." And my mother would sigh and say, "What a terrible woman." And James would bang his fork on the table and go red in the face and start to shout, she was *not*, she was *not*, and I would have to send him to his room.

I think I have only spoken twice to the boys about their mother. Once to tell them that she was gone for a long holiday. Then, when even they began to notice that most people would have returned from a holiday by then, that she was not coming back. "You mean she's dead," James said, in his clear, ringing voice. I winced. I said, no, she wasn't dead, she simply wasn't coming back, that was all. I never spoke of her again; I had to get on with my curiously shrivelled life.

• • •

I might have spoilt James. Always precocious, he was the golden child of the household, the first-born, imperial god made flesh (I'm exaggerating).

I skirted him carefully, hoping that in him my thwarted ambitions would be fulfilled.

At sixteen, though, came The Fall. Like a ripe fruit, James tumbled into The Socialist Workers' Party. He sported earrings in both ears, grew his hair long, and started bringing home white, long-limbed girls who draped themselves, fetchingly, over the furniture and said, brightly, "Oh, hello, Mr Chang," when I got back from the restaurant at two in the morning. Or, worse, tall underfed boys who clumped all over the house and played their mindless music at full volume. This louche behaviour maddened me. James and I had nightly rows, ridiculous arguments during which I yelled at him in Cantonese, and he, in English, lit into me for my ghetto mentality, my refusal to assimilate, my support for the *Conservative* Party, my God. Whereupon I told him that if he was ashamed of his heritage— at which quaint word he rolled his eyes—he could leave. Never darken my door again, etc.

Which he did, at seventeen. Walked out one day, into the sunset, to join a multi-racial repertory company, piously funded by a militantly left-wing local council, dragging its ideological baggage all over the country. We discovered later he does a skit on a Chinese restaurant owner whose English wife runs off with an insurance salesman. "Funny, poignant, moving," runs the blurb in the programme. Ha.

I admit I was stunned. My son, an actor. A left-wing stand-up comic trading on his ancestry for cheap laughs. For a time, I saw myself as a figure in a Thomas Hardyish novel of epic proportions, a man crippled and brought low by the cruel blows of fate and so on. (Now, I am simply resigned. Sardonic.) Prudently, James stayed away a year before revisiting the family home at Chinese New Year, to eat his way steadily through the festive spread, pocket the red packets, and depart trailing clouds of splendour. I suppose, if nothing else, he has style; I will grudgingly say this for him.

Now that he no longer lives at home, we get along much better. He deigns to visit us every month or so, during which visits we continue the rough, joshing arguments that are a feature (the only feature) of our discourse.

He will say, "Dad, I just heard that in Oxford they're not letting four Chinese restaurateurs join the Conservative Party. Not quite one of us, old chap."

I will say, wearily, that it is important to be engaged in the political process, and that, in my opinion, the Conservative Party is simply the lesser of two evils. For a Chinese whose parents fled communism, the mincing routines of the Labour Party are like the dances of a wolf in sheep's clothing.

And James will say, "Lovely analogy, Dad. But you know what I think? It's like Groucho Marx, see. You know—I wouldn't join any club that would have *me*. The more the right tries to step on you with its policies on immigration and education, the more convinced you are they're right. It's a kind of psychological sadism. Getting flogged is the price of acceptance."

And, losing my temper, I will say, "If you're so smart, how come you're such a loser?"

And, grinning, he will skip into the room he used to share with his brother, and I will hear the sound of laughter and music.

• • •

We christened the younger boy Richard, but lately he has begun using his Chinese name. He calls himself Khy for short. I do not know how much of this has to do with the fact that his mother's name is Kay. He looks remarkably like her: he has her eyes, large, grey, always her most expressive feature, and he has her brilliant, unnerving smile. But unlike his mother and brother, he is quiet, a little reserved, with none of their facility for collaring attention the moment they walk into a room.

Unlike James, he has seldom given me any trouble. He helps out in the restaurant when he can, he does well at school. He knows I want him to go to university. At the moment his chief vice is skateboarding in a manic fashion around the neighbourhood and terrorising the old ladies. I see him often in the company of a tall American boy called Lou, the son of a writer, I understand, here to gather material for her next novel. Lou has a careless athletic ranginess that the English boys lack, a long, tomahawk face affecting a stern, wary aloofness; he is always dressed entirely in black and has seven gold studs in his left ear. Once, going up to Khy's room, I found him lying face down on the bed, apparently fast asleep, while the American boy perched on the window sill, like a carrion bird, smoking and looking at Khy. Something in the way he was looking at my son made me tell him, sharply, that I did not allow smoking in the house. Amiably, he put out his cigarette. Another time—they were leaving the house—I saw Lou drape his arm around Khy's shoulders, draw him close and kiss him above the eye. Khy drew back and gave him a look of mildly rebuking surprise. They did not see me, I think.

The lives of one's children are such mysteries. Or perhaps it is better to keep one's knowledge within certain well defined boundaries.

• • •

My second wife is from Canton and I had never seen her before we got married. At least, I had seen a photograph of her, with her hair scraped back severely from her face, wearing a grave smile. By then, I was tired of living alone, tired of unsatisfactory one-night stands. The photograph showed no obvious deficiencies, and so I gave in to my mother's ceaseless importunings to find a wife. My mother's marriage was not happy—my father was a philanderer by profession—but the unhappily married always seem anxious to matchmake on behalf of the whole world. Delighted, my mother made all the necessary arrangements through the marriage bureau. It had been her idea to find me a foreign bride; she felt, I think, that someone with no ties in this country would be less given to bolt, would be self-shackled, to put it brutally.

Three months later, this unknown quantity—*my wife*—was duly deposited at Heathrow, speaking not a word of English. The customs officials somehow got it into their heads that, shy, stubborn and uncomprehending as she seemed, she had to be a drugs courier, and they kept her for hours. By then, I was furious at having to wait in the arrivals bay while the other passengers streamed past me, furious with myself for having yielded to my mother's schemes. But when she finally emerged, in tears, looking impossibly small and impossibly grateful to be met by me—the way she clutched at my hand, like a child homing in, instinctively, on the first trustworthy adult it sees—I knew, then, that whatever happened, this marriage would have to work. If only to save my face.

For she turned out to be much younger than I had been led to believe, nearer James' age, in fact, than mine. The boys looked at her, nonplussed. "Cradle-snatcher," James said in mock-horror. "*Child*-bride." It is a standard male fantasy—or so I am told—to marry someone half your age and twice as nubile, but her youth was an embarrassment to me. Still, here she was: one couldn't pack her off again like a defective TV set. We adjusted. She and I adjusted. I do not suppose it was easy for her, but she did not speak of it; she is the most silent and enigmatic woman of my acquaintance.

At first she seemed to me plain, her round, childish face contrasting oddly with the elderly floral dresses which were all she had brought with her. A dumpy, peasant woman, I remember thinking in the beginning, suitable only for bearing children and housekeeping. Mentally, I still kept comparing her to the other one, though I knew it was a self-defeating thing to do. A year after we were married, my second wife gave birth to twin sons, and we trooped, dutifully, to the hospital to view her lying, exhausted, in the cramped hospital bed, her duty done. I seemed to detect a look of determination on her face never to be a victim again.

Back home, she resumed her daily routine, but there was a difference. The weight peeled off, like a skin waiting to be shed; her face now revealed a spare, angular, I won't say, beauty, but something arresting, a little disturbing, her high cheekbones arching through and touched with rouge. She wore a faint, cheap scent; her nails were painted a colour which, on a trip to Woolworth's, I found to be Fiery Magenta. I watched her like a hawk, with a silent fear; she was conscious of my scrutiny.

Once, she asked me, "Your English wife, where is she now?"

I said, "I don't know."

"She was a bad woman?" (She had been listening to my mother.)

"No," I said. "She was just different." And I said, half-jokingly, half-fearfully, "And you—maybe you will leave me too, one of these days."

"Who would I run to?" she said, simply, a little resentful at being classed, even potentially, with the 'bad one'. I left the room, before she could say (as I felt sure she was going to say) that she was grateful to me and knew her duty—two of the most depressing phrases that the Chinese like to use.

No, she will not leave, if only because of the twins. I have seen her crooning to them, with that fierce, possessive mother-love that the Chinese poets love to eulogise; there is something in the strong line of her back that makes me think she would be prepared to lay down her life for them, these two black-haired, black-eyed babies sitting silkenly in their cots and shattering the night with their piercing cries. I had forgotten what it was like to have babies in the house—the smell, the noise, the sheer worry. She gets up, uncomplainingly, several times a night to tend to them; if I volunteer to help, she gives me that faint, resentful look, and I retreat.

Yes, she is a good mother, a good woman all round, I suppose, not in the least like the other one. After two years we have got used to each other and there is something companionable about our silences together. People sometimes ask me what it is like to enter into an arranged marriage in this day and age; their faces register polite incredulity. My answer is, I expected nothing, I am pragmatic, like all Chinese, and so I am content. Certainly, she will never fling a plate at my head or plunge me into a frenzy of jealousy, sending me out to scour the neighbouring pubs for her slender form and gurgling laugh before she takes her latest acquisition to bed. She will never put me through the humiliation of walking through massed ranks of Englishmen, propped against the bar, watching me, hearing my stuttered questions with amusement, and muttering, none too softly, about "Chinks on a bender." She has neat features, she stays at home, she looks after her sons. What more could a man want? Twice a day, I try to remind myself—it is all I ask for.

The Forerunner

My brother died, in the early hours of a Saturday morning, running, naked, arms outstretched, down the road into the path of an oncoming car. The car wasn't even going particularly fast. He died of concussion, later, on the way to hospital. He was seventeen. That made me the only son.

• • •

They did an autopsy on him and that was when they found the traces of drugs in his body. The pathologist called my mother to ask if she knew that her son was a dope-fiend. I can see my mother now, cradling the telephone between head and shoulder, her glasses perched on the top of her head and her eyes fixed in the middle distance, thinking of something else. "It could have been worse," she said. The pathologist hung up, disgusted. (Later, he included this anecdote in his best selling memoirs.)

I knew what she was thinking of. She had just read a life of Marie Curie and she had told us about the part where Pierre Curie is in a road accident, trampled to death beneath a horse-drawn vehicle. For months, his wife kept the scraps of clothing smeared with the remnants of his brains, poor matted nerves, muscles and blood impressed onto threads. Recounting it, my mother went pale. My brother was unimpressed. "Ma, you're so morbid."

All the relatives came to the funeral, all the ones I knew and hated, and some new ones I had never seen before but knew I would hate. They came to gloat over my mother. First my father (who had committed suicide a few months before my brother's death), now my brother: surely, now, she would betray some signs of being human? She did not. She sat through the funeral service, straight, composed, wearing what I call her Buddha look, made up of double-lidded, veiled eyes, an intimation of hidden secrets, a preternatural calm. I have seen the same transfixed, unblinking expression on the faces of lizards. When I was little, she could quell me simply by directing that stare at me. She did not cry.

• • •

If my brother hadn't been my brother, I think I would have hated him.

Things came easily to him. Too easily. Exams, games, friends, my mother's wide-eyed, chiselled looks. He did everything well, but not too well; because of that, he could seem facile, a lightweight to some. "That daring young man on the flying trapeze," my mother called him once, satirically, and that was the family image of him—heedless, flyaway. "I don't know whom he takes after," my father used to say, meaning, my mother. I, on the other hand, take after my father. Even as a baby, I had a certain recognisable solidity.

• • •

And of course there were the girls. When I was eleven and he was fourteen, we made a pact. If I would screen his calls for him, he would lend me the pornographic magazines circulating like an underground river among the older boys in school. (The prefects ran the racket, their source being a fatherly bookseller in a second-hand bookshop in Bras Basah Road.) My mother could never be relied on to be either possessive or strict; she'd say, "Oh, hold on, dear," and my brother would be stuck for hours on end on the phone with some girl whom he couldn't remember but who claimed to have met him at the bus stop. Whole battalions of girls claimed to have met him at the bus stop. They fascinated me, these girls, with their long, silky fringes and belts pushed low over narrow hips, but I would never have dreamed of saying anything to them.

• • •

My brother was an insomniac. In his whole life, I had never known him to sleep more than four hours a night. Often, it was less. Dark shadows circled his eyes: he looked perpetually hung-over, prematurely dissipated, irresistibly seedy.

He'd be up half the night, prowling about the flat, making surreptitious calls to friends, smoking incessantly. Sometimes he took long walks around the estate, sliding in at six in the morning, just in time for school. My mother never knew. She took a sleeping pill every night and went out like a light.

A few weeks before his death, my father, who'd magnanimously left home a year earlier when my mother said she couldn't stand to live with him any longer, came over and had a fight with my mother about this insomniac behaviour. According to my father, a friend of his had driven past the estate the night before and had seen my brother picking the lock of a car. And then, my father said dramatically, he *got* in and *drove* off.

My mother pondered this, and turned to my brother. "Is this true?"

"Of course not."

"Well," said my mother. "He's denied it. So what do you want me to do?"

She was always edgy when my father visited: guilt makes you fidgety, she said once, plants a tightly knotted coil of tension in you.

My father said it was clear that she was incapable of controlling the children and that he was going to sue for custody, my God, he was sick and tired of this. "Go ahead," my mother said. "Just go ahead." She was, is, a Catholic, though she never goes to Mass. She refused to divorce my father, who, still madly in love with her, agreed to a judicial separation for the sake of theological propriety. To everybody, this was yet another example of my mother's high-handed irrationality. My mother liked to say, wryly, that you could take a woman out of the Catholic church but you couldn't take the Catholic out of the woman.

My father called her implacable. Cold as ice. Hard as granite. My mother wore her faraway Buddha look, and I could understand my father's frustration. My mother and brother were elusive, evasive: when you thought you had them in the palm of your hand, they had already fled, with a swift, unthinking ruthlessness. My parents' marriage had always been a struggle, my father struggling to pin my mother down, my mother struggling to flee. Often, I had felt my mother's manic desperation, like that of an animal caught in a trap, willing to snap or chew a leg off in its single-minded desire to escape.

"Leave her alone," my brother said. My father hit him full across the face and he went down theatrically, like a ninepin. My mother snapped out of her gilded trance; I stood poised, ready to prevent a murder. Family life's better than Disneyland, my brother liked to say, there's never a dull moment. Magically, a red welt appeared across my brother's cheek.

"*Look* at him," said my father. "I mean, just *look* at him. He looks a mess. He's losing weight, he doesn't sleep, apparently. What sort of family is this, anyway?" To my brother, who was lying on the floor, staring at the ceiling and smiling beatifically: "Get up. You think this is some kind of game?"

"I've had enough of this," my mother said. She marched into the bedroom and locked the door.

My brother got up slowly, touching his cheek. "I think I'll wear this permanently. It's kind of cool. What do you think?"

My father sat down heavily, in the nearest chair. He looked old, defeated; for the first time I noticed that a whole new crop of white hairs had sprouted overnight on his head. "Promise me one thing," my father said. "Promise me you're not on drugs or anything stupid." He was a police superintendent in the narcotics unit. He was highly respected; he really was. It was only around his family that he wore the air of hurt bafflement that I'd come to associate with him.

"Dad,' my brother said. "I got all A's in the exams, remember? Come on. This is stupid. But I promise." You could see why old ladies would unhesitatingly entrust him with the money they had so cunningly stuffed into their mattresses.

My father gave us both a hard stare. "It's not easy being a father."

"No," we said in unison.

He looked towards my mother's bedroom, wistfully.

"Sometimes she stays in there for a whole day," I said.

"Why are all of you conspiring against me?" my father said. "Why do I get pushed out of my own home and continue paying the bills? What did I ever do?" He was shouting by now.

"Nothing," my brother said. It was meant to be soothing, but it came out different—accusatory. And we all knew, more or less, that that was the trouble. In anybody else's eyes, my father would have been the model parent and husband. But ordinariness, to my mother, in any shape, size or smell, was a death-knell. She would settle for nothing less than greatness. And it was no use expostulating, but who does she think she is? She didn't love him.

As he was about to go, he clapped my brother on the back. "So, tell me, did you really drive off in that car?"

"Dad, what do you take me for? One of those assholes you fuck about with during an interrogation?"

"*Watch* your language." He ruffled my hair (I hate that) and left.

• • •

Soon after this, my father killed himself.

They get confused in my mind sometimes, the two funerals. I have dreams where I'm not sure whom all the people in black are mourning, and my brother drifts past, asking, "Am I dead?"

Of course there are some details that belong exclusively to either occasion. Like the rows of policeman in uniform at the service for my father. They sat, perspiring stiffly in the heat, and afterwards they shook my mother's hand, one by one, carefully avoiding her eyes. They knew about my father's personal life and they knew whom to blame.

The thing I remember about my brother's funeral were the girls. Tall girls, short girls, mini-skirted girls, girls in long shredded skirts and feathery scarves, selfconsciously ethereal, hockey-playing girls with achingly sleek muscles. Skinny girls without figures, who huddled at the back of the church, hiding beneath their fringes, their long, slim legs tucked decorously under the seat, looking furtively around. "I didn't know he was a Catholic," they murmured. He wasn't. He was hedging his bets, or so he said.

All these girls were at the funeral. They all cried, silently, into handkerchiefs. As the cortege was leaving the church, one of them ran up to my mother, who was walking alone, a little ahead, and pressed something into her hand. It turned out to be a dried flower. She gazed at my mother directly, red-eyed. "He gave it to me," she said.

My mother turned on her the full, frightening serenity of her Buddha look. "Thank you, dear."

Outside the church, the girls held a heated discussion. Should they or should they not go with the family to the Columbarium?

Most of them elected to go. They were incandescent, alight with self-inflicted grief; they were proud of that grief, jealous of anyone who tried to wrest it away from them. Many had hardly known my brother and I thought it very peculiar that anyone would want to enter this charged, infected atmosphere of mourning for no good reason. I said, "Hi," to one of the girls, and she gave me a look of horror, as if I had indecently propositioned her or something. I wanted to tell her that it was possible to be anaesthetised by grief, that I'd had an excess of it in the past year. Years later, I imagined, they'd still be talking about this day, with nostalgia for the time when they could still love, purely and fiercely, from afar. My brother, the icon. My little groupies, he'd call them, lovingly.

• • •

Now and then I go to the Columbarium to put flowers in the little metal holder beside the stone tablets of my father and brother. It's a depressing place, I admit, miniature HDB grey blocks housing the ashes of the dead. My father and brother are placed side by side: my father's photograph shows him to be eternally forty-five, my brother is forever fourteen, gazing, wide-eyed and startled, at the camera. (After that, he refused to pose for photographs.) My mother never comes. I don't know why I do, unless it's a primitive suspicion that the dead are not really gone, that they need succour like everybody else.

. . .

The only girl who didn't go to the funeral was Rachel. She was sent to stay with relatives in Israel, or so I'd heard; she was supposed to purge her mind of all that had happened. I could see her at the beach, in some zebra-striped bikini and a pair of the blackest Africa shades, her little mouth set in a straight line. She would be outwardly demure and inwardly seething, plotting her escape.

When Rachel appeared on the scene, I knew she was different, somehow. She was quite mad, for one thing, and that appealed to my brother. Any streak of insanity appealed to him. He told me the story of Rachel on a combined schools camping trip. The instructor had fried a couple of slugs, to show how one could survive in the wild without provisions, and passed them around for consumption. No one, not even the boys, would touch them, except Rachel, who swallowed one unblinkingly.

I was quite keen to meet his slug-eating girl, but when I did, I was disappointed. She was small and slender, with a halo of hair surrounding an angelic, heart-shaped face; she looked terribly fragile, like somebody capable of breathing her last at any moment. When she smiled, her eyes narrowed and almost closed altogether, and her face wore an expression which I recognised from reproductions of the Mona Lisa. She was half-Jewish, half-Chinese, and had already been expelled from one school for disruptive behaviour. Without her parents' knowledge, she smoked a joint every morning for breakfast.

She was only two years older than I was, but the gap seemed vast, unbridgeable. "Hello, kiddywinks," she'd say when she saw me, and I'd go red all over. I didn't like her. She was dangerous.

The first time they made me try the stuff, nothing happened. Or rather, nothing seemed to happen. The three of us were sitting on the sofa, the two of them watching me benevolently, my brother's fingers entwined in Rachel's hair. "This is boring," I said. "You have to go with the flow," my brother said. They were both free falling, floating, moving in lunar time. I tried to get up to go to my room, and found I couldn't move. My legs wouldn't move. I broke out in a cold sweat; sweat was pouring off the bridge of my nose. "Hey, you guys," I said. And then I was sick all over. I was sick for the rest of the night.

"The stuff was too strong, I guess," my brother said, sorrowfully, after helping me to the bathroom for the fifth time and holding my head over the toilet bowl. But I knew that wasn't the real reason. I was meant for the straight and narrow. I had no wish to expand my horizons or climb onto higher planes of consciousness. I relished normality. It was just that, in my family, normality had been scuppered in its infancy.

• • •

So anyway, there was Rachel and there was my brother and there didn't seem to be any room for me in between. I watched them together, and I knew they thought they were the favoured ones, the ones who could glide through barriers and emerge on the other side, intact, more alive. "They'll learn," said my mother, who viewed all my brother's amorous escapades with detachment.

Rachel's family was exotic by our standards, "sickeningly liberal," she called them once. Her Jewish grandparents had fled the anti-Jewish upheavals in Baghdad after the Second World War. An uncle on her Chinese mother's side was a CPM guerilla. All this had bred in her parents a dour insistence on the importance of liberty and freedom of the individual. Dinner table discussions centred, relentlessly, on politics and the human condition in general; her father dabbled in human rights activism and more than once nondescript men had come to take him away for questioning. Rachel was the youngest of four children, the unexpected product of her parents' middle age—for her, they had always been elderly, embroiled in dead, antiquarian struggles.

"I believe in the three A's," Rachel said. "I'm amoral, apathetic, apolitical. I'm in the vanguard of the new youth."

All this meant nothing to me. When I looked at Rachel, I saw someone capable of walking on burning coals, who probably ate shards of broken glass for breakfast, with her inimitable jaunty air. She was destroying my brother.

"Destroying, piffle," she said. She was waiting for my brother at the corner of our block of flats, when I returned from school that day. I had never heard anyone say "piffle" before.

"He doesn't sleep any more," I said. "Not since he met you." Not since he started smoking pot and taking pills to help him relax through the night. He blanked out, drifted off, which was what he wanted. But in the morning he was more wrecked than ever. He was no longer pretend-seedy. He was genuinely seedy.

"You really admire him, don't you?" Rachel said. "It's quite touching, in a way."

"Why don't you leave him alone?"

"Please," Rachel said. "Please don't make him out to be some pathetic victim or whatever. He knows what he's doing." I stared at her and began to walk off. "It's just that he doesn't want to be ordinary," she explained to my back. "He wants to be extraordinary." She was *that* far gone.

• • •

Like some nocturnal creature, my brother only really came into his own at night. At night, his eyes lit up like 100-watt light bulbs and he was running about the flat in a passable imitation of those mice you see in pet shops, going round eternally on the toy wheels in their cages, expending energy uselessly, frantically. He was so febrile he looked as if his hair might catch fire of its own volition.

I couldn't sleep either. I had never seen him like this before and I was worried. I hovered around, scared he'd take a nose-dive from an open window (my mother had never got around to fixing metal grilles) and end up splattered all over the pavement; everybody loves a tragedy, as long as it happens to somebody else. The drugs did things to my brother: I saw him depressed, hysterical, ecstatic. But what really put me into a blue funk was his thinking he could fly. "I can fly," he'd say, looking straight into my eyes, and I'd look away, for fear of being mesmerised into believing him, he was so convincing. And he was forever dangling out of the damned windows.

I'm counting the lights in the block of flats opposite, my brother would call to me at night, dreamily. During the day, it looks drab, grey, and utilitarian, but at night this gigantic checkerboard takes on a symbolic, magical quality. It's a swarming warren of secrets, and I can decipher them, if I want to. Daylight is the spell destroyer. It picks out the cracks in the walls, it lays an accusing finger over the whole blighted landscape. I like the night, little brother.

• • •

I couldn't watch him all the time. Sometimes I nodded off, and then it was my brother who made breakfast, turned on the bathroom heater and got us both ready for classes. He'd be exhausted, but cheerful. All perfectly normal. Except that he would swallow a couple of brightly coloured pills with his coffee and, when he reached the bus stop, he was as high as the stratosphere, beatified, tanked up with gallons of euphoria to get him through the day.

When I was little, and prone to getting beaten up by the school bullies, I used to tell my brother I wished I was him, liked by everybody. "Don't ever wish to be me," he said. "Where's your self-esteem?" He got quite fierce. "Don't ever wish to be me."

• • •

The names were like an incantation. Downers, uppers, speed, Quaaludes, amphetamines, Benzedrine, acid, valium. (My mother took the valium.) Poetry. I liked the names.

• • •

We had a fight one night. "You're a junkie," I screamed at him, though, technically, I knew you had to be doing heroin to qualify as one. Lately, I'd started looking out for hypodermic needles—I hadn't found any in the flat yet, but I was far from complacent. Pills were already beginning to infest my dreams: they whirled, in gaudy-coloured arabesques, through my sleep.

My brother cocked an eyebrow, and wandered about, whistling.

• • •

His grades were slipping, of course, and he was dropped from the school tennis team, because his game was falling apart. But it wasn't the sort of thing that rang alarm bells: people put it down to our father's death, girlfriend trouble, the flu, whatever. Nobody would have believed me if I'd told the truth. Not my *brother*.

Rachel's father was a pharmacist; he was her unwitting supplier. She'd go down, after school, and have the run of the place, under the pretence of helping Daddy in his work. Rachel had the cool methodical efficiency of a genius, never creaming too many pills at any one time and never too many of the same. Her strength lay in her capacity for self-restraint, which sounds an odd thing to say, but it was true—she never once slipped up in her accounting methods, she never once went overboard. What she hated most in the world were crazed druggie types—no, what she was after was a managed detachment from reality. It wasn't her fault that it was my brother who betrayed her in the end, with his self-destructive messiness; he was her one conspicuous failure. Anyway, she looked so sweet, and serious, she had eyes like Bambi's, and hair like a sun-spattered cloud, who would've suspected her? Certainly not her father.

She caught my brother once with another girl, holding hands and strolling around a shopping centre. She watched from afar, wearing that ineffable Mona Lisa smile. The next day, she tracked the girl down, grabbed her by the wrist and twisted it hard; the girl gave a muffled scream.

Rachel never stopped smiling. "You leave him alone," she said gently. For someone so tiny, she was very strong, and no one ever doubted she meant what she said. She was convinced that she and my brother had a destiny together; she was oracular about this, and mean as hell.

I thought a lot about what to do. My mother, I knew, was hopeless, locked tight in her own remote Lapland of the mind. My father was dead. The day before my brother's death, I called the pharmacy where Rachel's father worked. "Mr Abraham," I said. "You don't know me, but I had to make this call." "What?" "Why don't you check the stores after Rachel's been through them?" "Who is this?" Seized by fright, I hung up. But by then, it was too late.

• • •

Picture this.

Picture a party at the flat, my brother and his friends, to celebrate the start of the holidays. I haven't asked any of my friends: they are only thirteen-year-olds and I don't want them to be laughed at. By now, in any case, I have become a twenty-four hour self-appointed guardian angel for my brother, and this unceasing vigilance doesn't leave me time for anything else.

Midnight. Most of the food is plundered and gone, or scrunched underfoot. The point of these parties is not to eat, anyway. It is to look and be seen and to make out. The sitting room is cleared of furniture, and someone is performing a complicated dance routine. Everybody claps. The music is loud, hypnotic, high-frequency; I imagine bats in remote parts of the island pricking up their ears, receiving the message. Someone has brought vodka and it is passed around, sacramentally. So as not to look out of it, I drink a glassful. It is colourless and tasteless, and I feel fine. My mother would not approve, but my mother is in Malaysia, visiting relatives. Out of the corner of my eye, at the knife-edge of my vision, I see Rachel threading her way in and out of the crowd, an evil, little elf in a tight, body-hugging, gold-patterned number. She is bite-sized and delectable, and moves with a confident, loose-jointed swing. Leaning against my brother, she barely comes up to his shoulder. He puts his arms around her and squeezes her tight; she laughs and pummels him, and he bites her ear, smiling.

I don't know who makes the suggestion to play strip-poker. The girls dissent, groaning. Rachel pops a pill into her mouth and slips one to my brother. It could be candy, for all I know. It's late and the excitement is growing, an excitement born of the hour and the heady vodka fumes, a boisterousness tinged, unspoken, with sex. Most of the girls leave, squeamishly, en masse—they are nice girls, and this sort of thing, on top of the vodka, is beyond them. A couple of boys gallantly offer to escort them home. I can imagine the rumours the next day.

Rachel stays, offering to play. "No," says my brother. "Yes," she says, glaring at him, and he has nothing more to say.

The rules are, footwear and accessories first, accessories being watches, bracelets, earrings, necklaces, scarves, caps, followed by the rest of one's clothes. The idea is to prolong the titillation as far as possible. My brother changes the music; no more House, instead The Doors come on, with *The End*, sepulchral, camp, ludicrous. "Yeucch," someone says, but by then they're far too engrossed in their game to notice. Things have got to the stage where a joint is being passed round and people are dragging on it, without really knowing what they are doing. They are all decent, middle-class kids, whose idea of depravity is to smoke a cigarette. They have no idea how far my brother has transgressed their unwritten boundaries.

My brother is losing, badly. He is down to his jeans and he is lying on his stomach on the floor, his bare feet thrust ceilingwards. He is too toked up to concentrate and he makes bad guesses, wild guesses. I think he wants to lose. I sit on the bed, watching the game; I haven't been asked to play. Rachel, on the other hand, sits demurely, her legs curled beneath her, her cards held high, primly, so no one can see them. Now and then my brother makes mock grabs at her cards and she swats him hard, with her fists, like a street-brawler. I can feel the exhilaration coming off my brother in waves of psychic energy: he is in love with the world, with humanity, but especially with Rachel.

Now The Doors are playing *Light My Fire*, and everybody has lost at least a shoe, except Rachel. The weed is beginning to take effect and everybody is shiny with perspiration: they think they're acting normally, but to me it's obvious that everyone is operating in a time-frame of his own and is puzzled why the others all seem to be too slow, or too fast, in their motions. It's funny, like a film where the sound and the action have ceased to synchronise. But it's a good feeling building up, a feeling that one can live forever.

My brother disappears into the kitchen to get more ice, and Rachel follows him. They are gone for a long time, and I'm sent to see what's happening. What's happening is that they're necking by the sink: Rachel's small hands have burrowed inside my brother's jeans and he is busy unzipping her dress. They move apart, unhurriedly, when they see me. "Hello, kiddywinks," Rachel says.

"Shut up," I say.

"Don't be rude," my brother says, smacking me. I hit him back and for a moment we glare at each other, heaving. I know, despite the fact I'm younger, that I can defeat him now in any fight; he has lost so much weight in the past few weeks that he's almost emaciated, the ribs in his chest are sticking out.

"Stop it," Rachel says, and places herself between us. My brother's arms encircle her waist. She is always between us.

The others are hollering for the game to continue. "Let's get rid of them," my brother says to Rachel. She nods, and slips him another pill, from her purse. He gulps it down with a glass of water.

I go and lie down on my bed. The vodka has gone to my head and I feel as if I'm being attacked by a sledgehammer. I'm tired of this party, though I like the jangling, demented guitars on *Light My Fire*, which my brother is playing again, defiantly. It sounds out of tune and yet in tune, pointless and yet full of cosmic meaning. This is the closest that my brother and I have come to a punch-up in a long time. I turn on my side and in a moment I'm asleep. In the one wasted minute I take my eye off my brother, he gets himself killed.

• • •

By this time, the brakes are off: in my brother's mind, he has circled the globe and back again, and is heading, feverishly, towards intergalactica. Everybody else is just so slow, winning, losing, playing, talking. All his life, he has been waiting for others to catch up with him. He wants, needs, to speed things up. By then his jeans have been dragged off, with much screaming ribaldry and sly glances at Rachel. My brother lopes about the room in bright red underpants, ignoring the protests of the others that he's trying to look at their cards. He leans out of the window, giving them his usual post-midnight rendition of how he can decipher the secrets of the night; they have to haul him back, bodily, from the window.

"I'll raise you," my brother says to Rachel. His cards are a mismatched motley. She shows her hand; she has four aces. My brother lets out a whoop; Rachel rolls her eyes. And before the others know what is happening, he has streaked out of the door, and down the stairs to the ground floor. They pelt after him in a rush, getting entangled in the doorway; laughing, out of breath, they glimpse him running, naked, ahead of them, straight across the grassy verge that marks the boundary of the estate, and hurtling into the road.

• • •

They stand at the top of the grass slope, staring at the body sprawled on the road. It looks white, unevenly marbled, under the light of the fluorescent street lamps. The driver of the car stands on the pavement, shaking his head and flailing his arms in stupefaction. He starts to shout: Why couldn't the stupid kid watch where he was going?

One by one, they step out of the dark and surround my brother, jostling for view. They are awed. This is the first person their age they know personally who has died. They wish, fleetingly, that it had been a more sublime death: this smacks of the faintly ridiculous. Still in this, as in everything else, my brother is the forerunner: they have yet to achieve non-existence. Someone whimpers. There is no blood. He lies very still, face-down.

They will remember this, and mythologise it.

• • •

Hours after they had taken the body away, Rachel was still sitting at the top of the grassy slope, clasping her knees. She was so rigid she seemed frozen. Nobody could get her to move and, in the end, they left her there, after calling her parents. I found her crouched, kneading her fingers into her palm. There didn't seem to be anything to say. We sat for hours, it seemed, without talking. Then her parents drew up in their car, and she was off and running towards the road, with some mad idea of flinging herself in front of another vehicle—I don't know—except that her father cornered her and dragged her back, she twisting and turning all the while, and that was the last I ever saw of her.

• • •

I don't hate her any more. I wish I did. At least you know you're alive when you hate someone.

Contingencies

He knows Kok Cheong, in a desultory fashion, from school: it is assumed that they are friends, since Kok Cheong says so. The truth is that Tom's primary emotion towards Kok Cheong has always been one of tepid indifference, though he has never had the heart to tell Kok Cheong, who has, over the years, taken his fealty for granted. Tom had drifted through school in a pleasant haze; his reports had always said, "has the intelligence, but won't make the effort." Kok Cheong, on the other hand, had been one of the golden boys, top student, fleet athlete, school prefect. Tom has always hated the guts of these golden boys, with a cordial, visceral hatred. But he has noticed that they frequently choose as friends someone less bright, less popular, grateful for whatever scraps of reflected glory are available. He knows that Kok Cheong has selected him for the role of sidekick, court jester; he ought to mind, but somehow he doesn't. In any case, he sees little of Kok Cheong these days, now that he is studying medicine at the university, and Tom is in business administration, fitfully trying to muster an interest in the details of business while his mind wanders into riffs, licks, snatches of Muddy Waters songs. He plays blues guitar in a pub at weekends, and he would play full-time if he could, except that his parents would have a fit if he failed to get his degree. (Tom is nothing if not filial.)

Occasionally, he sees Kok Cheong cruising around campus in a shiny black convertible sports car, which elicits untold envy in the mind of every right-thinking male student. Kok Cheong's father is a heart specialist with a lucrative practice. Tom's father is a primary schoolteacher with a homicidal dislike of eleven-year-olds.

Lately, the buzz around campus is that Kok Cheong is going out with a girl called Christie. Tom has seen her around, a tall, long-legged girl with a mass of kinked hair that changes colour every month. She is supposed to be Filipino, Eurasian, he is not sure. She is well-known for wearing red bustiers to class, causing the more fainthearted tutors to wilt, and for her string of boyfriends, all of whom are uniformly wealthy and, strangely, quite dull. Kok Cheong is wealthy, but rather less dull: he does, after all, have a black sports car and a fondness for baggy Italian clothes which do hang rather well on his athlete's body, admittedly. Soon, Kok Cheong, Christie and the black sports car are a combined fixture in the leafy lanes of Kent Ridge.

• • •

Soon after this, he runs into them at the pub where he plays on weekends. Cornered by Kok Cheong during an intermission, he is dragged, unwillingly, to where Christie is sitting by the car. She extends a slim hand.

"I like your bracelet," Tom says, for want of something to say.

With a swift, unthinking movement, she holds her wrist up to the light. The bracelet is composed of human teeth. "Oh, wow," he says. Now he really doesn't know what to say.

"I used to go out with a dentist," she says.

He senses that she is gently poking fun at him, and he decides to ignore her. Up close, he thinks her rather plain, even gawky; all her features seem a little too large for her face, and she is too thin and bony. She is smoking steadily, sunk into herself; her right foot taps with a sort of suppressed energy on the floor.

"She collects body parts," Kok Cheong says, and there is something in his voice which makes Tom look at him. Yes, the signs are unmistakable: the guy is moony, possessive, proprietary and quite ridiculously happy.

He is in the mood where everything and everybody seem good, kind and explicable to him, and he wants to share this feeling. Tom, conscious of a rising irritation, excuses himself.

Back on stage, he is acutely conscious of Christie's presence, without actually looking at her. He knows she is still smoking; he sees again the way she drags on a cigarette, with that tender, defensive flick of the wrist; he senses her looking over the heads of the crowd, in her distant manner. He thought her silly and negligible; he is wrong.

• • •

When his set finishes, they are still hanging around by the bar. Kok Cheong has seized him again and is suggesting they go to the beach. Tom says he wants to go back and sleep. "Sleep is for the dead," Kok Cheong says. Tom shrugs. Don't they want to be alone? But a lack of anything better to do, some instinct of curiosity, makes him agree.

They pile into the black sports car, Kok Cheong and Christie in front, he at the back with his guitar, which goes with him everywhere. Kok Cheong is a little drunk and drives erratically; Christie sometimes grabs the wheel, and Tom expects the police to appear at any moment and to ask them to pull over. Still, he likes the feeling of the wind ripping past and shredding the sound of the music from the radio. He studies the back of Christie's head, thoughtfully.

They make it to Changi intact and stumble out of the car. A sudden silence is ringing in Tom's ears, after the roar of the wind. He is amazed by the amount of activity still going on at the beach: barbecues in their last throes, people sitting on mats listening to radios. Now and then an incoming aeroplane roars overhead, so near that he can make out the shape of the wheels protruding as the plane, a gawky bird, prepares to land. There was a time when the idea of an all night vigil in itself used to excite him, but those days are past: it has been ages since he saw the sun rise.

They move further down the beach, to where it is darker and more secluded. Now they are stumbling over couples lying treacherously in unseen sandy hollows and beneath clumps of bushes; an angry murmuring begins to make itself felt underfoot, like the rumbles of an unseen giant coming to life. Christie is beginning to burst with suppressed laughter; taking off her shoes, she runs on ahead, pealing. Then she starts skimming stones across the surface of the water. The shadows of disgruntled couples can be seen retreating further down the beach.

Kok Cheong says, out of Christie's earshot, "We just got engaged today."

"Yeah?" Tom is surprised. Then, remembering his manners, "Congratulations."

"What? Oh, yes. Of course we can't get married for years yet. Not until I've started practicing."

"Well, if it's what you want."

"It is, it is." Kok Cheong is kicking at the sand, absently. "At least, I think so. It just sort of happened."

"You don't have to justify yourself."

"I guess not," Kok Cheong says, drily, and then he is grabbing Christie round the waist and they are scuffling, like unruly puppies. Tom flops on his back, and stares at the night sky. It is full of stars, and he wishes he knew their names, but he doesn't. He has never managed to identify the constellations on his own and he doesn't think he ever will; anyway, he likes them as random clusters, just as they are.

• • •

It is four A.M. on Sunday morning, but they won't hear of letting him go. Kok Cheong insists that they all go to his house for coffee. Kok Cheong, especially, is kind and solicitous towards Tom, while Tom, for his part, is succumbing to a deplorable savagery. He knows this smug self-absorption of fresh couples, their need to have an ordinary mortal around as a touchstone by which they can gauge their own radiance and reassure themselves that, yes, they are lucky.

Tom has been to Kok Cheong's house before, on a similar occasion, except that at that time the girl was a model called Janina, and Tom hadn't liked her at all. Light-headed with lack of sleep, he notes that Kok

Cheong's house, which is a gruesome pastiche of a Southern plantation owner's homestead, has acquired a second set of gates. Both gates are electronically operated and swing open in an impressive, squeak-free silence. Both are made of shatterproof glass, with a crystalline sunburst emblazoned in the middle. Would two gates keep out burglars better? He shelves this interesting question, momentarily.

"I heard you got engaged," he says to Christie, when Kok Cheong has disappeared into the kitchen to look for food.

"We were drunk," she says.

"Well, congratulations on having got engaged while drunk."

"Don't be sarcastic."

"I'm not. I'm trying to say the conventional thing."

"Well, don't," she says, frowning. She takes out another cigarette.

"Why do you smoke so much?"

"Why do you ask so many questions?"

He throws up his hands.

"You don't like me, do you?"

It is on the tip of his tongue to say she is wrong, but he doesn't.

"I'll show you something," she says, abruptly.

They go out to the garden, down some steps into a sort of sunken grotto. Leaves brush against his face, like webbing; he smells the cloyingly sweet, overpowering smell of frangipani, and bumps, unawares, against metal bars. Then he sees them, about a dozen white cockatoos, asleep on their perches in an aviary taller than he is. They look like carved, feathered statues, snowy white in the darkness.

"They cost a fortune," Christie says, "and they're as noisy as hell."

As if on cue, the birds awake; seeing the two intruders, they range themselves against the bars of their cage in an impotent fury, screeching with all the shattering intensity of a siren breaking the silence of the night; the din is amazing. He and Christie run for the house, pulling the front door shut; the screeching subsides to a distant crackle.

Christie is laughing. "The last batch of cockatoos they had," she is saying, "someone set them loose in the middle of the night. You can see them flying about wild, in the neighbourhood. I think that's why the ones in the cage are so furious—they can hear the other cockatoos, the free ones, mocking them."

An apocryphal story, he thinks later; then, he is struck by the proprietary air with which she recounts it, the air of a chatelaine showing a guest around. She would like to be the owner of this gruesome Southern plantation pastiche; she likes, he hazards, money.

"I hate birds," he says. Ever since he saw the Hitchcock film, as a matter of fact.

Lying on the sofa, she lights up one of her inevitable cigarettes. Her movements have a rangy carelessness as she blows smoke rings, very deliberately, at the ceiling. "Why don't you sit down?" she says; she is mocking him.

Kok Cheong comes back in with coffee. "We saw your pets," Tom says.

Kok Cheong rolls his eyes. "My father. His obsession. Once he got two parrots and was trying to teach them the National Anthem but they never got past the Majullah. Now he's moving onto guinea pigs and hamsters." He slips onto the floor, wraps his arms casually around Christie's long legs. "He keeps two of them in a cage beside his bed. He calls them Laurel and Hardy. When Mum isn't around, he slips them into the bed—"

Christie laughs.

"—and lets them twinkle over his stomach. Oh, hi, Mum."

Kok Cheong's mother is tiny, but lethal; the most impressive thing about her is her punk haircut, which stands up in waving anemone tendrils a half inch or so from her scalp; she is also clad in a kimono dressing gown with pink dragons imprinted on it. A fifty-year-old doctor's wife with a rock sensibility; Tom warms to her. She is, he knows, the owner of a string of very successful boutiques. Eccentricity, apparently, is not a bar to the accumulation of wealth in this family.

"Hello, Tom," she says. To Kok Cheong, "Have you been defaming your father again?" She nods, coolly, at Christie, while Kok Cheong unwraps his fiancée and does a fair impression of twiddling his thumbs. He is in awe of his mother; she was the one who bought the black sports car for him, after all.

"So what's happened to Janina?" she asks Kok Cheong, pleasantly.

"Over," he mutters, sulkily. "Over." As if in answer to an unbidden signal, he follows his mother into the kitchen.

"She hates me," Christie says, stating a fact. Tom nods; the mothers of sons always hate girls like Christie—it seems to be a universal law. She adds, dreamily, "I hope I have daughters later on. If I have a son, I'm going to leave him on the hillside to the elements. An ancient Chinese tradition." Seeing his face, she says, kindly, "I'm just joking, lah." But he senses that she means it.

That night, Tom dreams of cockatoos in flight through the trees in a white blur of anger.

• • •

Tom's band is called The Leopards. A dreadful name, coined largely because the lead singer, Hamzah, used to like to wear leopard-spotted trousers of a life-threatening tightness; now they are stuck with it, even though Hamzah has since discovered B.B. King and Otis Redding and John Lee Hooker and now wears torn jeans with army boots, the street-cred-prole look. Built like an American football player, he can do a high, mincing falsetto and a sexy James Brown growl.

The last band member is Animal (actually Anun Chandran), but he has been known as Animal for as long as anyone can remember. Very thin and hirsute, he is popularly supposed to change into a werewolf when there is a full moon. Animal plays the drums. He once studied law, but it gave him such nightmares he soon threw it up. On stage, he has been known to throw the drum sticks at the audience in his exuberance and to continue walloping the drums with his bare hands.

Tom is the quiet workhorse of the band; he prefers it that way.

They have come to an accommodation with the management. For every hard blues number they play, they have to do what the management calls "crowd pleasers." The management has definite ideas about crowd pleasers. These include, *A Horse With No Name*, *Speedy Gonzalez*, *I Just Called To Say I Loved You* and *Hello*. Among The Leopards, this is known as the List of Increasing Pukability, but it's either that or not playing at all. The Leopards are pragmatic.

• • •

"We'll be back," Hamzah promises the audience, "in half an hour." Scattered applause; most people are too busy roaring at two television screens propped over the bar, playing reruns of *I Love Lucy*.

Unstrapping his guitar, Tom sees Christie for the first time, sitting alone in a corner. She is looking directly across at him. It has been a week since he last saw her at Kok Cheong's house, and he hasn't been able to stop thinking about her. Her smile comes swimming at him out of dreams, like a Cheshire cat's; he finds himself mentally composing songs around the motif Christie; he wonders, distractedly, where it will all end.

He makes his way across and squeezes in beside her. Her hair has a light reddish tinge this week and is done up in a knot just below her neck. It is too difficult to talk above the din emanating from the speakers, so he orders two Cokes, and they sit in a companionable silence, waiting for his next set.

• • •

Backstage, Animal, who sees everything (like God), wants to know what Christie does.

"She's studying Economics at the university."

"Good grief," Animal says in horror.

• • •

Tom has no illusions about his looks. He is not good-looking, not in the conventional sense. Residual acne scars have given his face a craggy, weathered texture; he could be taller; his hair is thick and wiry and he keeps it cropped short, military-style, to prevent it from sprouting into an Afro aureole. On the other hand, years of swimming for his school have given him a good build and he does have nice eyelashes, as his aunts keep telling him, impervious to his embarrassment.

Tom is the youngest in his family. His two elder sisters have long since married and moved out; they visit on weekends, swooping down in a flurry of rackety children, morose husbands and a level of noise and bustle which seems inordinate but necessary, though Tom can't fathom why. His sisters, used to seeing him as the baby, pull his hair, tug his clothes and inquire with meaningful winks after his girlfriends, especially a girl called Li-Shen whom he used to date in his teens and was rash enough to introduce to his devouring family. She is now in the United States doing computer science and Tom can't even remember what she looks like, though she still writes to him regularly. In answer to his sister's queries, he says he intends to stay celibate.

"Please don't bother him about girls!" Tom's mother always cries, at this juncture. She is the antithesis of Kok Cheong's mother, a housewife who wears faded floral prints long after they have ceased to be fashionable and is letting her hair, heavy with pins, go grey; a gifted cook, her happiest moments are spent swapping recipes with her daughters. She is not happy about Tom playing in a band, but sees it as an aberration, something wayward and adolescent that will stop once he graduates, finds a job and loses his soul. A kindly, fussy woman who worries too much, she sees hidden traps and temptations for Tom everywhere: chief on her list of vices is Woman, followed closely by music.

Tom's father is a well of silence in this commotion prone family. Years of hectoring primary school pupils during the day have left him voiceless, averse to talk, at night. At night, he reads thick volumes of history in his room, all the wars, depredations and political ineptitudes throughout the ages. Reading history has made him dry and cynical: he believes firmly that all politicians should be shot.

Tom is the first member of his family to go to university. Because of that, he knows, he is treated with a sort of totemic reverence which irritates him, and frightens him, too: he is expected to bring home the goods.

• • •

Lying in bed, his radio turned low to Billie Holliday, Tom cannot sleep. The murmuring silence around him nudges him awake, every time he is on the verge of dropping off; as only true insomniacs know, the dead of night is the noisiest time of all. He tries counting sheep, tries counting the number of cars grazing past way below at the foot of his block of flats, but nothing works. He picks up the phone and dials Christie's number.

"Hmm?" she says into the phone, a sleepy cat's murmur; then "Tom?"

"Did I wake you?" he says, knowing it is a stupid question.

Long silence; he is afraid she will hang up, and he knows that sharp, definitive click of the receiver will finish him off forever. "No-o," she says at last. "I was waiting to be woken up. Talk to me, Tom." She came to him, he reminds himself, all gold and smoke-wreathed and confident.

So he talks to her about the first thing that comes into his head, the blues and how he discovered it, and his heroes and his burning, inchoate desire to escape, knowing he sounds like a fool and not caring, all through the long, slow slide to dawn.

• • •

The next time, it is she who calls him. He leaps for the phone, afraid his mother will reach, martyred, for it, and hear Christie's voice. The phone is in the hallway; he lies on the floor on a cushion, legs propped over the back of a chair, hand cupped over the receiver to muffle the sound of his voice. Living on the fourteenth storey, the only shadows cast on the walls of his living room are the humpbacked shadows of passing clouds. For the first time in years, he watches the sun rise.

• • •

They play twenty questions. Christie won't talk about herself; usually the most she will answer to a question is yes or no.

"What school did you go to?"

"A convent."

"Which one?"

"That's a secret."

"What did you like best about school?"

"Roller-skating. I used to go early every morning and skate like mad in the basketball court, round and round. I wanted to be a speed skater. Until one morning, I crashed into a wall bordering the court and broke my nose. I was in hospital for a week. After that Sister—Sister Mary—banned all roller-skating in school. I was so upset I cried."

He imagines her lying back in bed, amidst a welter of pillows and cushions, twirling a chain on her index finger.

"Do you love him?" he asks, abruptly, too abruptly.

"Who is *he*? she asks, innocently.

"Do you believe in love?"

A long pause. "Tom, you're getting sentimental," she says, and puts the phone down. The nightly teasing ritual is over.

• • •

"I paid a thousand dollars for the engagement ring," Kok Cheong says. "And I still haven't told my parents about us."

Kok Cheong's voice over the phone sounds very much the same as it does in person, low, precise, every word clearly articulated, authoritative, even when he is confessing to doubts. Tom, cradling the phone on his shoulder, draws tiny guitars on a memo pad. He wants to get off the line, but cannot bring himself to be dismissive. He has always found it difficult to shatter the images which other people have of him, and Kok Cheong's is particularly inviting. Tom knows he is seen as trustworthy, loyal: it has something to do with the deceptively open face he bears, a look which mothers and old ladies gravitate towards, instinctively. It has made him the repository of more secrets than he cares to remember. He cannot help having the sort of face he has.

Kok Cheong has been calling Tom, on the flimsiest excuses, which are merely pretexts to talk about Christie. A note of dissatisfaction has infiltrated his happiness; he has begun counting the flies in the ointment. He starts with the most trivial. He doesn't like the way Christie smokes all the time; it gives her nicotine-stained nails; kissing her is like kissing an ashtray. At this, Tom laughs out loud, while a tiny, internal polyp of hate grows at the thought of Kok Cheong and Christie, together.

Kok Cheong registers the laugh, grimly, and continues his litany. "I don't know," he says. "I think about her all the time; I try not to think about her all the time. I asked her what she wants, and she says she wants us to be together, the next minute she says, no, she doesn't want that at all, so I ask her, does she want to break off the engagement? And she says, yes, then no, then your mother doesn't like me, which is true, but that's never bothered Christie before. OK, that's bad enough, but she's got these mood swings, you know, first she's laughing, then she gets all furious and won't talk to me, then she gets hysterical and wants to fly a kite at East Coast at eleven at night, and this is driving me crazy, you know, and if I ask her, is it PMT, she storms out and slams the door—"

And then Kok Cheong says, "You know, that night at the beach, that was the best night of my life."

Tom is deliberately non-committal: "Uh huh," he says, or, occasionally exerting himself, "Gosh." He feels no obligation to be even minimally consoling; he has not sought out these confidences.

He does not tell Christie what Kok Cheong has said, and he does not tell Kok Cheong what Christie has said. He feels all the power and helplessness of an intermediary, caught in the middle of these telephonic dances; he feels, fleetingly, criminal.

Perhaps he simply likes betrayal. Perhaps he should have been a spy.

• • •

They go out once in a while, the three of them, always to pubs, discos, where the noise is such that any sort of normal conversation is impossible. The threesome is usually at Kok Cheong's insistence; he wants Tom along as an ally, Tom knows, a sort of silent witness to the incipient blood-letting which he feels, prophetic, to be in the air. As for himself, he derives a sort of perverse pleasure from the knowledge that when he goes back, he will call Christie, or she will call him. Kok Cheong's blindness makes him seem touching, almost lovable, in need of protection, a thing he hadn't thought possible.

Christie talks to Tom on the phone but she is sleeping with Kok Cheong. Or, has slept with him. Tom guesses this, from what he knows of Kok Cheong ("It takes two to tango" is one of his more infamous sayings) and from their showy physical intimacy in public. They are constantly nuzzling, reclining against each other, lacing and unlacing hands: Tom could have given them marks for the whole panoply which, he feels with some paranoia, has been put on specially for his benefit. Or he could be imagining things: his frame of mind is such that he imagines conspiracies, treacheries, where there are none.

Now and then Christie looks at him, mutely challenging; she is contemptuous of him, for sitting there, stolid and unbudgeable. "Voyeur," she says to him over the phone. "Spectator." It is true. He plays with his glass, looks round for people he knows, while all the time violent, unreal thoughts run through his head, thoughts of smashing the glass, digging the fragments into his palm.

Kok Cheong is trying to tell a funny story about medical school, something about a severed arm being missing from the mortuary. How a severed arm had then turned up in the locker of an unpopular student called Cheng, everybody assuming that it was a cruel, but fitting, prank. How it turned out that the severed arm was not in fact the missing limb at all, and nobody could figure out whose it was—

"Excuse me," Tom says, and runs for the bathroom.

He makes up his mind never to go out with them again.

• • •

The worst thing about love, Tom decides, is that it ruins your concentration.

Ragged, he hasn't opened a textbook in weeks. He skips lectures or doodles his way through them, his mind a blank. He can't even feign much interest when Animal manages to dig up a bootleg Jimi Hendrix record on which he has blown his life's savings. He stops calling Christie, and stops taking her calls; yet he waits, obsessively, for the phone to ring. His body and joints ache, for no apparent reason.

Hamzah and Animal suspect something is wrong. He has been downcast; he broods; he sings Speedy Gonzalez with such a tragic air that customers have inquired whether he is ill. The management threatens a termination of contract unless the act picks up. Froth and energy, though, are things Tom is currently deficient in.

"Forget her," Hamzah says, brutally. He delivers a stirring little homily along the lines of "plenty of fish in the ocean," etc., etc. All very well, Tom thinks, but what does one do if one's irrational hankering is for a particular fish?

He hears things. That Kok Cheong and Christie have had a public, enthralling row; that they have broken up; that they have made up; that she is seeing someone else; that he is seeing someone else; the gossip and the malice ebb and flow, as regular and cyclical as the tide—they are, after all, one of the more colourful couples on campus.

Once, he runs into Kok Cheong at the university tennis courts. Kok Cheong looks wrecked, beady-eyed, hungover. In answer to Tom's queries, he replies, abstractedly, "Fine, fine," and challenges Tom to a tennis match; he won't take no for an answer. Tom is pulverised: Kok Cheong plays like a demented hare, chasing every ball and giving uncharacteristic whoops whenever he hits a winner. Later, he asks Tom, not looking at him, "Have you heard from Christie?" Tom says, truthfully, "No." Kok Cheong nods, morosely, and walks off without another word, batting a tennis ball over his shoulder as he does so. Tom's hand flies out, mechanically, to catch it. Fellow sufferers, he thinks, we should get together and commiserate; he ought to relish the irony in it, but he doesn't. He gives the tennis ball to a child who has wandered on court.

• • •

"What a surprise," Kok Cheong says, flatly.

Christie is sitting by his hospital bed, biting her nails. She looks up as Tom steps into the room, bearing a basket of fruit. Tom stops short; he didn't expect to find her here, in the role of solicitous bedside companion. He hasn't seen her in weeks, and the vividness of her presence is like a slash, cutting him anew. He judges from their faces that they are not enthralled to see him. "Hey, I can come back," he says.

"Sit down," Kok Cheong says. "Join the party."

Kok Cheong has had a serious accident. A few days ago, he crashed his car through the central reservation barrier on the expressway, crumpling the front of the car like a concertina. He is listed in a stable condition at Mount Elizabeth, where his hamster-loving heart specialist father works. Christie was also in the car, but escaped largely unscathed, except for a few minor bruises.

Kok Cheong says, "Boy, do I feel stupid." From his bed, he looks from one to the other, turning his head slowly, painfully; his glance has a searching, unsettling quality.

Christie stays silent, so Tom says, "Why?"

"Crashing my car. Being a cliché. That's part of it."

The scene, the tableau, is somehow unreal, Tom feels. It is as if he and Christie have deliberately contrived this meeting, this opportunity to gaze at each other theatrically across the poor, mutilated body of the sacrificial victim, except that the sacrificial victim is refusing to collude and is, in fact, radiating a distinctly prickly hostility.

"Yes, I feel stupid," Kok Cheong says, ruminatively. "I've come to realise certain things. Christie knows what they are."

"Don't start," Christie says.

"I'm not starting anything. In fact, that's the whole problem, right? Endings. We're talking about endings here. Or am I wrong?" No one contradicts him.

And then he closes his eyes, suddenly. "I'm tired," he says. It is a dismissal. They stand and leave the room, like disciplined children.

"Thanks for the fruit," Kok Cheong says.

• • •

Outside, Tom says, "What was that all about?"

"Oh, don't pretend," she says, angrily. "Don't pretend you don't know."

"No," Tom says. "I *don't.*"

She starts to cry, standing there in the hospital corridor. It is a kind of crying he has never seen before, a furious, hate-filled stream of tears, completely silent, while she looks at him, steadily, as if she could kill him.

• • •

Of course, he guesses by now what must have happened. Accidents have causes; it's simply a matter of tracing them back to the one definitive, irreducible moment, the one when a teleologist says, "Yes, that's when the Universe began." It could have been the fact that she chose to tell Kok Cheong, in the car, that she was leaving him, which decision Kok Cheong refused, stubbornly, to accept, without an interrogation as to the rival whom he persisted in believing had cut him out, running through a list of potential swains, each more preposterous than the last, while Christie issued her denials, wearily, then with increasing fury. Then it must be Tom, Kok Cheong said, expecting incredulity, hilarity, until he saw by her face that none of these were forthcoming; and, in the fraction of a second that he took his eyes off the road, he lost control of the car. It could have been any of those facts; or none of them.

"It's funny, isn't it," Christine is saying. "I know everybody is going to think I was somehow to blame for the accident. That I provoked him or something. When the truth is, there was no causal connection at all."

She looks at him, wanting affirmation as to the arbitrariness of life and death, wanting absolution. He wants to say he is not the person to give it, but he cannot bear her supplicating tone, so unlike her, and so he says, no, there was no connection at all. He senses the relief in her, while fear rises in him, setting the ends of his nerves on fire: he knows, as sure as he has ever been of anything, that they are bound together inextricably by this.

• • •

"You live here?" Tom says.

She nods, impatiently. She has already paid the taxi-driver and clambered out, while he is still looking out at a block of pre-war flats.

"I thought you were rich," he says, wondering, following her past an overflowing rubbish truck above which flies buzz, luxuriantly, and up a dark hallway lit by a single bulb. She gives him a scornful look; she seems to have recovered, during the long, silent ride back.

The flat is small, and cluttered. Vases, books, newspapers, bits of cloth, stationery, lie jumbled together on the shelves, also plates of half-eaten, moulding food, he cannot help noticing. Two large armchairs, smothered in moth-eaten antimacassars, take up most of the space in the living room. The TV is an old black and white set that stands on an upturned box against one wall. One shelf is given over to dozens of photographs in rusting frames: sepia-coloured, stiffly-posed, curling at the edges, they are of some antiquity. He examines them, while Christie flies about, tidying up, emptying plates, wiping, straightening.

The photographs show a polyglot of races: an Edwardian man with a walrus moustache; a young woman in a Peranakan blouse; an Indian man in a 1920s duck suit and spats. The more recent ones show Christie as a child, suspended between two adults, her parents, he supposes; by then the ethnic blend is so complete it is impossible to tell the origins of these three people, assuming anyone thought it interesting. Tom does; he has always been curious about the genealogy of Eurasians; it has always been an unconscious, heretical regret of his that he is, unexcitingly, only Chinese.

"These are your parents?"

"They died in a plane crash when I was two," Christie says. "I never knew them."

"Then who...?"

The unspoken question is answered by a tentative, "Christie?" and an elderly woman comes into the living room, blinking at the light. She is small and stooped and very frail; as she settles into one of the massive armchairs, she seems to be swallowed up in the upholstery, a tiny floral dot against the cerise leather. Her hair is completely white. "Hello, Auntie," Christie says. "Some tea?"

"Yes please, dear," the old lady says. She gives her hand, trustingly, to Tom, as though extending an audience. She seems not to notice that it is past midnight and that Christie has brought a strange young man to the flat.

• • •

The kettle comes, wailing, to the boil, and Christie makes three cups of tea. Great-aunt Eugenia is handed a plate of biscuits and this she puts decorously on her lap, nibbling at each biscuit with tiny, mouse-like movements. She talks about her childhood during the 1920s.

"We were well-off then," she says, regally, to Tom. "We had a house in Nassim Road, and every weekend there were parties. My mother loved fancy dress parties. She would dress up in silk and feathers and beads and I would help her. All gone now, of course. My father drank, you see. Then the Depression came, and the War, and we shed the house, and the servants, until one day there were none at all and my poor mother had to do her own washing."

Tom straddles a hard-chair brought out from the kitchen. He glances across at Christie, wondering whether she has heard these stories before. Christie looks impassive, walled-in, her eyes fixed on her great-aunt; he cannot tell what she is thinking. It seems very quiet, except for Great-aunt Eugenia's spidery, rhythmic voice, a voice from the past. He has a sudden vision of Kok Cheong lying in the hospital bed, connected to various tubes and catheters and wires, no, they are growing out of him, he is sprouting them, organic stems and roots and tendrils, forming a flowerbed. He gives himself a little shake; he needs to sleep, badly; it has been a long day.

"Can we put the television on, Christina?"

"They've stopped broadcasting, Auntie."

"Strange." She turns to Tom. "I've forgotten his name," she says to Christie, puzzled, her young-old face uplifted expectantly.

"Tom," Christie says, patiently, for the fifth time. She has the briskly efficient manner of a nurse with her great-aunt—kindly, firm, but never really listening to the patient.

"I think," says Great-aunt Eugenia, "I should like to go to bed."

She wedges the plate with its heap of biscuit crumbs between two books on the nearest shelf, extends her hand again to Tom, and vanishes into her room. The door closes with a soft click.

• • •

"She took me in after my parents died, and brought me up. Two years ago, she had a stroke, and her memory has been failing ever since." They are in Christie's room, a Spartan affair. The bed is an ancient, creaky metal contraption like the ones in army barracks; a single chair stands beside it. A small table doubles as a desk and a dresser. He knows now where she derives her lack of sentimentality from, the capacity he has glimpsed in her for making a clean severance at the root in all matters.

Christie lights up and sits hunched on the bed, knees drawn up to her chin. She holds her hand out for the ashtray; he hands it to her.

"You smoke too much."

"You've said that before."

Her bed is hard and springy, uncomfortable; he cannot imagine that she has been sleeping in it all these years. He unfurls her legs and she flops back, the hand holding the cigarette raised above her head to avoid singeing the bedclothes. Ash scatters in an arc on the pillow. Arms propped on the bed, he lies on top of her, length to length, a pair of cards. He runs his finger along her cheekbones and removes her cigarette.

"I'm not rich," Tom says, temporizing. "I don't think I ever will be."

"Pity," Christie says, drily, a little wistfully, he thinks. Then she asks, "Do you think we'll pay for this?"

He reminds her, "There's no causal connection." Then he says, incorrigible honesty getting the better of him, "Yes, probably, but who cares." He has to ask as well, the thing that has been bothering him for weeks, "Why me?"

In answer, she touches his face.

Hell Hath No Fury

The road to Damascus for Grandma occurred on a hot Sunday morning in the church of St. Aloysius, Roman Catholic, ten-thirty A.M. Father Le Mesurier, the old French priest who normally conducted Mass in a thickly incomprehensible French accent, was away on holiday. In his place was Father James Hsien, newly graduated from a Taiwanese seminary.

Father Hsien was so short that nobody in the congregation realised he had streamed in until an admonitory reedy voice piped over the sound system, "Brothers and sisters in Christ, PLEASE STAND!" Startled, the congregation leapt to its feet. Over the top of the lectern, the beginnings of a crew cut and thick tortoiseshell glasses of a type not seen since the 1950s could be glimpsed. From what they could see of him, he appeared to be all of twenty-one years old. (He was, in fact, ten years older). He looked like an infant swaddled in sacerdotal robes for a joke.

In his opening remarks, he told the assembled throng there was much sin about and little grace and redemption. With this unpromising start, he steamed into a sermon that managed to antagonise everybody from the large expatriate American community ("America is a land of sin and fornication, plagued by crime, drugs and Aids"), to the society ladies who organised charity lunches and thought themselves remarkably benevolent ("And I say to you, think of how you treat your maids. For the gospel says that the meek shall inherit the earth, so how will your diamonds, your cars and your travels avail you?"), to Grandma ("And I know of old ladies who waste their last years playing mahjong and living from one meal to the next, instead of reflecting on their sins and the life that is to come..."). With that last salvo, Grandma came awake with a look of murder on her face. It was all the Tan family could do to prevent her from marching up the aisle and clouting Father Hsien around the head with her handbag. Quivering with indignation, she refused to go for communion; she wanted nothing to do with "that man."

On the ride home, she fulminated against the Catholic Church, its bossy patriarchy and above all Father Hsien. "I should never have sent you to the convent," she told her daughter, Mrs Tan. "I should have known that colonial institution would have you rushing into the church. What does that man know about anything? He's still wet behind the ears. I've given birth to six children—"

"Mother," said Mrs Tan, patiently, "I don't think he was referring to you personally."

"He was looking," said Grandma, "right at me."

Her grandchildren, Peter and Jonathan (good Biblical names) groaned. Mr Tan drove on with a long-suffering look on his face. He was thinking that if Father Hsien managed to wean his mother-in-law off her marathon nocturnal mahjong sessions, he would, like a good disciple, drop all and follow him. Not exactly drop *all*, of course, but he would certainly be a lifelong devotee. Mr Tan was an engineering lecturer with a propensity towards migraines who craved above all peace, quiet and tranquillity. There was very little of any with his mother-in-law around.

The next Sunday Grandma announced that she was a fully paid up member of the Renewal Charismatic Free Church for All Brethren. She had washed her hands of the Catholic Church.

• • •

"She's joined *what?*" said Mr Tan.

Mrs Tan, close to hysterics and convinced her mother was doomed to hellfire, repeated the name of the church. Again, Mr Tan, good at engineering terms and bad at civilian discourse, missed it by a mile.

"Oh," he said.

"It's one of those fundamentalist Protestant groupings where they speak in tongues and insist that everyone pays ten per cent of their income."

"She hasn't got an income."

"That's not the point. The point is, she's been led astray."

"Oh, now really," said Mr Tan. "We all believe in the same things in the end."

"No, they don't. They don't believe in the Virgin Mary or acknowledge the Pope or—this is *horrible*."

As it turned out, Grandma had very little idea what her new brethren *did* believe in. She had joined the renegades because her friend Mrs Sinnathuray was a member and because the pastor, the Reverend Michaels from Peoria, Illinois, was so handsome and so kind. Not at all like the vituperative dwarf at St. Aloysius. And she liked the rousing services, where there was a good deal of arm-waving, breast-beating and being born again. ("Everything short of Mardi Gras," said a distraught Mrs Tan.) So very different from the Catholic Church, where people slumbered through Mass in an agreeable stupor and had only the foggiest notion of the Bible's contents. Grandma, in a most moving personal testimony to a packed assembly, laid the blame for her years of waste and error squarely at the door of the Pope.

But Grandma was nothing if not broadminded. She went right on reciting her rosaries and praying to the Virgin Mary. And her mahjong parties increased in bonhomie and amplitude, as her new church members took to her like ducks to water, in spite of her theological shakiness.

"*So* delightful!" they said to Mr Tan. "At her age, with her energy, her mind, remarkable!"

Mrs Tan resolutely stayed in her room during these proceedings. When she did appear, she drifted through, wraith-like, hollow-eyed. The Brethren left her alone, recognising that here was a woman who had closed her mind to the Message. Mr Tan's chief emotion at these times was a wishful desire that his wife would stand up to her mother, but that, he knew, was beyond her. It was beyond him, for that matter. Grandma was an Act of God.

However, no matter how much the Brethren smiled, chirped and wolfed down the food in the refrigerator, they never shook off the air they carried with them of venturing into the home of infidels and pagans. Mr Tan recognised the familiar battle-light gleaming in the eye of the keen proselytiser as, one by one, they bore down on him.

"Don't you want," they invariably began, "to join a church where you feel you belong, where you know you're at home?"

Mr Tan, a man of limited spiritual needs, felt his head beginning to throb. They wouldn't leave him alone in the office and now they were invading his home as well. "I do go to church," he pointed out.

They smiled disbelievingly. They never stopped smiling, but there was a range of meanings compressed into those smiles. This was the gently humouring smile. Did the secret of their success lie in those never ending, fixed smiles? Come to think of it, Catholics generally went around dour and indifferent, hardly beacons of light for their faith.

"We believe," they said, "in a participatory church. Where you take part in a service that glorifies God. We don't believe in passively following ritual."

Mr Tan waved a feeble hand at his sons, returning noisily after football practice. It was a signal for help but they ignored him. "Gosh, hi, Dad, bye, Dad," they said. "Got to rush, Dad." They bolted themselves in their room.

Mr Tan was not a particularly religious man. It had to do with the fact, he sometimes thought, that he was a man of little imagination; the thought of death, the afterlife, the sense of a higher, divine being, seldom disturbed him. He wasn't given to asking why. He was a Catholic by marriage and that, it seemed to him, was as good a reason as any. The histrionics, the sheer *energy* involved in becoming a born-again Christian, appalled him. And there were times when he told himself that if the Europeans hadn't flooded Asia with their missionaries and their schools, he would still be a Buddhist, comfortably subsisting in the darkness where there was supposed to be weeping and gnashing of teeth. What if the so-called act of faith was nothing but a historical accident?—He realised, with relief, that it was time to go to bed.

• • •

Grandma's rebirth was akin to lobbing a stone into a still pond: it created ever-widening ripples. One of its immediate effects was that Grandma became tremendously interested in the Apocalypse and the Antichrist.

"You will know the end of the world is nigh," she reported, "when there are earthquakes, famines and volcanic eruptions."

"They've always been around," Mr Tan said dampeningly.

Grandma gave him a shirty look. "The point is," she said, "that we always have to be ready, no matter where we are or what we're doing. Imagine! If the Lord came to earth while I was in the bathroom, what would I do?" (Nobody could find a ready answer to this either.)

Then she discovered that the Proctor & Gamble trademark was thought by some to be depicting the Antichrist. She hot-footed it home, determined to eradicate all use of their products, but *everything* in the nature of a cleansing agent was apparently manufactured by P & G or a subsidiary. This struck Grandma as even more sinister. How could a single multinational have a monopoly on all the soap circulating in the world?

"I guess it's a case of being clean or being pure,' Jonathan said. The whole family soaped away, P & G-style, doing its best to boost capitalist exploitation and ignoring Grandma's warnings.

Next, Grandma took it into her head that Ronald Reagan was the beast himself; 666 was the number of the beast, was it not, and there were six letters in each of his names. 'That only makes 66," Mr Tan pointed out; in spite of himself, he was becoming quite interested in all this.

'This is totally infantile," Mrs Tan declared. "Numerology under the guise of Christianity—honestly!"

There was nothing she could do, however, to stop Grandma from giving a delicious shudder every time the avuncular features of Mr Reagan appeared on the screen, or to prevent the boys from yapping and howling in dire imitation of a werewolf whenever his name was mentioned. Mrs Tan, who was supremely rational in every area outside Catholicism, told anyone who would listen that it was simply mind boggling that the man who had acted with Bonzo the Chimp could in any way be associated with the forces of evil. She was discovering the labyrinthine and peculiar byways of Christianity and they appalled her.

The next Sunday, Peter Tan, fifteen, electrified his family by announcing that he had became a Buddhist and wouldn't be attending Mass any longer. After a heated argument about transport convenience (the family usually went for lunch after Sunday Mass) he sulkily accompanied the rest to church.

Later, in his room, they discovered a book called *Zen and the Art of Motorcycle Maintenance*. "Have you been corrupted by this book?" Mrs Tan demanded.

Peter shrugged sleepily. He was tall for his age, slender, and surreptitiously growing his hair whenever his parents didn't notice. Dreamy and dissociated, his parents feared he might never become the lawyer/doctor/accountant/banker they wanted him to be. Jonathan, sixteen and aloof, said, distantly, "Don't ask *me*," when cornered. He was going through a family-phobic phase and his whole manner implied he was not his brother's keeper.

"*Why* are you doing this?" Mrs Tan asked her son, with a sort of petrified tranquillity.

"I just happen to find Buddhism a lot more compatible, Mum."

"Compatible!"

"Catholicism is a patriarchal and bureaucratic religion, Mum. It's drifted away from its roots. Sure, maybe it was a good idea in its time but Jesus would be horrified if he came down now and saw what his followers had done."

Mrs Tan made a gurgling, semi-strangled noise.

"Buddhism doesn't require any structures. That's the beauty of it. It's inner-directed. It's not egocentric. You can be a force for good wherever you are—"

"*Wah*, his language improve so very much, one, hor, when he become Buddhist, so funny, what, what," said Jonathan. His father told him not to be sarcastic. Ostentatiously, he joined the choir at St. Aloysius as head choirboy.

Meanwhile, Peter said that animals were as worthy, if not more worthy, of respect than old Homo sapiens and he was becoming a vegetarian. He prowled the neighbourhood collecting stray cats and dogs; he even launched a Stop Killing Flies campaign. At mealtimes, he lectured his family on the unsavoury practices of the meat industry, and one choice anecdote about veal in particular had Jonathan rushing to the bathroom. The odour of sanctity carried about him, the family felt, was positively sickening. "I hope you're reincarnated as a cockroach, so I can step on you," Jonathan told his brother; Peter flew across the room and landed on him—it took both their parents to tear them apart. The situation, it seemed, was rapidly approaching West Bank flashpoint level.

"This is all your fault," Mrs Tan said, between gritted teeth, to her mother. These days she went around in a frozen calm, a self-willed deep freeze which was rather alarming.

Grandma had the grace to look a trifle disconcerted. "I don't know what you mean."

"Yes, you do, Mother! You started a revolution! You're breaking up my home!"

"Such melodrama," said Grandma, briskly. She skipped out, nimbly, with a little stack of pamphlets titled, Get On The Nearest Hotline To God! (blue covers for non-Christians, red covers for Catholics). She was going to the City Hall MRT station to distribute them to the uninitiated.

"If she gets picked up by the police and spread all over the front pages, I'm renouncing her as my mother-in-law," Mr Tan said.

"This is *not* funny," said his wife.

Just then, the Reverend Michaels arrived.

• • •

It was with some difficulty that Mrs Tan could be dissuaded from slamming the door in his face. She considered him the author of, the perpetrator behind, her mother's behaviour. This large, corn-fed American with the very blue, porcelain eyes and the very white teeth, who did he think he was, leaving America to spread mayhem and dissension in once united families? She looked at him with the sort of defiance that the Catholic Mary Queen of Scots must have brought with her to the gallows, or was it the executioner's chopping block? She couldn't remember.

"Ah, Mrs Tan," said the Reverend Michaels. He took both her hands in his. It was the first time she had met him face to face since she had hitherto assiduously avoided him. He had a long, slow drawl, and a brilliant smile. He wore a short-sleeved, open-necked shirt, undone to the second button, above which tufts of luxuriant chest hair could be seen, and a pair of Levi's 501 chinos. He was very good-looking—this knowledge slowly filtered through the haze of indignation with which she regarded him. (Also the fact that his size twelve feet draped all over the front doorstep made it impossible to dislodge him.)

"It's so *varry, varry* nice to meet you, Mrs Tan," said the Reverend Michaels.

"Your mother has told me *so* much about what a wonderful daughter you are, Mrs Tan," the Reverend Michaels added.

By this time, he had somehow insinuated himself into the front hall and seated himself in an armchair in their living room, legs crossed, beaming in response to a somewhat dazed offer of a drink from Mrs Tan.

"Just water, if you please, ma'am. The religious life is such thirsty work."

Left alone, the Reverend Michaels and Mr Tan contemplated each other's knees. Mr Tan had met him before and had found the charisma somewhat overpowering, like musk. "Do you—er—often wear jeans?" he asked feebly.

The Reverend Michaels laughed genially. "They're my disguise," he confided, "for slipping in behind enemy lines, you know. Folks see a guy in jeans, they figure he can't be a minister and that lowers their guard. The only problem," he said thoughtfully, "are the girls. Young girls, especially."

"Have to beat them off with a stick, eh?"

The Reverend Michaels dug him in the ribs and grinned. "*Exactly.*"

Mrs Tan returned with a glass. "What can we do for you?" she asked, somewhat abruptly; in the kitchen she'd had time to recover from the impact of the gaze from those eyes. "I'm afraid my mother's not in."

"*Wa-al*, actually, I was rather hoping she wouldn't be. You see, it's like this." He leaned forward, clasping his hands earnestly. "Your mother wants to donate a large, antique lacquered table to our church, to function as an altar. Now, under normal circumstances, I'd be more than happy to accept it—more than happy. As you know, we're desperately in need of what businessmen call startup capital." Flash of teeth. "We're a fledgling church and we welcome all the donations we can get—"

"Wait a minute," said Mr Tan. He turned to his wife. "Isn't that the antique table she promised to leave us in her will?" (They'd had it valued some years ago: the expert had put it at a conservative estimate of $10,000.)

Mrs Tan nodded, distracted by the slender golden hairs, glistening in the sunlight from the window, on the Reverend Michaels' wrists.

"Are you aware," demanded the Reverend Michaels solemnly, "that it has an emblem of a Chinese dragon on the surface? In gold leaf?"

"Yes, of course. It's a very good example of the art flourishing in that period..." To think of the legacy, which they had always taken for granted, going to this man made Mr Tan feel faint. Not for the first time, he thought his mother-in-law ought to be certified.

"But we can't accept it," said the Reverend Michaels sorrowfully.

"Oh," said Mr Tan, taken aback.

From the depths of his armchair, the Reverend Michaels rose to a rhetorical splendour. "How can we start a church, sir, tainted with symbols of a pagan culture? Of a pagan civilisation? Our mission is to rid the world of superstition and fear and let the light flood in. To accept such an object would be the sheerest of bad luck." He realised what he had just said and laughed, uproariously. "Oh my, I've cooked my own goose, haven't I? *Wa-al*, you know what I mean."

"My mother will be disappointed," said Mrs Tan. Her husband looked at her, wondering; she was speaking in a peculiar, constricted tone of voice.

"We aim," said the Reverend Michaels, "not to please, but to do the right thing." He spread his hands, disarmingly. "We need an altar table, ma'am. Just not one with a dragon. You *will* let her know? Thank you.—And have you thought of joining your mother, and coming down to one of our gatherings?"

"Not exactly." Desperately, she focused her eyes on a point beyond him; she had the sensation of drowning.

"I understand you're a Catholic, but, please, don't be put off, we welcome everybody. As I said, we're a new church, but we're dedicated. Dedication is the word. We demand a huge commitment but we also give a lot back..."

When he was gone, an hour later, Mrs Tan rushed to her bedroom and sank to her knees. For once, praying had little effect, however; instead she splashed water on her temples and paced about angrily, telling herself to calm down and not to behave like an infatuated schoolgirl. For she had a weakness for terribly good-looking men in the old fashioned mould, which forty-odd years of living had failed to dampen. One would have thought that at her age, with two teenage sons, she would get over these attacks, which left her suffused with confusion and a burning sense of embarrassment, but no, here she was flushing again. She tried to invoke the image of her husband, placidly going through the Sunday papers in the next room, but she could only dredge up a blank. He was the ideal husband: he was safe, steady, constant and never caused her the slightest anguish. Truth to tell, he was rather dull. She smacked her forehead in despair. "Jesus, Mary, Joseph,' she said aloud.

"Where are you off to?" queried her husband, as she tore through the sitting room, jangling the car-keys.

"I'm going to Mass."

He grunted. He was used to his wife's piety. As far as he was concerned, all that mattered was that the legacy was safe.

• • •

Grandma returned with Mrs Sinnathuray at ten P.M., victorious. They had pinned various quivering youths to the wall of the station and had refused to let them go until they promised to attend the next service at the Free Church. "I tell you, I'm having more fun every day since my husband died," Mrs Sinnathuray declared.

"Oh, the Reverend Michaels was here today," said Mr Tan.

Grandma sat up straighter. "Really? What for?"

He told her.

Grandma's eyes snapped. "We'll see about that," she said. She strode to the telephone and called the church; it was true. Grimly, she replaced the receiver. "Oh, darling," said Mrs Sinnathuray despondently. She recognised all the familiar warrior symptoms in her old friend.

"Mother, you promised that table to us," Mrs Tan protested.

"Yes, I know, but it's a question of who has the greater need. You and the children are comfortably off. The church is just starting. I can't tell you how *exciting* it all is."

"Mother, the Reverend Michaels has said he doesn't want it."

"That's what he thinks."

"Mother, why are you *doing* this?"

"The Greeks called it hubris," Jonathan informed everyone. "We did it in literature."

Grandma launched herself into a flurry of activity. She decided that the thing to do was to get signatures for a petition urging the inclusion of the table, but she ran into some unexpected opposition. A few people—unbelievably—shared the Reverend Michaels' reactionary views on Chinese dragons. "Philistines," fumed Grandma. "What about St. George and the Dragon? I've never heard anyone objecting to that."

That, it transpired, was because St. George's Dragon was impeccably English, a well established part of myth and folklore and the traditions of the early church. But, in any case, the Free Church frowned upon St. George and his unfortunate Dragon, seeing that the pair of them were so bound up with the fossilised structures and rigidity of High Church Anglicanism, which, after Catholicism, was Public Enemy Number Two in the Free Church's impressive canon of objects of vilification.

"It's just a dragon," insisted Grandma. The table, after all, would be covered with a clean white cloth during the service and nobody would have to view the offending beast. In Grandma's opinion, this refusal to accept her table was nothing less than a personal insult. Her weekly mahjong parties for the faithful lost some of their sparkle, as members took sides for and against the issue; there was a positively un-Christian tinge of rancour in the atmosphere.

"Hell hath no fury like that of one Christian loathing another," Jonathan said sagely.

The Reverend Michaels tried to reason with Grandma. He sat her down in his office, fed her biscuits and turned on her the full blast of his charm. He showed her pictures of himself as an angelic little boy in Peoria, Illinois, and of his favourite spaniel, Pooch. He told her she was invaluable, *invaluable*, in the church.

"But do you remember, ma'am," he said, earnestly, "the day you testified that you had become a new person? When you promised to sublimate your will to that of the Holy Spirit?" He was walking back and forth across the carpet, fists clenched to emphasise his point. Grandma nodded, mesmerised.

"Far be it that I should try to tell you what to do. *I* can't do it; only *you* can decide for yourself what action to take. The Good Lord gave us free wills to distinguish us from the animals so that we might exercise them. But there are ways and there are ways of using our talents." He perched on the arm of her chair, smiling beatifically down at her.

At this point, Grandma's resolution wavered a little. But then she caught sight of the good-humoured look in those cornflower-blue eyes, the serene conviction that *he*, Edward Danforth Michaels (a man to whom no one, and certainly no woman, had ever said no), would prevail. And the contrariness that coursed through her veins as surely as blood ever did led her to whip out the petition once again, and draw his attention to the two hundred and fifty signatures. The Reverend Michaels, his smile fading, stood, and pressed the tips of his fingers together, unavailingly. He pursed his lips; he was vexed, most vexed, and he made the mistake of saying so. They parted burgeoning enemies.

Finally, Grandma hit on a brainwave. She would hire a furniture removal company to transport the table to the church and install it while the Reverend Michaels was out fulfilling his pastoral duties. Presented with a fait accompli, he could hardly object, could he? She confided her plan to her supporters, a militant group who wanted the Reverend to take a more aggressive approach towards proselytising, and were exasperated by his high-charm, low-ferocity tactics. They saw this as a good way of registering disapproval.

So it happened that on a cloudy Friday afternoon, while the Reverend Michaels was conducting an infants' class at the home of a member, a large furniture truck rolled up to the front entrance of the church, Grandma ensconced in the front seat beside the driver, to whom she recounted the whole affair in high-velocity Hokkien. She felt like a military leader commanding a convoy. A dozen or so of her supporters milled around, hindering rather than helping in the unloading of the table. Grandma's mood was triumphal, imperial—first the table, then ... the possibilities were endless.

"*What* is the meaning of this?"

The drawl, the lilting cadence, was the same, but the geniality was gone. The Reverend Michaels hove into view, blond, Nordic, towering. There was a stunned silence. A frisson ran through the assembled rebels; what was he doing here? (They discovered later that he had dismissed the infants' class early.) As he came towards them in a furious rush, the thought that was uppermost in their minds was that he looked as if he were the wrath of God personified. They fell back on either side to let him through—someone remarked later that it was eerily reminiscent of the parting of the Red Sea. He stood before the table, heaving; out of nowhere, it seemed, he produced a stick and—everyone gasped—thrashed the delicate curved legs of the table. With an almighty, ominous CRACK, it settled down with a thump, a good five inches shorter. Then the Reverend Michaels, without so much as a backward glance, vanished, leaving a distinctly post-apocalyptic flavour in the air.

• • •

Grandma took to her bed for a week. (The table, sent to the workshop, cost several thousand dollars to repair; the bill was duly despatched to the Renewal Charismatic Free Church for All Brethren.) The Tans, victorious but feeling it unseemly to crow, wore the mantle of quiet dignity as they tiptoed through the house. The mahjong parties ceased; the Brethren scattered their spiritual largesse elsewhere. Peter met a Catholic girl from the convent school down the road, and thought, perhaps, that Buddhism, well, wasn't exactly meant for him. The next Sunday, the whole family was back at St. Aloysius, Grandma barely blinking an eyelid while Father Hsien expatiated on the theme of spiritual pride. Her spirit was broken, her flesh subdued.

"I *told* you there was no need to panic," Mr Tan said to his wife.

That's what *you* think, she thought privately, though she did not answer. Absently, she fingered the crucifix around her neck. One needed a very strong faith to get through life.

THE GUNPOWDER TRAIL AND OTHER STORIES

The Gunpowder Trail

Lina

Lina sometimes thought she should have been a double agent, or an undercover detective. Her life often seemed to her not hers entirely, like a fictional construction foisted on her by an over-zealous intelligence case officer. With this imaginary person, she'd waged a battle for years over the ill-fitting roles that he'd required her to assume: compliant daughter, dutiful mother. In only one persona had she ever felt completely at home: her job as an investment banker. The other roles she made up as she went along, often stumbling, blundering and hurting the people she'd meant to protect. Not surprisingly, she lived life with one eye fixed, unwaveringly, on a quick, speedy exit. Only once before had she had to pull off a similar disappearance, and that had been easy, too easy. Steve, poor, besotted fool, had been no match for her. This time it was different. This time, the exit would have to be final. Any traces would have to be kicked over as cleanly as a beach scoured by the tide.

These thoughts ran, quickfire, through her brain as she lit a cigarette and checked her watch for the umpteenth time. Another cigarette lay, half-smoked, in the ashtray; she'd laid it down and forgotten about it in her nervousness. For she *was* nervous, and surprised to find herself so. She'd thought through her plan, and acted on it, with a clinical precision that hadn't allowed, so far, for doubts, compunction, second thoughts. She'd been determined to keep it so. She'd seen plans fail for all kinds of reasons, chief among them being a lack of momentum and a wishy-washy donnish even-handedness that wanted to "explore all sides of the question." God, how she hated those words. Peter had always quoted them at her. Peter, her former boss, who had once been a fellow at Oxford. She felt a brief, exhilarating spurt of dislike at the thought of him; it left as quickly as it'd come. Peter wasn't important this morning.

Six-thirty A.M. The dawn a greyish hue, burdened by an overcast sky. A wind stirred the curtains, bringing the smell of rain. It hadn't started to pour yet, but it would. It was the kind of morning she'd loved as a child, snuggling deeper down into the bedclothes, listening to the wind whip harder and harder, and finally the rain clattering down like gunfire on the metal awning outside her windows. She was supposed to send her daughter to school that morning—well, why not, it would be for the last time. Wen Shan had shrugged when Lina had made the offer the night before; if she was surprised at her mother's offer, she didn't show it. Her face wore the same wary look she always wore around her mother, impossible to read. She had been cute as a child, with that wild, brown, springy hair; now she looked merely unkempt, grungy.

Six-forty. She couldn't bear the waiting around any longer. In her nervousness, she'd got dressed far too early—black pencil skirt, white v-neck silk blouse, her usual functional work ensemble rescued from dowdiness by her lithe, athletic frame, a frame she'd managed to preserve at thirty-six, and a way of walking which someone had once described as slinking. (It hadn't been meant as a compliment and Lina hadn't taken it as such.) She'd had two cups of coffee already and the caffeine was already setting her head buzzing. She called up the stairs to her daughter: "*Wen Shan.*"

Get it on, get it on, get it on ... the words to a pop song the name of which she couldn't remember. She checked her watch again. Her flight was at nine. She'd made sure not to take a direct flight to her destination. There would be two connecting flights, a detour to a small, hick town she'd transited in years ago on a business trip and thought ideal for vanishing.

Her final destination did not have an extradition treaty with her country. She'd checked.

Wen Shan

Funny how you always know when your mother's gone. Even though she's never been remotely maternal and her life is as mysterious to you as calculus, or Sufism. Blood thicker than water and all that? I never believed that, but who knows. Anyway, when I got back from school that day, I just knew. Standing there in the hallway, I couldn't breathe. All my life, I'd been expecting my mother to run out on me, but all I could think then was, why now? Racing up the stairs to her bedroom, I kept hoping I was wrong. Her bedroom *looked* the same. Like the rest of the house, except for my room, it had the white, uncluttered severity of a modern art gallery: stark, cream walls broken by a black and white Robert Mapplethorpe print of a nude, black man, futon bed, recessed spotlights. My mother disliked *cosy* intensely. The only mess was the welter of perfume bottles on the table. My mother used little makeup, but she had a weakness for scent.

Her blue silk dressing-gown lay in a crumpled heap on the bed where she'd tossed it that morning. Her book of the moment, some trendy doomsday schlock like *Future Shock*, the only kind of book my mother ever read, lay face-down, spine cracked, on the side-table. I registered the details mechanically. I don't know why I had that weird certainty something was wrong. Maybe a concatenation of factors, too small in themselves to have merited attention.

Like the fact that she'd left the windows in her bedroom open, a thing she never did. My mother was fanatical about dust. Like the fact that she'd got up at the, for her, unearthly hour of six to send me to school that morning. When she'd made the offer the night before, I hadn't known how to refuse. In the car, she seemed preoccupied, eyes shielded behind sunglasses. The cascading jazz she always played when driving masked the silence between us. "How's school?" she said, making a visible effort. I wished she wouldn't. "All right," I said; I knew she didn't really want to hear about A-levels or my boring friends, such as they were. Thankfully, it started to pour, the world through the windscreen dissolving in a wash of rain, and she had to concentrate on the road. At the school entrance, she swung in too fast and braked, wheels squealing, a little too abruptly. I saw students casting speculative glances at my mother's black, miniscule sports car, its size inversely proportional to its cost. That was why I preferred to take the bus to school. "You need a haircut," my mother said. I jerked away, sharply, too sharply, from the hand on my head. Pure reflex, motivated by a sudden, prescient alarm. My mother hardly ever touched me. She let her hand fall. Like I said, I couldn't see her eyes. How was I to know that was the last time I'd see her?

Flinging open her wardrobe, I grabbed armfuls of her clothes and heaped them on the bed. I knew my mother's clothes the way an art connoisseur knows his paintings. (How I'd envied and resented her unerring dress sense. She had the sort of figure that would've looked good in anything, but she played it up devastatingly. Outside the house, she only ever wore varying shades of black, white and grey, offset by the barest of accessories. Her style was sleekly austere and made everyone else look overdressed or not dressed at all.) I saw immediately that her favourite items were gone: a sheer white organza blouse that I would've balked at wearing, her black blazer with the satin lapels, her black pencil skirt with the Balinese-style silver scrollwork belt. There would have been no reason for her to bring them to work.

Unless she was really gone.

The message light on the phone by her bed was on. I hit the button. There were six messages from her office, all increasingly urgent. Most of them from Peter Holbrooke, my mother's Australian boss at the American investment bank where she ran the private banking unit. uLina, are you there? What kind of hell game do you think you're playing? Where the *hell* are you?"

I sat on my mother's bed and put my head between my hands. My mother had sent me to school that morning, ostensibly on her way to work. But she had not reported for work. After dropping me off, she must have driven to the airport, her few, favourite items stashed in an overnight bag in the trunk of her car, and vanished.

I wondered why.

Lina

Lina liked the adrenalin of driving too fast, the cheap, childlike thrill of overtaking some lumbering four-door that had the temerity to wander into her lane. She liked the feel of hugging the road in her sports car, the illusion it gave that she herself had become, *was*, pure motion. She'd been called a rotten driver by all her boyfriends, given the tinker by more drivers than she could remember. "This is so adolescent," Peter had said, referring to her driving, the last time he'd sat in her car. That was the time he'd told her she was being retrenched. Their bank had just been the subject of a hostile takeover by a German commercial banking giant, and things were in flux. In turmoil. The old, entrepreneurial free-for-all culture, of which she was a part, had to go. What the Germans liked above all was order. Implying that she was too wild for the new scheme of things. She listened to him without comment. She'd always been a good listener; what she gleaned, from hearing people talk, were not so much the words themselves, but the motives that animated them. She was a wholly political animal, but it seemed she had lost this particular manoeuvre. Smiling, she hit a hundred-fifty on the speedometer, skimming a heavy-duty truck with seconds to spare. By the time they arrived at their destination, a meeting with a client, Peter was a whiter shade of pale. Teeth still clenched, he called her a bitch. She left him yelling in the carpark. She knew there was no point asking him whether he would have let her keep her job if she hadn't ended their affair. Lina never indulged in wins and what-ifs.

She was reckless, but lucky; she'd never been involved in an accident. Until that morning, the last morning of her old life. Driving to the airport, the road uncharacteristically empty, her attention wandered, and she failed to see a taxi shoot out of a side-lane into her path. Braking, her car skidded across two lanes to the left and beached up against the pavement.

She heard the sound of metal crunching, while her neck whipped back against the headrest.

She wasn't sure how long she sat there, gathering herself together, while cars tooted angrily from behind. Touching her neck, gingerly, she was relieved to find that, though sore, it could move. She got out of the car to inspect the damage. Left fender and headlight were crushed in; black car paint streaked the pavement. She felt a fleeting, regret; she liked her car, more than she liked most human beings. Including, she suspected, her own daughter. Who, incidentally, had been the cause of her first and only accident.

The final parting with her daughter had unsettled her more than she cared to admit. She saw the scene again, with a cold clarity: Wen Shan, in some trick of the rainy-light, looking more like Steve than ever, with that mass of brown hair, that high line of cheekbone. She could've looked stunning, if she'd only taken the trouble, but of course she wouldn't. (Lina knew very well, of course, that Wen Shan's sloppiness—the jeans cut-offs and frayed t-shirts—was a way of repudiating her mother's chic. Lina didn't mind, or rather, didn't care; motherhood in general bored her too much to get into generational disputes.) She scorned sentimentality in general, but that morning the weight of memory was having an unpredictable effect on her and she reached out to touch her daughter's hair. Mistake. She saw Wen Shan's recoil, and her confusion at the recoil.

Well, what had she expected? Her mothering style was best described as one of indifferent, benign neglect. The late, only child of middle-aged parents, she'd suffered through a childhood of unstinted parental adoration, and had been determined not to repeat that mistake with Wen Shan. It seemed she'd succeeded only too well. Regrets, at this stage, were merely self-indulgent.

In the car, she lit another cigarette and briefly closed her eyes. The past was all around her that morning. Strange, that Steve should be so much on her mind, when she hadn't thought of him in years, even though he was Wen Shan's father. Particularly because he was Wen Shan's father. She had not behaved well towards him, and Lina had the useful trick of neatly excising people from her mind to whom she had not been nice.

Steve was a fellow student at Berkeley, where she'd been sent on a government scholarship. Her major was economics, his musicology. The giddiness of being away from home for the first time had got to her; uncharacteristically, she'd let her guard down, invited Steve in. Steve, whom she would ordinarily never, in a million years, have bothered with. New Age-leaning, tofu-eating, acoustic guitar-strumming Steve, the embodiment of every West Coast cliché. Steve wanted to form his own rock band one day. Please. She'd fallen for the fluid arch of his cheekbones, the long-lipped, almost too pretty mouth, the square, ail-American jaw. In those days, she was still susceptible to such things.

In the first panic of discovering she was pregnant, she'd blurted out her secret to Steve. Bad move. She knew this immediately from the solicitude crinkling his face; she sensed him mentally squaring his shoulders. He was going to be—*responsible*, when the last thing she wanted was to be the grateful recipient of his beneficence. She left a note in his letterbox, informing him baldly about the abortion. She should have foreseen that he would come hurtling into her room, threatening to create a scene, set off the fire alarm, unless she talked, *talked*, to him. Lina hated talking, or at least what Steve meant by talking. Where she came from, people didn't discuss emotions; they discussed food, weather, stock markets, property prices. He refused to accept that she had broken up with him. He wanted to marry her. She laughed, incredulously. What were they going to live on, his royalties?

He nodded, very slowly, when she finished. "You know," he said, "it's kind of interesting, in a way, to see the care you take to destroy anybody and anything that wants to love you."

She hadn't liked that. But she'd already come to suspect that she was incapable of love, and the thought that Steve might catch her out in this scared her. He was like all the American men she knew, ridiculously idealistic. He thought that, beneath her flip, sardonic manner, was a warm, fuzzy person waiting to get out. Lina knew her own insides: they were spiky, studded, not a shred of fuzziness there. So she'd deployed all the venom of which she was capable to get rid of him; she'd believed she was being kind.

She was right about him, of course. He never became famous. Another wannabee in a country full of wannabees. She could imagine him now, at the age of almost forty, a session musician on the fringes of the music industry, scraping a living. He'd have an ex-wife, a daughter he seldom saw, and an amphetamine habit. Steve had his charms, but backbone was not one of them. Still, the episode with Steve had been useful; it had taught her the dangers of slackness, of letting a moment of vulnerability escalate into a full-fledged disaster. She'd told herself: *never again*.

Lina opened her eyes. Seven-forty-five. It would be ludicrous to miss her plane after all the elaborate planning. The hell with insidious, parasitic memory. She chucked her cigarette out the car window and started the engine. Mercifully, it cranked into life.

Wen Shan

"She was your mother."

That's what the police kept saying. Mow could I not know? How could I not suspect? What sort of mother takes off without a word?

The repetitive questioning was beginning to get on my nerves. Ten P.M. They'd invited me down to the police station tor a 'talk', put me in a freezing interrogation room, brilliantly lit with cheap fluorescent lighting that seemed to angle behind your eyelids even when they were closed. I was shivering; they'd given me a sweater. I was thirsty; they'd given me coffee. But there was no suggestion I could cave.

I said we weren't close. They seemed to find this unsatisfactory. *Why* weren't we close? Did she hit me? Was she abusive?

The police are so unimaginative.

I was indignant: "Of course not!"

Then what—?

Little things. So difficult to explain if she's not your mother. For instance. I was four before I even met my mother. My grandparents, my mother's parents, whom I lived with, had always glibly explained that she was "studying," a word that came to signify, for me, permanent absence. I knew what she looked like, though; my grandparents had created a veritable Lina shrine in their sitting room. Lina in a tutu, Lina at the piano, Lina grinning from the winner's stand at a swimming meet, Lina shining at a whole panoply of middle-class accomplishments. (Mv grandparents, needless to say, adored my mother, and adored me. Unlike my mother, who felt stifled by adoration, I lapped it up.) When I had nothing to do, I'd study the photographs, looking for clues, some genetic link.

I didn't see any—my mother's straight black hair was disturbingly different from mine, so brown and bedraggled. Yet I'd memorised her face so thoroughly that I recognised her at the airport before my grandparents did: a tall, lanky figure dressed in black, hair tied back in a ponytail. (My mother, having graduated summa cum laude (whatever that meant) from Michigan, was back for good. "For *good*," my grandparents had been repeating for the past few days, dutifully trying to be delighted, but clearly apprehensive.) I grew suddenly shy, and screamed when my mother tried to pick me up. My flailing hands scratched her cheek. My mother swore, and dropped me. "Stupid kid," she said. Her voice was very low, almost like a man's, unhurried. She sounded vaguely amused.

What else? For example. For the longest time, I thought Jim Morrison was my father. Of course I'd always known I didn't have a father, but it never bothered me until Primary One, when I got teased about my corkscrew brown hair, and the teacher-middle-aged, inquisitive—asked me why I had my mother's surname. I dutifully reported all this at home. "That bitch," my mother said. Then, with that adult detachment with which she'd always treated me, she said that she'd had a brief affair with my American father when she was nineteen. That they had not parted on good terms, and she didn't know where he was. Did I understand? I understood enough to know that she would never speak to me about him again. I said I wanted a picture of my father. To keep me quiet, she gave me a picture of Jim Morrison. It seemed plausible—I mean, he had my hair, after all. For years, I carried the picture in my school folder. When I was twelve, I discovered the truth. I was flipping through a music magazine at the newsstands and his picture stared up at me. all pouty-lipped ethereality. I confronted my mother. She admitted the deception freely, couldn't understand why I stood there with tears of rage running down my face. I shouted, "*I hate you!*" There, it was out, the dirty little secret between us. My mother stopped laughing. Her face snapped shut. She cut me dead for a week. By the end of that week, I was exhausted by the stand-off. I forgave my mother, because I had no choice. She was my mother, and I needed her more than she needed me.

The day my mother gave me the picture of Jim Morrison, she also asked me to call her Lina. She said it sounded nicer than Mum. What she meant was that she was only twenty-seven, and didn't want to be reminded that she was the mother of a seven year old. I nodded, dubiously; I was a horribly conventional child, and it seemed wrong to me. In the end, I avoided addressing her at all, though I secretly called her Lina in my head when I got mad at her or wanted to be impertinent.

It didn't sound much, I know. I wished I could come up with something more authentically lurid. I could see the police were still stuck in that whole mother-daughter paradigm. The one that says that, even if mother and daughter don't get along, the rocky relationship is itself a manifestation of the blood-tie. That is, you don't get under somebody's skin unless that person lets you. The fact was, my mother and I seldom talked, seldom fought. We orbited different planets in different solar systems. The disjunct in our lives was so great I had no idea what she liked to eat, or who her friends were, or what she did at work. Let alone imagine that she would run off with US$50 million that didn't belong to her.

Yes, why be coy about it? My mother was never coy. So, my mother stole US$50 million from the accounts of her private banking clients.

It was the police who told me what she'd done. I was ready for them when they arrived, the evening I discovered she was gone. They came in an unmarked police car that attracted no attention, both male, both plainclothes detectives, one Malay, one Chinese. It was the Malay officer who broke the news to me. He had the scrappy, wiry physique of a football player, and a thin pencil moustache.

"*Allegedly* stole," the Chinese officer corrected. He wore thick, black-rimmed glasses that gave him an owlish, academic look. Though younger, he seemed to be the Malay officer's superior. From his accent, and his mannerisms, I guessed he was a graduate, maybe even a scholar.

The Malay officer gave a wan smile that suggested an all-encompassing cynicism about mankind. He seemed a little disappointed that I wasn't more shocked, but I couldn't muster up the outrage. My mother had never cared a fig for convention, and the line between the permissible and the impermissible was hazy in her mind, though it was true she'd never committed a crime before. She must've had her reasons; my mother always had brilliant, warped rationalisations for whatever she did.

Yet I also had the instinctive feeling that, being older, having seen more, the Malay officer was, paradoxically, more likely to forgive. He asked, politely, if he might take a look around the house; it didn't occur to me to object. I was shivering, though the night was warm. My mother was gone. I don't know how long I'd sat on her bed among her clothes, that one thought running through my head.

I followed the police about the house while they went about their work. They took their time. Looked about the living room, Japanese in its spareness, intently, as though the walls themselves might yield some clues. Peered at the photographic prints on the walls: the Ansel Adamses, the Diane Arbuses, the Mapplethorpes. Walked round the gigantic rice-paper lamps suspended from the ceiling and grazing the floor that resembled nothing so much as giant cream pupae. Their expressions were quizzical. I knew what they were thinking: who would *want* to live in a house like this? And then, for the first time, it came to me. I wouldn't have to live with my mother's pretensions anymore. I could get rid of the pupae. Tuck away the Arbus freaks. I held my breath, blinded by a fleeting, treacherous feeling of liberty.

Lina

The check-in queue snaked past three booths. Lina, stuck three-quarters of the way through, wanted to put a bullet through the head of the man arguing for excess luggage capacity at the counter. She had a precise image of him slumping over the counter; a thin trickle of blood oozing slowly from the head wound. Lina was in the habit of concocting imaginary, usually execution-style murders for the people who annoyed her. She was not squeamish about death. As a child, she'd had to attend more funerals and wakes than she could count, the consequence of having elderly parents whose relatives and friends had taken to dying at an alarming rate. Dead people just looked so—*dead*. As an adult, she'd had to identify the mangled bodies of her own parents at the morgue, after their fatal car accident. Which she'd done without turning a hair, although the sight had not been pretty. Peter had said, more than once, that she would have made a great assassin. He had a vision of her in black leather, packing a gun; in some ways, he was very conventional. What he didn't know-was that the thought of causing someone's death, as opposed to merely imagining it, didn't appeal to her at all. Put it down to some atavistic scruple from her convent schooldays, which she professed to scorn and was often flippant about, but the teachings of the nuns had been more insidious than she realised. Sitting in the waiting room of the abortion clinic, face in her hands, she'd known she couldn't go through with it. (Coming out into the California sunshine, she'd had to fight her way through a pro-life group picketing the clinic. "You did the right thing," one of them, a thin, intense-looking man with a scraggly beard foghorned her. Why was it always the men who were so intent on preserving the unborn, when it was the women who bore the burden of bringing up the born? Lina shoved his placard in his face.)

Having made her decision, she moved swiftly. Spinning a fictitious and libellous story about how she needed to escape from an abusive relationship from Steve, she swore the sweet admissions officer to secrecy about where she was going. Then she decamped to Michigan, where she'd been promised student assistance. (Her pregnancy had cost her her scholarship—among other mediaeval conditions, it forbade her from getting married or pregnant.) Where it was cold and snowy and she could bundle up and look fat with impunity. And where Steve was unlikely to venture in any case. (Steve liked the sun. He was like a cat, in many ways.) Pregnancy didn't suit her. She chafed at its restrictions on coffee, alcohol and cigarettes, all the things that made life bearable. She resented the selfish, importunate demands the baby made on her body. (Childbirth, a month early, came almost as a relief, though it was hardly in the most ideal of conditions. She went into labour in the bar where she'd taken a part-time waitressing job to supplement her scholarship income. The bartender, a six foot film studies major with a grizzled beard, became hysterical, and she had to instruct him, slowly, from a booth, to dial for an ambulance. The baby, in a rush to enter the world, was out minutes after she was wheeled into the delivery room. Mewling, bloody, inhuman-looking, it was dumped on her with the uncut umbilical cord attached. She almost threw the thing away in horror.

Her feelings towards it didn't improve in the days to come. Post-natal depression, the doctor said, glibly, but she knew better. She wanted to give it up for adoption, but her parents, for once in their life, had put their foot down. If Lina didn't want the child, they did. Her parents were almost as staggered as Lina at their temerity in standing up to their daughter. Arriving in Michigan to collect the baby, they tried, unsuccessfully, to curb their delight in their granddaughter. Lina shrugged. The only condition she'd imposed was to call the child Wen Shan; she didn't want a phony Christian name or any other reminder of the father's heritage. A month after delivery, Lina saw parents and child off at the airport with indescribable relief.

Where was it written, that you had to love your child?

Wen Shan

My mother didn't return to Singapore because of me. She returned because America was in an economic downturn and Southeast Asia was booming. An American bank made my mother an offer to work back home she couldn't refuse. In her first year of work, she was earning more than my grandfather had in twenty years of teaching.

My mother moved back into her old home for a year. Her first day back, she walked through the house she'd grown up in, wearing a look of incredulity. My grandparents, a mild, gentle, old-fashioned couple, would never have dreamt of changing a stick of furniture in the house. They'd had the same uncomfortable rosewood for years, lovingly polished every day to a slippery sheen that left a dark patch on the seat of your pants. Doilies, which my grandmother knitted as a hobby, covered every available surface. I saw my mother wince at a particularly winsome picture of herself astride a pony in the Lina shrine, and tap out a cigarette from a case cached in the pocket of her black pants. I made a sound: my grandparents hated anyone smoking in their pristine sitting room. My mother caught me peeking at her from behind a chair. "What are you looking at?"" she said, not unkindly. I fled.

My mother was seldom in. She worked long hours, so long I was often unaware she'd come home and gone to work again. I saw her, briefly, on weekends. An hour each Saturday before she went out with her man of the moment, when she'd let me watch her dress and apply her makeup. At such times, her manner with me was indulgent, amused. She'd ask me desultory questions, though, even then, I noticed that she never really listened to the answers, because she often asked the same question again. Sundays she spent most of the day sleeping, or engaging in some sport like water-skiing or diving, all fortunately unsuitable for young children. Very rarely, she'd breeze into my room, very early in the morning on a weekday, and give me, still sleep-cloudy, extravagant hugs that left her expensive scent clinging to my clothes for hours. (Later, when I became more critical of her, and we navigated each other as warily as ships traversing a narrow strait, I'd wonder if I dreamt those hugs.)

Then my mother bought her own place, a studio apartment which I visited once with my grandparents. We registered the futon bed on the floor, the charcoal etchings of nudes on the walls, a huge, ugly pod thing which my mother said was a sarcophagus. An unnamed man's shirts and trousers hung alongside my mother's on the clothes stand. I opened the fridge; there was no food. "Very nice," my grandmother said, unhappily. They were silent on the way back in their car; bewilderment hung about them like a cape. I think it was the first time I thought to wonder how people like my grandparents had come to produce someone like my mother. Perhaps there was some truth after all in the stories about changelings, those human cuckoos who come to squat in your nest and turn your life upside down.

We never visited again.

I saw my mother even less after she bought her own apartment, sometimes not for weeks at a stretch. (There was no suggestion that I would live with her.) Then she'd descend out of the blue on a Saturday afternoon, screeching to a stop outside my grandparents' house in the secondhand red convertible she drove in those days with the top down. "Lina, *sunblock*," my grandmother would say, faintly, as she bounded in with an armful of presents for me, all of which I greedily unwrapped. "Yeah, yeah, yeah," my mother said. My mother was at her spirited best when she made her brief, whirlwind stops, and, frankly, I preferred her guilt-ridden irresponsibility to a grim dutifulness, since the former at least produced presents, while the latter, I knew, would produce nothing but resentment on her part.

Sometimes a man would accompany my mother on these lightning visits of hers. If they were child-phobic, which they often were, they stayed outside in her car, the engine and radio running. Sometimes they came in with her, tall men (they had to be tall, because my mother was five eight, a giantess as far as Asians were concerned) who draped themselves over the sofa and watched the mother-child reunion indulgently behind dark glasses which they kept on indoors. They asked me stupid questions (*How old are you? What toys do you like?*) and talked about me as though I wasn't there (*She doesn't look a thing like you, Lina!*).

My grandmother would purse her lips when they came in, and when they didn't. "Marriage settles a person," she'd say, hopelessly. My mother would roll her eyes, but she never took anything her parents said seriously. "Can you see me doing the little woman act?" she said to me. I didn't know what she meant. My grandparents had been happily married for more than forty years.

I didn't take much notice of the men. With my mother, there was always a man, and in those early years she went through them fast, with breezy contempt. I did remember one man, a black American who was co-owner of a jazz bar along Orchard Road. He didn't seem black to me at all; he was the most beautiful coffee colour, in fact, he was the most beautiful man my mother ever went out with. (Yes, my mother had her own weaknesses.) My grandparents disliked all my mother's boyfriends on principle, but they were virulently opposed to Lester. They had the prejudices of their generation, and black men were particularly taboo. They were barely civil to him; they offered him no drinks, and didn't ask if he'd eaten. Lester didn't notice the cultural slurs; he was completely at ease wherever he was, even in my grandparents' house with the rosewood and the doilies. Complete self-possession was something he shared with my mother.

I liked him, for a change. He talked to me like an adult, in a musical Southern accent, and he'd play what he called honky tonk on my mother's piano, infectiously twitchy music that shook the rafters and had the neighbours complaining to my grandparents. I stopped liking him, however, one Sunday when he was waiting for my mother to finish her business with my grandmother in the kitchen, and looking at the pictures of my mother scattered around the sitting room.

Lester started to laugh, softly. "Your mama," he said, "she's something." He looked at me and winked. "It's not everyday you meet someone who knows exactly what she wants. It's a rare thing, knowing your own mind. I wouldn't want to cross your mama."

I stared at him.

"I'm not saying she'd go so far as to kill to get what she wants. But there's a lot of stuff you can do before you get to that point, you know what I'm saying? No, I wouldn't want to cross your mama."

I froze; I was instinctively protective of my mother. "I don't know what you mean."

Lester's shoulders shook again. "You sound just like your mama when you said that. You know what I mean all right."

Lester didn't last long; he was replaced by a local guy who worked in my mother's bank. He was one of those who made the mistake of getting serious. One night, I picked up a call and he was on the phone, asking if I knew where my mother was. "My mother doesn't live here," I said. "She has her own place." I heard an odd noise over the line, which sounded like snorting, and which I realised, with some panic, was crying. I had never heard or seen an adult cry, and here was a stranger sobbing over the phone about my mother. I replaced the receiver and tiptoed back to bed.

Two days after I turned twelve, I was called to the principal's office. My mother was there, in her office clothes, looking a little pale. The principal told me, as gently as she could, that my grandparents had been killed in a car crash. Without thinking, I blurted out, "Oh ... good for them." This sounds callous, hut it was the best thing that could have happened to them: they were so devoted to each other that neither could have survived the other's death. The principal looked shocked, but my mother darted me a quick look of complicity. She knew what I meant. She did not hug me or touch me. Outside the principal's office, she lit up in relief. "Do you know she used to teach me?" *She* meaning the principal. (My mother had sent me to the same convent she'd so disliked as a girl, simply because she couldn't be bothered to look any further for schools for me.) I shook my head, dumbly. "She said I would go far, but that she wouldn't care to know how I got there." My mother's mouth twisted. She blew smoke rings, elegantly. (Only later did I discover that she'd already been to the morgue to identify my grandparents.) She looked clown at me, reflectively. "I suppose you'd better live with me from now on."

Her sense of duty was idiosyncratic, and spasmodic: you didn't question it when it was functioning.

That was how I came to live with my mother.

I cried at the funerals; my mother, eerily striking in her black mourning wear, did not. At the wake, I noticed the relatives gave her an extremely wide berth, as though she might be contagious, or bad luck.

Any gratitude I felt at my mother not abandoning me lasted as long as it took her to move in and throw out all the familiar, dowdy furniture I'd grown up with, and redecorate the house in her minimalist, ultra-modern style. The Lina shrine was ruthlessly dismantled. Where once the house had been dark and cluttered, it was now starkly white. It became my mother's house, and ceased to be mine. I was allowed to leave my room the way I wanted it—cluttered, messy—and it was to my room that I increasing retreated over the years as I got older.

Older, I became less enamoured of my mother. She no longer appeared to me the glamorous, quicksilver creature of my early childhood, trailing scent in her wake. At close quarters, she was impatient, wilful, drainingly energetic. A workaholic, my mother never seemed to sleep. Back from the office at ten or eleven, she'd work another hour or so, then stretch out on the sofa with a drink and a cigarette, listening to jazz until the early hours of the morning. The house was an extension of her office; faxes spewed through all hours of the day, and I wasn't allowed to use the phone much, because overseas calls were constantly shrilling in. "*Max* (or Felipe or Thansin or whoever), *hi*, got your fax, five basis points ... yeah, market's down, I understand ..." Meaningless, cryptic conversations, conducted in the staccato financial jargon that my mother spoke as a first language. Her mathematical brain chafed at my innumeracy: she'd leave me money to pay the newspaper or gas man, and I'd forget to ask for a receipt or else I'd wander down to the secondhand bookshop for some paperbacks. Either way, I couldn't account for where the money had gone. "*God*," my mother would say, drawing the word out; her intake of breath was sharp enough to snap a twig. My mother's adrenalin level sapped me; around her, I always felt fagged, as though I'd run a hundred miles.

Older, I became more critical of my mother. I saw she had no female friends, at least not what women consider friends. My mother was not interested in women, just as she was not interested in housework, cooking, children or anything remotely domestic. For their part, women instinctively disliked my mother. I saw them stiffen when she walked into a room; I saw the tight smiles they gave her. I think there might have been a time when my mother had made a token attempt to disarm the women. Be part of the camp. But, rebuffed once too often, she must have rapidly got bored and accepted her outsider status. It was different with men; it always had been.

My natural instinct was to side with the women. I felt comfortable, safe, with women; I felt wary around men. The ease with which men fell for my mother, betrayed the ties—wife, children—binding them, made me despise them. Men only ever looked at my mother in one of two ways, either with guarded fascination, as though they were prey waiting to be snared, or desperation. I'd seen my mother walk down the street, wearing nothing more provocative than a t-shirt and jeans, and have total strangers swivel their heads to stare at her. Desire, my mother taught me, is a weakness.

I didn't blame the men entirely. My mother was not a femme fatale, or a seductress, or any of the less complimentary terms I'd heard applied to her. She didn't set out, professionally, to entrap anyone. But she'd been born with something she couldn't fully control and didn't, I think, completely understand. And she wasn't, of course, above taking advantage of it. She was a hedonist and a sensualist, and if the man pursuing her seemed interesting enough, she didn't let principles stand in her way.

Younger, I thought *la ronde* a lark, the boyfriends a running joke. That was how my grandparents had tried to camouflage it to me, using the imagery of innocent courtship. Now, of course, I knew what my mother and her lovers got up to. I was from a convent; sex had its own taboo allure among teachers and pupils alike. What I couldn't imagine was the physical part of it, the shedding of clothes, the tumbling around in bed. The whole thing seemed ludicrous, in grossly bad taste. Thinking of it in connection with my mother gave me the tormented sensation of a flock of ants crawling over my skin.

With my mother, I was apt to become the parent, she the errant child. She usually rang to say if she would be late, which was almost every night. One night, she didn't ring. At four A.M., sick with worry, I was about to call the police when she stepped through the door. I knew she'd been on a tryst: her colour was high, her clothes very subtly dishevelled. Relief made me voluble. I shouted that I would not be hedonistic, manipulative or promiscuous. My mother stood in the hallway, tugging her blouse out of her skirt, unclasping her neckchain. She grimaced, comically: "So many *syllables*." She went up to bed. I was speechless.

For her part, I think my mother regarded me the same way her parents regarded her: with mystification. I was bookish, withdrawn, badly-dressed, uninterested in money, everything my mother was not. After we started living together, she made a few token attempts to dress me better. She had a good eye; I resisted her efforts, and after a while she gave up. Sometimes, on a Sunday morning, she'd call up to me, still sprawled in bed, to ask whether I wanted to follow her for coffee. We'd go to the local Coffee Bean; within five minutes, we'd both realise it was a terrible mistake. That we had nothing to say to each other. Gulping our coffee down, we'd exit in relief, my mother to disappear to the office, even on a Sunday, or to the gym or some other youthful urban professional activity, while I crawled back into bed.

I used to wonder if I were adopted, except that the idea of my mother adopting a child was so manifestly absurd that I knew she had to be my mother. In this world, you accept what proof you can.

Lina

There had been a time, long ago, when the condition of being wanted, desired, had troubled her. The nature of men's desire for her had nothing to do with popularity's mainstream appeal; she'd never been popular, with either sex. Men wanted her for other things, it seemed, usually to star in some dark, mordant, sometimes mordantly funny, fantasy of their own. They saw something in her—a kink, a twist, a controlled recklessness. Once sparked, their interest in her rapidly turned to obsession. It'd seemed to her almost a sickness; she'd never courted or sought it and she'd thought, for a time, that she only wanted to be left alone. Now she was simply matter of fact about it: the smallest nuances of desire were transparently, boringly obvious to her.

Sometimes, however, it still had the capacity to surprise her. As it did that day, more than a year ago, when she ran into Peter in the lift for the first time without knowing who he was. The attraction had been instant, mutual, a little bewildering; he'd looked at her with grave, puzzled eyes all the way up to their floor, where awkward introductions were exchanged.

She'd resented his entry, ascribing it, correctly, to the jobs-for-the-boys principle that still prevailed, ever so subtly, at the bank; she'd been prepared for a long, dirty bout of political infighting between the two of them. What she hadn't expected was the complication of a sexual undercurrent, so strong that it seemed to suck the air out of any room they were in.

What made Peter so dangerous, of course, was that he was essentially a male counterpart of herself. She wasn't stupid enough to discount the potency of narcississm. He could, as everyone liked to tell him, usually within five minutes of meeting him, have been a film star; he bore an uncanny resemblance to one of the best known American film actors of the day. Like her, he had the reflexive self-regard, the unconscious assumption of entitlement that good looks conferred, though, in his case, he'd become careless, perhaps even a little ashamed, of his appearance. To most people, he gave the impression of restrained control: he said little, as a rule, and he'd retained the don's habit, acquired through five years of teaching economics at Oxford, of crisp summary, of listening, patiently, to half-baked arguments before demolishing them summarily. To Lina, that control hinted at something else, something he wanted kept hidden: a capacity for sublimated, intense feeling, or a sexual fetish, or (perhaps mundanely) a bad temper. Whatever it was, she recognised in him someone similarly skilled in dissimulation, capable of leading various lives simultaneously.

They skirted each other, warily, in the beginning. *Common sense, rationality*: Lina repeated the words to herself like a mantra. It worked, up to a point. On their second business trip to Jakarta (one of Lina's favourite places before democracy ruined it) the plane hit an air pocket and plunged ten thousand feet. Seatbeltless, she flew, levitated, out of her seat and smacked her head on the overhead locker. Around her, babies wailed; passengers picked themselves off the aisle; coffee stains marked the cabin walls. Peter, belted (naturally) a row behind, leaned over the headrest. "Are you all right?" She nodded. He touched her eyebrow: "You're bleeding." The familiarity of the gesture startled them both. She went to the bathroom to clean up.

In Jakarta, they were plunged straight into client meetings. She was the one who usually did the talking, the buttering up; Peter, a product specialist, was not especially good with clients. He couldn't do the gladhanding, the social trod, except with a stiffness that quite took the fun out of it. The meetings failed to whiz along with Lina's customary energy; freefalling in a tin can had shaken her more than she cared to admit. It was with relief that she gravitated to the hotel bar in the evening.

Peter was there. It seemed rude to avoid him. He was more silent than usual, and she had plenty of opportunity to observe his profile in the mirror over the bar. She couldn't decide whether his silence was a way of trying to appear mysterious, or whether he was simply a gigantic bore who had nothing to say anyway. She was about to go up to bed when he turned to her and said, "You know, you're unnervingly beautiful."

She had to laugh; it was such a direct, untrue remark. Whatever it was that she had, she knew she was not conventionally beautiful. "You're unnerving me."

"I find it hard to believe anything could unnerve you." Eyes steady, unblinking, on her face; it was she who had to look away first.

"Look," she said, "this is a mistake." She did warn him, after all.

"Aren't you tired," he said, "of leading the invariably safe life?"

He was married, she remembered, even as he leaned forward to kiss her. (Like many good-looking men, he had a nondescript wife whose face Lina could never remember, who looked after the two children and did the expat wife circuit with a kind of exhausted diligence.) The tension between them was paradoxically having a narcotic effect on her; she felt drugged, unable to exercise her usual clear-headedness. They went up to her room.

Never get into anything you can't control. She'd ignored her own maxim in Peter's case. It was too sudden, too much. In public, they were punctilious to a degree with each other, but in every other way they were reckless—lunchtime trysts in obscure and not so obscure hotels, where they ran the risk of running into people that they knew; gropings in the lift; dirty phonecalls from Peter to her across the hallway that separated their offices. At meetings, she was conscious of his studiously averted gaze, the way he was ferociously willing himself *not* to look at, touch, her. As she'd guessed, beneath his formality was a voyeur, a fellow-experimenter willing to go to lengths that surprised even herself. A British politician died from auto-erotic self-inflicted asphyxiation and the newspapers had a field day; Peter said, suddenly confessional, that that could have been him. She didn't care to pursue the subject; she was not, in truth, into any kind of *ism*; it struck her as a kind of mental slavery.

Once they made love, late at night, on the floor of her office, the place empty except for a junior officer toiling down the corridor. She had to bury her face in Peter's shoulder to stop herself bursting out laughing at the tackiness of the whole enterprise. Peter, whose sense of humour was not especially active, watched her convulsions wonderingly.

The nondescript wife went back to Australia for a visit. Reluctantly, Lina agreed to accompany Peter back to his rented house in District 10; as a rule, she didn't frequent the homes of her married lovers. The nondescript wife's taste in interior decoration ran to English chintz, stuffed cushions and porcelain animals. Lina was apt to confuse taste with character; the awfulness of the furnishings relieved any incipient stirrings of conscience. In the dusk, they lit candles, Peter saying, with a small boy's glee, "I *always* wanted to do that." With mock ceremony, he brought out some vintage wine. "Tell me about yourself. You never talk about yourself." "I don't like talking about myself." "For someone as self-obsessed as you, I find that odd." He might be obsessed with her, but that didn't preclude a clinical dissection of her faults.

She said, dryly, "What do you want to know?"

"Your daughter, for instance. How did she come about?"

She began to laugh. "The usual way. A colossal mistake on my part." For some reason, she found herself telling him about Steve, the past suddenly taking on flesh again. In the flickering candlelight, his fingers traced the contours of her face. She was surprised to find her cheeks suddenly wet, herself in the grip of a maudlin, overwhelming sense of loss. *Bloody wine*, she thought. Peter, mistaking her mood, drew her in: "Oh, my dear." She caught the note of tenderness, stray, unexpected, in his voice; she allowed herself a moment of wild fantasy, herself married to Peter, living in the house with the English chintz. She was slipping.

Partly to make up for that moment of weakness, on the way to lunch the next day, she pulled the car into a shaded layby. Engine running, she began to undo her skirt. "Lina, for God's sake." His resistance was token, feeble. Cars whizzed past them at a hundred kilometres an hour. Nothing restored Lina's humour better than a judicious flexing of her power.

He'd had affairs before—he admitted this, matter of factly—but not like this, he said, never like this.

Lina never went into an affair without mentally sizing up the exits she could use if things turned sour, but she'd been shoddy in this case. An accumulation of incidents brought this home to her. An innocent lunch with a male ex-colleague became fraught when she ran into Peter at the entrance to the restaurant. He was icy, already convinced of her betrayal; the ex-colleague was flummoxed by Peter's rudeness. One Sunday night, Peter called her in a rage, demanding to know where she'd been all day. As she'd spent the day, as it happened, platonically, with an old boyfriend, she refused to tell him. His voice barrelled down the line, apoplectically loud. She hung up. He was becoming imprudent, walking past her office more often than was required, checking on her. He had always been something of a control freak, wanting to know where his staff were, where every file and memo was. Now he was applying these techniques to her. He wanted to know she was always available, where she was at all times. The clerks were beginning to gossip. Lina hated being the object of prurient speculation.

"You're getting careless," she told him, not without contempt.

"I think about you," he said, by way of apology, "all the time."

She sensed him hovering on the verge of a declaration; she didn't want to hear it.

The weeks passed; he continued to be wifeless. At least, he showed no inclination to return home at all, and his sporadic mentions of the nondescript wife ceased entirely. "We are not separated," he told Lina, coldly; she didn't investigate further, having got the assurance she wanted. Peter, married, was paradoxically safer than Peter untethered.

Returning home from the gym one night, she found Peter slumped in his car outside her house. She watched him for a few minutes in the rearview mirror; in the reflection from the streetlamps, his face, eyes closed, looked cratered. She got out of the car.

"I don't appreciate being followed."

He opened his eyes. "The safe life," he said, "is looking more and more attractive."

"Then go back to it."

He looked at her with something approaching hatred. "You know I can't."

Against her better judgment, she went back with him to the house with the chintz. It was a mess, overflowing ashtrays, empty pizza boxes stacked in a corner, newspapers and books strewn everywhere. It was a house, plainly, without a woman. He made a token attempt to clean up. He brought out the wine again, lit the candles, but it was not the same; his mood was brittle, his eyes, on her, mistrustful. *I should leave*, Lina thought, but she found herself hijacked by an unexpected sense of pity. For him, naturally.

Two A.M. She'd fallen asleep without realising it. The candles were gutted. Peter breathed, heavily, at her side, his arm slack across her waist. She disentangled him, gently, and began pulling on her clothes.

"Do you have to go?" His voice, looping out of the dark, startled her.

"Yes. Sorry."

"Your daughter's asleep. She won't know."

"Yes, she will." Lina had a rule, admittedly meaningless, that she would not stay overnight at a lover's. She could not imagine herself explaining to Wen Shan where she had been, and she couldn't lie.

"I don't understand," Peter said, reverting to the precise, academic tone that Lina particularly disliked, "why you feel you need to maintain this facade of moral rectitude in front of your daughter. She's not stupid."

Lina shook her hair out from the collar of her blouse. "It's none of your business, how I choose to conduct my relationship with my daughter."

"It's your specialty, isn't it," Peter said, "walking out on people."

"It's better if we don't continue this."

"This conversation, or this affair?"

She shrugged, and slung her bag on her shoulder.

"Time's running out for you, Lina. You don't think you can lead this sort of merry go round forever, do you? Age is catching up, even for you. What do you think you'll be like at fifty? A pathetic, raddled figure, propping up bars, scaring off all the men within a fifty yard radius." Sounding, momentarily, more Australian than ever, the vowels getting flatter and more elongated, the voice more nasal. Usually, he managed a sort of fluctuating estuary British/transatlantic accent. Lina had never particularly liked the Australian voice.

He'd come up to her and was kissing her again, even as he spoke.

Sugarcoated viciousness: that was *his* specialty. His mouth probing, insistent, at her mouth, the hollow at the base of her neck. Lina closed her eyes. Being with Peter was like being swept into an undertow; after a while, you wanted to stop battling the current. With an effort, she pulled away, and slapped him across the face. The ring on her finger, an intricate silverwork design, nicked him across the cheek. A thin line of blood foamed up across the skin. He stared at her. "I should hit you," he said, tonelessly.

The affair dragged on for another month, Peter alternating between bouts of abject grovelling and bouts of slashing viciousness. The thought occurred to her that Peter was, ironically, right; she was too *old* for this sort of thing. She was thirty-six. For the first time, she began to wonder about her future.

The merger with the Germans was announced at the annual Christmas party. Dead silence; everyone present was mentally calculating what this meant for himself. At the dessert buffet table, Lina ran into Peter, newly reunited with the nondescript wife. "Shannon, I believe you've met Lina." The wife inclined her head, without enthusiasm. Lina said, "Peter, a word."

"I want to know whether I have a future in the new regime."

He said, with stultifying formality, "I can give you no such assurances."

She began to walk away.

"Lina," he said, in a quite different tone of voice.

"Don't," she said. There were some things she was not prepared to do to salvage her career.

The next day, mulling over some discrepancies in client accounts at her desk, the thought came to her that it would be easy, too easy, to rifle through these accounts. The controls at the bank were notoriously lax, and there had already been one or two minor scandals, which had affected the price the Germans were willing to pay for the acquisition. Her mind, which liked puzzles, deconstructing problems and financial wizardry, worked rapidly: she saw how it could be done, the labyrinth of offshore accounts through which money could flow, smooth as butter.

She'd once worked on an anti-moneylaundering project for the bank, and the ingenious techniques had remained lodged in her memory. That was how it'd started, almost as a lark. An intellectual game. As a girl, she'd played chess, one of the few girls to do so, and it'd trained her to think several moves ahead.

A month later, she was retrenched. "I'm very sorry," the managing director told her. He wore an air of puzzlement; he'd been her champion from her very first day; he knew her worth. He would have fought to keep her, except that his own job was on the line. Furthermore, though he didn't say so, but which Lina heard anyway, Peter was the one who'd recommended her retrenchment.

He'd made a few trenchant remarks about deteriorating performance, more in sorrow than in anger, it seemed. He was gambling that she wouldn't reveal their affair. He was right: Lina would rather die than have her private life made public.

She had three weeks left in the bank. She went to work.

Wen Shan

"You have to know *something*."

The police were insistent on this point. In their experience, people didn't vanish without leaving a residue, a gunpowder trail that could be analysed and made to yield results. They urged me to *think*. Travel brochures lying around the house? Unaccounted movements in bank accounts? Changes in my mother's demeanour?

I thought of my mother's hand on my head that morning, when she dropped me off at school.

I thought of the day, a week ago, when my mother said, casually, "Oh, by the way, I've transferred the house into your name." The house, once my grandparents', then my mother's, now mine. I couldn't think of anything to say, except, "Oh." My mother sighed; she'd always considered me an idiot about money. She seemed on the verge of saying something, then changed her mind. Instead, she'd given me an envelope containing the papers for the transfer. Naturally, I hadn't looked inside.

I thought of the night, some months ago, when I'd got up to get a drink and met Peter Holbrooke in the kitchen. I knew who he was; he had been to the house once to pick my mother up. He was by the sink, rinsing a glass. He wore nothing except a towel round his waist. He stopped in mid-rinse. "So you're the daughter," he said, more curious than anything else. He seemed in no hurry to leave, drinking me in. His manner was, if anything, proprietary; I was the intruder. He had the sort of careless, windswept good looks that attracted my mother; I noted that, mechanically. I also sensed a sort of heaviness about him, a capacity for melancholy, an unarticulated yearning. He seemed to me vaguely dangerous. Malevolent. Capable of going off the rails. Which, no doubt, was also what attracted my mother. Lina, I thought, you're getting sloppy. She was normally discreet about bringing her boyfriends back to the house. I backed out of the kitchen, and fled to my room. In the morning, I wondered if I'd dreamt the incident.

I didn't tell the police any of this.

There was a commotion outside. I heard an Australian voice, precise, controlled, but tight with rage. "You can*not* do this to me, I have my rights, I *demand* to see my lawyer. I will not be put through the kangaroo justice of your tinpot republic—"

Peter Holbrooke. I said I needed to go to the bathroom; in truth, I wanted to catch a glimpse of him. Our paths crossed in the waiting area. Each of his arms was held, firmly, by a police officer half a head shorter than he; together, they made a lumbering, six-legged shuffle across the floor. Peter was in office attire: rumpled suit, loosened tie crazily askew. He looked unshaven, bone-tired. He saw me, and I saw him trying to register where he'd seen me before. Recognition flashed. "Christ almighty," he said. His voice turned silky.

"Your mother's a clever little bitch, isn't she? Too clever by half. Are you half as clever as Mum, darling? Why don't you tell the policemen here where the money is and save us this bother? You know where it is, don't you? Of course you do. You're your mother's daughter. I can see it in you. Of course you'll never be the looker that Mum is, but looks aren't everything, are they? You've got brains, obviously. Why don't you use them, darling, *and tell us where the money is!*"

His voice rising to a sudden screech on the last words. He seemed a little drunk; no doubt it'd been a long, frantic day at the office. Sorting out the havoc my mother had wrought. He lurched; the police, thinking he was about to make a bolt, gripped his arms harder. "I'm all—right," he managed to choke out, before they hustled him off to an unseen interrogation room.

At the entrance to the police station stood the nondescript wife. I got an impression of badly-frizzed hair, a floral dress that looked like a housecoat. She held her handbag tightly across her chest. We stared at each other. I wondered what she thought of my mother. Hated her, probably. I don't know why, I raised my hand and gave her a tentative wave. She didn't wave back.

It transpired that my mother, in taking the money, had somehow implicated Peter. Her co-signatory on the discretionary client accounts, he'd signed one too many cheques blindly, not realising that the transferee was a certain dummy company in an offshore tax haven. A dummy company set up, incidentally, by my mother. When the news came out, the office wags began to talk. It seemed that people had not been as oblivious to their affair as Peter and my mother had thought. The Germans, not about to let the scandal derail their takeover, personally called the police to take Peter into custody.

I learnt this later. My immediate problem was fending off my two interrogators, who'd been given a new lease of life by Peter's little declamation. The money. *Did* I know where it was?

I remembered that, in the police car, on the way to the station, the Malay officer had turned round in the front passenger seat to ask me how I was going to live. Was anybody going to take me in? It was typical of me that I hadn't considered this question. My mother was not close to her relatives, and I didn't relish living with any of them. I said I was going to live alone. Gently, for I must have seemed more naive for a sixteen year old than he was used to, the Malay officer asked what I was going to live on. *Money*, he added for emphasis, in case I didn't understand. I tried to think. I had the house, but I couldn't sell it if I was going to live there. My grandparents had left me a small legacy, about a hundred thousand dollars held in fixed deposit. "Legacy," the officers had repeated, as though it wasn't a word they were used to hearing every day. I don't know, was it an odd word for a teenager to use? Something in their tone made me say, defensively, "I'm not rich." This time they laughed.

"I've told you," I said.

"You're not close," the Chinese officer finished for me. He saw me looking at the wallclock over the door. Eleven P.M.

"Why would that man think you know where the money is?"

"He had an affair with my mother. She left him."

"You knew that? Although you and your mother were not close?"

I shrugged. "You know these things."

"Your mother was good with money?"

"Yes."

It was my mother's other preoccupation, besides men. My mother liked money. She liked making it, talking it, spending it. She earned a tidy sum at work, where her rise had been meteoric and where the compensation was largely bonus-based. Her investments were shrewd, her instincts unfailing. She could talk shop for hours with the money men; it was one of the reasons women disliked her. Deals fuelled her life; taking her numerous calls at home, hearing the roar of dealing rooms in the background, the electronic urgency of billions of dollars being traded communicating itself down the line even to me, standing in the sitting room in my oversized night t-shirt, I thought of her as being at the centre of some vast, spider's financial web, a queen arachnid to which all the subject arachnids brought their daily offerings.

"And you?"

I didn't know if they were trying to have fun at my expense. "Not very," I said.

"Because it's always been there," the Chinese officer suggested. I was beginning to dislike him. "You've always had an easy life."

"You can think what you like."

"You're not protecting your mother, are you?"

If I said no, they would think I was lying. If I said yes, they would think I was being flippant. I couldn't win. "I didn't approve. Of her lifestyle." Which was not an answer, but I hoped it would pass muster.

"Still," the Chinese officer said. "She was your mother."

Yes, there it was. The nub. The non-sequitur. Funny, all my life I had been conditioned to think of myself as my mother's ball and chain. Now our roles were reversed. She would dog my life. There would be the brief burst of notoriety, the reporters circling like hounds, the whispers behind my back.

"If I knew anything," I said, trying to look honest and not too bright, "I would tell you."

"That's all we want," the Chinese officer said. "The truth.

The truth, in my opinion, was overrated. I could have done without the truth about my father, the truth about my mother. I could easily have lived in a parallel universe, one where my two-parent family lived out its safe, suburban existence without any hankering for the occult. A week ago, my mother had asked me, out of the blue, what I wanted to do with my life. (Another sign, which I'd ignored?) I'd said, unthinkingly, that I wanted to be a writer. It was the first time the thought had occurred to me. As soon as I said it, though, I knew it was what I wanted to do. What I could do. My mother had said, wryly, "Then you'll really need to have money." Like many people from her world, she thought the arts an indulgent pastime, suitable only for the independently wealthy.

"So do I," I said.

Lina

The long nightmare of check-in was over. Finally. She'd breezed through, her only luggage being a hold-all compact enough to fit into the overhead locker. It was surprising how little she'd found compelled to bring: a few favourite clothes, some items of jewellery, a photograph of her parents with Wen Shan at the age of seven, the last a reluctant concession to memory, sentiment. Her passport, some personal papers, and a key to a safe deposit box in a Swiss bank in Lucerne. A box that, incidentally, held the paper trail of how she'd managed to siphon off US$50 million from her clients' accounts.

A new life, a new identity. An exhilarating thought.

Lina's greatest dread was boredom, the rut. Even before Peter's little bombshell, she'd been mulling over her future. She'd been coming to the conclusion there was no future, not with an almost adult daughter who wouldn't need her in a few years, not in a country where she'd always felt out-of-kilter: too driven, too unsentimental, too sexual, too much of everything. She didn't dislike her country; she simply had no feelings for it. Someone had once told her, thinking Lina would share his sentiments, that the departure lounge at Changi airport was the most beautiful sight in the world. Lina had given him a cold smile. She didn't care to be lumped with the fashionably disaffected. What she felt was that her birth had been a secret wheeze of the gods. For some reason, they had seen fit to give her the parents they did, the country they had. Left her with a sense of dislocation so powerful she had serious difficulty comprehending other people's use of the word *home*. She'd wondered whether they were subscribing to an emotion that they thought they ought to feel or, worse, whether they actually felt it. Hundreds of times, returning from overseas business trips, she'd been tempted to peel off and vanish; the thought would bubble, irresistible, iridescent, to the surface as she made her way to the airport at Bangkok, Jakarta, Guangdong or wherever it was, to go *home*. She never had, because of a tiresome, intermittent sense of responsibility—to her parents, to her daughter—that came and went like the flu and never allowed her to recover sufficiently to take flight. Well, she'd discharged those responsibilities, God only knew, and she'd always made sure to provide for Wen Shan. She was free to go. She *wanted* to go.

(Oddly enough, her sense of responsibility did not embrace the clients whose money she'd pilfered. They were not, on the whole, attractive human beings; rich people, as she'd had ample opportunity to observe in her line of work, seldom were. As a rule, she withheld moral judgment, because it was unprofessional to allow morals to intrude at work, and because her own life did not, admittedly, bear much scrutiny either. But she had little compunction for them.)

She needed a drink. She found a serviceable bar, where she could keep an eye on the clock over the counter, as well as the span of the departure lounge. She had an hour before the plane took off; a lot could happen in an hour, including being frogmarched across the departure lounge by the police. It was a bit early for alcohol, but she didn't care.

A man at the end of the bar was looking at her. She went still. A day ago, she would have guessed that he was trying to hit on her; now, she couldn't be sure. She had no real apprehension of being caught at this stage; she'd calculated that it would take at least a day for the bank to discover what she'd done. Officially, she was on holiday in the Seychelles. All the same. The man, olive-skinned in a European-cut sports jacket, caught her eye and smiled, a bit too engagingly. He got no response from her. Giving a Gallic shrug, his gaze shifted down to the newspaper next to his drink. She relaxed.

For the first time, it occurred to her that this was going to be the tenor of her existence from now on. A life on the run, a life spent sitting with one's back to the wall, scanning everyone who walked through the door. Not sure whether the prickly sensation at the back of your neck was simply due to the heat or the certainty that someone connected with law enforcement was trailing you. She knew the risks; she was not a panicky person. Which was another way of saying she had few, if any, nerves. Lina had always had a conveniently fluid sense of right and wrong, the legal and illegal, and if a line was a fine one, she seldom hesitated to walk it. However, this was the first time she'd unequivocally crossed the line. She had a dim inkling that the crossing was irrevocable. That, having entered a netherworld, you didn't come out of it easily. She might thrive; she might just as easily end up in a back alley with her throat slit. Her hand, as she held her glass, was steady.

Wen Shan

I thought how easy it would be if I could only light a bonfire in the back garden. Heap all my mother's papers into it, watch the flames leap towards the sky. But it was not the seventh month, and any fires would be regarded with suspicion. I had to make do with putting a match, sheet by sheet, to my mother's paraphernalia, and flushing the charred pieces down the toilet.

I was certain the police would be back the next day with a court order to search the house. I wasn't sure if there was anything incriminatory in the dozens of files in my mother's study—the papers were filled with meaningless financial jargon to me—but I was determined they wouldn't find anything.

They, the police, had to let me go in the end, past midnight. I'd told them a little of my life and my mother's life, what I knew of it. Told them with that sense of betraying a trust which I couldn't shake, even though I knew I owed nothing to my mother in this respect. She was pragmatic; she would've said I had no choice. The sense of betrayal lingered, even though the police clearly found what I told them unsatisfactory. They didn't want family history, they wanted the gunpowder trail. Where was my mother? Where was the money?

Towards midnight, worn out from the questioning, I'd simply tucked my head into the crook of my arms, folded on the table. I wanted to block out the white brilliance of the fluorescent light overhead; I wanted to sleep. I'd lain my head down for only a second; when I lifted it again, I caught a fleeting look of commiseration on the officers' faces. I felt a momentary surge of chagrin; I didn't want anyone feeling sorry for me. I knew they were thinking, *Poor kid*. They probably had kids of their own. Anyhow, it worked. Fifteen minutes later, I was released. The Malay officer dropped me off at the house. "You may be required," he said, formally, "to come down to the station again for further questioning."

He was telling me they didn't trust my denials. Perhaps I should have cried? But, except for the time my grandparents had been killed, I did not cry easily. I was like my mother in this. Or perhaps it was something in my demeanour, that unyielding, unhumorous look I tended to wear when my back was against the wall, what my mother used to call, with irritation, my opaque look. It made people think I was deliberately not telling them the whole truth.

Well, what is truth?

I did not know where my mother had gone. That much was *true*. All I knew for certain was that she was in some large, cosmopolitan city, where she could disappear into its anonymity and reinvent herself. My mother, quintessentially urban, would have died of boredom anywhere else.

Or perhaps truth is not the right word here. What the police wanted to hear was *relevant* evidence. What I had told them was filler, irrelevant to the larger scheme of their investigation. And it was *true* I had withheld certain *relevant* pieces of evidence.

I did not, for instance, tell them that, a week ago, my mother had called to say that she would be home early. She suggested I order in something. I was a little staggered, that my mother wanted to eat dinner at home, that she wanted to do it with me. I couldn't remember the last time I'd had dinner with my mother. I called one of the upmarket takeaway places I thought she'd like. In spite of her call, she was still late; the food was cold when we sat down to it. She drank more than she ate. She'd clearly rehearsed the conversation. She told me she had been making financial arrangements for me. A bank account had been opened for me in the Cayman Islands. She would give me the details; I was to memorise them or store them where third parties wouldn't be able to have access to them, and then destroy the papers. She seemed serious. The account was a temporary measure. She would give me further instructions. She gave me a short, precise lecture about being almost an adult and fiscal responsibility. Coming from my mother, the lecture was almost funny, but I didn't laugh. "Is something wrong?" I said. She considered this. "Nothing more scandalous than a little tax avoidance." Her flippant answer stupidly reassured me; my mother disliked paying taxes as much as she liked making money.

Nor did I tell the police that, when I'd burst into my mother's bedroom that afternoon after school, I'd found an envelope on her dressing-table addressed to me. There was a short note explaining that US$10 million had been banked into my Cayman Islands account, and would be transferred out shortly thereafter to another account in another tax haven. The note asked me to store the details of the accounts somewhere safe, and ended, "You'll know soon enough what this is about. Don't turn all moralistic and judgmental on me. I know you better than you know yourself."

The note made no sense. US$10 million? It might have been Monopoly money for all the reality it conveyed to me. All the same, I was in the habit of following my mother's instructions, at least on financial matters. I dutifully transcribed the details of the accounts into my notebook and destroyed the note. Long ago, when I was into detective stories, I'd devised a childish code. A letter for each number, a word for each letter. I chose the names of cities, exotic, flowery names of places I'd never been to. Tierra del Fuego. Bukara. Lhasa.

Then I'd settled down to wait for the police.

Now it all made sense.

Relevant evidence. I felt it sticking in my throat, about to burst, during the interrogation. I was not, technically, lying, but I was withholding, and both were the same to the police. During the interrogation, a silent duel waged in me: should I tell, should I not? If I did, my mother would inevitably discover that I'd talked, and I'd be as good as dead to her. I knew her—she was testing me. I couldn't lose the hope, however faint, however desperate, that I might see her again. I kept searching the officers' faces, wondering if they really expected me to turn my mother in. Which is what telling the *truth* would have amounted to. Didn't they know that if I'd learnt one thing from my mother, it was loyalty to those who'd given you life, to those whom you'd given life? Even if it was a loyalty that was grudging and often resentful?

And the money. Ah, the money. My mother had been clever, too clever. A lesser amount, and I would have felt no sense of loss in giving it up. But it was a dazzling sum, dizzying: I could feel myself already beginning to make a helpless, parasitic accommodation with it. My school had drummed into me that money was a curse. My mother, the serpent in the garden, had always taught me otherwise. Money was freedom. The truth, as always, was probably somewhere in between.

Tierra del Fuego. Bukara. Lhasa. The words danced through my head like an incantation. I had a little of my mother's need for escape in me. I had always wanted to see those places; now, I realised I could. I could do a lot of things. If I didn't tell. I felt the touch of my mother's hand on my head again that morning. A blessing, or a curse? Letting my head fall onto my arms on the table in the interrogation room, the decision was made for me. Swift, irrevocable, painless.

Driving Sideways

At last he could bear it no longer. "Look," he said, "can we turn this thing off?"

This being the hotel inhouse pornographic movie which had been playing for the past half hour. Made in Taiwan, it had a kind of jolly slapstick crudity which he'd found mildly amusing in the beginning, but it was starting to get on his nerves. He didn't understand how Jek and the girl could sit and conduct a conversation with various sexual acts being performed on TV, but apparently they could; Asian sexual prudery was a myth he'd discarded a long time ago. It was just another in a long series of cultural dislocations which he should have got used to by now after a year in Southeast Asia, but he hadn't. Which was odd, because as a Chinese-American, switching between English in school and the Hong Kong Cantonese of his parents at home, he was used to feeling out-of-kilter, schizophrenic, an inhabitant of dual worlds that met only in his head. He'd thought that, by taking a year out from college to wander around Asia, he might resolve some of this irresolution, but he'd found only that he felt more American the further he strayed from upstate New York (and conscious, all the time, of a heretical, shame-faced, relieved thought: *thank god my parents had the sense to leave their hometown/ province/ continent*). And never had he felt more irredeemably foreign than here, in a sleazy hotel room in southern Thailand, in the company of Jek and the girl, both overseas Chinese like him, but, unlike him, born and bred in Southeast Asia and at home in the accommodations and compromises which the culture of the region demanded and which he, with his straight-arrow American rectitude, found at best incomprehensible and at worst offensive. Or perhaps he was just using cultural differences as an excuse, and refusing to admit that the real cause of his irritability was the fact that he was certain—no, he *knew*—that Jek and the girl had once been lovers.

Jek and the girl looked at him. Jek reached out from the bed and turned off the TV, plunging the room—coffin-sized, claustrophobic with its drawn blinds—into a sudden silence in which the only sound was the asthmatic wheezing of the airconditioning. "Thank you," he said, sounding, and intending to be, sarcastic.

There was a pause.

"So, Russell," Jek said, "what's your excuse?"

"My excuse?"

Jek leaned forward, giving Russell a good glimpse of how his Hakka genes had coalesced into a hateful, fortuitous combination of broad cheekbones and a wide, surprisingly delicate mouth. "Why are you here? Why aren't you on Wall Street like the rest of your overachieving second generation Asian American peers?"

Jek had studied law for two years in London University before calling it quits. The Singapore government, which had awarded him a scholarship, had not been pleased. He was vague about what he'd done in the seven years since.

Russell said, lamely, "They're all in Silicon Valley actually," and heard the girl give a short laugh.

She said to Jek, "Isn't it obvious?"

"What's obvious?" said Jek, lighting up, though a sign on the wall said in English and Thai, *No smoking in the rooms.* There was a hint of boredom in his tone; he was, as Russell had already gathered, easily bored. There was a lounge lizard quality in Jek, though at other times he gave the impression of being a hyperactive kid. Russell had not taken to him from the moment that Jek had opened the door of his hotel room. One look at Jek's long-limbed athleticism made Russell feel even more of the over-intellectualiscd, life-starved Asian studies postgraduate that he in fact was. *I have to meet a friend*, the girl had said. *He's supposed to pass me something*. He'd been tired from tramping around the dusty, unlovely city, all cracked cement and trailing overhead telephone wires, with not a stick of greenery in sight. Without thinking, he'd agreed, *ok*. It hadn't occurred to him to ask the usual questions; he was used by now to the imperatives which governed life with the girl, her Delphic silences, her unfathomable decisions. He knew only that he was in thrall to her, in a way he didn't fully understand himself.

"He's finding himself."

Russell said, grimly, "Always glad to be a source of entertainment," as they both grinned. Twin Cheshire cats.

He said, "Care to tell me what's *your* excuse?"

He was surprised when the girl answered first. "I used to work in a bank. I used to drive to work, listening to Aimee Mann sing *Driving Sideways* on the radio." She brushed an imaginary hair out of her eyes. "After that it was just downhill the rest of the day. So I began to think, what's the point?" It was the longest speech he had ever heard her make. He looked at her in some surprise, trying to imagine her in a bank. Imagination failed.

"Life's too short," Jek agreed. They had a habit, Russell had already noticed, of finishing each other's sentences. The knot of irritation in his neck began to pulse again.

"I don't have an excuse," Jek said. "Unless it's die young, stay pretty."

"Oh please," Russell said. He felt depressed. He hadn't travelled halfway round the world to find the same cheap pat alienation.

"What were you hoping for? Something more profound?" Jek seemed, if anything, genuinely curious. "People are the same everywhere. They're shallow everywhere." He said this, if anything, gently, as though he knew and understood Russell's frustrated idealism.

"I need air," Russell announced abruptly. He said to the girl, "Are you coming?" He half-expected her to say no, but to his surprise she nodded. She motioned, *one minute*. While she was in the bathroom, the two men soaked in a heavy silence. Russell was wondering whether it was politic to ask Jek about the girl, in particular his carnal knowledge of her, but was afraid it might sound too adolescent. As though sensing his thoughts, Jek said, politely, "You like her, don't you?"

"Any problem?"

Jek waved the aggression away. "All that's over." Glumly, Russell noted the *over* and what it implied. Jek looked round for an ashtray, found none and stubbed his cigarette out on the dresser.

The girl emerged from the bathroom; Russell stood in relief. "See you around," he said to Jek with patent insincerity. Jek raised a hand in farewell; the girl exited without a word.

It was only when they'd hit the traffic-snarled street that Russell thought to ask, "So what did he pass you?"

She glanced at him sideways, a stray, ghostly smile flitting across her face. He felt the familiar, helpless twist in the pit of his stomach. "Wild mushrooms," she said.

He first saw her in Koh Phangan, walking across the hot shimmering sand to the sea. She wore a white bikini and black sunglasses, her black hair coiled in a careless, unravelling knot on top of her head. She walked a little unsteadily, arms held slightly away from the body, as though she were, ever so gently, biplaning. An adolescent's body, all slender bones and not a superfluous ounce of flesh anywhere. A memory of desire stirred in him; he put down his book and watched as she waded into the water and struck out for the open sea, swimming with precise, powerful strokes. She swam a good way out; at one point he lost sight of her, in the haze of heat over the horizon, and he sat up worriedly. Then he saw the flash of her bare arms and relaxed. She was, he estimated, about half a kilometre from the shore. It was high noon. Time for lunch, but he had no appetite. Watching the girl swim, thinking of the energy she'd expended, left him exhausted.

When she drifted back to shore, floating on her back in the shallows with her dark glasses still on and her hair spread about her like a rock-chick Ophelia, he turned back to his book, not wanting to be seen to be staring. He continued to pretend to read even when she stood over him, her small shadow darkening the pages. He had no choice but to look up.

"You've been watching me." She said it as a statement of fact, recorded for posterity. She spoke in English, in an accent he had come to recognise as Malaysian or Singaporean.

He said, mock-boisterously, "Hey, it's not a crime looking at a pretty woman."

She ignored this. Nodding at his book: "Is that interesting?"

He had to admit, "Not particularly." His intention of combining some worthy reading on the polluting effects of globalisation with bumming around Thailand had been scuppered by beach torpor; he felt a twinge of embarrassment at the graduate-school earnestness of his reading matter.

She'd been ringed by sun, casting her in shadow. As she moved out of the shadow, he saw that she was older than he'd imagined, older than he was, her skin lacking the fresh suppleness of youth. Saw, too, that the trunk of her body was stippled by a faint constellation of coffee-coloured spots, just discernible under her tan. Again, he tried not to stare.

"Café au lait," he thought he heard her say.

"What?"

"They're called café au lait spots. I have mild neurofibromatosis."

He had no idea what she was talking about. She stood bundling up her hair, one foot drawing circles in the sand just inches from his face. A particularly dark spot ringed her ankle like a tattoo. Without thinking, he began to trace its outline; she looked down at him, consideringly. He felt sun-drunk, his mouth dry. He got, slowly, to his feet. She came up only to his chin, but her smallness had the density of rock.

She was alone, as he'd guessed; she radiated the self-sufficiency of a cat. In her rented hut down the beach, she tossed her keys on the camp bed and shod her bikini nonchalantly and turned to face him. He could smell the sea on her still. Her directness disconcerted him; desire for him, was at its keenest when the object of desire was just out of reach. Anticipation, he'd discovered, was always preferable to fulfilment. Sensing this, she said, with infinite contempt, "It's all right, we don't have to do anything," and instead of feeling his manhood impugned, he felt only a surge of relief.

"It's not that I'm not attracted to you," he began, in his circumlocutions American way. She rolled her eyes.

It was odd, how he felt he'd known her forever, even though they'd just met. He lay propped on one elbow, wedged against her on the tiny campbed. The ceiling fan whirred creakily, barely stirring the warm afternoon air. He bent to kiss a spot on her shoulder. "Don't," she said. They went to sleep.

He woke to find the light fading fast, night drawing in rapidly. The fan continued its lopsided whirr; he felt a chill across his bare skin. The girl was propped up in bed, watching him. While he was sleeping, she'd got dressed: tie-dyed boxer shorts and a white t-shirt. Her hair was plaited and she wore a pair of black-rimmed, rather severe-looking spectacles; he remembered her unsteady, shortsighted walk down the beach. She looked like a bookish schoolgirl. Her backpack stood, squat as a troll, on the floor.

"Let's go," she said.

In the next town, he developed a raging fever. He woke one morning, his throat dry and raspy, and fell back on the bed with a groan. Shivering, he allowed himself to be piloted by the girl to the nearest doctor, a man who spoke no English and prescribed him an array of primary-coloured pills that caused his eyes to puff out like ganglions an hour later.

"You must be allergic to something."

"Penicillin."

"You should have said so."

"I have *no* idea what the hell you and the quack were talking about." He'd sat in the clinic, tame as a lapdog, while the girl conversed in fluent Thai with the doctor; they could have been conspiring to poison him for all he knew. He was aware of a querulous note in his tone; illness had been rare in his healthy American life and it was not his best state. The girl sat with her chin uplifted in thought, training on him the cool, detached stare which he imagined assassins wore. He guessed she would have no compunction about shooting him like a dog and leaving him by the side of the road.

She said, as though she hadn't heard, "You'd better rest. I'll get lunch."

It began to rain soon after she left. It rained as though the heavens meant to deluge the earth. He had to close the casement windows; the stuffy room immediately became stuffier. With exquisite timing, the air-conditioning also failed. He cursed and thought with longing of the beach at Koh Phangan, its bone-white brilliance. Their itinerary since then—was it really only a week?—had been dictated by her: waking up each morning in yet another fleabag backpacker's hotel, she would announce that they were heading for such and such a place, and he would just nod, a willing captive. Time with the girl had a fluid, amnesiac quality: minutes turned into days and the days swallowed up memory, leaving him born anew each morning. Home seemed increasingly unreal, like the fakely upbeat American sitcoms that populated cable television wherever he went; the only reality was the girl. He wondered if this was what Stockholm's syndrome was like. Their mad perambulation interrupted momentarily by his fever, he thought to wonder for the first time what he was doing here. What he was doing with *her*.

Back at Columbia, there'd been a girl, quicksilver-bright, raven-haired. They'd met at a sit-in to protest World Bank policies. Besides global economics, they'd shared a mutual interest in Miles Davis and Chinese history. His parents were not thrilled: Ellen, they told him, was the wrong colour, while he tried to persuade them of the absurdity of their bigotry in the land of the free. His parents needn't have feared. He and Ellen eventually drifted apart; she complained that he seemed to be experiencing life through a pane of glass. He worried that she was right. He hadn't thought himself capable of a *coup de foudre*; he hadn't thought himself capable of a lot of things.

He woke in the late afternoon. He was puzzled; he didn't remember falling asleep. Experimentally, he sat up; the fever had broken and the swelling around his eyes had subsided, but he was aware of a gnawing hunger. He had not eaten all day. The girl, he remembered, was supposed to have bought lunch. She had left in the morning and had not returned. Her knapsack was gone.

He rushed down to the reception; no, they hadn't seen anybody leave. He bought a sandwich from the cafe and went back to the room, which looked more desolate than ever. Down the corridor, he heard squeals of laughter, the sound of clinking glass. He waited an hour. Two. At some point, he slept again. When he next woke, it was dark.

Travelling alone had a different dynamic from travelling with someone. Travelling alone, you answered to no-one but yourself. Travelling with someone else, you developed a viscous, vicious dependence on the other person. At least, *he* had; he didn't deceive himself that she was with him on anything other than a whim. He began a feverish crawl through the town, ducking into stalls, shops, bars. The town had seemed drab by day, but at night it took on a mysterious life. Winking coloured lights decorated the meanest stall and scooters carrying crazily heaped human cargo zipped along the pavements. He heard a great deal of laughter, which he couldn't account for, unless it was just one of the phantasmogoric effects of travelling alone, to imagine that everyone else was having a never-ending party from which he was excluded. The laughter, the coloured lights, all seemed vaguely sinister; he grew clumsy in his movements, began bumping into people and backing off with exaggerated apologies. Someone shoved him from behind, shouted, "Farang!" *Foreigner*. He whirled round; shadows flitted past him in the dark. He'd been mad ever to think he could blend in. He started to run.

She was waiting for him in the hotel room. Propped up in bed against the pillows like a doll, reading a Thai newspaper.

"Where have you been?"

"I got detained."

"What detained you?"

"Business."

"Yes, tell me, what *do* you do?" This wasn't her first disappearance *on business* by any means, but it was the longest.

"I'm a middleman," she said. "I make deals. I get commissions." She paid for everything, he'd noticed, in cash. She had wads of it, fished airily out of the pouch she wore around her waist like rabbits pulled out of a hat: the supply seemed inexhaustible, inexplicable. Whereas he lived from one American Express traveller's cheque, cashed carefully every week, to another and drawn from a dwindling scholarship fund.

"Wild mushrooms," he suggested, bitingly.

A smile lurked in the corners of her determinedly straight mouth: "Yes."

"*Bullshit.*"

She said, coldly, "What do you want me to say?"

He tore the paper away, raged at her. The violence he felt in himself surprised, then frightened him: he was enjoying his rage, enjoying the thought of what he could do to that small, stippled body of hers. She watched him with narrowed, interested eyes. Then he was suddenly exhausted, anger spent.

He said, curious now, "Why did you come back?" and worked it out, slowly: "I'm useful to you in some way."

In answer, she pulled him down. In her hair, her clothes, he could smell the freeze-dried, smoky air of some bar; he tried not to think where she could have gone. Her lips tasted of rain. He closed his eyes. With an effort, he held her off: "Did you really work in a bank?" An absurd non-sequitur, given what she was doing with her tongue in his mouth. But he felt, rightly or wrongly, that it held the clue to who she was.

(She spun lies, figments, as easily as a pious child recites his prayers. At times, he found himself almost enjoying trying to detect when she was lying, and when she was inadvertently telling the truth. His questions were asked mainly for the pleasure of seeing her concoct.)

She stopped long enough to say *yes*. But he had already lost interest in the answer.

Where are we going?"

She named a town on the Thai-Malaysian border. "Right. Where are we *really* going?"

"Where I was born," she said.

He did not like the country—prosperous, humourless, a toenail on the slender foot of Malaysia—where she was born. When he was there, the papers had been filled with a fretful anxiety about being left behind in the race towards globalisation. Which was ironic because he had never seen a people that embraced economic colonisation by Western multinationals with such fervour.

"Why don't we just take the train?"

She looked at him, as though to say, *don't be so anal*. He didn't ask again.

It was a hot day, the sun slung high in the sky, the light spearing down pitilessly. There was no escape. At the border, a long queue shuffled towards Malaysia. Backpackers, mostly Westerners, pickled red by the sun; lorry drivers ferrying goods; an army of motorcycles spewing choking black smoke. Thai immigration officials waved them on, looking smart and sinister and vaguely Latin American in gold-rimmed sunshades and military-style uniforms. The delay was on the Malaysian side. Craning his neck, Russell could see Malaysian customs turning luggage inside out with a zeal that seemed positively criminal in this heat. Popping gum, Russell tried to stifle the instinctive unease that border crossings roused in him. He couldn't account for it, this irrational fear that he or his papers would somehow be found wanting and he'd be held back, left in limbo, stateless. Put it down to a family history of ancestors being smuggled across borders too numerous to mention, always fearful of being caught and repatriated. Or perhaps he'd watched one political thriller too many (the righteous man fleeing injustice in his own country—fake passport—his face on a wanted poster at the border crossing post, the close-up of the immigration official looking from passport to fugitive—the slow, reluctant descent of the official stamp onto the forged papers...).

He hadn't given a thought to the girl, shuffling alongside him, until she had her fit. He heard the man behind him exclaim *look out* just as they stepped up to Malaysian customs. Her eyes rolled back into her head; she turned blue and keeled sideways, with the straightness of line of a felled tree; it might almost have been comical if he hadn't been so scared. He caught her just before she hit the ground. A thin line of froth trickled from the side of her mouth. He was trying to remember his first aid— something about a bit between the teeth and the victim biting off his own tongue—when he found himself being shoved aside by two customs officials, who lifted the girl without ceremony and carried her round the main building to a side door. "Hey," he said, "*hey*—"

He found himself in a small, air-conditioned office reeking of cigarette smoke. They'd laid the girl down on a sagging sofa, and a woman official was undoing the top button of her t-shirt. "Hey," he said, "she needs help, she's sick—"

The woman official, an Indian Tamil, stood, blocked his way. "She's all right, understand? The fit has passed. She's sleeping now. She'll probably sleep for an hour. I've seen this before." She spoke clearly, slowly in English, as if he were an imbecile or a foreigner who didn't understand English. He felt a bubble of hysterical laughter rising in his throat. *I'm American, don't you understand?*

One of the men said, "Sit down."

The interrogation began. Was she his wife? No. Girlfriend? He started to say no, because his relationship with the girl was nothing like any of his previous relationships, then checked himself in time. This was not the place for hairsplitting. Yes. Was this the first time she'd had a fit? Did she have a history of fits? What did he mean, he didn't know whether she was prone to fits? Wasn't she his girlfriend? Had she been tested? Tested? His mind slow, fumbling, unable to grasp immediately what they wanted to know. One of them pointed to a sign on the wall. It was in a foreign language, but he saw the letters HIV. Understanding dawned; he was used, by now, to the reflexive hostility he'd encountered in the region about the disease. No, the girl did not have Aids. She was not HIV positive. She had (the word came back to him in a rush) neurofibromatosis. A neural disorder. Fits were one of the symptoms. It was not contagious. (He hoped to God this was true.) He'd recovered himself. Remembered the role he was supposed to play. Ugly American, ever ready to assert his rights. Making sure he wasn't getting railroaded in some developing country where (he saw another poster on the wall) they hanged drug traffickers. Forgetting, momentarily, that his own country still had the death penalty (yes, but only for murder, murmured his pedagogic, inner voice). He was sweating, despite the blast of cold air from the air-conditioner.

Where was he from? America. Chinese-American? What was he doing here? (The same old dreary question. It was because of his skin colour, he knew. Asians found it hard to believe that fellow Asians would take time out to bum around. If you were white, they couldn't care less.) Yes. Is she American? No, Singaporean. He saw their interest drop. She was almost one of them, and therefore uninteresting. They stared at him, fixedly, for a minute that seemed like an eternity, then turned away; they seemed almost disappointed. Relief flooded him. He asked whether the girl could rest in the office until she woke. Grudgingly, the men nodded and clumped out. The woman official settled herself behind the desk. There were no spare chairs. Russell leaned against the wall.

The woman official was speaking to him. He leant forward. She wanted to know which university he was from.

"Columbia."

"It's a good school, right?"

"The best," he said, immodestly.

"Do you know how my nephew can get in?"

He was furious, but not surprised, to find Jek waiting for them outside Malaysian customs. In a battered blue Toyota, a car you wouldn't have given a second glance and in fact he hadn't, until the girl said, "That's Jek." Said it so that Russell knew she'd been expecting him, that they'd planned this all along and that he was the biggest stooge they'd ever encountered bar none. The sensation that he was being taken for a ride had been growing ever since the girl had walked calmly out of the immigration shed after waking from her Sleeping Beauty stupor, shouldering her heavy backpack with the expert, military heave of a little sabra. (What *was* in that rucksack? Why was it so damn heavy and why wouldn't she let him help her carry it?). No explanation from her, no questions as to how she'd ended up in that office. She seemed as devoid of curiosity as an android.

"You took your time," Jek said. "I need a drink, man." He cut the engine. "Hello, Russell."

They were in an emporium near the border. *Emporium*, Russell had learnt, carried a different meaning in Southeast Asia. It meant a Chinese-style, bargain price department store, stocking specialist Chinese food items and vaguely kitschy examples of chinoiserie. Jek and the girl were leaning over a glass, metal-rimmed case of a type Russell hadn't seen at home since the early '70s. Looking at rows of sweets. "Wow, haven't seen these for a long, *long* time." "Hacks!" (A type of sweet, apparently.) "Coconut flavour!" "I used to love them in school."

Russell said, "Anybody care to tell me what the hell is going on?"

His voice was louder than he'd intended. The security guard standing by the cashier looked their way. Jek and the girl stopped flirting with nostalgia long enough to give Russell wordless, reproving looks. They moved towards the entrance, Jek swigging the mineral water he'd come in to buy. They moved like two people who'd walked side by side countless times and knew the body rhythms and pace of the other by heart. He was surprised by the rush of heat, or anger, or jealousy (he wasn't sure which) spreading across his chest. This wasn't love, not even desire, more a paralysing compulsion than anything else.

So following her outside into the afternoon heat was not an act of will but of predestination, though he much preferred to stay in the air-conditioned, muzak-filled air of the emporium. (He was tired of the relentless heat, the humidity that soaked his t-shirt through in an hour, the sun. The *sun*. He found himself at times dreaming about winter, snowfalls that muffled sound and cold that stung.)

Outside, Jek and the girl were regarding him as if he were a persistent, rather amusing stray that refused to go away. And he realised that was his trump card with them: he refused to go away. He stood planted on the pavement before them, blocking the sun, blocking their path.

Jek said, "Shall we tell him?"

The girl had her arms crossed over her chest, each hand gripping the opposite shoulder, as though she were cold, or shivering, or hugging herself, or all three. "Why not?" He couldn't understand what he was looking at at first. Six square plastic packets of a white powder. Like flour. No, not flour.

He said, "You gotta be kidding."

He had smoked the odd joint back home of course. It had always been a post-supper kind of thing (like mints, he thought inconsequentially), the pasta dishes cleared, the scented candles flickering, the wine making everyone sleepy and mellow anyway. He never knew who brought the stuff, and he'd smoked it mostly to be polite. He had never seen hard drugs. Until now.

"Why?" the girl said.

She sat cross-legged on the bed watching him, the plastic packets spread before her like wares. Wearing her unflattering glasses, which somehow made her look younger than ever. The bed yet another hotel bed, the hotel another featureless backpacker's lodging which Jek had led them to in this featureless border town. The same dusty blinds drawn against the sun, the same harsh fluorescent lighting, the same air-conditioner wheezing and leaking tiny plops of water onto the concrete floor. *Déjà vu*. A simulacrum of hell.

"Don't they hang people for this in this part of the world?"

"Only if you get caught," Jek said. He was sprawled on his front on the bed, looking up at Russell like a big, lovable puppy. Oh, how they wanted him to love them, to understand what they were doing! He could feel the emanations from them, powerful as magnetic rays.

"And you don't plan to. Get caught."

"No," Jek said. "We've always been lucky. We plan to continue lucky."

We. "You picked me up in Koh Phangan," Russell said to the girl.

She smiled. "You had the look."

"You think I'm a fool," he said, bitterly.

"No, no," Jek reassured him. "You look trustworthy. You look *exactly* what you are. A hardworking postgraduate student taking a summer break. You know how rare that is or not?"

"And that's why you needed me? For my *face*?"

"You lent—what's the word?"

"Verisimilitude," the girl said.

"The customs people like that," Jek said.

"Was that real?" Russell wanted to know. "That fit?" He couldn't absorb it: the fact of the girl lying on the sofa in that immigration shed, the contraband just a few feet away in her backpack. (And he couldn't help but think perhaps *this* was punishment for what he'd been thinking back in that shed: what it would be like to make love to a comatose woman. He'd seen himself maneouvring until he was propped on his elbows just above her, but without touching her. Kissing her on those lips that only minutes ago had been tinged with blue, and finding it almost creepily enjoyable until the woman official had started scratching in a file with a pen and he'd snapped out of his necrophiliac fantasy with a pounding heart.)

"Of course." She said it without heat.

"Why don't I believe you?"

She shrugged.

"Why," Russell wanted to know. It wasn't even a question.

Jek said, "It beats nine-to-five."

Russell was outraged. "Hell. What do *you* know about nine to five? When was the last time you did an honest day's work?"

Jek stared at him; burst out laughing. "You're serious. You're *shocked*. Russell, you're so sweet."

The girl laughed too. She reached out to touch Russell's hand but he recoiled, instinctively. Even then, he had time to think: *not in front of Jek*.

"Don't fucking patronise me. If you want to be some lousy drug dealer, for God's sake just be a lousy drug dealer. Don't wrap it up in some pathetic existentialist crap that would disgrace a sixteen-year-old."

"Actually," Jek said, "when I was sixteen all I wanted was to be a lawyer. I was going to get a Mercedes. Live in a bungalow. Buy some koi fish."

In Jek's drawling voice, Russell could hear the various telltale inflections: the broad a that was a relic of the British colonial legacy in Southeast Asia, the slurring gonna that spoke of the pervasiveness of American popular culture, all darting through the flat intonation of Jek's own local accent. Russell thought: I'm looking at the *ur*-product of globalisation. It didn't look pretty.

"OK. I'm sorry. You're a case of arrested development. You're having your adolescent crisis now."

"I don't think you're in a position to judge, Russell. What are you, twenty-four?"

"Twenty-five."

"Right. And you've never worked a day in your life. You're the eternal graduate student. In ten years time you'll still be writing that thesis that seemed such a great idea when you were twenty but now you're not so sure. Personally, I agree with Pink Floyd. We don't need no education. But, hey, who am I to judge?"

"Fuck you. I'm not the one breaking the law here." Aware, even as he spoke, that he was losing it—the argument, the upper hand. He fell into vulgarities only when he felt vulnerable. They were older then he was, Russell had to remind himself, he was the kid brother here. Reproving, censorious beyond his years. He felt—was meant to feel—ridiculous. Which itself was ridiculous.

"Admit it," Jek said. "It's a rush. Knowing you didn't get caught."

"And that's why you do it. For the rush."

"And the money of course." Jek swung off the bed, began punching numbers on his mobile phone. He sounded bored.

As though the girl had sensed Russell's thoughts, she said, "Several hundred thousand U.S. dollars. That's the street value. If we get it back home."

He said, humouring her, "And I get a cut."

She looked at him, narrowly. "If you're in."

If you're in. He was, perversely, flattered: he'd always suffered the shy person's need for any kind of social inclusion.

"And if I'm not?"

"We kill you now and stuff your body in the *longkang* outside," Jek said. He snapped shut his mobile phone and sprang on the bed, making it bounce. "You're not going to the police, are you, Russell? You wouldn't betray us, would you?"

"Think of the service I'd be doing to society. One drug dealer less on the face of the earth. There's got to be something to be said for it."

"But, Russell, you don't give a shit about the wasted youth, do you? Russell? The victims of the unwinnable war on drugs? You're not that much of a hypocrite. Are you?"

"You like to talk, don't you, Jek? Why didn't you ever graduate? Find your true calling as a morally bankrupt lawyer?"

"The law bored me. *Life* bored me. I never thought I'd live to be thirty years old, but I have and it's killing me. Every day I hope to God I manage to do something self-destructive enough to finish me off but somehow self-preservation always kicks in at the last moment, so here I am. Yes, I despise myself and I'm filled with self-loathing, so now you know. Why," Jek demanded of the girl, "are we wasting time on him?"

"It's not the money," Russell said to the girl, "is it?"

Strange, how she'd suddenly become the centre of power within the room, the deity to whom they made their supplications.

"No," she said, "it's the power." And before either he or Jek knew what was happening, she'd produced a penknife out of nowhere and nicked a clean hole in one of the packets and was sanding the floor with it. A cloud of powder rose in the air.

Jek swore, something in the Hokkien dialect which Russell didn't understand but understood to be vulgar, and lunged at the girl. She held the penknife to his face, at the same time as Russell unleashed a long-forgotten football tackle and wound one arm around Jek's throat. He was surprised at how easily Jek choked and collapsed on the floor; that athletic frame was deceptive.

The girl sheathed the penknife and grimaced. In the sudden silence, Russell heard the continued drip drip of the water from the air-conditioning unit. He stared at the mess on the floor. Money counted in grains of white. He felt a kind of awe at the prodigious waste. And a twinge of fear as well, not of Jek, not of the girl, but of himself, because, although they were callous people—callous above all about themselves—he was beginning to see the seductiveness of their philosophy.

Later, Russell would wince at the memory of how, snapping out of his state of suspension, he'd grabbed the girl and bundled her out of Jek's room, kicking the door shut behind them; of how he'd said to her, with low, missionary urgency, *You don't need to do this. Come away with me*, and realising how patronising it sounded. Her smile was contemptuous. *Are we going to get married and have babies?*

He wasn't sure but he thought he heard a muffled laugh from behind the door of Jek's room. He had a vision of Jek, whom he'd left doubled up on the floor, lying now prone on his back and listening with malicious pleasure through the flimsy walls. It brought Russell up short. What was he thinking of? That he could reform her? Save her from herself? It was his country's perennial folly—to think that the rest of the world wanted to be led into the light.

He took her face between her hands and rubbed his thumb, slowly, along the line of her jaw. Below her left eye he could see the faint smear of another cafe au lait mark. He kissed the mark, then her mouth—all scarily soft, deceptively yielding sweetness—then bolted. There was no other word for it. He *bolted*. He tore down the corridor of that shabby, slovenly hotel as though fire were licking his heels. If she'd called him by his name—which, it struck him now, she had never used—he would have turned round even then, but she never did.

Jek told him a story about the girl.

He had met her on his first visit home after dropping out of law school. Home had been a frosty place since his decision not to graduate, but his brother had just got married and it seemed like a good time to repair the breach. The girl was in the queue ahead of him at the moneychanger's. She was wearing (he grinned at the memory) a pearl-grey office suit, her hair up in a bun. She looked desexed, packaged. He had known. Just known. He'd followed her out and she'd tried to shake him off, walking faster, then slower, at one point darting into the post-office. Then she'd stopped and confronted him. *What do you want?*—*You.* In plain view of dozens of office-workers, she slapped him; he received the slap stoically. Waited just long enough for her to scribble her address down for him on a slip of paper fished out from her Prada bag.

He wasn't sure if she'd open the door to him, but she did. Away from work, she'd changed into shorts and t-shirt and let down her hair, and she looked about twelve, a serious, unsmiling child. Stepping inside, he thought, *Oh shit.* She was married. She wore no ring, and he saw no wedding photos about the very ordinary apartment, but he knew he was right, he could sniff this sort of thing a mile off. Coupledom, domesticity, filled him with horror, and he was in the thick of it: the cosy chats on the sofa in front of the TV, the dinners for two whipped up in the dinky little kitchen. But where was the husband? She said, *Away on a business trip*. She was making no attempt to be a good hostess—she hadn't even offered him a drink—and he was thinking whether to go, whether to tap on the decency that lay buried in him like the basalt in the earth's crust when she took his hand and pulled it under her t-shirt.

He met her every night for a week until she said that her husband was coming back. Coincidentally, it was also the day his brother was returning from Bangkok. (His brother was in the foreign service). He was a little relieved; he needed to come up for air. And he had family obligations: dinner at his parents' place with his brother and sister-in-law. He had not seen his brother in years. They were not close; they were too different, his brother having spent his life doing exactly what was expected of him. Nothing wrong with that, but it severely limited conversation between him and Jek. Still, Jek was fond of him, as he would have been fond of an old family dog. He was in his parents' sitting-room when the bell rang that evening. He sprang to open the door.

Imagine, said Jek, his befuddlement when the girl walked through the door. She reacted quicker than he did. "Hi," she said, "I'm Jun Leng," squeezing his hand with a painful, warning pressure that belied her size. His brother was a second or two behind, snapping shut an umbrella against the drizzle. "Jek!" he said. He gave Jek a bear hug, the sort of thing his brother *would* do. "Shao," Jek said, wanly.

Somehow, he and the girl got through dinner. Of course it was over, sexually, between them the moment she walked in; he was capable of a lot of things, but he wasn't capable of knowingly sleeping with his brother's wife. She left his brother the very next day with nothing more than one suitcase and a note (typewritten) pinned to the pillow. *I'm so sorry. The mistake was all mine.* Never had he seen a man more crazed than his brother after the girl's departure. He wept; he stormed; he raised hell in the police station where he made his missing person's report, demanding that they find her *immediately* while the policemen shook their heads sadly and didn't have the heart to disabuse him, though privately they were all thinking the same thing. Runaway wife—how many times had they seen this before?

Jek couldn't tell Shao that the girl was holed up in his hotel room, where she lay in bed with the covers drawn to her nose, watching cable television. He left her alone, knowing she was still in shock. At night, she slept huddled against him for warmth, and he held her as he would have something maimed: gingerly, without daring to breathe. After a week of this, when he was beginning to wonder what he'd taken on, whether he wouldn't be better off just foisting her back on Shao, she got out of bed and turned to him. *What happens now?* The pinched, devastated look had left her face, and he knew she'd renounced her previous life as completely as a nun entering the convent. He approved of what, to someone else, would have appeared as callousness. Too many people led cluttered lives. You could never know who you really were until you were stripped down to nothing. Had nothing. That was purity, that was zen. Of course, it was only in a metaphorical sense that the girl had nothing, because she actually had about fifty thousand dollars in savings, earned through five years of hundred hour work weeks. Which (he had to admit) was a help, because he was running low on reserves at that point.

He'd been waiting for this moment. The thing about drug running was that you quickly developed a sense for who was game and who was not, because your life depended on it. The girl didn't seem surprised when he told her what he did for a living; he had the impression she was not so much amoral as completely neutral in her moral judgments. He had a delivery to make that day at an apartment that he suspected was being staked by the police. The girl was his lookout. Within a minute, she spotted the police sitting in their unmarked car in the grounds. Went up to them, pretended to be a property buyer wanting more details of the development. She could, when she chose, simulate a kind of childlike innocence that was heartbreaking. She was a natural. He made the delivery, paid her her share.

They were a team. *A team.* (Stressed this, so that Russell saw that, oddly enough, this meant something to Jek, the natural loner who went scuba-diving, did middle-distance running, any activity that didn't require other people. The kind of guy you never wanted to have on your team, because he didn't see the sense in being a cog in a seamless powerful machine.) She never looked back. Someday she would cut him off too, as cleanly as she'd struck his brother from her life. He knew this with the certainty of someone who'd read the tea leaves. Knew, too, that it was useless to cavil at this. It was what made her what she was.

Jek told him a story about the girl and he listened because he was still stunned by his defection from her and hungered for mention of her name like an addict for his fix and because he had an hour to kill anyway before the bus to Penang for the flight back home. Leaving her, his one coherent thought was how he needed to get out of this country, this region, as fast as mechanical means could transport him. The airline he chose had just suffered its worst crash in history but the fare was a song, so he took it. Emerging from the travel office, he saw what appeared to be a tourist class hotel across the street and knew that what he needed right then was hard liquor to addle the brain fast and good. From experience, he guessed there would be a bar—the town was not overtly Muslim and the Malay women he had seen had their heads uncovered—and he was right.

Jek was at the bar. Russell hesitated, then strode up grimly. It would have seemed childish, churlish to walk away. Not to mention cowardly, though he knew he had nothing to fear from Jek in person. Contract killings were more Jek's style than personal violence.

"Russell," Jek said, meditatively. He looked none the worse for wear.

"Listen," Russell told him. "I'm not in the mood."

"I was going to buy you a drink." *You left her.* It hung in the air between them, loudly unsaid.

It was only after the vodka arrived that Russell thought to mumble, "Thanks."

Jek lifted his glass. "To the wasted youth."

Sitting in the nocturnal gloom of the bar, Russell had a fantasy. In ten years' time, he will meet Jek again in another bar, probably in another town in southern Thailand. Jek will look wasted and it will be obvious to

Russell that Jek has broken the first rule of drug-dealing—never sample your wares. The girl is out of the picture. That much is clear too.

This time, Russell will offer to buy him a drink. Jek is still able to talk—in his emaciated, deracinated state, it is something he can still do. What Jek talks about is the girl. Talks a streak, eyes glinting and feverish, that lopsided smile even now getting glances from bystanders who don't know better. Russell lets him talk. He bears Jek no ill-will, after all this time. And he is curious about the girl. The memory of her is still something incendiary, untamed, capable of bursting into awkward life at all the wrong moments and making him sweat.

He ends up sitting at the counter with Jek until closing time. Bides his time, waiting, with increasing impatience, to ask his question. *What happened to her?*

"She died," Jek says. "Of Aids."

Russell is horrified. "I didn't know—"

"She had neurofibromatosis. You knew, didn't you? There was a tumour. She needed a blood transfusion and the blood was contaminated."

He suddenly wants to get away. Sordidness is infectious. Which is why he has never gone off the rails like Jek or the girl. They were too hubristic, thinking they could maintain their sanity and youth and wit amidst the effluvium. He knows it isn't possible. That's why phrases such as *taking time out, discovering yourself* and *getting away from corporate America* infuriate him. Russell is now an investment banker, flying first-class in the air and staying five-star on the ground. (He has escaped the fate prophesised for him by Jek—the eternal student—and the satisfaction of proving Jek wrong is not the least of the motives that drives him.) His one quirk is frequenting squalid little bars that his colleagues are too squeamish to enter.

He says, as diffidently as he can manage, "Need money, Jek?"

He reads Jek's bright, thin smile (taut as a wire) correctly. Together with the generous tip he leaves for the bartender on the counter, he places a thick, separate wad and fishtails out the door so that he doesn't have to see Jek pocket the cash.

It was a satisfyingly sick revenge fantasy. Russell played several variations of it in his head over the next few hours, played it even as the plane was preparing to land for its transit stop in Singapore and the captain made his usual deadpan announcement about drug trafficking inviting the death penalty. Played it even as the plane landed and disgorged him into Changi Airport; it served to quell the panicky, agoraphobic feeling that was wont to seize him now that he'd emerged from his subterranean existence with the girl. He'd just closed his eyes to stem another wave of giddiness when two uniformed men came up to him and said, "Russell Liu?" "Yes," he said, yielding up his identity unthinkingly, stupidly.

"Come with us please."

Alarm bells pealed in his head. "No, wait—"

They took him to a room with a table and three metal chairs. The first thing he noticed was the sniffer dog, an Alsatian, straining at its leash to get at the table and barking madly. He stared at the table, across which were scattered the contents of his backpack, his sole check-in luggage. It was a meagre, typical backpacker's display: water-bottle; bedroll; hopelessly worn t-shirts, everything faded to a dull grey; his tome on globalisation and a cheap thriller, picked up in a Vietnamese guesthouse in desperation for something to read; a packet of (he winced) ribbed condoms. Then he saw it. A white plastic packet that he'd last seen lying on the bed of Jek's hotel room.

He thought wildly. He'd left his backpack in the lobby of Jek's hotel when he rushed into the town to look for the nearest travel agency. It would have been the easiest thing in the world for Jek or the girl to slip in the packet, place an anonymous call to Singapore customs and incriminate him. Hang him as surely as though he'd hung the rope around his own self-deceiving neck. It had to be Jek. Even in the midst of the incredible fear that tore through him—a fear that he hadn't thought possible, it was as acute, as terrifyingly real in its every pang as a heart attack—he clung to this thought. *It had to be Jek.* Not the girl. Above all else, he didn't want it to be her. His *faith* in the universe depended on it.

One of the officers picked up the packet and threw it in his direction. He was too stupefied to duck; it struck him full in the chest.

"What's *that?*"

They were, he realised, more contemptuous about his stupidity than anything else.

"Listen," he said, "I can explain—"

A mistake. An innocent man would have simulated outrage, demanded to know what was going on. The sniffer dog, hearing his voice, lunged at him and he lurched back against the wall. In any event, he was brought up short by the looks of polite incredulity on the officers' faces. They were young, younger than he was and shorter (in Asia, his American-fed physique towered uncomfortably over everyone), clean-shaven, acne-scarred. They looked like twins. They must have heard dozens of tall stories by now, the concoctions spun by desperate couriers twisting like reeds in the wind to avoid the gallows. The gallows! Even then, he could think, irrelevantly, about the quaintness of the expression, its archaic flavour. And how it was cheaper than electrocution or lethal injection, though he didn't suppose that was the reason for its continued usage. He faced it: they didn't believe in quick, easy deaths here.

He abandoned the attempt to explain. "I want a lawyer."

They seemed amused. One of them snorted, "Americans!" The other interjected, more gently, "It's not part of the procedure here." Tweedledum and Tweedledee. It was just his luck.

"What happens now?"

"You wait."

He was taken to a remand prison to wait. There was nobody else in the cell, which was warm and fetid-smelling but otherwise unremarkable. The wait was the longest of his life, longer than the wait he'd endured as a nine year-old at the dentist to have an aching tooth pulled out and hearing the howls of the kid who'd gone in before him, longer than the wait he had suffered at twenty for Mary Beth Jablonski, his first girlfriend at college, to return from her date with a former boyfriend and knowing, just knowing, that she wasn't going to. Time froze, congealed. He was going to suffocate in its abundance. In this surfeit of time, his mind kept sliding, like a man rolling helplessly towards the edge of a precipice, towards a mental image of a noose freeze-framed against a grey sky, at which point he'd spring up from his wooden bench and hurl himself dementedly against the bars, yelling fit to burst. After an hour of this, a middle-aged officer trotted over and looked at him weightily. That was it. Time resumed its slow, interminable progress.

Sunshine. The sweet roar of traffic down a four-lane highway. Old, matured trees unfurling their branches across the highway and creating a natural canopy. He had no idea where he was but it was all beautiful. *Beautiful.* Even the grey remand prison from which he'd just been released in what was clearly monumental disgust. "What's happening?" he'd kept saying, as two men unlocked the door of his cell and frogmarched him down the corridor. Jeez, were they going to hang him *now*? Without benefit of a trial? Without the appearance of a trial? What kind of country was this anyway?

"What the hell is going on?"

That got their attention. They stopped rubber-stamping a pile of forms long enough to look at him properly for the first time. Apparently, they didn't like what they saw, because they returned to rubber-stamping with renewed fury. "Think you're smart, don't you?" he thought he heard one of them say.

The next minute, he was standing in the parking lot of the remand prison with his backpack dumped rudely at his feet. Late afternoon sunshine poured from a yellow sky.

Did that count as a near-death experience? Russell decided it did. He'd been given a new lease of life, and he meant to *enjoy* it, dammit. He was going to celebrate the first day of the rest of his life by blowing his travellers' cheques on a one-night stay at the Ritz-Carlton while waiting for the next flight back. The Ritz-Carlton, the cab driver who drove him there assured him, was the swankiest hotel in Singapore, and Russell wasn't about to argue with him.

The luxury of a bath in a genuine bathtub with little wrapped bars of soap on a porcelain side-dish and little jars of shampoo and lotion! The old Russell would have scorned these Lilliputian mementoes of a five-star hotel, but the new Russell revelled in them. To hell with roughing it and the whole bullshit about authenticity. He wanted creature comforts, manufactured experiences, mass tourism. He wanted theme parks! To hell with reflexive guilt about coming from the richest nation on earth. To hell with worrying about globalisation, the consumer culture and the End of History. He didn't want the weight of the world on his shoulders any more. He wanted to eat a burger whenever he felt like it (something he'd avoided religiously for months and now felt a ravenous craving for) and let someone else worry about the rainforests. To hell with unearthing your roots; in the new global order, ethnicity meant as much or as little as the shade of your briefcase. To hell with—

The phone rang. "Mr Liu? Someone's waiting for you in the lobby. Sorry, I don't have a name."

He was not thinking of the girl. He was most resolutely not thinking of her, and it was working. It worked up to the point that he stepped out of the lift into the lobby and saw her sitting in one of those sunken sofa chairs that swallowed you up whole and left only a severed head bobbing above the armrest. He saw her head, her profile, that neat, uplifted chin, before she turned and saw him. He had a second to decide whether to stay or flee. He hesitated.

She was wearing a slip-dress that seemed to be all straps and filmy material and slingback sandals that barely covered her feet. He'd never seen her in a dress before. He swallowed.

He said, in a voice that didn't sound like his own, "That was a cute trick you pulled." Of course he'd figured by now it was her.

"You walked out on me," she pointed out.

In the warped logic in which she dealt, this seemed perfectly reasonable. In spite of himself, he found himself nodding. "I got scared."

"I know."

He couldn't take his eyes off her; he imagined that the hungry, adolescent quality of his gaze was apparent to anyone looking at them and, though more fully clothed than she was, he was the one who felt naked, exposed.

"So tell me," he said, "why'd they let me go?"

There was the glimmer of a smile. "Probably because they couldn't analyse enough heroin to hang you."

His brain worked slowly, too slowly, for her. "You mean—?"

Impatiently, "It was baking soda."

But the sniffer dog was going nuts, he wanted to say, but didn't. Hell, maybe the dog just didn't like him. He said, wryly, "So I guess you made your delivery safely."

"You don't have to like my job. You just have to like me.

"And to hell with the wasted youth."

"They're everywhere," she pointed out. "You can't save everyone. I don't create the demand. I just feed it."

Somewhere the argument was flawed, but he didn't know where to begin. He wasn't sure he wanted to begin. Moral ambiguity was a landscape she painted in pastel, soothing colours; it was a pure line of melody, light as a plume of smoke, from an unseen saxophonist in the park on a Sunday afternoon.

He tried to summon up his indignation—he almost got hanged, he was lucky not to get a *coronary*—but indignation was having a hard time muscling through the fog of kinkiness and hapless desire that was his usual state of mind with her. He wanted to put his hands around that slender neck of hers and squeeze the life out of her, he wanted so badly to taste her he was getting dizzy just thinking about it.

"So what happens now?" he wanted to know.

She shrugged and started to walk away. In a minute, she would be swallowed up in the mass of people milling by the hotel entrance. He waited. He always liked waiting until the last moment; it gave him the comforting illusion he had a choice. When she disappeared, he broke into a run.

Do What You Have To

5:00 P.M. When he arrived to fetch Sunil from his Sunday art class at the country club, the child was gone.

"What the hell do you mean, *gone?*"

The young teacher, clad in jeans and a smiley-face t-shirt that made her appear a child herself, quailed. Vivek, six feet tall and drawing himself up to his full height, seemed to fill the room with his anger. The girl stammered that Sunil had gone off with a woman whom he'd called "Auntie." He'd slipped his hand in hers, swinging it happily. Pressed for a description, the teacher wrinkled her nose in despair. The woman was young. Chinese. Small. Slender. Hair pulled back into a ponytail. Nothing special. Unless you counted the diamond earrings in the design of a hex.

Vivek's first reaction was relief that he was not imagining things or losing his mind. For days now, he had been haunted by the feeling that someone was following him. He'd acquired a shadow, a ghost whose presence he thought he saw trailing him in shop windows and the mirrors of office lobbies. Sometimes the phone line went dead when he answered his calls. The thought had crossed his mind that it might be Elin, but he had heard that she had gone abroad to do her MBA. So he had shrugged off the sensation as an aberration; as he liked to say, he was about as psychic as a doorknob. The supernatural, the spiritual, the world's buffet of religions, all struck him as a tremendous bore. He had no time for things that were not explicable.

Sunil had called her "Auntie." Which suggested a prior acquaintanceship. Had she been hanging around SuniPs school or contriving to meet him accidentally in the park with the maid on their evening walks? Vivek felt something approaching nausea at the thought. But Sunil's greeting was not conclusive. For reasons that Vivek could never fathom, Sunil, though a physical miniature of his father, was friendly as a dog with strangers. He was a happy child, indiscriminate in his affections. Watching him trot up to other children ("Hello, my name is Sunil, I'm four and three quarters") Vivek would experience a blast of contradictory, powerful emotions, the main one being an urge to sit Sunil down and warn him about other people. That they were duplicitous, untrustworthy and as ready to stick a knife in you as smile at you. In other words, they were exactly like his father. Yet he also envied Sunil his unclouded nature. The happy might be naive but they were happy.

"I thought she was a family friend—" The young teacher's face was beginning to look blotched, teary.

Vivek forced a smile. His anger at her had now fastened on himself. It was not her fault. He walked out of the classroom, through the air-conditioned hall of the club and into the warm humid afternoon. The sun continued to burn in a mercilessly blue sky. He crossed the road to his car.

5:10 P.M. "I'll be late," he told his wife on the handphone. "Sunil and I are going for ice-cream."

"Vivek. He has a *cough.*" Parvati was ill in bed with fever, which was why he'd had to chaperone Sunil to his art class. In the background, he could hear the strains of Mahler, which he detested. Wrist-slitter music, he called it. Life was grim enough without suicide-inducing audio stimulants. Parvati called him a philistine.

He said, "*One* ice-cream won't kill the kid," and rang off.

He continued to sit in his car outside the police station, drumming his fingers on the steering wheel. Where had he seen that long low roof and pale-blue institutional facade before? A long-forgotten memory stirred: whirring ceiling fans; Brother McCabe's mild Irish voice explaining the periodic table on a hot drowsy afternoon. There, at his mission school in Bombay, he had got his first whiff of the possibility of escape. An old boy who'd founded a software company in Silicon Valley returned to give a talk to the student body: it was the usual alumni speech about the debt he owed his school, and Vivek was struck less by what was said than by the way the software entrepreneur carried himself. He noted the expansive gestures, the hands thrust casually into pockets (in direct violation of the brothers' warning to the boys to take their hands out of their pockets), the rangy, easy physicality of his movements. At fifteen, it often seemed to Vivek that he inhabited a world of hunched, shrinking, timorous, defeated people moving crabwise through life. In this group, unfairly, he lumped his father.

His father had wanted to be a historian, but lack of means had propelled him into the civil service instead. Thirty years as a government clerk had put the finishing touches to an already fatalistic disposition. But you make your own freedom, Vivek argued over the kitchen table, you don't let the world shape you, you shape the world to your own ends! (How was he to know that the software entrepreneur's company would collapse in a year in a blizzard of debts and indictments? Even so, there seemed something rather magnificent about the scale of the software entrepreneur's ambition and spectacular fall from grace.) Vivek's older brother was to fulfil their father's hopes of having at least one academic in the family; the day he came home with news of his assistant professorship Vivek announced, not quite facetiously, to his unamused parents that his aim in life was to make money, and lots of it. Later, much later, it would occur to him that he could have been less rough on the old man, but at that time he was consumed only by youth's merciless need to puncture the certainties of the middle-aged. When he won a scholarship to an Ivy League university, he thought, That's it. He never looked back.

He had to do something. Inaction would drive him crazy. He cut the engine and entered the station.

Name. Vivek.

Nationality. U.S. citizen. A look of some surprise; twelve years in New York had not eradicated Vivek's fairly thick Indian accent.

Address. Somewhere in the expatriates' ghetto of District 10.

Age. Thirty-eight.

Occupation. Executive vice president of a prominent local bank. Youngest ever in its annals. "Foreign talent," the young police officer attending him—a pimply kid with brylcreemed hair—said sotto voce to his colleague at the next counter.

Nature of complaint. Someone has taken my son.

Here Vivek immediately ran into difficulties. He had £one to fetch his son from art class. The child had apparently gone off with a stranger. No, not a stranger. It might be someone he knew. A woman. He had no idea what her intentions were. Not kidnapping, surely. Dear God.

"But you know the lady, sir."

Not quite a question, not a statement, more an insinuation.

Yes, he thought, someone who used to work in the same bank as I do, someone I barely know, except that we had a one-night stand. (Or rather, twenty, to be precise, and he knew that, with her meticulousness, a quality he'd valued when she was working for him, Elin would be.) Someone whose career I deliberately destroyed because her very presence in the office was a taunt to the vow I had made that I was not going to see her again.

He stood, the half-completed report in his hand. "I—I've changed my mind. This was a mistake. I'll sort it out."

"If you suspect that a crime has been committed," the pimply kid intoned, portentous with officialdom, "you have a duty to report it, you know."

Vivek felt like smacking the kid's head. "Look, I know my rights. You can't hold me. OK?"

The kid stared, open-mouthed, as he tore the report into shreds and dropped them in the bin.

The problem with high-flyers was that they reached cruising speed too soon. They got bored. They got antsy. Which was how he felt after twelve years in New York, nine of them in an investment bank where he had risen so rapidly that, at the age of thirty-five, he'd bumped his head against a glass ceiling that his contemporaries would take years more to hit. There was also the fact that his mentor, Eduardo Alvarez, had retired, and the new man showed no particular love for Vivek. Vivek knew, in the cycle of revolution and counterrevolution that was life in investment banking, that the tumbrils were coming for him. It was only a matter of time. Which was why, when the call came from Eduardo, drawling down the line at two A.M. in the morning, he did not immediately dismiss it out of hand.

"Viv" (he liked to call Vivek "Viv") "how often do you get the opportunity to build something from *scratch*, to get in at the *ground floor* of an enterprise with guarantees of *no interference* and the sky the limit?"

Eduardo was the son of Chilean immigrants to the United States. Political idealists, they were, like Vivek's parents, disappointed that their son had chosen mammon over the higher calling they'd envisaged for him, this being public life in Eduardo's case. Perhaps it was true, as Ed liked to say with a wink, that men who disappoint their parents share a special bond.

The *fact* was, Viv, the Singapore government was liberalising the financial sector and welcoming skilled foreigners with open arms ... No matter what you thought about their political record (and frankly, Viv, he *never* thought about politics if he could help it) you had to give them kudos for facing up to the challenges of globalisation and a rapidly-evolving economic paradigm ... Foreigners like Ed, who had been headhunted to become chief executive officer of a Singapore bank. Foreigners like Vivek, whom he wanted to run the entire treasury operations.

"Face it, Viv, how many people your *age* get such an opportunity handed to them on a *platter*?"

Vivek immediately spotted the worm in Ed's hyperbolic apple.

"And what do the locals think of this initiative?"

"Well, jeez, Viv, they don't have a hell lot of choice, do they?"

No, they' didn't. They had no choice; they were whacked, steamrollered, shell-shocked, pummelled into submission. "You have to *understand*, Viv, this place has been run for *years* like a miniature arm of the civil service masquerading as the free sector. It's safe as houses and dull as paint. They wouldn't recognise a synthetic derivative if it came and slapped them in the *face*. That's what we're dealing with."

Arrogance was not something that Ed had ever lacked though he hid it well most of the time, and Vivek, under his tutelage in New York, had been encouraged to give free rein to his natural contempt for those less intelligent than he was. Since young, Vivek had been afflicted by a rabid consciousness of other people's slowness on the uptake. His so-called leadership qualities, his ability to dominate business meetings, was nothing more than the product of a horror of boredom, of having to wait while others puzzled out issues that he'd already worked out in his sleep the night before.

So it was that on his second day on the job (his third day in the country) he saw no reason to dissimulate or be tactful about the bank's shortcomings at a meeting with external lawyers and one of his young officers. The lawyer was English, an associate from one of the foreign law firms operating in Singapore.

The discussion was about rating triggers. Namely, the ability of lenders to the bank or its counterparties to call an event of default if the bank's grading by a rating agency dropped below investment grade. "Surely," the lawyer was saying, "there must be a system in place to monitor and track such covenants."

Vivek shook his head. "No such system."

"Well, it's normally the purview of risk management in other banks—"

"No risk management systems here to speak of."

It was possible that they were all conscious of the serious breach of form that was taking place, of the bank's dirty linen that was being washed in front of third parties; possible, too, that this was a spur to Vivek, who enjoyed the occasional bout of recklessness.

"Or a credit issue—"

"Credit doesn't look at such issues. Credit hasn't even seen fit to separate itself from relationship management yet, despite the inherent conflict of interest."

The Englishman laughed, and if his laugh was a little nervous, Vivek didn't notice and didn't care. The meeting had already exceeded its time slot and he was about to rap out the things he wanted done when he caught the young officer's eye. Her hair was scraped back from her face into a severe little bun at the nape of her neck; her ears lay close to her scalp like the pricked ears of a cat. In her earlobes, tiny diamond earrings in the shape of a hex caught the light.

Her expression had remained blank, poker-faced throughout and she had said nothing except to offer facts when requested. Nor had she made a single note of the meeting; her pad lay lily-white before her and he felt unaccountably nettled (had he said nothing worth recording?). In her eye, he thought he detected an amused contempt. It was not what he expected: in two days in the bank, he'd run the gamut of fawning servility to outright hostility. He checked her name again after she left (these Chinese names were hell to remember). Elin.

5:30 *P.M.* His handphone rang.

"Surprised?"

His heart thudded so hard in his chest he thought he was having a seizure. "*Where is Sunil?*"

"I can't tell you that."

"You're crazy. You know that? I could report you to the police."

She asked, reasonably, "What's stopping you?"

He was silent. Then: "You've been following me. Haven't you?"

"You noticed."

"You're very inept at stalking."

"I'm learning."

"I want to talk to Sunil. I want to know he's all right."

A small voice came on. "Daddy? Daddy?"

"Sunil? Are you all right?" Without knowing it, he lapsed into the Hindi that he hardly ever spoke: "Are you safe?"

The line crackled; the small voice was fading in and out. "… having ice-cream, Daddy."

Not crying, Vivek thought; he wasn't sure whether that was a good sign.

Elin's voice was in his ear: "I'll talk to you again."

"Don't cut me off—"

The line went dead.

Two years ago he had touched down one muggy evening at Changi airport and, still groggy after his twenty-two hour flight, had been borne down the East Coast Parkway, where he caught his first glimpse of the financial centre, a sweep of illuminated glass down Clifford Pier. It was the first and last time he'd felt his heart race at the sight of anything in the landscape. In this tiny island, he still got lost driving out of the city centre. The so-called heartlands—the public housing estates—baffled him with their utilitarian sameness; he was used to the picturesqueness of squalor.

Parvati had resisted the move out here. Not directly, of course; that was not her way. She had talked about cultural wastelands, the lack of seasons in an equatorial climate and the paucity of good international schools in an oblique, maddening way until Vivek told her to get to the point. Relations had been cool between them for months. So it was ironic that she had settled in better than he had. She'd found a group of expatriate friends to embark on assorted arty projects intended to raise the cultural awareness of the deprived local population; on weekends, she and Vivek ate at restaurants that she had discovered during the week. She was not *happy*—her frustrated intelligence, her thwarted ambitions, had been undercurrents in their marriage for so long that Vivek had ceased to pay attention to them—but she had adapted.

He, on the other hand, had no interest in the country. It was a place to work and make money, not to sink roots. Together with the other expatriates he met, he lived and breathed in a kind of rarefied, borderless international ether of conference calls, video link-ups, twenty-four hour emailing and breakfast meetings in five-star hotels of the business capitals of the world. With all this connectivity, he didn't, strictly speaking, *need* a physical body; he could have existed as an astral emanation, or a scooped-out brain stuffed in a jar and giving out electromagnetic signals and accomplished the same amount of work.

And if he could have existed as pure mind, pure intelligence, of no particular race or creed, he would have. It annoyed him to be pigeonholed as Indian or Asian or Hindu. He was Vivek: entire, unique. It was such an integral part of his conception of himself that he would have been surprised to be accused of arrogance. The problem was that this sense of himself as pure mind sometimes ran aground in the shoals of daily life.

His height, for instance, which had not seemed out of place in New York, made him feel oversized, afflicted by gigantism, in this country; he'd developed a kind of apologetic hunch when talking to people. Matters of the heart. Emotions. The fierce, almost primitive love he felt for his son. Natural, certainly, but not, perhaps, a good thing; he was held hostage by it. The vagaries of sexual attraction. Why he felt little of it for his wife; why it could ambush you like a thief in the night when you were least expecting it. As it did the morning of the photoshoot for the Mission Statement Working Group. "Can you bend a little?" the photographer had called out to him. So he'd jackknifed himself to get into the frame and his nose had brushed against Elin's hair. He inhaled the smell of her shampoo and something else, a whiff of mingled perfume and skin under the coiled hair held in place by an enormous tortoiseshell comb. "Sorry," he'd said, and she'd turned and flashed him that crooked rent smile of hers. That was how it had started.

He hardly knew her. He didn't know her at all. For a year, his only glimpses of her had been of her crossing the trading room floor: a neat, criminally self-possessed figure. She did not report directly to him; he had little reason to speak to her. Yet she occupied his thoughts much more than her status in the office would have warranted. If she had been more stunning, or more senior, he might have been worried. but she was none of those things. Vivek had never been unfaithful, but the fidelity was lightly-worn: he had never yet met anyone for whom he'd felt inclined to risk his reputation and his career.

The Mission Statement was the brainchild of Ed who, ever since he had thundered into the bank like a conquistador, had deplored its lack of corporate vision and *espirit d'corps*. The bank that pulls together pulls up the share price, was one of his favourite sayings. What this place needed was a mission statement. A working group was swiftly set up, comprising the usual bunch of toadies and reluctant conscripts. Vivek was press-ganged to lead the group. Running through the list of members of the group, Elin's name had caught his eye; he found himself circling it. He kept his own feelings about the project (that the only reliable motivator of men was self-interest and that mission statements were pure hogwash) under wraps; no-one would have known, looking at him, that he was keenly aware of the absurdity of debating the nuances of whether the bank should be known as *a leading regional bank* or *a bank with a leading Asian footprint*. No-one except, perhaps, Elin; often, bringing his mind back from the outer galaxies to which it had drifted during a particularly inane patch of the proceedings, he would find their eyes involuntarily meeting across the heads of the other participants, co-conspirators in mirth.

It might have stopped at that: a harmless flirtation, a slight frisson at seeing her in the office. But then this *thing* had happened. And she had seen his face. (He had straightened up, stunned, and looked round a little wildly. No-one had witnessed their little byplay. Not for the first time he thought how strange it was that whole inner lives could be contained within you without anyone having the slightest inkling.)

She had seen his face and she had made the first move. That was how he justified it later. The working group had celebrated its last session with a drink at Boat Quay; one member had puked into the river and Vivek had excused himself early to head back to the office. It was not late by his standards, but it was Friday night and the place was deserted except for the handful of night dealers studying their screens.

She had come to his room, the glass-walled generously-proportioned cage in which he sometimes felt like an exhibit in a zoo. There was only one reason why she should have come. He felt, if anything, a sense of relief that she had decided to bring matters to a head. She'd knocked on the door and closed it behind her and leant back against it, looking at him with her disconcertingly direct gaze. Saying nothing until he'd felt compelled to break the silence himself: "You didn't join us this evening."

He could not say that he had looked out for her and, when she did not appear, had been seized by an irrational despair.

She shrugged. "I don't drink. And I don't like groups."

He suggested, sardonically, "You're not a social animal. You keep your own counsel."

"I don't," she said, as though confessing to a minor, embarrassing vice, "like people very much on the whole."

Neither did he. Maybe that was what had pricked his interest in the first place: he'd sensed in her a similar contempt for others that was a form of self-dislike. And she had the same manic work ethic that he did—he had seen her at her desk past midnight many times—a work ethic that seemed born of a desire to keep something at bay. Self-reflection, perhaps, or the realisation that to stop working for a moment was to acknowledge the abyss at their feet.

He said something next that was so out of context, so out of character, that later he thought he must have been mad. Or drunk. But he had not drunk much; he was stone-sober and yet there was a lightness in his head like inebriation. "You know I'm married."

"So am I."

He wished she would look away, or down, or at any rate turn off that laser stare of hers. It was he who blinked first. He got to his feet. Later, he was not sure how he had made his way out of the office, down to the Stygian gloom of the carpark. He must have said something to her about picking her up down the street; they could not be seen to leave the office together. She was waiting at the corner for him. It was beginning to rain. He saw lightning fork the sky, beautiful and brazen, and then the world was deluged, water coursing down the windscreen and obliterating the world outside. Her mouth on his tasted of mints and coffee; her hand on his chest had the heat of a branding iron. She pulled away long enough from him to say, "Isn't this like the movies?" She was laughing, though he didn't know what the joke was. He seldom watched movies. He didn't have the time. Just as he didn't have the time to read a book, listen to music, take his son for a walk in the park, make love to his wife. He'd grown up too quickly, married too young and worked too hard. Perhaps at that moment he felt his hunger for Elin as a hunger for all the things he'd missed out on in life; without knowing it, he was already composing his *mea culpa* to an unseen audience composed of his family and his conscience.

"What's your excuse?"

She said, "I don't have any. Do we need one?"

He suspected this was the correct answer. There was no excuse, no reason, except that Vivek, engineer by training and banker by default, couldn't stop searching for one. He did not believe in *coups de foudre* or eyes meeting across the room or kismet or what his father would have called sentimental balderdash. So he had no explanation to fall back on, and no explanation for why he needed an explanation, unless it was to drown out the timpani of the words *midlife crisis* ringing in his ears.

She was an orphan. Given up for adoption as a baby by her unmarried mother, rescued from the orphanage at the age of five by a middle-aged couple with two teenage boys of their own. They were Pentecostalist Christians, with a strong missionary bent. They meant well, but she'd felt like an alien in their household. She did not agree that the material world was an evil, contaminated place. Her rebellion was not noisy or boisterous, which would have been a relief to her foster parents, because then they could have prayed and wept over her. What they found hard to bear (she did not say this, but Vivek filled in the blanks for her) was her obedience; obedience without belief was a mockery, a goad. University, then a young, hasty marriage, had been her escape. About her husband, she would say little. They were separated.

She told him this their first night together in the unprepossessing room in the budget hotel that she'd expertly directed him to. (He had the disquieting feeling that this was not the first time she had come here.) The rain had stopped, but he was curiously reluctant to go. He continued to lie in the hard bed with her, watching the red glow of the bedside clock.

She said, "Why all these questions?"

He could not say, *To make it seem less of a one-night stand* . Not to spare her feelings, but his own.

He wondered if that was her excuse. The wary, distrusting orphan. Betrayed once and most fundamentally by her own mother and finding her only revenge in a cool appropriation of others for her own ends. (But if he had given voice to this, she would merely have fixed on him that slightly incredulous smile of hers and he would have felt like a fool.)

At last he had left, and he was secretly relieved when she declined his offer of a lift back. She would sleep over, she said. The thought of spending the night in that cheap hotel room appalled him. He drove home through empty streets, eyes blinking with fatigue, to a wife who murmured, "Vivek. Another all-nighter?" and turned over and went back to sleep. He could not believe that betrayal was so easy. It was *too* easy. He got into his second bed of the night and slept heavily until noon.

"What's your excuse?"

Elin said, as he expected her to, "Not *again*." Exactly as Sunil did when he was forced to perform some loathsome chore.

It had become a game, pinpointing the reasons why they returned, again and again, to the cheap hotel room with its faint smell of antiseptic, half-drawn blinds and its view of the backyards of a row of old terrace houses. They were always given the same room. ("Maybe it's cursed," Elin said, "and they can't rent this to anyone else.")

She hazarded, "Because you're tall, dark and handsome?"

"Too easy."

"Because you're the boss and I need a raise?"

"Which you're not getting."

"I don't know then. What about ... getting into bed with the enemy. Self-survival."

"Am I the enemy?"

She said, lazily, "Oh yeah. Don't you know? You're part of the New Colonial Order. The New Empire. Western technology and Western financial markets and Western jargon. We need you but we don't like you. And we have to abase ourselves all over again." She made the gesture of a sign on the wall: "'No dogs or coolies allowed.'"

"Do you really believe this nonsense?"

"I've thought about this a lot."

"I think you've got your colourful metaphors a little mixed. I'm Indian. Insofar as that means anything. We fought to kick out the British too, don't forget."

"You know what I mean, *lah*." (He had never understood this linguistic tic of the *lah*, slipping unexpected out of the mouths of even the most culturally deracinated locals.) "Credit doesn't look at such issues." She wouldn't ever let him forget their first encounter. On cue, she started laughing again. She found him amusing. This, in itself, was a novelty. Vivek was used to being taken seriously, too seriously. He let her laugh.

The detritus of an affair: snatched memories darting into his brain at the most inconvenient moments:

Tracing the whorl of her earlobe and the earrings she always wore: "You like these earrings, don't you?"

"They're my lucky charm."

"Who are you trying to ward off?"

She held him off by the shoulders. "You?"

Performance appraisal at work. A time of intense emotional upheaval and horsetrading for some. Not for Vivek, who usually made up his mind about someone's work performance within a couple of weeks. He was not always right but at least he was decisive. In his book, that was the cardinal virtue. He signed off on Elin's appraisal, done by her immediate supervisor, without comment. (*Highly motivated. Willing to go the extra mile. Excellent performer.*) He went out and took his customary mid-morning stroll across the trading room floor. In the time since he'd arrived, he'd transformed the place. Stripped out all the grey systems furniture that had made the place seem like a morgue, papered every available surface with mock-Scandinavian pine, infused the place with a vitality that had been missing. He wanted his people to have fun at work. Best of all, he'd banned the cheap instant coffee granules that were all the previous regime was willing to provide and installed ground coffee machines in every meeting room. The smell of freshly-ground coffee pervaded the place. He wanted everyone on a caffeinated rush. The more manic people were, the more they made money. He loved that five-minute walk every morning through the controlled little patch of aggression that he'd created.

She did not look up from her trading screen as he passed.

"Ho Sin Thye?"

"I don't know him."

"He's the management trainee you recruited three months ago. The Stanford MBA and CFA."

He could have kept up the pretence, but decided not to. "What about him?"

"He says you're cold-shouldering him. That you told his supervisor not to pass him any deals if possible."

"Since when do you talk to management trainees?"

"I ran into him in the pantry."

He waited. She should have seen the ground she was treading on, but she didn't. "He was upset. He asked me what had happened."

What had happened was that Vivek had decided that the boy was the academic type who should never have set foot on a trading room floor but it was not his style to spill the bitter truth to people. Those who hated his guts—and there were plenty—would have been surprised to know it, but he disliked confrontation. He left it to his victims to deduce that they had been left out in the cold to freeze to death (the deduction was always a slow, agonising process) and accepted their inevitable resignations without comment.

He said, icily, "It's none of your business."

"Oh, what, I'm just your once-a-week fuck? I can't say what I think?"

"Don't be crude. What I decide in the office is out of *bounds*. You should know that."

He started pulling on his clothes.

She said slowly, and she seemed genuinely surprised by the revelation, "You can be horrible, Vivek."

His tone was sarcastic: "I thought you didn't like people on the whole."

"I don't like meanness either."

He said, "Spare me the grandstanding," and slammed the door on his way out.

The next time: "I thought you weren't going to come." The closest he would ever come to an apology. She said, "Why would you think that?" The density of her small frame in his arms. The sensation of drowning, of the waters closing above his head—he should have panicked earlier. But he didn't, because pure mind was still telling him that he could kick free at any moment and because he found he liked this new subterranean world.

5:55 P.M. His handphone rang.

"When will you be back? I need to tell the maid when to get dinner ready."

"I'm not sure. An hour maybe. Maybe more."

"Is Sunil asking you to buy him a toy?"

"No. Yes. Yes."

"Vivek. Is something wrong?"

She had asked him the same question a year ago. He had reached out to take her hand in his across the table of the very expensive Japanese restaurant that he had insisted on taking her to, on the grounds that "we never spend any time alone together." He had been affectionate and solicitous and Parvati had immediately smelt a rat. It was the evening following the photoshoot. He had arranged to meet her there. She was late; he'd had time to read the menu twice, raising his head only when he became aware of a stir of interest in the room and knew that she had arrived. Parvati had that effect on people. She was the most impeccably groomed and elegant woman that he knew. He did not love her. Theirs had been an arranged marriage. He had agreed to it to mollify his parents, who were upset by his plans to migrate to the States. It had been a good business proposition on paper. Parvati's family was wealthy and cosmopolitan and she had trained expensively to be a lawyer before she gave it all up to marry him. She at any rate had loved him. Sometimes he wondered why. He had no illusions about himself. Still, the ice-core in him, the part that could view even his marriage as a statement of debits and credits, would point out that she had not done too badly either out of marrying him.

"Nothing," he had said then, "why do you ask?" It was not until that moment that he had explicitly acknowledged to himself that he was going to betray his wife.

"I'll he back," he told her now, "in an hour. Yes, an *hour*"

6:00 P.M. She had called him; her number must have been recorded in the handphone memory. He located it and punched her number with suddenly nerveless fingers that kept sliding off the tiny digits. A mechanical voice told him that the system was not responding.

He had not moved his car from outside the police station. A squad car pulled out of the compound, the driver looking at Vivek curiously. He had to leave soon, or he would attract attention. He closed his eyes briefly. Tried to think. There had been a great deal of noise in the background during Elin's call. Traffic. People chattering and laughing. The clink of glasses. Booming American voices from a movie trailer dissipating into the air. In his limited knowledge of the country, there was only one place where you could get this particular aural mix. An outdoor cafe at the traffic-riddled intersection of Scotts and Paterson Road. He released the handbrake.

6:10 P.M.. He had read somewhere that traffic jams were the result of a random confluence of freak events: a sudden surge of cars into a street, a red light, a car idling in the left lane; their build-up defying all prediction. A wall of cars reared up suddenly in front of him without warning; he braked sharply, cursing under his breath.

He wondered when Sunil would tire of the thrill of ice-cream and ask to go home. And what he would do when Elin said no. Cry, probably, or else the corners of his mouth would turn down in that sad-clown expression he had perfected so well when he didn't get his way. Nightfall would only increase Sunil's confusion and anxiety; he had a favourite blue blanket from which he was inseparable once the sun vanished and he would be whimpering for it. Vivek's hands tightened on the steering wheel.

Yes, he loved his son but he was not an exemplary father, not by any means. He was too little around and when he was the constant refrain of, "Daddy, Daddy, play with me," got on his nerves. Left alone to mind Sunil, he would head speedily for the park to let the child run himself ragged, much to Parvati's annoyance. Fatherhood for him was chiefly a series of tactile, sensory moments: the smooth little body squirming seal-like and shrieking with laughter in the shower; the deep, heavy sleep of an exhausted child, so deep that Vivek could undress him without his eyelids once fluttering; the back of Sunil's head, as he ran ahead of his father, with its tuft of hair sticking upwards and looking absurdly small and vulnerable from Vivek's height.

Death. Dying. Sunil had lately become obsessed with the topic, after Parvati had enrolled him in a Catholic kindergarten. He had come home brimming with the story of the crucifixion, particularly the gory bits (the nails hammered through the hands and feet, the piercing with a spear in the ribs of the dying Son of Man) and Vivek had wanted to pull him out of the school immediately. He didn't want his son's head filled with religious nonsense, whether of the Hindu or Christian variety. Parvati told him he was over-reacting. Sunil was not scared; quite the contrary. ("When you die, you go to heaven. Heaven's a nice place." Parvati: "Yes, very nice." "What do people do in heaven?" "They enjoy themselves." "Yes, but what do they *do*?" "They have parties." "Nice parties?" "With balloons." The kid had almost laughed himself to death.)

He envied Parvati's light touch with the kid, but it was beyond him to joke about death where his son was concerned. A year ago, the maid had taken Sunil for his usual after-dinner walk and a dog had lunged at him and bitten him on the forehead, narrowly missing the optic nerve by some miracle. Still, he had required major surgery. He woke from his five-hour operation with no memory of the attack and his faith in humanity unimpaired. It was Vivek who was scathed. During the time it took the surgeon to operate, Vivek had managed to sack the maid, threaten the neighbour who owned the dog with grievous bodily harm and generally make his presence felt in the expensive private hospital in an extremely unpleasant way. If someone had pulled him aside and asked him why he was acting in this manner, he might have offered several excuses. That Sunil was a late unexpected arrival, after more than a decade of marriage during which he and Parvati had given up all hope of children. That they were unlikely to have others. That he never forgot the sense of amazement that engulfed him when the baby was placed in his arms for the first time and he saw his own genetic legacy in the long prominent nose and the light, almost Caucasian tint of the skin. All this might just plausibly have accounted for the sense of shock he felt when he arrived at the hospital to find SuniPs head swathed in a gigantic bandage that made him look like a mummy and Parvati's blouse caked with dried blood. What he did not say was that, at the exact moment when Sunil had been bitten by the dog, he had been making love with Elin in their shabby hotel room and he could not forgive himself.

Parvati had tried to restrain him during his rampage; he had shaken her off. It was only towards the end of the operation, when the surgeon emerged briefly to reassure them, that he had calmed down and Parvati had said, apropos of nothing, "You've been pulling a lot of all-nighters, Vivek." She had phoned him repeatedly at the hotel; he had turned on the handphone only as he was getting out of bed and then he had rushed off without a word of explanation to Elin.

He could not be absolutely sure of her meaning. A finger of ice seemed to be drawing itself across his gut. He would brazen this out, he thought rapidly, bluster his way through... He was surprised how much he minded Parvati's knowing. If she knew. He liked being in control, and her knowledge would introduce that element of human unpredictability he so hated unless it was something he could turn to his advantage. His headlong affair with Elin had used up whatever reserves of impulsiveness were left in him. And he was suddenly conscious that he reeked of Elin; she was all over him, his hands, his body, his mouth. He'd had no time to shower. He was getting careless, failing to take the basic precautions that any practitioner in betrayal would have taken.

Parvati looked exhausted: wan, red-eyed, hair tousled, quite unlike her usual immaculate self. Exhaustion, he knew, led people to do strange things; in her case, it might even cause her to abandon the reflexive civility with which they had treated each other all their lives, a civility that had its roots in the fact that they were practically strangers when they got married and knew no other way of living with each other. He had not always been kind, but at least he had always striven, with some stumbling, to be civil, and he suspected she was as tired of it as he was. But this was not the time—this was the worst possible time—to start injecting some honesty and transparency into the gilded eggshell of their marriage.

She was saying, "I wish we had never left New York, I wish you didn't have to work so *hard*—" and he looked at her, not quite understanding her words, until the realisation sank in that his thoughts had been horribly, unnecessarily, off-tangent and the moment of nerves that had assailed him passed as he put his arm around her shoulders and felt the weight of her head on his shoulder.

6:15 P.M. His phone rang again; he pressed it to his ear.

"Elin?" It was months since he had spoken her name. Even now a sour taste of desire rose like acid in his mouth.

"*Vivek.*" The lilt of mockery in her voice unmistakeable.

"What is this, some kind of elaborate revenge fantasy?"

"You mean like *Fatal Attraction*? Are you afraid I'm going to start boiling a bunny?"

"Don't be facetious," he said through his teeth. "Is it money that you want?"

"I don't need *money*, Vivek."

"Then what the hell do you want?"

"What do you think?"

"Don't play games with me."

"I was thinking about atonement. Contrition. Retribution. An eye for an eye."

They're not synonyms, he was thinking. As though on cue, she added, "Any one would be nice."

Yes, he could hear it all right. The traffic, the metal scraping of cutlery and, in the background, the throb of the movie trailers. *Keep talking.*

"I was wondering," he said, "why you left so quietly. Knowing you, I kept expecting something. A letterbomb. A bolt from the blue. You were biding your time. Weren't you?"

"Not exactly. I was just trying to survive. What you did, Vivek, it gets *around*. People I hardly knew were asking me whether I had robbed the bank. I got hired and fired by another bank within a month. No explanation except that it had something to do with you."

"I never," he lied, "spoke to any third party about you."

"You're such a lousy liar, Vivek. Your voice has this funny tremor in the middle."

How would she know? He had never lied *to* her before. *About* her, yes. And then he remembered—while he was being questioned by the bank's internal investigation team in a conference room, the doors had swung open. A tea lady had come in bearing refreshments and he had turned in mid-flow to catch a glimpse of Elin standing in the hallway outside. It had taken him some moments to register that it was her, and by then it was too late. She must have heard him.

"And how does it feel? The eye for an eye? Or whatever you choose to call it?"

She didn't answer this directly. "He's a nice child. I can't imagine he's yours."

The traffic in front of him was inching forward again. He did a wild left turn across the paths of two cars and plunged down the short-cut he had been aiming for, the sound of car horns blaring in his wake.

"If you hurt him *at all*—"

She cut him off: "It feels good. It feels fantastic."

"What happened?"

He said briefly, "My son. He was bitten by a dog."

Her eyes widened. "It's not serious?"

"He had an operation." He made a gesture. "He's fine."

She did not press him. They almost never spoke of his family; he never volunteered any information and she never asked any questions, though whether it was tact or a lack of curiosity on her part, he did not know. The fact that she made no demands on him made it even harder to act on the resolve that he'd formed while waiting outside the operating room for Sunil to emerge. He had to end the affair. Sunil's injury changed everything. When he looked at Elin now, he saw the dog leaping for Sunil's forehead. He could not imagine it: the canine teeth crunching the soft skull, the pain, the terror, the blood that had spattered Parvati so liberally. Because he had not been there, it took on a magnified significance in its mind. What had been pleasurably illicit between him and Elin now became an action with consequences. Yet he could not think how to disentangle himself. He could not simply tell her, it's over; he could not get his tongue round the words. She was an addiction, to be stoked and fed. He was in the grip of something far stronger than pure mind, with its feeble attempts at rationality, could hope to grapple with.

It was in this state of mind, some weeks after the attack on Sunil, that he buzzed for her to appear in his sanctum. She knocked.

"Close the door," he said. "Have a seat."

She had her ubiquitous pad with her. She looked at him with the neutral expression that she always assumed towards him in the office. It occurred to him that, as her boss, he could have her make coffee or perform some other demeaning task simply to drive home the power that he wielded. He felt the tiniest lick of cruelty, of the desire to make her suffer as he did.

"I just needed to see you," he said by way of explanation. He had not slept the night before, a series of images crowding his brain irresistibly even as he tried to shut it down. He was with her by the beach. In the sitting room of a house that looked uncannily like his own. Walking with her along a tree-lined road. Not doing anything, not going anywhere, just being with her. He did not know where those images came from because he had never been anywhere with her other than the hard bed in their hotel room.

Her expression changed. He saw the bright anger in her eyes, the glint of her earrings as they caught the light from the quick, impatient turn of her head.

She said, "Don't *ever* do this again."

"I can't meet you next week. I'm going up to Malaysia with some friends."

"What friends?"

She said vaguely, "Friends. We're going scuba-diving."

Swimming among the sharks, she'd added for his benefit, but he did not laugh as he was meant to. It was the first time she'd given any hint of a life apart from him. *It's over,* he thought, but the words echoed emptily back at him.

For the first time in weeks, he spent Friday evening at home, dribbling a child's football with Sunil in the garden of his rented bungalow. Night fell with its usual guillotine swiftness. Still they played on, while Parvati called from the patio for them to come in to dinner. Sunil had recovered faster than expected from the operation; the wound had stayed free of infection and the big swaddling bandage was gone, replaced by a piratical pad over one eye. He was delighted to have his father to himself for the night. Each "goal" scored (a kick into the battered hedge by the driveway) saw small arms upraised in glee, followed by a squeal of triumph. Then, heartstoppingly, he tripped and fell and lay unmoving facedown in the grass. Sprinting over, Vivek swept him up, with hands gone suddenly cold: how slight, how breakable, the body of a five year old seemed. "Did you get a fright, Daddy?" He looked down into the innocently mischievous face and, instead of the scolding he'd meant to deliver, hugged the boy tight. Sunil protested, wriggling out of his father's arms like the escape artist that small children become when smothered by unwanted affection. How could he have known what Vivek was thinking—that he could have Elin or Sunil but not both and that this was a conundrum that never got any better or more solvable the more he thought about it.

After dinner, he put Sunil to bed, reading him one story after another with growing desperation until Sunil's eyes, against all odds, finally began to close. He made some excuse about having to pop down to the office and got into the car.

He drove to Elin's home; it was in one of the identikit public housing estates and he went round in increasingly confused circles, cursing the bad signage and the dark, until by pure good luck he turned into the correct carpark. He recognised her car at once, the small white tincan known as a Vicki. He had not quite known what had brought him here so late, or what he had expected to find, until he saw the car sitting in its slot. He had not really believed her story about going on a trip with friends; she was the lone, backpacking type, who would have found a group intolerable. In her bald statement about going scuba-diving, he must have sensed the shadowy figure of some other man. Another boyfriend, perhaps even her estranged husband. Had he wanted to, he could have gone up to her flat and rung her doorbell and verified what he had come all this way to verify, but he did not. Sitting there watching her car; he felt the tiniest stirrings of a release, the very slight loosening of a bolt. He understood that his obsession with her was slowly unhinging him; the obsession was far from over but for the first time he began to glimpse the possibility of its ending.

The treasury division was on course for its best year ever, "buoyed by the volatility of the markets and the best team of traders assembled outside of the major financial markets in the West" (the official line he fed the board at its quarterly meetings). The bonus pool promised to be obscenely large. Then Vinnie Matheson resigned for personal reasons.

Vinnie ran the equity desk, a hatchet-faced beanpole from the North of England whose uncanny resemblance to a Mafia hitman hid a great tenderness of soul. It was Vinnie who participated in every charity drive organised by the bank and kept a series of interchangeable hamsters under his desk, feeding them lettuce leaves surreptitiously throughout the day. Vinnie was Elin's boss. Vinnie had lounged, arms folded, against the door of Vivek's office, as was his wont, explaining that he had been working for twenty-four years without a break, twenty-four years of shite, excuse the language, Vivek, but he'd had enough and wanted to smell the roses for a change. Vivek had listened with his feet up on the desk as was *his* wont and watched the lines of fatigue deepen like rutted roads in Vinnie's forehead. The man did not appear to have slept in days. Before Vinnie was quite out the door that same day, toting his single box of personal effects and his hamsters enroute to catching a connecting flight to Ibiza, Vivek had called up a list of all the transactions recently done by the equity desk.

He stayed past midnight, running and re-running the numbers. The next morning, he was back before seven, timing his arrival with Elin's whose movements he knew by heart. "I need to see you," he said without preamble. She was just back from her "holiday"; he noted clinically she was a good deal more tanned, but that was evidence of nothing in particular. His tone made clear this was business. In his office, he showed her the unsustainable position in a certain stock that Vinnie had been building up over the last few weeks and which Vinnie had managed to conceal from settlements, operations, risk and Vivek himself.

"Do you know anything about this?"

"Should I?"

"You were his star pupil, his pet. He must have mentioned something." She said evenly: "No, he did not."

"Sorry," he said, but he wasn't. "I had to ask."

Her expression didn't soften. One part of him was thinking that he had not seen her in days and all he wanted at that moment was to be alone with her in that hotel room he'd come to think of as his own; the other part was thinking that if she was lying to him he would not hesitate to flay her. He closed his eyes briefly; he was bone-tired.

Then she said, with a misguided attempt at levity, "Well, it's not quite Barings," and he opened his eyes again. Had it been anyone else, he would have slapped her down. True, the downfall of the bank was hardly imminent, but the sums involved were large, way too large for any sort of calm, measured explanation. The sums involved almost certainly required the rolling of heads and he did not intend his own to be among them. He could not get over the fact that Vinnie—sweet, hamster-loving Vinnie—had perpetrated this right under Vivek's nose, making him look like a colossal fool. In Vivek's scale of things, that was quite possibly worse than the collapse of any bank.

What was it he had said? "We have to manage this position. Fast." The markets were opening in fifteen minutes.

She had nodded; how collected and contained she'd seemed to him, how he'd loved her at that moment, with a sudden fierce intensity that took him still by surprise. "Do you want me to do it?"

How could he have seen how it would all play out? "Do what you have to."

She'd gathered the pile of papers to her and stacked them up. "And tonight?" He always wondered where she got that forthrightness from, that ability to look him without embarrassment in the eye. Perhaps it was because she was not the hypocrite that he was. Perhaps it was as simple as that.

He said, without looking at her, "Same time."

She sold down the position and they made love for the last time that night.

He had saved the bank's bottomline but it did not prevent the charade that was to follow.

"I'll be frank with you, Viv, this does *not* look good." Seven-thirty in the morning in Eduardo's office, a room even more vast and palatial than Vivek's, with CNN and a Bloomberg screen humming away in a low, soothing murmur in the background. Like Vivek, Eduardo worked inhuman hours and had done so all his life; yet, at sixty, he still looked impossibly youthful and puckish. Vivek, more than twenty years younger, had been startled by his reflection in the mirror that morning. Middle age was advancing on him as surely as the lines of crow's feet fanning out from the corner of his eye.

Eduardo had received a call from the regulators at home. Something about wild gyrations, wild rumours, in the market the day before. The source of the disruption had been traced back to big sell orders placed by the bank. Unpleasant questions were now being slung. Had someone attempted to manipulate the market? What exactly the hell was going on?

Vivek explained briefly, crisply. There had been a lapse, a failure of controls. He'd identified the problem and it wasn't going to happen again. He'd done what he thought was necessary to minimise losses. One of his staff had been instructed to sell down the position. He had explained all this in a long email to Eduardo and all relevant parties the day before. The employee in question would never have done what the regulators were hinting at. There had to be some mistake.

"Viv, you know and I know this is horseshit but we have no choice. We have go through the motions." The habitual ironical emphasis was gone; the tonelessness, as Vivek well knew, signified finality, deadly seriousness. He could expect no charity from this particular quarter; Ed's reputation for the swift kill if a person became a liability was legendary. The fact that he and Vivek had more than ten years of history between them back in New York would mean nothing. They both understood this.

He said to Elin: "We shouldn't see each other until this is over."

She was silent for so long he thought the line had been disconnected. Then he heard the one word. "Yes."

Do what you have to.

The games began. An internal investigation team was empanelled. Four men, one women, all from the top echelons of management and sworn to secrecy, all idiots as far as Vivek was concerned. He felt demeaned, slimed, sitting in front of them and answering their questions. The proceedings dragged on for a month in fits and starts. Elin gave her testimony with icy precision. She had used several brokers to sell down the position. They had been told to get the best possible price in the circumstances, given the size of the order. The tape recordings of the conversations were retrieved and analysed. Their quality was bad; the trading floor had been particularly rowdy that day and only snatches could be deciphered. Three words in particular became the subject of intense, furious debate. "Ramp it up," Elin could be heard rapping out at various intervals.

"What did you mean by that?"

"Just that he was to speed it up. He was slow."

"Were you asking him to try and move the market to get a better price?"

"I was not."

"Were you aware of rumours about a possible takeover of the company?"

"Not at all."

"The regulators suggest someone in the bank started those rumours. Do you know anything about this?"

"I don't."

As one of the most senior people in the bank, Vivek was privy to her testimony but she was not privy to his. It might have been a minor breach of protocol but what use otherwise were the privileges of rank? He could imagine her steadfast, unemotional denials. *I have a really slow heartbeat*, she'd told him once: at moments of pressure, the world seemed to slow down and fragment into discrete units of time. Was character fundamentally a physiological matter? These were the irrelevant, absurd thoughts that kept flitting into his mind while he was supposed to be answering the panel's questions.

Parvati asked, "Who is this Elin?"

He said tersely, "One of Vinnie's traders." His tone was steady; his eyes did not blink.

He'd felt compelled to tell her a little of what was happening, to cushion the shock in case the tumbrils came for him. He picked what he chose to be the best time: Saturday night, after dinner at another of her culinary discoveries, an Italian restaurant in the Glub Street area. Past midnight, she kicked off her high heels and sank deep into the patio sofa and he'd sat down and told her what he had to.

"But I don't *understand* what it is that you're supposed to have done." She'd twisted round on the sofa and was holding him by the forearms, with a surprisingly strong grip. Just so, he guessed, she would hold him on his deathbed, to prevent him ebbing away. She had always been loyal to him, with a fealty he had never quite understood and had taken for granted but which he now saw, with belated clarity, was what kept him afloat. How quiet, he thought abstractedly, the neighbourhood was; only if he strained his ears could he hear the low metronomic buzz of insects in the garden. The still-sharp tang of the grass that had been cut just that evening lingered in the air. In the garden, the dusty yellow glow shed by the street lamps pooled with the pale silver from the sliver of moon that hung in the night sky with the unreality of a paper cut-out pasted on velvet. It was not his country, his house was rented and in the morning he knew he would notice again that the garden was not properly weeded and that the roof tiles needed replacing. But there was something in his wife's grip on his arms, in the night scene before him, that staunched the habitual reflexive cynicism.

Gently, he disentangled her hands and held them in his. "I shouldn't worry," he said, "everyone will make the appropriate noises and it'll all blow over."

6:35 P.M. The fierce heat of the afternoon was gone; a fine gauze of cirrus clouds hid the sun. A wind was picking up, rustling the tops of the dusty trees in Angullia carpark. Luck favoured him for the first time that afternoon. He shot into a slot that another driver had been patiently waiting to enter and strode off to the sound of the man's imprecations. A right turn and then he was on the broad walkway of the country's main shopping artery. A booth hawking cellular phones had been set up in front of one of the buildings; a simpering celebrity was giving away prizes and a crowd had gathered, forcing the rest of the heedless throngs clacking along the pavement into a wide oxbow bend. He plunged into the open-air courtyard of one of the fast food joints that lined the walkway. A sea of heads glanced up at his whirlwind entrance. He saw indifference, fleeting curiosity, etched into the faces around him; faces that, in his heightened state, seemed like the distended, ugly caricatures one saw in a hall of funny mirrors. He tried the next cafe. A waiter accosted him. "Did you see a boy—an Indian boy—with a Chinese lady?" The waiter—hideous dyed-blonde hair, a crescent of acne across his nose—shook his head. In his eyes, level with Vivek's shoulders, Vivek saw a faint spark of alarm as Vivek—too tall, too loud—towered over him. For the first time he realised the absurdity of his quest. He had come here on a wild hunch and now the possibilities multiplied around him like a host of viruses. They could be anywhere.

6:45 P.M. His phone rang.

"You've had your fun. Give me back my son."

"Not just yet."

"He's only a child." His voice rose, broke; he despised himself for it.

"Well, I'm sorry, but I didn't know how else to get through to you."

"Atonement," he said; he could not keep the heavy sarcasm out of his voice. "Contrition. What's the rest of the mantra? Retribution? An eye for an *eye*?"

"So you *were* listening."

"Come off your high horse. You had an affair with a married man. Or are you forgetting?"

She said, her voice so low that he could barely hear, "I haven't forgotten." *I have no excuse,* she had said. She had taken his infidelity on its own terms: that he was old enough to decide for himself and she would not waste time debating fine moral distinctions with him.

"So whatever it is I'm supposed to have done, you've equalled it in the turpitude stakes."

"What did you tell them that morning, Vivek? They said you'd made some statements."

"I told them nothing."

"You can't do this to people, Vivek. You can't stamp all over them and think that *you can get on with your life*—" (When, he wondered, had she turned whiney and self-pitying? What he'd always liked about her was her tough, unsentimental streak.)

It was so exactly what he thought that he stopped listening to her and strained to hear the background to her voice, but there was too much noise around. He looked round for a quiet corner. A bunch of teenagers walking past jostled him with the breezy insufferable insouciance of youth, causing him to drop his phone. When he picked it up, the line was disconnected. Damn.

Do what you have to.

"It's getting ugly, Viv," Ed had said to him. "You've got to watch your back." The ironical inflexion had still not returned. Vivek nodded. Ed would do no more; could not be seen to do more.

His last meeting with the panel of five dwarfs. "What did you mean by 'do what you have to'?"

Was he supposed to tell the truth? An idea so risible he almost found himself smiling. What he had *meant*, of course, was that Elin was to do whatever was necessary to sell down the position, including breaking the law provided she could get away with it and he didn't have to know about it. Someone like Vinnie, for example, who never needed to be told where his limits were because they were gloriously elastic, would have read the sub-text perfectly and executed the instruction like a trooper. (But then it was Vinnie, with those elastic principles of his, who'd caused this problem in the first place.) Vivek's mistake, he saw now, was to have entrusted the job to someone as relatively inexperienced as Elin; he'd been misled by that cool, competent, façade of hers.

What he *said* was that Elin was supposed to have done all that she could, within the framework of the law and all applicable regulations, to get rid of the stock. All his dealers knew they had to be as pure as the driven snow when it came to regulatory compliance and ethical standards. Purer. They knew he was merciless in dealing with rule-breakers. His disclaimers were emphatic, punchy, to the point. Exactly the way he'd been taught during the media relations course his former investment bank had forced him to sit through.

"Did she misunderstand you?"

"I'm not sure what you mean."

"Come on, Vivek. Did she think you were asking her to push the envelope. Take chances. And, if so, why would she think that? Maybe she thought you were prepared to cover for her. You know what we mean."

Vivek looked into the face of the speaker, one of the relics from the previous regime that had run this place like the civil service. Jobs for life, don't rock the boat, risk is a dirty word, we're happy with our return on equity of eight point nine percent per year. He had been the most craven of the old bunch, clinging on to his job like a wrecked mariner to his plank of wood while the others had drowned one by one. He loathed Vivek. Vivek didn't reciprocate the loathing (to have done so would have been to accord the man a greater consideration than he deserved); he simply despised him.

He saw he was missing something, had been missing something all along. The tone of the discourse had changed. Someone, somewhere, had decided that there had been an infraction. In the words of the thriller writers that Vivek sometimes read on transcontinental flights, his long legs cramping slowly in front of him, she was dead meat unless he tried to rescue her. He had seconds to adjust to the situation. His expression did not change.

"I would say what I have already said. That I do not countenance and have never countenanced any kind of irregular behaviour by my staff. You know that and I know that. Vinnie Matheson was an aberration. But I would point out that his appointment was vetted by not less than eight people in the bank. Including yourself."

His interrogator shifted in his seat while a nervous ripple of laughter went round the room. He let out the breath he hadn't even been aware of holding.

They had just one more question for him. Elin's record was excellent. What she'd done seemed out of character. And character was the issue here. It was understandable that Vivek, as her ultimate boss, would feel bound to defend her. But they wanted his honest opinion. Did he think Elin capable of what she was accused of?

Capable, he thought, what did that mean? Everyone was capable of anything, given the right circumstances. He was even capable, himself, of decency when the stars were aligned in their firmament and the sun suffered an eclipse. It was a stupid question. He saw again the garden at night with its dusting of pale moonlight, felt Parvati's grip on his arms drawing him back into the charmed circle he had left so heedlessly. He had been here before. He could save himself, but not Elin; the raft wouldn't accommodate both of them. The instinct for self-preservation was kicking in with a speed, a force, that was like an adrenaline rush, pure mind working overtime to contain the damage and divert the effluent away from himself.

"Yes," he said, "yes? Of course she's capable of this. That's why she and Vinnie worked so well together. Look, when is this going to be over?"

She was escorted off the premises that very afternoon, flanked by twin security guards and carrying only her bag. They were going to send her things along later. She walked across a trading floor grown disquietingly quiet, the silence broken only by the shrilling of the phones. From his office, Vivek watched her go. He was not the one who'd had to break the news to her; it was Vinnie's replacement, a Taiwanese with the creased face of a crushed paper bag, who'd been handed the unpleasant task. Vivek could have stopped the security escort, which he felt to be excessive, but he did not. Pure mind was back in control, and pure mind was telling him, with the cold clarity he'd once taken for granted but which he'd misplaced during the past few months, that it was best not to interfere. He had tried so hard to tell her it was over and now it was. Still, he had to stifle the impulse to crash out of his office and take her by the arm. Plead with her to leg it to the airport with him and book the first ticket at hand, perhaps to South America. He had never been there and it had always seemed to him redolent of a kind of cheesy romance. Even the names themselves had an impossibly concocted ring. Ecuador. Patagonia. Curacao. A city named after a drink, or was it the other way round? She never once looked in his direction. He would never know.

7:00 P.M. He saw her and Sunil. Or rather, saw the back of her head, the swing of the ponytail as she brushed a crumb off her shoulder, the flash of diamonds in her ears. ("I only wear diamonds," she'd told him once. What was it he had said? "Bully for you if you can afford them." She'd said, teasingly, "Who says I have to buy them myself?"). She was talking into a handphone. The child was crying, loud wails piercing the wall of noise around them. The sign over the entrance read Café Montmarte. Vivek plunged in, knocking past waiters and diners. He placed a hand on Elin's shoulder, turning her roughly round.

It was not her. It was only someone who looked like her from afar; he was beginning, frighteningly, to forget what she looked like. And the child was not Sunil; he was not even fully Indian, one of those mixed-race half-Indian kids that he saw increasingly in the country. The mothers were always Chinese. Why was that the case? And he wondered, fleetingly, what his child and Elin's would have looked like.

The woman had risen from her chair. She was getting ready to call for help. And now he saw she looked nothing like Elin at all; she was taller, heavier, with a square, determined jaw. He threw up his hands in apology and began backing away.

"I'm sorry," he said, "I thought you were someone else—"

His handphone rang again. He snatched at it and dashed through the blockade of waiters that had begun to surround him, his legs carrying him rapidly past them and out to the pavement, where he was quickly swallowed up in the crowds.

"Yes? Yes?" He should've remembered to charge the phone battery that morning. Either that, or he needed to get a new phone.

"Vivek." It was Parvati, and in her voice he heard the telltale note of panic. Parvati, with her infinite calm, her maddening serenity, never got excited, passionate, heated. Certainly not panicky. He knew, even before she spoke again, what she was going to tell him. "I got a call from the police. They have Sunil. They said a woman dropped him off. He's all right, but he's crying a little. I thought you said the two of you were having ice-cream—I don't understand—Vivek, what's going on? Are you there?"

He was, but he did not answer. Light had leached out of the sky; it was not yet dark but soon would be. Soon, the fairy lights, as Sunil called them, would come on one by one in the buildings around him. A necklace of lights girdling the island, winking diamond studs visible from ten thousand feet. Just so had he seen the island for the first time that night two years ago as the plane banked and got ready for its descent. He looked up involuntarily at the sky but all he saw was a Planet Hollywood helium balloon making its stately ascent into the atmosphere. He wondered when it would burst.

Story told in two levels of time—
Fast & exciting
Slow

Personal — Business

Judged by outside bosses, p 315

find scapegoats

Back to colonialism) 302

In Memoriam

The British High Commission
Thailand

By fax

Dear Ms Tan

I understand you have spoken to Mr Alan Johnson at our Bangkok office. I am writing to notify you officially that the body of your brother-in-law, Mr Scott Ransome, was discovered in Room 217 of the Pattaya Golden Hotel last Tuesday, the 26th of May. The Thai police were alerted and an autopsy will be performed shortly to discover the cause of death. There is no suggestion of foul play.

Apparently Mr Ransome had been dead for several days before he was found, as the body was in an advanced state of decomposition. I say this not to cause you any further distress but because I have been informed by the undertaker that, under the circumstances, it may be disturbing for Mr Ransome's next of kin to view his remains. I understand from Mr Johnson that Mr Ransome left a wife and three children in Singapore. If they intend to fly to Thailand for the funeral, a closed coffin affair would probably be best.

Alternatively, we can also make the necessary arrangements to cremate the body and courier the ashes back to Mrs Ransome.

I should be grateful if you could let me have your instructions as soon as possible. I would also need to know your intentions regarding Mr Ransome's personal effects...

The High Commission has also written to the Lockwood Shipping Company, Mr Ransome's employer, to inform them about his death...

Please accept our condolences in the matter...

....

Schedule of Scott Ransome's personal effects

British passport
One thousand Thai baht
Fifty Singapore dollars
Wallet containing Singapore work permit and Visa credit card
Letter from Lockwood Shipping Company regarding shore leave
One Samsonite suitcase containing three shirts, three pairs of trousers

....

The British High Commission
Thailand

By fax

Dear Ms Tan

We have received your instructions regarding the cremation of Mr Scott Ransome's body. This can only be done after the coroner's office releases the body, which is expected to be within the next few days. I am informed that the cost of cremation and of flying the ashes back to Singapore will be

We don't have them

approximately____baht. I should be grateful if you could
arrange to wire this amount to the British High Commission
in Thailand as soon as possible.

The official autopsy report has not been released yet but it
appears that Mr Ransome, although only thirty-seven, died
of catastrophic liver failure.

Strange, the Reverend Stephen Mullins thought, what a life can be reduced to. Personal effects in an impersonal hotel room. A practical problem as to the disposal of one's remains. Ashes in an urn. And yet, even through the dry officialese of Her Majesty's servant in Bangkok, it was possible to glimpse the shadowy departed figure of Scott Ransome. Not the individual, but the prototype to which he belonged. Ransome was a merchant seaman after all. Not academically-inclined, probably none too bright, but sturdy and with a strong practical bent. One of those restless young men the British Isles had always produced, who set out in search of adventure and never returned. A hundred years ago he would have been striding forth in a pith helmet under a colonial sun, his restlessness dignified in the name of Empire. Now they were called expatriates, staggering from one alcoholic watering spot to another around the world, a world which paradoxically looked more and more the same the more they travelled.

"Reverend Mullins?"

His reflections interrupted, he looked up from the two letters he held in his hand into the face of Ms Tan seated across the desk from him. Tan Shu Meng. Senior Vice President of Corporate Planning at the country's largest shipping line. She had made an appointment to see him that morning, in his capacity as the resident chaplain of the Mission to Seafarers in Singapore. From her rather low, husky voice over the phone, he'd formed the impression of an older, heavier woman, not the professionally elegant woman in her early forties who sat before him in a well-cut pearl-grey suit and well-trimmed bob.

Handing the letters back to her, he said, not for the first time, "Please, call me Stephen."

She ignored this. She was, he could see, a stickler for protocol. Her slightly broad face was strong rather than pretty, the make-up a touch heavy, possibly to hide teenage acne scars just visible beneath the powder. Good figure, though. He imagined that she worked out. No wedding ring, though that might not mean anything these days. Her gaze was disconcertingly direct, holding his eyes without a trace of vulnerability or embarrassment, even as she'd handed him the two letters to read. And he wondered now why she had done so, because she did not seem particularly confiding or upset, and he would have imagined, looking at her, that face mattered to her. Her English was almost accentless, without the local nasal intonation that he sometimes found hard to follow.

"As I was saying," she said, with a touch of reproach at his inattention, "we wanted a memorial service for Scott because there was no funeral. That's something my mother can't get over. And it's hard for the children—my sister's children—to understand their father's gone if there's no funeral. They keep asking about him."

"Yes, it's always hardest for the children, isn't it?" He had learnt, in such situations, to stick to well-tried, innocuous statements.

She said, surprising him, "That's what everybody says, but I don't think it's true. Children forget and adapt faster than we think. It's the adults who brood and don't let go. But then—" and here he saw the glimmer of a smile; she'd been resolutely poker-faced so far—"I could be wrong. I don't have children of my own."

"How is Mrs Ransome coping?"

"Mrs—?" For a moment, she seemed at a loss. "Oh. My sister." He heard again that ambiguous tone which she'd used earlier in relation to her sister. "She's upset. Naturally. That's why she couldn't come today." She was doing it again, he noticed; explaining things unnecessarily, revealing more than she had to.

"Will she be able to manage financially? Was Mr Ransome the sole breadwinner?"

"Yes, yes, he was. It's a worry ..." her voice trailed off. "He had an insurance policy that he took out a year ago. I made him do it. But you know you can't claim on it if—"

He completed the sentence for her; it was instinctive: "—he committed suicide."

She flashed back, "The autopsy report was inconclusive." She'd obviously found his response wanting; her glance was now very distinctly a glare.

"I'm sorry." He felt some sort of explanation was due: "I used to be a policeman. I'm afraid the training is harder to get rid of than I thought it would be." The observant—too—clinically observant—eye; the ability to file away trivial details about a suspect that would come in useful later; the tendency to treat people as guilty until proven innocent.

She asked, genuinely curious now, "You were a policeman? How did you become a priest?"

He corrected her, "I'm not a priest in the Catholic sense," but saw that these nuances were lost on her. He added, smilingly, so as not to appear rude, "It's a long story." Uncapping his pen, he went into professional mode. "Right. A memorial service. Just some details, if you could. Was Mr Ransome an Anglican?"

"I don't know. I never saw him go to church. I think," and he heard the dryness in her tone, "the pub was his church. But he was married in one."

"That's fine. I have to ask, that's all." And he felt again that prick of loneliness, of being the last defender of an obsolete faith in a foreign land. In the pecking order of fashionable religions and denominations, the Church of England was right at the bottom. He was used to it; it was, ironically, what had attracted him. The hard, solitary grind. The mining of a difficult lode. But when he passed the packed congregations of the Pentecostalist churches that had sprung up like wildfire in this region, it was hard not to feel a pang. "What about Mr Ransome's family—will they be flying out for the service?"

She shook her head. "Mr Ransome's mother is too ill to fly and his father can't leave her."

"I'm sorry to hear that."

"So are we." She glanced at her watch. "I have a meeting soon. What other details do you need? My sister's name? Jonquil Ransome nee Tan Shu Lin. The children—Belinda Ransome, aged five, Brenda Ransome, aged three, Mary Ransome, aged one. Scott's parents? Mr and Mrs Peter Ransome."

She reeled off the facts with the precision with which she must have conducted her meetings and he thought in some amusement that he would not want to cross her. His pen scratched rapidly.

"Jonquil. That's an unusual name."

"She *calls* herself Jonquil." There was a waspishness in her voice she couldn't entirely disguise. She is angry at her sister, Stephen thought. Curiosity stirred in him. "My mother didn't give either of us English names. She's a Taoist. I'm a freethinker and so's my sister, although she got married in church." All this was said with a touch of aggressiveness, as though he'd tried to convert her. "But it's the fashion to use English names. If you've noticed." He said, mildly, as though her little outburst had never occurred, "Very well, then—next Wednesday, three P.M.

How many people are you expecting? Our premises, as you saw, are not large."

"My mother, myself, my sister and my nieces. My sister"—again, he heard that quick, angry inflection—"might invite some of Scott's friends. If you can call them friends. I don't think there'll be many of them."

"No particular preferences as to hymns? Or readings?"

She surprised him by saying, "There was that song Jerusalem, wasn't there, in the film *Chariots of Fire*?" (A film he couldn't stand for its sepia-tinted view of England.)

"I liked that."

She stood and he stood as well, feeling for a moment as though he were the one being dismissed. He wasn't quick enough getting out from behind his desk and it was she who preceded him through the door of his office and into the hallway of the Mission to Seafarers, with its colonial high timbered ceiling, and faded lithographs of ships dating back to the Cutty Sark (pride of place among the lithographs went to a stained-purplish photograph of Princess Anne visiting the Mission back in 1974 and wearing a white hat—or what had once been a white hat—with feathers). He saw Ms Tan look round again and register the worn armchairs, the chipped coffee table and the unpainted staircase banisters with that faintly incredulous look that all Singaporeans, with their mania for newness, brought to bear on objects that were not in mint condition. He had not mentioned financial terms, but he felt certain that a donation—a generous one—could be expected from her.

They shook hands at the front door. The roar of the rushhour traffic outside engulfed them like a wave; he raised his voice to make himself heard. Once, this had been a sleepy road with a backpackers' hotel round the corner; many mornings he'd thrown open the doors to find a group of young people lounging on the steps, expecting to be given coffee or tea as a matter of course, and he'd been happy to oblige. Now the hotel was gone and the young people too. He knew he wasn't supposed to complain about 'progress'. He was a guest in this country, a white man in a place where, for all the lip service paid to the skills of 'foreign talent', resentment of the colonial past could flare up in sudden, unexpected quarters.

He said, "If your sister would like to call me—any time, any time at all."

She said, with a sudden fierceness that he couldn't account for, "I'm doing this for Scott, you know. Poor man. He didn't have a chance."

He watched her trip across the road in her high, murderous heels until a bus blocked his view of her and then he retreated into the safety of the Mission.

He rang an acquaintance that he knew at the British High Commission.

"Smithy."

"Well, if it isn't the Reverend Mullins." That insistence on using his job title again, though the inflection this time was ironic, the irony a defensive mechanism against—God forbid—taking religion seriously. "What can I do for you?"

"I've been asked to hold a memorial service for an Englishman who worked for the Lockwood Shipping Company. Said Englishman was found dead in a hotel room in Pattaya in a bad state of decomposition. Left a wife and kids in Singapore. Know anything?"

"Always pithy, always to the point, aren't you, Stephen? As a matter of fact, I do. Colleague of mine met the grieving widow. If you can call her that. Very calm, very beautiful, didn't turn a hair. Apparently, she wanted to know if her husband was really dead, because no-one had made a positive identification of the body. The Thai police just assumed it was—what was his name?"

"Scott Ransome."

"—because of the circumstances in which his body was found. Grieving widow says, I need to know this before I can claim on the insurance. Then, realising that this might sound just a *mite* heartless, she puts on her sunglasses and her lower lip trembles on cue."

Stephen said, drily, "Grief takes people in different ways."

"Yes, and I'm an old cynic. That's what this job does to you."

"Did she have a sister with her?"

"How did you know? The kind of female that can easily run an army and put the fear of God into every man?"

"You take the words out of my mouth."

"Sister did all the talking. Made the arrangements. Even suggested that Mrs Ransome might like to ship some of the ashes to Mr and Mrs Ransome senior back in old Blighty. But grieving widow shoots sister such a look of murderous contempt that sister drops the idea at once."

"Your colleague seems to have been totally indiscreet."

"He's a happily married man with two children but he says that if the grieving widow had given him even the tiniest encouragement—"

"Did anyone ask what the husband was doing in a hotel room in Pattaya?"

"The subject never came up." A slight pause. "Anything ... untoward? That I should be mentioning to the police? Here or in Thailand?"

"Not at all. Just an ex-policeman who can't help asking too many questions."

Another pause. "Haven't seen you for some time, old man. You must come round. My wife will be glad to see you." Stephen had difficulty recalling Smithy's wife: he had the impression of a faded woman in a floral print dress and a shapeless haircut with grey bangs. Smithy was an ex-army officer. Stephen had met him at a garden party at the British High Commission and the two had hit it off, cautiously. As Smithy said, it was the short back and sides sported by both men that did it. *You don't look like a clergyman, I must say*, had been Smithy's first encouraging observation.

"Thanks. I'm up to my ears." This was said mechanically; he wasn't up to his ears, far from it. He had been used to fourteen hour days as a policeman and then at his first posting in a parish in south London; this job was a sinecure by comparison, though he knew it was wrong to think of it in those terms. *The point is, you're serving God*, his bishop back in England had said to him, and he had agreed, doubtfully.

"How long have you been out here, Stephen? A year?"

"Fourteen months."

"Any home leave coming up?"

"I turned it down." There was nothing for him in England. His parents had died long ago; he had one sister, but she was very married and houseproud and though he was fond of her he found her very domesticity stifling. They had little in common. He had an ex-wife, whom he had not seen in years and whose features were beginning to dim in his memory. The friends he had from the police force—used to have—belonged to another life. Once they had learnt of his new vocation, they had begun treating him with a peculiar stiffness, born of the sudden belief that they had to mind their p's and q's around him, and so he had mostly avoided them, to spare them (or himself?) the embarrassment.

He could sense tiny tendrils of concern beginning to unfurl across the telephone connection. This was hugely ironic—he the clergyman supposed to dispense succour, Smithy the agnostic bracing himself to buoy Stephen up. "I won't keep you, Smithy. Many thanks for your time." And he hung up before Smithy could invite him formally to dinner.

There was a pool of regulars at the Mission: English, South African, Australian and the odd Canadian or United States citizen who plied the South-east Asian-routes and never failed to pay a visit when they got shore leave. Stephen did not recall meeting a Scott Ransome. That night, as he watched a game of snooker being played in the converted games room on the second floor of the Mission, he asked one of the players if he'd ever heard of Ransome.

"Scott? Scotty? 'Course I know him. He's gone native, Scott has. Married a local girl. Lives with the mother-in-law in some place I can't pronounce. *Ang Mo Kow*—"

Stephen said, though his own pronunciation was not much better, "Ang Mo Kio."

"Yeah, that's it. Painted the mother-in-law's flat too, he told me. Old lady was terribly chuffed."

"Did he ever come here?"

"Only once. It was the night the tree knocked down the gate. *You* remember."

And now Stephen did remember. Last year's Boxing Day, the night of the memorable storm. A combination of the North-East monsoon and a low-pressure system causing the rain to fall for two straight days without a break, while winds gusted up to thirty-five miles an hour. (You remembered these things in the balmy weather of the tropics. It was the lack of seasons and the consequent difficulty of tracking the passage of time that he'd found hardest to adjust to.) He'd just finished bolting down everything that could be bolted down when the most enormous crash sounded. The few men in the Mission that night dashed out into the driving rain to find that the giant angsana tree that used to stand just outside the Mission had fallen in the tiny garden, wrecking the gate in the process. "Leave it," he'd shouted to the men, "I'll call the contractor in the morning." But one man, rather drunk, had insisted on trying to shift the tree from the pathway. Nobody, he explained, could get in or out, though they tried to persuade him they had no problem climbing over the trunk. He would not be dissuaded; he applied his big, red hands to the trunk and heaved and heaved, making no impression. There had been something comic in his futile endeavour; that, and the rain plastering his straw-yellow hair to his head and dripping off the edge of his nose. The men could not help laughing, until it passed the point of being comic and became merely the obsessive, pathetic behaviour of a drunk and two men plunged into the rain and yanked him back forcibly. Soaked through, shedding water like some newly-emerged creature from the deep in the hallway of the Mission, he'd towelled himself off and apologised to Stephen: "Got a bit carried away." There had been nothing remarkable about him: a big man, about five feet ten, mid-thirties, large, pale, slightly protruding eyes, skin ravaged by teenage acne and still cratered, at his age, like the surface of the moon. A front tooth in his lower jaw was missing; it gave him the lopsided grin of a child. And it was a child that he'd reminded Stephen of, a big, overgrown, unhappy one.

'Why did he come that particular night?"

'Had a quarrel with the wife. Said he needed some air."

"Do you know the wife?"

The man winked. "Who doesn't?"

The man was a ship's engineer, with red, bristly hair and the aspect of a friendly fox. His name was Jones; at least, that was how he introduced himself. He seemed to have no first name that anyone had heard of. He was prepared to be loquacious but Stephen was suddenly disinclined to discuss Ransome further. "Scott died in a hotel room in Pattaya," he said briskly. "Three days ago. His family's arranging a memorial service next Wednesday. You might like to attend."

The man's jaw fell open. "Died? Oh Christ—sorry, Stephen. Poor bastard."

To escape the man, Stephen made an excuse about having some letters to write and made his way downstairs to his office again.

He wanted to look for the speech that he always used at memorial services. He used "speech" for want of a better word: sermon sounded too pompous. It was not a speech he had to make too often; at most, two or three times a year, and he needed to refresh his memory. There was no reason to look for it now—Wednesday was a week away—but he liked to be prepared. (The religious life was, after a time, a job like any other, one that you had to organise with a certain amount of efficiency if you wanted to get anything done.) That, and the thought of Scott Ransome lying in a pool of his own vomit and bile in a hotel room in Pattaya, undiscovered for days. Twenty years as a policeman had taught him that people generally do not die in hotel rooms in squalid circumstances unless they intend to do so or unless they are on an inexorable downward course that ends in such a death.

He was reaching up to retrieve a file from behind the filing cabinet when he felt the old, familiar stabbing pain in his chest again. *Oh Christ—sorry.* His hand groped, blindly, for his chair and he fell into it with a gasp. There were whole days when he could almost forget the fact that he'd been beaten half to death at his first parish in south London—one femur shattered, one lung ruptured—by a group of boys who had been part of his youth group, until something as simple as taking a deep breath or raising his arm could bring it all back: the teenage cries of *get him*, the smooth possessed faces of the boys milling round him, the black iron rod silhouetted like a snake against the glow cast by the study lamp on the ceiling before it came crashing down on his chest. Before they struck him, he'd almost succeeded in fighting them off, and he took some unChristian satisfaction in the fact that he'd broken several of the little buggers' ribs.

It had transpired that, in his former incarnation as a murder detective, he had locked up one of the boys' brothers for manslaughter and the boy had simply been exacting revenge. The episode had taught him a useful lesson about hubris. He had thought he was making progress with the youth of the parish (deprived, sullen, frankly sociopathic). He'd avoided wearing the dog collar; he'd asked them to call him Stephen; he'd talked to them about pop music and their hopes and fears. Now, at least, he could look back on that time with a kind of grim amusement, even though it had cost him the rude physical health he had always taken for granted. There had been no question of his going back to his parish: too strenuous, the doctors said, overriding his objections. And so he'd accepted the posting to the Mission to Seafarers instead.

He no longer expected to work miracles. The kind of muscular Christianity he'd envisaged when he'd entered his new life had given way to an altogether paltrier desire simply to take things one at a time. "I hope you're not disillusioned," his bishop had said to him in hospital. "I'm not a defeatist," Stephen had replied. But not wanting to be seen to give up easily and ploughing ahead because of unshakeable belief—those were two different things and he knew it. The trouble was that there were days—and there were more and more of them—when he had difficulty distinguishing between the two.

"Reverend?" One of the men was in the doorway, looking at him with some concern. Stephen felt again that surge of irritation he'd experienced while on the phone with Smithy. He did not like being pitied, helped; it was one of his failings. "Everything all right?"

He got to his feet. "I'm fine. Did you want anything?"

"Thought you might like to join us for a beer." He knew that the men liked him. There was some consolation, was there not, to be obtained from that? He was tired; he didn't want to think anymore. He would look for the speech tomorrow. He shut the door of his office behind him.

It was the usual story (said Jones, when he sought Stephen out the next night and insisted on telling him what he knew about the dead man). Man comes East in search of some adventure, man meets pretty little thing and shacks up and next thing man knows is that the pretty little thing is leading him down the aisle and he's dandling some Eurasian infant on his knee less than the regulatory nine months later. Man is snared, well and good. Except that in this case Scotty had seemed to be genuinely in love with his pretty little thing. He'd met her in a bar (don't they all) a bare two months after leaving England. She was a waitress. He'd pulled playfully on the knot of the frilly apron she was wearing, causing her to trip and spill her drink over him. The manager had bustled over, threatening the pretty little thing, and Scott in an excess of chivalry had knocked him to the ground and fled with the girl. That was the end of her stint in *that* bar.

No-one knew anything about the girl. All right in the looks department, but hardly a knockout, not drop-dead gorgeous, nothing of the sort. (Recalling the words of Smithy's colleague, Stephen wondered if Jones could possibly be talking about the same woman.) Bit on the quiet side. Everyone had urged caution on Scotty. Go slow. Take it easy. Plenty of fish in the ocean. Even if she's got a bun in the oven, don't buy her line that it's yours. But Scott wouldn't listen. Became indignant, in fact, if anyone impugned the purity or virtue of the beloved. They'd taken to calling her

VM after that (short for the Virgin Mary). *She* called herself Blossom or Hibiscus or some such name—

"Jonquil," Stephen said.

Yeah, right (said Jones, obviously not liking this interruption). Knew it was something fanciful. Well, you've met Scott. He wasn't exactly Adonis. Not ugly, not handsome, just ordinary beyond belief. In England, he was heading precisely nowhere until he signed up with a shipping company and they sent him out East. The East went to his head. Everyone talks about how the world's getting exactly the same, y'know, globalisation and all, but that's not really true. The women in the East are different from the women in England and that's a fact. In England, women wouldn't give Scott the time of day. Here, out East, there's a certain type of woman for whom the sun has never set on the Empire and if your skin's white, Bob's your uncle. *You* know, Stephen. Oh, sorry, you wouldn't, would you? Though to be fair to Jonquil she didn't seemed the type. Seemed more educated, less showy, than the usual sarong party girl.

So they got married back in England. White wedding, the works. Girl was rather keen on living in England, but it was Scotty who wanted to return East. He hated the cold. So back they came and because the wedding had nearly bankrupted Scott they had to live with her mother in her government housing flat. Old lady was a lamb, Scott had no problem with her. There was a sister, though, one of those super-achieving unmarried females that manage to cast a chill whenever they enter a room. A good woman in her own way, no doubt, but absolutely no fun and that was a fact. Hard to believe that she and Jonquil were sisters, really, they were like chalk and cheese. The sister was one of those who always know their duty; she doled out the cash and they took it, unblushingly, because Scott was rotten at money management and Jonquil was even worse. Never mix money with family relations; any fool knows that, but it wasn't clear if Scott did. Then the babies started arriving. Jonquil got pregnant at the drop of a hat, and if she wasn't actually having one she was either miscarrying or aborting it.

Those were the facts of Scott's existence. His thoughts, his state of mind, about those facts was less clear because Scott wasn't the most articulate of men. And he was too much a gentleman to say anything against the ladies, the harem he was stuck with; you had to read between the lines. Scott with a beer in his hand, propping up a bar and grinning, a second too late, at some idiotic joke that someone had just regaled him with—that was the image of Scotty they all had. Oh yeah, one other thing. He'd adored his children. His duchesses, he called them, though they took after the mother and looked remarkably little like him. He used to carry their pictures around in his wallet and talk about them to anyone who would listen and his face would light up so that it was almost painful to watch him.

"You mentioned something about his wife."

But now the man with the red, bristly hair and the aspect of a friendly fox was feigning deafness, or ignorance, or forgetfulness, or all three. Death had transfigured Scott Ransome and all those related to him; it was part of its exasperating, terrible power. He simply shook his head.

"Poor Scotty."

It seemed to be Scott Ransome's epitaph.

The first person to arrive for the memorial service on Wednesday afternoon was not Ms Tan, as Stephen had expected, but a stocky, dark-haired man with a neatly-trimmed moustache. "Hans Fuchs," he said, shaking Stephen's hand. His accent was South African.

"So glad you could make it. Were you a friend of Scott's?"

"You could say that," Hans said and he stood to one side with his hands in his pockets, looking short and glum.

A bunch of people came all at once. Jones, uncomfortable in a tie; a couple in late middle age with the telltale nutbrown wrinkled skin of the Caucasian who's spent too many years pickled in the sun, the man bald as an egg, the woman wearing a smock, her long grey hair pinned up in a straggling knot; a young couple, the man a tall, good-looking Indian, his companion a Chinese woman in black low-slung pants. "Welcome," Stephen said, "welcome," motioning them into the hallway of the Mission. Jones and the middle-aged couple brightened at the sight of each other: "... spent the week *plastered* in Sydney," the bald man could be heard braying, until his wife poked him in the ribs and he guiltily re-assumed the solemn expression with which he'd entered.

Stephen motioned to Ronald Chan, his assistant, to take the attendees up to the small chapel on the first floor. (Ronald was twenty-seven, good-natured and blessedly free from introspection. Faith came to him as easily as accountancy, which was to say that he was eerily adept at both and could have become a partner in one of the big accounting firms had he chosen to. That he had not chosen to was a sore point with his parents and Stephen never failed to feel a stab of guilt whenever he met them for having been partly responsible for Ronald's lapse.)

He looked at his watch. Three ten. The main protoganists were still missing. Unpunctuality did not seem typical of Ms Tan; he would have credited her, if anything, with Swiss precision timing. He was debating whether to call her when the front door opened.

His first impression was of a swirl, a gaggle, of women. Ms Tan herself, elegant as ever, supporting an elderly woman—her mother—clad in the kind of traditional black pants and samfoo that was dying out with the older generation. Darting in and around them, like a shoal of tiny restless fish, were three girls in identical sleeveless blue dresses. They brought with them a cloudburst of femininity that the Mission had not seen in years.

The old lady smiled tremulously at Stephen and said something in the Hokkien dialect.

Ms Tan translated: "She says Scott painted her flat for her." The high colour in her cheeks told Stephen that it would be prudent to skip the pleasantries. Turning to her nieces, she said sharply, "Belinda, Brenda, Mary, stand *still*."

The darting stopped; six large light-brown eyes, set in similar heart-shaped faces tapering to slender chins and ringed by identical bell-like bobs, stared up at Stephen. Their gazes had the same disconcertingly direct quality as their aunt's, and something else as well, a kind of unchildlike knowingness. They would be stunning later on; Scott's only legacy was in their colouring and their last name.

He said, "How d'you do," to the girls, which was the signal for them to run and hide behind their grandmother.

He was just about to ask where the last member of their sextet was when a slightly-built woman stepped in and shut the door behind her. She seemed young, far too young, to be the girls' mother, but the resemblance was unmistakeable. In her, the girls' features had taken on a kind of high-Orientalism: her hair was very black, very sleek and very long, twisted into a rope that skimmed her waist; her skin was very fair and slightly translucent, its fairness accentuated by the thick vividness of her eyebrows and the dark red lipstick that she wore. Beneath her black slip dress, she was pregnant, the slight bump of her belly just visible. It was not an obvious beauty—it was haughty; it depended on the contrast in her colouring; it required a certain kind of taste (and Stephen could not help feeling surprised that Ransome—poor, maligned Ransome—had tastes that ran in this direction)—and Stephen could see why Smithy's colleague and Jones had differed on the subject of her looks. It was also possible to guess—even without the look of exasperation that Ms Tan directed at her sister, even without the sublime obliviousness that Jonquil Ransome manifested towards Ms Tan—the family history of those two siblings. What rotten luck it must have been for Ms Tan to have had this late, lovely intruder muscling into her world and claiming all the attention that had once been hers: she must have decided early on to parlay her only trump card—that of the clever hardworking girl—into unimpeachable career success and financial clout. As for Jonquil Ransome, her enigmatic, slightly blank expression gave nothing away—was meant to give nothing away except her shifting beauty and the corrosive sense of entitlement that good looks bring.

At her entrance, the children eddied round her and she picked up the youngest expertly and hoisted her on her hip, while holding the hands of the other children. And it was in this manner, festooned with children, that she ascended the rickety stairs to the chapel on the first floor.

The low murmur of voices in the chapel died down as he entered. The chapel, a converted store room, was ridiculously small—three pews arranged on either side of a narrow aisle and within spitting distance of the altar—and had the slightly musty smell of a room that is opened up only once a day. The ferocious afternoon sunlight pressed itself unavailingly against the windows, which had been closed to prevent the air-conditioned air from escaping.

Ms Tan had settled herself, the mother and the children in the front row; Jonquil Ransome was exchanging kisses, ceremoniously, with the bald man and his wife. Hans Fuchs was seated in the back row by the door, his hands clasped in his lap; there he was to remain, never moving a muscle, as far as Stephen could tell, during the service. The young Chinese woman was checking the numbers on her handphone.

At the lectern, Stephen looked down at his speech, the one he always gave at memorial services. He had worked on it, painstakingly, for the very first such service he had ever given and he'd mastered the rhythms of the language since then. He knew it was not a bad speech of its type, a comforting, uplifting parable about an oak tree and of how in the midst of death we are in life. Yet it seemed too easy, too practised, for this occasion. In the few seconds before he cleared his throat and began speaking, he realised that he was not going to use it. The thoughts that had been germinating at the back of his mind ever since the morning crowded to the fore: he decided to wing it.

"I won't pretend," Stephen said, "that I knew Scott Ransome well. In fact, I didn't know him at all. It's always awkward when you have to hold a memorial service for someone you don't know. So I won't waste your time or mine talking about the kind of man he was. But I do know that he is important to you because you have taken the time to come here on this Wednesday afternoon, a working day, to pay homage to his memory. I know he is important to his wife and his children, his sister-in-law and his mother-in-law. And to his parents, who cannot be here today. He was a more fortunate man than most in having this at least. The comfort of friends. The love of family."

The grieving widow, as Smithy had called Jonquil Ransome, had put on a pair of sunglasses. Silver-rimmed, small, incongruously glamorous in those sombre surroundings.

"I want to talk about something else. Most of you know how Scott died. It was not a pretty death from what I understand. I'm sorry if mentioning this brings pain to anyone. But it is pertinent to what I'm going to say. Scott Ransome was also a relatively young man who should have been in the prime of life. He was ten years younger than I am. Some of you may ask, where was God when he allowed this to happen? Why wasn't Scott Ransome allowed to grow old and die a peaceful death like many of us do?

"I don't know the answers. But I do know that even in the midst of the most dire distress, at our darkest hour, at the scene of the worst atrocity, *God is there*. I know, because I was a policeman once. I investigated murders. I knew nothing of God and yet he was there."

He had seen bodies stabbed, shot, strangled, drowned—in one case decapitated—all the myriad ways in which it is possible to dispose of a human being intentionally. How many times had he stood over the battered body of some man, woman or child and thought to himself that this was just one more piece of forensic evidence for the case, already overwhelming, that God did not exist?

"I accommodated myself to the absence of God. I felt it as a void, a force sucked out of the universe, yet I thought it was normal. Part of the bleak fabric of life. I was a policeman and I dealt in facts, not speculation. My motto was *get on with it and don't whinge*, and that was what I did. I held nothing sacred." Certainly not his marriage, which had ended after five years when he came home one day to find a short scrawled note from his wife: *I'm leaving you in case you happen to notice*. Her divorce petition cited, among other things, his inability to communicate and his emotional repression; she was a youth counsellor and her language was peppered with the jargon of her profession. He instructed his solicitor not to contest the petition: he was not going to fight this kind of airy-fairy nonsense. Fortunately, they'd had no children.

He'd become aware of a series of snuffles, like the scrabbling of mice, from the front row, where Scott Ransome's daughters sat with unchildlike decorum. Their aunt produced a tissue, which was passed down the line. Jonquil Ransome's gaze seemed to be trained directly in front of her, though behind those impenetrable shades her eyes could have been pinwheeling for all Stephen knew.

"What I was living with was the absence of hope. Of love. The possibility of redemption. Of course I didn't know this at the time. I was forty years old before I realised this. And it took a dead child to make me see it. I'll spare you the details but she was another victim in a very busy year." A ten-year-old girl, the victim of a horrific sexual assault in a field less than a mile from her house. The killer was a paedophile who had progressed from molesting small children to acting out violent sexual fantasies; the cover-up was clumsy, the capture swift and satisfying. "We caught the killer in a guesthouse literally in bed. He was very ordinary-looking, a man you wouldn't have looked at twice in the street. And I remember I was outraged—that he was so very ordinary—and I was hitting him with a rage I hadn't known I'd possessed"—a rage that was like a cloud of black flies swarming around his head, blinding him—"until I heard a nasty cracking sound and I knew that I'd broken his arm."

A cough sounded from the back pew. Jones took out a large handkerchief and tugged at his nose. In the front row, Ms Tan wore a little frown that suggested she was not entirely happy with the way the service was proceeding. Perhaps, Stephen thought, he should have stuck with the oak tree. But it was too late now. He plunged on.

"Whatever you may have heard about police brutality, we're not encouraged to hit suspects. I think once I started, I didn't know how to stop. I remember the man's scream of pain. Then my police officers were grabbing me and dragging me headfirst into the corridor. I did the only possible thing possible under the circumstances. I went to a pub and drank myself blind and passed out in the street."

A muffled guffaw erupted from the back. The bald man's wife dug him in the ribs again. At the periphery of Stephen's vision he was aware of a shift in the angle of Jonquil Ransome's gaze, so slight as to be almost imperceptible were it not for the fact that he had been preternaturally conscious of her black-clad presence ever since the service began.

"The next morning I woke to a pounding head. And a message on my answering machine that my superintendent wanted to see me asap. But it wasn't the disciplinary action that I feared. It was the loss of control, the chink in my unflappability. It had never happened before, it wasn't supposed to happen, and I was afraid. I decided to walk to work, thinking that the winter air would clear my head. But every step I took was like a jolt of pain through my head. I knew I had to sit, or I was going to faint. So I turned into the first building I came to. It happened to be the small church down the street." A hideous late Victorian gothic chapel sandwiched incongruously between a stationer's and a deli. "I had passed the church every morning for years without ever having gone in and I had no idea what denomination it represented. It was empty at that hour of the morning." No, not quite true. There had been an old woman, sweeping the aisles. She'd paid him no attention and so he'd sat in the last pew, staring blankly at the cross plastered to the wall behind the altar and the dust dancing in the weak sunlight slanting in through the narrow windows.

"It was very quiet, though the rush hour traffic was hurtling past just outside the doors. I was just glad to sit." After a while, he began to be aware, as never before, of the shape of his thoughts: pulpy and unformed at first, then assembling themselves themselves with a rapidity, a rush that began to resemble a waterfall and he leant forward and buried his face in his hands.

"I thought of what had happened the night before. And I realised that the rage I'd felt at the killer was actually rage at God. Rage that he'd looked away once again while the killer went on his rampage. What kind of God was it who allowed this kind of thing to happen? I knew the theological answers, of course, because I'd been educated at a parish school, but the answers never made any sense. Still didn't. What was *different*, that morning, was that for the first time in my life I was acknowledging that He existed. I'd got tired of denying His existence. It struck me that I had been clinging to non-belief with as much strenuousness and fervour as a believer might have clung to his beliefs. Somewhere along the line, although I couldn't pinpoint the moment, that non-belief had turned itself inside out, like a pocket that seemed empty but wasn't, to reveal what lay hidden." Belief had caught him unawares that evening in the guesthouse while he was assaulting the man; his anger had been quicker than his brain, fastening with an almost personal venom on God.

A belief born in rage did not sound propitious, at least not to the head of the theological college that Stephen applied to join, after resigning from the police. (His boss had said, "Are you mad?" and advised him to take a month off to go to Ibiza.) The head had made various token objections. Stephen was not young. Stephen might be better off joining one of the more fire and brimstone denominations ("not my cup of tea," Stephen said doggedly). He was patient but persistent, in the way that he'd learnt to be in the interrogation room and the head had finally relented, probably thinking that Stephen would drop out of his own accord. He hadn't, though there had been days when he wondered what he was doing, when the old unbelief, the blankness, would descend again with the old familiar flatness. It was in part a fear of failure that saw him through the course and to his first posting in south London.

"The rest is just a matter of detail. How I joined the church, how I happen to be standing here in front of you today. My story is a message of hope. Of the good that can come out of great evil and great unhappiness. Of course you may ask what consolation my conversion— my redemption—brought to the family of the dead child. The brutal answer is: none whatsoever. It didn't make her parents sleep better, it didn't lessen their grief or their bitterness. Yet, if her death managed to bring peace even to one person, I believe that she did not in the larger scheme of things die in vain."

Yes, now *she* was staring at him all right through those sunglasses, its small oval shades resembling the black unwinking eyes of some malevolent statue. He licked his lips. Almost there, he thought; he could see the elusive punchline beckoning him, tantalisingly.

"I don't claim to know what good if any will come out of Scott Ransome's death. And you may be outraged at the very idea—of the dead as sacrificial victims for the living. But it's a natural human instinct to try and make some kind of sense out of his death. Of any death. Of course some deaths are easier than others to accept. For the man who dies in his own bed, surrounded by his children and grandchildren, having lived a long and useful life, there is no sense of waste. For the believer—any kind of believer—there is a ready answer. There is a theological framework in which you can put things. But even if the death is not easy to accept, even if you are not a believer, still you must try. For the dead man's sake if nothing else. For the children that Scott Ransome had. For the child that his wife is going to have. If Scott made you laugh—hang on to that memory. If he once did you a service—lent you money, consoled you when you were down—remember that. If his untimely death teaches you that life is all too short and that you have to make the most of every minute—well and good. In their own way, the dead tell us, the living, how to live. Please rise."

Ronald broke into *Jerusalem*, the CD player grinding out its karaoke musical accompaniment. Ronald had a fine tenor voice, carrying the high notes easily. The hymn brought Stephen back, as it always did, to those sleepy Sunday morning services in his childhood church, where his barrister's clerk father had been a verger for thirty years. How interminable those services had once seemed; how cold the air within the vaulting confines of the church, no matter how cheerily the sun shone outside. He was aware now of an overwhelming feeling of disappointment, and exhaustion. He had used the story of his own conversion for cheap theatrical purposes and still he had not nailed the ending: it had drifted away from him on a tide of platitudes and a strained, confused striving for significance.

The hymn had ended. The small gathering of mourners was looking at him expectantly.

"Let us pray," he said.

"Please help yourself to the tea," Ronald was saying. "There's also coffee if you prefer." Boh tea and Nescafe instant granules—he made them sound like the lap of luxury. The young couple accepted cups from him gratefully; they were friends of Shu Lin, they said, and Stephen had to stop and think for a minute whom they meant. Ms Tan took hers absently. "What are they all doing outside?" she asked, *they* meaning Jones, the bald man and his wife and Hans Fuchs, who had all disappeared into the tiny garden of the Mission after the service with the air of escaping prisoners.

"Having a smoke, I expect. I'll call them back if you like."

"No, please don't." Ms Tan peered into her cup, as though surprised to find it still empty. "That was—an interesting speech."

"I hope I didn't disappoint you."

"No, no. The only thing is, I don't know how much of it the girls understood. We haven't told them how their father died, you know. They think it was some sort of accident. The younger ones don't even really understand the concept of death. I just hope they don't get any ideas from what you were saying." That direct, piercing look of hers again. This sidelong thrust was her way of reproaching him for not sticking to the anodyne; he saw, with resignation, the generous donation that she might have made slipping away forever.

"I think," he said, apologetically, "I was trying to do justice to Scott Ransome." But now he wondered whether he had gone too far in this quest to be fair to the memory of the dead man and whether it had been at the expense of the living. "This was an unusual case and I'm afraid I might have got a bit carried away." Damned if he was going to apologise anymore; for the first time in a long time, he felt the old angry defensiveness that had marked every day of his life as a policeman rise to the surface. He changed the subject: "Can I get you or your mother anything? Tea?"

"Thank you. My mother and I will help ourselves."

The old lady and her granddaughters had arranged themselves on the sofa in the sitting room, the little girls sunk unmoving into the deep dusty cushions. Jonquil Ransome was nowhere to be seen.

"Would you like anything?" he said to the mother. "Tea?" She smiled at him uncomprehendingly. "Girls? Would you like anything?" *I'm beginning to sound like a bloody waiter.* Very slowly, the eldest girl shook her head. He could still see the shiny patches on her cheeks where the tears had dried.

Clumsily, he patted her head—he had never been good with children—and opened the front door with a growing feeling of hopelessness.

Outside, as he'd expected, Jones and the bald man were puffing away on cigarettes with greedy gulps. Hans Fuchs again stood to one side, hands in pockets, not smoking, just standing, always somehow apart.

"Reverend," Jones said. Now he was Reverend again. "Never knew you were a copper."

"People always find that a source of fascination. I wonder why."

"Must be a damn sight more interesting than this God business, anyway," the bald man said. He had a thick Scottish accent.

"Peter," his wife said with resignation.

"Damn, my tongue just seems to run away with me today."

Stephen said, "There's tea, coffee, inside ... and beer," he added in a moment of inspiration.

"Never too early," Jones said, brightening.

He was wondering where she could have gone when she answered his unspoken question by unlatching the gate and coming up the short path to the front door where he stood like a parent waiting for an errant child to return. And, like an errant child, she said, "I needed some air," though he had not uttered a word. It was the first time he had heard her speak. Her voice, like her sister's, was very low. She was still wearing her sunglasses.

"You're not feeling sick because of the child?"

"You mean this?" Her fingers stroked, absently, the black cloth stretched over her belly. "No, I don't get morning sickness."

He said, formally, "I haven't had the opportunity to tell you how sorry I am about your husband—"

She listened with her head slightly cocked as though trying to decipher a code and his words petered out.

She asked, apropos of nothing, "Were you really a policeman?"

"Why, did you think I was making it up?"

She admitted, "Yes," a smile suddenly escaping the confines of her resolutely straight mouth and he could see now why Scott Ransome had fallen for her that night in the bar. It was a smile hinting at both aloofness and vulnerability, a Giaconda-like quality that Ransome might have mistaken for Oriental inscrutability. For the first time in years he felt a slight quickening of the blood. He thought, *This is insane*, and damped down the impulse as hastily as a man in a leaky boat might have battened down the hatches.

They stood there on the front step in silence for some seconds. He could feel the perspiration begin to pool around his dog-collar. They ought to have gone in; it was hot; she was pregnant. Yet she continued to look cool and immaculate, as though nothing would melt her. She did not seem particularly grief-stricken, he thought, recalling Smithy's words, but that might mean nothing. It was too easy to confuse heartlessness with a failure to mimic the emotions that convention demanded.

She said, suddenly, "I have to tell you, I didn't really go out for some air. I went out for a cigarette. I had to go round the corner so my sister wouldn't see me or she'll go crazy." She added, "I thought you would understand," and all of a sudden he was back in the interrogation room again with a murder suspect who, weary and in turmoil after hours of relentless questioning, was leaning towards Stephen Mullins, his accuser and saviour, repeating the self-same words. *I thought you would understand.* And the battle-cry would go round the department: *Mullins does it again.* It was how he had secured most of his convictions. He was never entirely sure himself what prompted the suspects to break down: they must have seen something in his face or heard something in his voice that gave them the comforting illusion he empathised with them, and he never did anything to disabuse them of the confidence trick he was perpetrating. Except that he was not soliciting a confession now and he was suddenly on his guard.

"Well, no-one's going to blame you for one cigarette in your circumstances."

"I didn't want this memorial service, you know. My sister insisted. She thought Scott was an idiot when he was alive but now he's a saint. Untouchable."

"I imagine your sister is the sort that always wants to do the right thing."

"Oh yeah, she's always been good. She always does the right thing. She makes me sick. But I can't say anything because she has the money."

Oh yes, she was in full flood now. How many times had he seen that reckless, heady unburdening in the interrogation room, the need to unload overwhelming the instinct for self-preservation, even as the suspect's solicitor repeatedly warned his client that every word he was saying was incriminating him? In those days, he had simply turned on the tape recorder and let it run.

He said, slowly, "You're very different from your sister, aren't you?"

"She's the good sister. I'm the bad one."

"Oh, come now," he said, irritated. "That's too facile. Easy," he added, unnecessarily.

"I know what it means," she said, sweetly.

"I didn't mean to imply—"

"That I'm unintelligent? But I did drop out of school at seventeen, you know. So you see. I *am* unintelligent."

"You're being disingenuous," he said, and resisted the impulse to explain what this meant too. "You're clearly not stupid. In fact, I'd say you were trying to manipulate me, though I don't know to what purpose."

She seemed, if anything, pleased by his laying all his cards on the table. "I met Scott. In a bar, where I was working part-time. I wasn't supposed to be working there—in fact, I told my parents I was going for night classes. He was sweet. Not handsome, not even very bright. But he had a strange kind of decency. I ran away with him. I got pregnant. That's why I left school."

He said only, "Why *strange*?"

"I knew a lot of men. I met a lot of them in that bar. White men. I know what they call women like me, but Asian men are so dull. Especially Chinese men. They don't know how to have fun ... I was going out with an American, a married man with two children. He would cry about his wife whenever he was with me and then he would want to tie me up ... Scott was different."

"He was genuinely in love with you." In spite of himself, he was falling into the rhythms of the interrogation room: goad and counter-goad, prodding her on to the next level of self-incrimination.

She flashed him a quick look of dislike and in spite of himself he felt a small, perishable sense of triumph. She did not answer him directly. "I have fun. I do what I want. I smoke when I'm expecting. I love my children but I'm a bad mother. I get bored easily. I'm a bad daughter. I steal money from my mother when I need to. I take money from my sister but I don't like her. I married my husband because he said he would die if I didn't marry him and he was crying and I felt sorry for him and after we were married I kept wishing he was dead. I didn't love him. I was a bad wife. Eight years is like eternity if you don't love someone. Then he was dead. Maybe—" and now he could hear clearly the mockery, like a silvery undercurrent of laughter, running through her voice—"you can help me." Her fingers still stroking, rhythmically, the black cloth shielding her stomach. He blinked; the contrast between her demure appearance and what she was saying was like a disjointed dream.

"Mrs Ransome, I don't know what you want."

"You were trying so hard back there. To give some meaning to Scott's death. Trying to make something out of nothing. I thought you'd want to know the truth. You're a policeman. You work with facts. You said so yourself."

And suddenly the illusion that he was back in the interrogation room snapped; he was standing on the front step of the old pre-World War I shophouse that housed the Mission where he was the resident chaplain and his black short-sleeved clerical shirt was drenched through with perspiration and clinging unpleasantly to his skin. He registered the slip she'd made about him being a policeman but did not correct her. He took out his handkerchief and wiped his face. "I'm not your father confessor. This is not a confessional. You don't have to tell me anything."

"I didn't murder him. If that's what you're thinking. I just wanted to let you know what he was doing in that hotel room in Pattaya."

He placed his hand on the doorknob. "He wasn't a saint. He went there for some R&R during his shore leave. I think we all know that."

"I told him I wanted a divorce. He wouldn't give me one. He said no way he was going to give up the children. So I told him I wasn't expecting his child. I was expecting another man's baby."

How persistent she was, how relentless the drip drip drip of poison that was her voice. He wished he could shut it out, but instead he asked, mechanically, as she clearly wanted him to, "Whose baby is it?"

"I said it was Hans' baby."

He said, confused, "Hans?"

"Hans Fuchs. Hans was his best friend."

He was aware of a fleeting, insane sense of jealousy, that the short, unimpressive South African should have claimed her attention at all. "Stop," he said, violently. "I don't want to hear anymore."

"He went to Pattaya to drink himself to death."

"You don't know that."

"The doctors had warned him to stop drinking. His liver was already damaged."

At last she was finished and she removed her glasses and perched them on her head, blinking in the bright afternoon sun. Her face looked briefly naked without her glasses, and he saw now that she was not as young as she'd first appeared. He wondered when Ransome had first realised what he'd fallen in love with. How long had he managed to preserve his illusions through that dead-eyed arid remorselessness of hers? From all accounts, he'd been a man unable to bear too much reality. And he, Stephen, stood implicitly accused of the same sin of sentimentality. Of trying to raise Ransome, metaphorically, from the dead. Well, it was his job, wasn't it, to spin the fairytale. All the same, he should have stuck to the oak tree.

Somehow he had found the strength of will to turn the doorknob he'd been clutching: the door yielded an inch. He heard the rustle of voices inside like the twittering of birds in an aviary. He had never wanted to get away from someone so badly in his life, but even as he prepared to turn his back on her, something that she'd said earlier came back to him.

"You told your husband that was Hans Fuchs' baby. Is that true?"

She looked startled for a moment then her eyes narrowed in appreciation at his astuteness. She gave a tiny vulnerable shrug of the shoulders. "I'm not sure. I'm not sure of the dates."

He shut the door on her and on the merciless afternoon sun. The cool air-conditioned air of the interior came as a slight shock and he thrust his handkerchief back into his pocket. He noticed absently that his chest was hurting again; it was not the stabbing pain of the other day but a discomfort like a muscle ache.

"Reverend," Jones called somewhere from within. "We were wondering where you'd gone."

"Just taking a breather," he said. "That's all." And he crossed the narrow hallway of the Mission to join them.

The Pool Boy

I dreamt of my father again, and it was always the same dream. He lay at the bottom of the swimming pool in his suit and tie; the tie wavered upwards, like a frond of seaweed. His head was resting on a bed of waterlogged leaves. His eyes were closed; he looked peaceful; he might have been sleeping.

When the police recovered my father's body from Hong Kong harbour, it was bloated beyond recognition. My mother identified the body by his watch, a gold Rolex, the watch of choice of Hong Kong businessmen. I wasn't allowed to see the body. It was a closed-coffin funeral, the coffin inordinately long on its bier, because my father had been a tall man by Chinese standards—almost six feet. The smell of wreaths and incense was overpowering; unable to stand it, I sneaked a packet of cigarettes from one of the monks leading the mourning and, though I didn't smoke, surreptitiously lit fag after fag, gulping down the fumes greedily. Those monks were cheerful, pragmatic souls; one of them arrived in a Mercedes and later I saw him talking into his handphone, checking the Hang Seng index with his broker. Their chanting was irritating at first, then consolingly numbing; when the funeral was over, the silence in the house was the hardest thing to bear. I was thirteen years old.

After the dreams started, I refused to swim. This was awkward, because the pool which my father so inconveniently inhabited was one of the key attractions of the English boarding school where I had already spent three years. In the glossy brochures sent to parents, the pool resembled something from a luxury spa, lined with mock-Roman tiles and surrounded by French windows that looked out on verdant rolling grounds. The reality was that the tiles were cracked, the water was always cold even though it was supposed to be heated and the pool seemed to attract dead leaves like a gutter. Once a week, we were forced to lower ourselves into the water, shivering, and complete two laps in the name of physical education. I hated cold, hated the pool.

As I wouldn't swim, I was made to wait in the changing room for the allotted one hour. "We don't make exceptions for spoilt young women," the sports mistress said. I didn't mind; the changing room reeked of disinfectant but it was quiet and sunshine streamed in through the high casement windows in dusty motes. I'd sit and read, always travel books about long, random treks where the whole point of the journey was the journey itself. I liked the idea of perpetual motion and never arriving; I saw myself as a full-time itinerant on the railway, rattling round the world until my money gave out.

It was when I went to retrieve one of these books from the changing room that I met the pool boy.

I must have seen him on Mondays, trawling the pool for dead leaves with a long net, but I had never really noticed him until that morning, when a prickly sensation at the back of my neck told me that I was being watched and I turned to see the pool boy propped against one of the French windows having a cigarette. For one hallucinatory moment he looked bathed in a halo of fire, a pop-comic saviour sent to save the world and I caught my breath, but it was only a sudden blaze of the sun through the glass. We stared at each other across the pool. I was at a disadvantage: his face was in shadow, mine in the light. After a moment's hesitation, I walked over to face him. He continued to smoke.

"Stop it," I told him.

He said, and his accent was the local burr, "Stop what?"

"Looking at me."

"A cat can look at a queen."

While I was thinking of an answer to this, he remarked, "I've seen you around. You're Chinese, aren't you?"

"No," I said, "Eskimo."

A very faint smile rippled across his face, all planes and unexpected, fluid angles and high, jutting cheekbones; I was reminded of light glinting off water. I was looking at his hair; it was fabulously corkscrewed and ringleted and tied back in a thick ponytail and it was red, a red that had caught the sun and made me think he was on fire. I wondered, idly, what it would feel like to hold it in my fist. He must have seen the thought flit across my face, because he reached out his hand to touch my hair—black, straight as a board—with the curiosity of a child. And I let him.

We didn't exchange another word, even as his hand slipped down from my hair to my cheek and then my neck. I was so close to him I could see the individual threads on his frayed dirty white Arran jumper and the stubble on his imperfectly-shaved chin. I knew nothing about boys, but I knew I wanted him then, with a desire so sudden and perfectly formed that I had to catch my breath. It was very quiet and it was hard to believe that barely a hundred feet away the rest of the school was going about their routine on this mundane schoolday. I don't know how long I stood there before I disengaged his hand and walked to class.

The following Saturday afternoon, I took the 49 bus to his home on the outskirts of town. There was no suggestion I should visit him, oh no, none at all, even though I did find an address on a slip of paper in my pigeonhole with no name. The address given was a narrow council house on the ribbon of road that led to the expressway to London, and it had the look of all those houses that are never part of somewhere, only on the way to somewhere else. It was forlorn, scabby-doored, broken window mended with sticking-tape and a potted geranium on the sill that had long since wilted. I stood at the gate looking up at the house, which seemed blind, shut in within itself. Heavy metal music thrummed from the house next door. A woman pushing a stroller down the road stared at me; I stared back at her, truculently, until she looked away. The next bus was in half an hour and a wind was blowing that brought with it fluttery droplets of rain. I rang the bell.

His face was suitably blank when he opened the door. He jerked his head, meaning *come in*, and I followed him into a house that smelt powerfully of stale cigarette smoke and congealed cooking grease and up a narrow stairway to his room. It was still a boy's room, horrendously untidy, clothes and magazines heaped everywhere, faded posters of rock stars running in a frieze round the walls and childhood mobiles bumping our heads from the low ceiling. There was a sharper, sweeter smell I couldn't identify. "Here," the pool boy said, holding out what looked to me like a very limp cigarette. He saw my face and mocked me gently: "You're kidding me, right? I thought everybody at that school was a dope fiend." I had a toke, just to be polite, and while I was coughing, he said, "You know you're not supposed to be here." I stopped coughing and considered this. I thought about taking the 49 bus back to the town centre and wandering around the shops until it was time to head back to the school while the wind picked up and the rain began to fall in icy needles. Here it was warm and the pool boy lay sprawled in bed in his dirty white Arran jumper with his hands clasped behind his head, waiting for my decision. "I know," I said. "*All* right then," he said, as though we'd just sealed a pact and he peeled off his jumper.

His body was milky-white, freckled and bisected by a long, badly-healed scar down his chest. I ran my finger down the bump of the still-livid scar and he looked down in some surprise, as though he had only just remembered it. He said he'd been knifed in a fight; said it casually, as though such things were part of the air he breathed, and then he put his hands on my shoulders.

Up close his eyes were very green and opaque and his mouth tasted of the joint he had been smoking. There was a practised ease in all his movements; he had not, I guessed, encountered many girls who said no. I was curious to see what he would do and I was also curiously detached from the proceedings. It was not me who was having her shirt tugged off; it was not me kissing him back with an abandon I'd never thought myself capable of; no, it was somebody else altogether.

Afterwards, he jumped up from bed to fling open the windows. Cold air swirled into the room, stinging our bare skins. He laughed when I started to shiver. His mum, he explained, would kill him if she smelt marijuana.

"What's your name then?"

After a moment, I said, "Jade."

It was not Jade, not really, but it was the closest equivalent of a difficult Chinese name that many people found difficult to pronounce and so I had taken to using it. In the beginning, I had felt I was betraying who I was, but then I began to see possible advantages in the ruse. "Jade" could be whoever she wanted to be, unburdened by her past.

"Jade," he said, savouring it, drawing it out, "I like it. You're all right, Jade." And after that he called me Jade at every opportunity.

He had a name, of course, one of those clunky English names like Nigel or Graham, but I always thought of him as the pool boy. Not long after we met, he asked me, "Why've you let me into your life, Jade?" I considered this. "Have I *let* you into my life?" He traced a line down the inside of my thigh and said, "What do you call this then?" I had to get out of bed after that and sit on the chair, until he coaxed me back in.

I told myself that three hours on a Saturday afternoon, even if we did spend them in the narrow bed in the narrow house in which he'd lived all his life, did not, in my scale of things, amount to letting him into my life. Often all we did was drift in and out of sleep until we were rocked awake by a blast of heavy metal from next door. Or I would take his head in my arms and slip off the rubberband that held his ponytail in place and run my fingers through the hair that sprang out with wild irrepressible life; I could do this for hours, trying to comb out the tangles, trying to impose order on what couldn't be straightened, the rhythmic motion of my own fingers lulling me into a trance until the pool boy caught hold of my wrist and broke the spell: "D'you think I'm a doll, Jade?" Not quite angry, but on the verge of it.

None of this meant anything, surely? But I was beginning to see that what I thought was not always the decisive factor; that there were other points of view that could be radically, disconcertingly divergent. Not naming him kept him at a distance. Stripped him of the power of his living, breathing reality. Or so I thought.

I was the first Chinese girl he had known. Those long Saturday afternoons, while his mother worked her nurse's shift at the hospital, he would look down the length of my body with an almost anthropological sense of wonder until I had to cover his eyes with my hands. "Why do they call Chinks yellow? You're not yellow at all, more a kind of nutmeg or olive—" I told him, primly, that it was politically incorrect to use the word *chink* and he said, nonplussed, "yeah?"

He had *known* other girls of other races and other nationalities—black, Indian, Italian—meeting them up north in the nearest city that passed for a metropolis in this part of the country. English girls bored him; all they were interested in was getting knocked up and getting married. He told me this matter-of-factly; artlessly, even. I looked at him. Possibly he sensed some implied criticism.

"You get around," I said.

His smile was slow and lazy and appeared in distinct stages like a Cheshire cat's. "Don't pretend to be moralistic. You're not moralistic."

He would have told me anything that I asked him. So I stopped asking. Since my father's death, I had shied away from frankness; my father's example had taught me that openness was self-defeating, like someone revealing all the cards up his sleeve at once.

He was nineteen and he cleaned the pool at my school. Those were the bare facts of his existence and I tried not to know more.

There were certain things I couldn't avoid knowing. Sometimes the front doorbell would ring and he would slide out of bed and take a quick look out the window before pulling on his clothes and reaching under the bed to extract a small brown envelope from a shoebox. Then he would return with a wad of cash that he counted openly in front of me, before stashing it in a rusted Thomas the Tank Engine money box on the desk. Once, while he was taking longer than usual, I pulled out the shoebox from under the bed and opened the lid to find what looked like very shrivelled tea leaves. It took me a while to realise what I was looking at.

I was sitting up in bed waiting for him when he returned, the shoebox in my lap. He stopped when he saw me.

"Aren't you afraid I'm going to squeal on you?"

"Now why," he asked reasonably, "would you do that?"

He prised the box gently away from me and fished out the afternoon's pickings from his pocket. Fifty pounds, paid for in very dirty ten pound notes, which he stuffed into his absurd child's money box. He was making me watch; I could feel the complicity envelop me like a mist.

"Why don't you put the money in the bank?"

"Don't trust banks."

The swiftness of his reply, juxtaposed with the flimsiness of his child's money box, made me laugh. He didn't blink. I asked, curious, "What are you saving up for?"

He shrugged. "Beer. Fags. To get out of this hell-hole. What do you think?"

He kicked the shoebox under the bed. His anger came in spurts like little licks of flame that died as quickly as they sprang into life. He fell on the bed and lay face-down; in a few minutes, I knew, he would be asleep.

Early every Sunday morning, I called my mother on her handphone in Hong Kong. Sunday mornings were evenings in Hong Kong and she would usually be out for dinner with a business acquaintance or her mahjong friends. It was not a good time to talk, which was why we had both settled on this hour.

My mother was once an actress, a movie starlet specialising in swordfighting epics where she was always the tomboyish sidekick to the hero, never the romantic interest. Her strong-boned, wide-eyed beauty came at the wrong time; the rage was for waifs with tiny heart-shaped faces. Probably she realised she had a limited future in the movies. Then she met my father at one of her film premieres (his family's company was sponsoring the event). I have an old press cutting of their encounter: my mother wears a silver lame high-slit dress that lays bare her athletic legs and slender shoulders and my father is debonair in a tuxedo. They are shaking hands. Nothing in the grainy photograph hints at the conflagration between them.

Within days, my father had broken off his engagement to the girl of good family that his parents had selected for him from within their circle of rich Shanghainese exiles. Within months, my parents were married in a high-profile wedding splashed across the tabloids. His family was outraged. They had all the aristocratic pretensions of the Shanghainese and more, while my mother was poor, ambitious and (it was whispered) had slept her way to whatever minor success she'd had in the movies. It was not until I was born that they deigned to speak to her. Within a few years of her wedding, my mother, who'd abandoned her career to become a *tai-tai*, would come home from an afternoon of aimless shopping and fling her purchases in the hallway, loud, ugly sobs racking her as she stood with manicured hands to her face, not knowing that I was watching her from the stairs. I knew that at such moments she did not want to be comforted; that she would turn, like an animal in pain, on anyone who tried to approach her. I understood that she was unhappy, but I did not know why. All I could do was wait for the crying to stop. It always did, just in time for her to wash her eyes and re-apply her makeup and put on the smile that my father always expected to see when he returned from the office. The conflagration, you see, never died for my mother.

My father's death liberated my mother. Barely a week after the funeral, she booted my grandfather, my father's father, off the board and installed herself as chairman. People talked about my mother in hushed tones as a Frankenstein in the making. I was the only one who wasn't surprised. Only I had seen those crying jags of her; only I had seen her plough her white Mercedes like a heat-seeking missile down some narrow alleyway crowded with hawkers and foodcarts, scattering people and animals out of her way. She could have killed someone; she probably wanted to. When my father died, all that rage and frustration went into the family business, where she exhibited the same headlong approach as she did in her driving. It worked, and she was very successful, and I was glad for her, but it only increased the distance between us. My mother liked to say to me, in a vaguely dissatisfied way, "You take after your father."

Conversation with my mother this Sunday was more difficult than usual. Static kept breaking up her voice, and I kept saying, "What?" while in the background I could hear the intermittent roar of a Hong Kong restaurant at dinnertime. I told my mother what I usually told her at such times. I was progressing in French. I was discussing my future with the careers officer. I always told her good news, never bad. The pool boy lurked at the back of my mind like an incubus. My mother would have considered him *very* bad news. Even though she had the same weakness as me for good-looking, not very effectual men (like my father). Then I ran out of things to say, as I always did after five minutes.

"Jade?" my mother was saying. "Are you there?"

I shouted, "Yes!" I said, "I want to come home."

"But you'll be back for the summer holidays soon, darling!"

That was not what I meant, but I didn't correct her. I don't know why I said it either, except that, standing there in the school hallway with the receiver in my hand, I felt a sudden powerful sense of dislocation. I had forgotten who Jade Wong was or what she was supposed to be. The last time I was home, my mother and I had played a cat and mouse game. I'd opened all the windows every chance I got, while my mother just as determinedly closed them every chance she got. My mother believed the wind would blow all the luck out of our house. Or so she said. (What she did not say was that the last day of my father's life had begun with a typhoon warning which my father, a fresh air fiend in an air-conditioned city, had ignored. While he was alive, we hardly closed the windows, and that day I remember the wind twisting the curtains up into strange, fluted shapes near the ceiling and my mother trying to seize them to tie them back, all the while biting her lip to hold back the sharp words that longed to trip off her tongue.) We were both secretly relieved when term started.

"Yes," I said. "Of course. You're right."

The nearest Chinese restaurant was a takeaway in the town centre; the food it served resembled nothing that I knew back home. It was run by immigrants from Hong Kong, a couple with twin daughters who had grown up thick as tree trunks in the clammy English air and with the rosy complexion of milkmaids. The awfulness of the cooking, their isolation in this godforsaken place, when they had the world to choose from, all depressed me and I tried my best to avoid the takeaway until my longing for any kind of Chinese food got the better of me and then I would make a furtive trip there, doing my best to avoid looking the daughters in the eye. They, on the other hand, had no qualms about staring at me while I paid my money and waited at the counter. It was strange that I thought of them as prisoners in that landscape of gorse and hills when I had even less freedom than they did and when they could take the bus down to London at any time. But they never did; they were always there when I visited the takeaway and for some reason I always found their sentinel presences unsettling.

To say that food is important to the Chinese is an understatement. During my first weeks at the school—an autumn of mist and endless driving rain—I thought of nothing but the food back home. I didn't miss my mother; I didn't even miss my father. I thought constantly about the taste and texture of delicacies such as smoked duck, dragon's feet (really braised chicken claws), the smell of steamed pork buns at a street corner on a winter's day. Food haunted my dreams; I began to regret all the times that I'd passed up second helpings or failed to finish the food on my plate. I found the mashed potatoes, the stringy slabs of meat that we sawed with blunt knives at dinner, disgusting. I couldn't eat; I lost weight. When my mother came for her first visit, she brought me down to London where I gorged until I was nearly sick in one of the five-star restaurants in Chinatown. She observed me with alarm. When we got back to school, she confronted the principal.

Waiting outside the principal's office, I could hear my mother in full cry. My mother's English was emphatic, idiosyncratic ("my *daughter*, you're not *feeding* her, at home eating is *no problem*, why only in England she cannot eat! Why I pay thousands of pounds a year for her to become *famine victim*?") Then the rivery, soothing murmur of the principal's voice. I wasn't intended to hear, but still I caught the words "dissociative state" and then my mother's voice rose again. She wasn't having her daughter psychonalysed; Chinese people didn't *believe* in psychoanalysis!

When I was called into the office again, I saw the high colour in the principal's cheeks and the look that my mother always wore when she knew that she had gone too far.

"Jade," my mother said in Cantonese, "I want to know if you are happy here."

I understood that, depending on my answer, she could whisk me away immediately. I had not wanted to come and I had never seen weather like this—weather that was a tangible, malevolent presence—but I had also come to feel a certain safety within the walls of the school. At home, it would be just myself and my mother. My father would not be there to mediate between me and my mother's gorse-like personality. My father was dead. I felt a slight electric shock at the thought; I think it was the first time I absorbed the full reality of it.

I said in English, "Yes, I'm happy here."

Anyone looking at my mother then would have thought that she had suddenly sunk into deep, consuming thought. Her eyes focused in an intent stare at nothing in particular. I took a step back. I was as familiar with my mother's moods and expressions as the terrain of my own face, and I knew that the stare meant only that she was livid at my having tripped her up in front of the principal.

"Good," she said, still in Cantonese, "good, you're happy here, I hope you continue *being happy* here."

She shook the hand of the dumbfounded principal and walked out without another word. She had perfected her exits in the movies, and I couldn't help admiring her elegant turn of heel even as she abandoned me. The next thing I heard was the wheels of her rented Jaguar scrunching the gravel in the driveway.

My mother's whirlwind visit taught me a lesson. Always dissimulate. Never wallow. I'd never thought myself capable of a low, shallow cunning, but within days of my mother's visit I'd stopped obsessing about food and avoiding people and applied my mind to blending in. It was not easy. I had been a solitary only child and I never got used to sharing a room or the unconscious ease with which the English girls stripped for games. Still, I did what was required not to draw attention to myself. I worked on my halting English, to the point where it began to scramble through my brain like a computer virus—I woke up one morning and found that I was thinking in English and having to translate the sentences back into

Cantonese. I kept up my marks; I bided my time. In my third year, I got lucky. I was allotted a room of my own, of broom cupboard dimensions, to be sure, but the privacy was what I prized. I had few friends, but I didn't want friends. I preferred to travel light, like the terrorist who empties his life of all baggage while waiting for the coded call to action. Then I met the pool boy.

Once the pool boy said to me, "You must be rich."

I said, automatically, "No, I'm not." Denial came naturally to me, even of the truth; especially of the truth.

"Everybody at that school's rich." He had a kind of reductive logic sometimes.

"A lot of girls are on scholarship."

"But you're not."

I stopped denying it. "No, I'm not. What are you going to do, kidnap me?" The words were out of my mouth before I knew it. I kicked at him clumsily and swung out of bed.

"Hey," he said, startled. "It was just talk." He propped himself up on his elbows. "Come back in. You'll catch your death of cold."

I got back in and hid my face in the crook of his shoulder, my legs scissored in his; it was the only way we could squeeze in his bed. His hand continued to stroke my hair but there was a new tautness in him that destroyed the usual easy fit of our bodies, a tautness sprung from all the questions that he would have liked to ask but didn't.

When I was growing up, I had little sense of my family's wealth. I took for granted the luxury cars that my parents drove once a week, if at all; the fleet of *amahs* who looked after my mother and me; the safe, hidden behind a portrait of my paternal grandfather in the study, in which my mother kept her jewellery, including her favourite jade earrings. By the standards of Hong Kong, we weren't particularly ostentatious, nor were we even particularly rich. We lived halfway up Victoria Peak, which perfectly exemplified my father's mid-level standing in Hong Kong's strict pecking order of tycoons. At night the glittering tapestry of the city spread itself out just below our garden; it seemed like a display put on for our benefit. I was used to hearing my father say, "Now, so and so has serious money—" so that I somehow formed the impression that our own money was never, quite, serious enough.

I was always ferried by car to and from my exclusive girls' school, where all the other pupils came from similar backgrounds. Occasionally, I would accompany my mother on shopping trips to the city centre; I would loll around, bored, on the sofas of the trendy boutiques where she shopped with a desperation bordering on the manic. Or she would bring me to high tea with the other skinny brittle women who formed her social circle after her marriage where I picked at the *hors d'oeuvres* while a pianist tinkled *Rhapsody in Blue* on a baby grand. (Once I went up to the pianist and told him, "My father plays much better piano than you," before my mother could yank me away, red-faced.) Every Sunday we had lunch at my father's family home, where we ate in a high-ceilinged dining room dwarfed by a chandelier that always swayed dangerously in strong winds, where we were served by ancient retainers in full uniform. In my grandfather's study, a photograph of himself and Chiang Kai-Shek took pride of place on the mantelpiece.

The world beyond the tinted glass of our car, beyond the boutiques and five-star hotels was a fetid panorama that I observed at a safe distance. As a very small child, I saw beggars on the street and asked my mother in all innocence, "Why don't they go home?"

I gradually became aware that not everyone lived the way we did. I remember, when I was five, being brought by my mother to a nasty-looking block of public housing in the outermost reaches of Kowloon. The paint must once have been white but it was hard to tell. We walked up four flights of rank-smelling stairs and stopped at a door marked 44. My mother fished in her Prada bag for her bunch of keys and fitted one into the lock. I was confused: was my mother going to burgle the place? We stepped into a flat so cramped there was hardly space to move. Boxes took the place of furniture and a strong odour of cat litter pervaded the rooms. In the sitting-room—or what passed for the sitting-room—a small elderly birdlike couple watched a swordfighting serial. The wife wore the kind of quilted sleeveless jacket that streetsweepers wear on cold days while the husband—and this was a point of horrified fascination—had lost part of his right thumb. My mother said, "Mama," then, "Ah-bah." I clutched her hand and stared in astonishment at the people who were my grandparents.

It was hard to say who was more petrified, my grandparents or me. My grandparents had refused to visit their daughter in her new house, fearing they would feel out of place, and my mother had baulked at returning to the home that she'd fled with such relief. It was my mother who blinked first: hence this trip. But she was not happy having to cave in, and my mother's unhappiness was always a palpable, bracing thing. I saw immediately that my grandparents were cowed by my mother, and I wasn't surprised. I couldn't make the connection myself between these two homely figures and their polished, gleaming daughter. My grandmother smiled at me with trembling eagerness, revealing a mouthful of gold teeth, and offered me a plate of biscuits. I shook my head and buried my face in my mother's shoulder. "I want to go," I said. My statement fell into one of those deafening silences that opened up between my mother's scattershot utterances. The trip was not a success.

Later, my mother moved her parents to an apartment in one of Hong Kong Island's better districts. It was not large but still my mother's parents seemed almost intimidated by its size. Boarding up two rooms, they lived and ate out of one bedroom, which they also piled high with the ubiquitous cardboard boxes. My mother nagged them to no effect. Her visits were like military inspections: her parents seldom passed muster and there was no disguising the relief in their faces when it was time for us to go. They had spent years as factory workers; my grandfather's thumb had been torn off in an industrial accident. I used to stare at that mutilated finger until my mother said sharply, "Jade?" and I looked away guiltily. My grandparents would have liked to get close to me, their only grandchild, but it was difficult. They were beyond the tinted glass.

They fled one weekend the year that I turned nine. We walked in to find a bare apartment, the boxes gone. My mother turned white; she swayed and would have fallen if my father hadn't caught her. He laughed; she snapped that it wasn't funny. Of course my grandparents had decamped to their old home, boxes and all. I never saw them again. They had made my mother lose face and she never forgave them. She paid for their upkeep but her filial piety stopped there.

Oddly enough, it was always my father who had put my mother's parents at ease, whose large affable presence soothed away the sting of my mother's remarks. He had a simple trick of leaning forward in his chair, his hands clamped on his knees, a look of intent concern on his face as he faced his interlocutor; it made you think you were the sole object of his attention, that he really, really *cared*. In life, when it mattered, my father was a much better actor than my mother. His fake empathy made him enormously successful with women—it was one reason for my mother's afternoon crying jags in the hallway—and with people in all walks of life.

"Life is a façade," he liked to say. He meant, let the masses think you care, anything goes that oils the wheels of life and lets us all get along. "Relax, just relax," he told my mother, after her parents pulled their disappearing trick on her; he sprawled on the sofa in his study, a whiskey in his hand, enjoying my mother's consternation. Life for him was not only a facade; it was a cabaret, a gallery of grotesques which he used to stave off the boredom that always lurked just below the surface of things for him and which, for him, was the most horrifying thing possible. Once I heard my mother exclaim, "My God, nothing touches you, *nothing*" and suddenly the whole trick of his personality was laid bare in that one sentence. His wealth insulated him from most things, including his own emotions; his encounter with my mother had pierced that carapace briefly but like a lizard's tail it regenerated itself. The numb are, for the most part, easy to live with. It was my mother, with her strong passions and even stronger will, who made the air electric with her entrances and set nerves on edge. She liked to say, "The rich have it easy *all* ways," forgetting for the moment that she had joined their ranks. And she would look accusingly at me (I was always a convenient proxy for whatever happened to vex her) and I would look away. I felt no guilt about wealth. It was the luck of the draw and it was self-evidently better to be rich than to be poor.

Anyone who professed otherwise was either crazy or an idealist or a saint and I was none of the above.

The pool boy was my secret. I was good at secrets. They came naturally to me and, after I turned thirteen, became a necessity. The trick to keeping secrets was simple. It was a matter of compartmentalisation: knowing when to bring things out at the right time. Blanking out the other life when it wasn't needed. To guard against the possibility of slip-ups, you checked all spontaneity on your part. It made you a wary, watchful person. But since I had never been a particularly fun-loving, spontaneous child anyway, this was not difficult.

In the changing room of the school, I overheard some girls discussing the pool boy. "He's *rather* dishy, isn't he?" I walked quickly away. I didn't want to know if other girls before me had also taken the 49 bus to the narrow brick house.

One Saturday afternoon when I got off the bus, I saw a girl leaving his house. Olive-skinned, Mediterranean-looking, with straight long black hair, large hoop earrings and a gypsyish flowered skirt. She walked in quick, confident steps in high laced-up boots. Passing me, she gave me a quick smile and nodded. Stranger to stranger.

The pool boy's face betrayed nothing when he opened the door. But compartmentalisation, the ability to clean up after the scene of a crime, was not his forte. In his room, a hair-clip—not mine—lay on his desk. Beneath the fug of fag smoke, dope and rain-soaked Arran wool, I detected the whiff of perfume. I hated perfume; it made me sneeze; I never wore it. The pool boy began his usual peacock's dance, easing my shirt out of my jeans, his mouth at my ear. I put my arms up against his chest, resisting him.

"I saw her."

His arms fell away; he didn't try to pretend. "She's an old friend."

"Does she console you when I'm not around?"

" Console?" He plunked himself on the edge of the bed, folded his arms and considered this. He looked sly and unguarded all at the same time. "What if she does?" I didn't answer. "Come on, you're not going to tell me there's nobody else in your life, are you, Jade?"

"What do you take me for?"

"I thought everybody at that school was a sex fiend."

"Listen, you ignorant bastard. That school is top-rated academically. Nobody's got any time for dope or sex or anything else in your poor, pathetic life." I heard my own voice and I couldn't believe it was mine. Where did those clipped English vowels, that upper-class sneer, come from?

"Except you."

I pushed at him and we fell to the floor in a heap, dragging the clothes stand down with us. I kicked him in the side and he swore and clutched my ankle, twisting it hard enough to make me cry out in pain and for him to release me. Then I was hitting him everywhere in a blind frenzy, in what was almost a joyful delirium of hate. He tried to duck, then to retreat, then his arm came up, whether intentionally or not, and I was knocked to the floor.

Neither of us spoke for a while. I crouched by the window, touching my face and wondering if I was going to bruise, while the pool boy rummaged under the bed and broke out a new packet of dope and collapsed at my feet.

"You *crazy* cow."

I didn't answer, and after a while he took my face in his hands and began running his thumb along my jawline, tenderly at first, then more insistently, until I turned my face away: it was beginning to hurt.

"It's not like I see her that often, you know?"

It took me a moment to puzzle out who *she* was, and I almost laughed. He thought I was jealous; I didn't want to disillusion him. I was thinking how little I knew about him, even though I was familiar with every crevice of his body. What I knew would scarcely have filled up a missing person's dossier. He had one GCSE in woodwork. He had spent two years on the dole after that, with an agreeable sideline in selling dope. To get his mother (she of the Protestant work ethic) off his back, he had answered an ad in the local paper for a pool boy at the school, but the sight of all those rich, pubescent girls was driving him crazy with lust and anger and class consciousness. When he spoke, I listened with half an ear, or I would cut him off. I didn't want to know more. I wasn't interested anyway. He was not stupid but his conversation was limited. What interested me was his hair and his body and the restless, yearning heat he gave off. My interest in him was narrow, selfish, monstrously egotistical. He was my creation, my fantasy, a golem I conjured into being between the hours of two and four on a Saturday afternoon. I was not angry about the girl with silver hoop earrings; I was angry with him for daring to exist outside the universe in which I'd placed him.

"Do you think about me when I'm not here?"

"What?"

I repeated my question and he rolled off me onto his back and stared at the ceiling. His face wore the frustrated look of someone whose day was not going to plan. "Sometimes. All the time. I don't know. Sometimes I think you're a dream, you know? You're not real. You're not here even when you're here." He said my name with a sudden venom: "*Jade.*"

"Sometimes I don't think I'm real either."

"What's that supposed to mean? Huh?"

I told him, "I don't know."

I learnt the art of compartmentalisation by watching my father's clumsy attempts at it. My father had secret lives galore but he was half-hearted about concealing them; he simply didn't care enough. He was deeply in love with my mother for the first two years after their wedding, then he was chronically unfaithful. Often, he didn't bother to disguise the lipstick stains or calls to the house: he'd shrug and wear that slightly rueful smile he'd perfected while my mother tore into him. (His carelessness might have been partly intentional because, when he was beginning to tire of a woman, he found it easier to have my mother give her the chop.) Like monogamy, the business life did not come easily to him either. He had taken over the family business only because it was expected of him; his heart was not in it. Conviction can be mimed for a time but can't be sustained for a lifetime. I think my father simply woke up one morning and realised that he was in a job he disliked with a wife for whom he no longer felt the same intensity of passion.

In this, he was no different from many other men (and that, too, was another tragedy because my father was keenly aware of the banality of his dilemma) but unlike other men he had better resources for self-destruction. He was—had always been—a heavy drinker, and not just in the ceremonial settings (weddings, reunion dinners) where the Chinese do most of their drinking. He had a drink every evening after work and one before bed; the liquor cabinet was always well-stocked and kept under lock and key. I can't remember when I began to notice that the drinks were no longer spaced out at intervals, that he was pretty much drinking steadily from the time he got back until he collapsed, still in his office clothes, on the study sofa in a stupor. It must have been around the time that my mother began to talk about resuming her movie career and started volunteering at a shelter for battered women. My father took exception to all this. He ridiculed her acting skills; he poured scorn on her suddenly re-discovered social conscience. She was his wife, he said; why wasn't that enough for her?

They always had their arguments in the study, in the belief that its thick walls and carpeted floors would muffle their voices, although everyone in the house, from the cook down to me, somehow always managed to discern every word they said.

"It would be enough ... it would be enough, if you still loved me."

"Love, love, why do you keep bringing up that absurd word?"

"It's not absurd to me."

"We've been married thirteen years; it's not reasonable to expect us to behave like teenagers."

"I can't go on like this."

"Well, I don't want my wife whoring it in the movies."

This would be greeted by the sound of splintering glass—my mother flinging one of his precious liquor glasses against the wall—followed by a brief struggle. It always ended with my mother running out from the study, her hair in disarray, and up the stairs to the bedroom, where she would slam the door and not emerge again for the night.

I blamed my mother. She was an easy target. I was with her most of the day and so I got the brunt of her personality. She was beautiful but argumentative; restless, impatient. Captivating from afar, but flinty and only intermittently maternal up close. I seldom saw my father and so it was easy to invest him, like a mythical creature, with all the qualities that were so lacking in my mother. I was not blind to his weaknesses but because they did not affect me directly, I could discount them. I adored him.

One afternoon my father came back early from work. It was about four; I was just back from school and doing my homework. Hearing him, I ran down the stairs.

"Where's Mummy?"

"At the shelter."

He rolled his eyes. I had no views about my mother's volunteer work, except that it was probably good for her to expend some of that volcanic energy of hers outside the house. I only knew that I did not like battered women; I did not like their despair and messy emotions. I did not, since the quarrels between my parents began, like emotions, period.

My father said, and he sounded surprised, "How you've grown, Jade."

It was the signal for me to hunch my shoulders; I had shot up over the past year, losing my baby fat, and discovered an awkward self-consciousness.

My father seemed to be pondering something. At last he smiled and said, "Shall we go for a ride?"

I could smell the liquor on his breath; he'd started early today. But he seemed cheerful and he was humming to himself, although he and my mother had had one of their worst fights the night before. I said, quickly, too quickly, "All right."

The last time I had been out alone with my father, I was about five. He had brought me to the dentist to treat a toothache; I was yelling in anticipation of the pain and was so uncontrollable that it was decided I should be put under general anaesthetic to extract the tooth. The last thing I remember was clutching my father's hand and screaming, "Daddy, Daddy," as the gas mask was clamped over my mouth. When I woke again, I saw blue sky and my father's face bobbing above mine: he was carrying me across the street to the waiting car. The sense of security his arms gave me, after the nightmare visit to the dentist, was immense; I pretended to be out for a good deal longer, just so he would continue cradling me. It was one of the rare occasions that I remember my father taking an unqualified interest in me as a small child. (That he was disappointed I had not been a boy; that he was furious my mother did not want more babies; all this had been drummed into me from a young age by my amah, a great gossiper.)

He called for the driver and we climbed in and the Jaguar with the cream leather rolled smoothly down the hillside. "Where're we going?"

"To a little place I know."

It was a place near the harbour; an area of warehouses and shipping agents and men who sat around on crates around their shopfronts, smoking heavily. I had never been here before. It had been raining and the rain had left long dirty streaks down the sides of the warehouses. My father tapped the sliding glass panel that separated us from the driver. "Stop."

My father seemed not to notice the stares—not entirely friendly—that he was attracting as he placed his perfectly-shod feet on the pavement. I wondered how my father had discovered this place, but I was not surprised. He'd always cultivated a liking for curiosities, for the offbeat and the wayward: it was a way of keeping the boredom at bay.

We stepped inside a small bar that was practically a hole in the wall. It was so dark I stumbled over the front step. The smell—of years of stale beer and cigarettes—was blanketing. I started to cough. When I stopped, and my eyes started adjusting to the gloom, I felt a battery of eyes trained on me. In actual fact, there were only about four patrons in that sinkhole that afternoon, but the intensity of their stares made it seem like a roomful of hundreds. My face started to burn. Unperturbed, my father hoisted me up onto a high stool by the bar counter.

"My kid," my father said to the bartender, a middle-aged man thoughtfully sucking a toothpick.

The bartender nodded; he seemed to know my father well. Nothing that my father did, I could tell, would faze him. "Pretty girl."

"Takes after my wife. My family all look like horses."

"Girl like that could make it in the movies."

My father said, and his tone had dropped a notch in cordiality, "Her mother tried."

The bartender had overstepped his mark and he knew it. He said, urbanely, "The usual?"

"The usual."

While the bartender poured. My father asked, casually, too casually, "M— not here today?"

The bartender looked at me and then at my father. "It's her day off today. I thought you knew."

I was given a bowl of peanuts and a Coke. After a while, the four patrons stopped staring and resumed whatever they were doing. An old Cantonese love song played over the scratchy speaker, sung very dolefully by a famous singer from the Fifties. I recognised it as one of the songs that my father liked to play late at night, when he was very drunk. My mother hated such music, just as she hated it when my father started banging jazz standards on the grand piano that took pride of place in the sitting room. I'm not sure why my mother took such exception to my father's musical interests and minor musical talent. Perhaps she saw them as a species of affectation; perhaps she sensed, rightly or wrongly, that it came from a part of him that he deliberately kept from her and which she wouldn't have understood in any event and so she felt threatened by it.

From where I sat, I could see the sun setting over the harbour. It was very pretty, an explosion of salmon pinks and oranges that lit up the sky and drenched the drab surroundings briefly in flame. Then the dark carne, but we continued sitting there. My father was talking to the bartender, who sucked his toothpick and polished his glasses. No-one else came in while we were there.

My father talked about a lot of things. He talked dreamily, desultorily, not always making sense and looping round in circles. He talked about my mother, and how he'd felt about her the day he'd met her all those years ago, all young and ambitious and with that indefinable spark of hers ("everybody in my family is dead, they've been dead for years and don't even know it"). And how their marriage had somehow evolved over the years into a battle of wills so intense he'd somehow forgotten the point of the contest, except that he'd never yet met anyone he didn't want to control. He talked about the family business. How it would be better off in somebody else's hands. How there were days he thought of setting fire to the family properties and collecting the insurance and running off to San Francisco with a nice young girl that he knew. The bartender didn't interrupt. He seemed to have heard this all before. I listened until I got bored or lost the thread and finished all my peanuts. My father's confessional streak did not surprise me; how many times had I heard my mother admonish my father, after he'd said one too many indiscreet things to total strangers, "You don't tell people things like that." To which my father invariably replied, "We're all human, aren't we?"

"Daddy," I said at last. I was thinking that my mother would be back from her battered women's shelter and would be frantic if I wasn't there.

His eyes focused on me for the first time. "Jade," he said, and his voice was thick with whiskey. I'm not sure he really recognised me. He put out his hand and it caressed my cheek and I felt a mild electric shock. He seldom touched me—like most Chinese fathers, he was not demonstrative—but when he did it had never been like that. I shied away. "'Scuse me," he muttered. He stumbled off to the men's.

The bartender looked at me, not unkindly. "You should be at home doing your homework."

He was right, but he also had no right to judge my father. I looked round for my father; he was taking a long time. I felt rising panic; what if he didn't return? The place seemed to stink worse than ever. What, I wondered, was its attraction for my father?

The bartender remarked, "Your father's a very, very strange man. Not a bad man. Just strange."

I slipped off the bar stool and started in the direction of the men's, just as my father stepped out.

"I'm here," he said, as though he knew what I was thinking.

In the car, he said, "You're not going to tell your mother, are you?"

I said, "No." I liked the idea of our keeping a secret from my mother. I sat close to my father as we sped through the rain-slick city back home. The streetlights glimmered hazily through the streaming windows. His arm was around my shoulders and his hand was stroking my hair, slowly, rhythmically.

On Monday, I decided to walk down to the pool during my free period. The pool boy was trawling the water and at first he didn't see me and when he did he stopped for a moment and looked round. But when he saw I was not going to do anything, he resumed his trawling, more slowly this time, all the while looking at me. It was an expressionless gaze, his usual blank slate, but he brought the whole weight of him to bear in it. I'd come to kill some time by taking a peek at him as though he were an animal at the zoo, but now I found I couldn't move; I was trapped in that gaze, held fast, a moth pinned to a mounting-board. I raised my hands, I don't know why, perhaps to shield myself from his eyes. Then we heard a burst of chatter in the distance and whatever it was that held me in thrall was broken. I turned and ran, but I could still feel the pool boy's eyes on my back.

I fell asleep once in the pool boy's room and dreamt of my father in the pool again. Something was happening to the water: smoky pink tendrils were unfurling around my father's head; they were few and delicate at first, then mushroomed rapidly into a red mist that blotted out his face. I realised it was blood, seeping out from the wound at the back of his head where he had been shot execution-style and I woke with a start, a scream stillborn in my throat. "Easy," the pool boy said, "*easy*." He held me by the arms; I'd been thrashing around in my sleep. I subsided. The neighbour was playing some heavy metal record, the keening guitars weaving a feedback loop that never seemed to end.

"Bad dream?"

I nodded.

"Want to tell me about it?"

"No." I said, "Do you see things in the water when you clean the pool?"

He gave me a funny look. "Of course I see things in the water. Dead leaves. Drowned beetles. Stuff. Why?"

"Nothing."

"You don't tell me anything, do you, Jade?"

"I told you my name."

He started to croon, *Keep me searching for a heart of jade. And I'm getting old.*

He must have felt me twitch in his arms, because they tightened around me. How could he have known that the last person to call me heart of jade was my father, on our last family holiday in Bali before his death? We were seated, my mother, my father and I, at the alfresco hotel restaurant set prettily on stilts just above the seaside rocks, the table lit by a single flickering candle and tapers of flame tied to wooden poles. It was the latest in *au naturel* resort settings and the only sound, apart from the lapping of the waves and the murmur of the other diners, was the crackle of mosquitoes being electrocuted. The first course had not arrived and already my father was drunk.

We had arrived only that afternoon after a delayed flight and already I was wondering how we were going to make it through the next three days before we went home. (I had not wanted to come; it was my mother who had said, "If you make a fuss, I will never forgive you.") My father had started early at the pool bar, while my mother took a nap and I went for a swim. I had nothing else to do. When it was time to change, I had had to walk past my father on his bar stool. "Jade," he said. There was a note of curiosity in his voice. His hand was on my neck. He had not touched me since the last time, though I was always conscious now of him watching me, steadily, ruminatively. I could not see his eyes behind his sunglasses; all I could think of was the heat of his skin against mine and how I wanted it to continue forever. I put up my hand to touch his wrist, and his hand fell away at once. He said, "You'd better ask your mother to get ready for dinner."

Just before we left for dinner, my mother asked me, "Are you going out like that?" I looked down at myself. I was wearing jeans and a tank top; it was warm. It was Bali, after all.

"Leave her alone," my father said, amiably; he did not look at me.

"She's not a child any more."

"Of course she is."

I said, "I'll change."

At dinner I ordered roast chicken with rosemary and coriander while my mother asked for a salad and my father a large whiskey.

My mother said, "You're not eating."

"I'm not hungry."

She was quiet for a while, and then her voice was low and unlike her usual voice, "You could at least pretend. For the sake of the child. To be happy."

Their faces flickered in and out of the shadows cast by the candles and the tapers of flame; I could not see their expressions easily. This was a place for lovers, not families: at the other tables, heads bent together conspiratorially. It was the worst possible place my mother could have chosen for a holiday.

"Now she's a child. A moment ago she wasn't."

"You're twisting my words."

"Isn't it bad enough that we're all here on a holiday that we don't want to be on, eating food that we don't want to eat? We could have given it to the battered women. *Couldn't* we, Jade?"

"Please," I said. "Stop it."

My mother said to my father, her voice rising, "God, you're sick. I hope you're happy now."

"Jade," my father was saying. "I named you. Did you know that? Your mother wanted something worthy; I wanted something decorative. And you've grown up decorative like your mother. But with something else as well. Something at the heart of you that you keep hidden. That's right. That's how it should be. Jade. That's a good name. My jewel, my mother of pearl, my diamond of fire, my heart of jade—" His voice had grown thick, slurred, again, as it had the day in the bar.

My mother scraped her chair back noisily and ran off into the darkness.

"Heart of jade," my father said again. "No, not a child anymore."

He got up heavily and went off to look for my mother. The food arrived; I finished all of it. I was not hungry but I felt it was important not to waste anything.

See p. 378

I said now to the pool boy, "It doesn't rhyme."

"Heart of jade," he said to the air. "What's it like in there?"

One Saturday afternoon I overstayed my allotted time and, running down the stairs, met his mother letting herself in the front door. "Hello," I said, beaming madly; I didn't know what else to do. The dope had blunted my nerve ends, dulling speech; I spoke through a fog. She said nothing. I could see where the pool boy had got his hair, but hers lay in a limp frizz close to her scalp. She looked like every other middle-aged defeated Englishwoman I had seen in the high street, with bad hair, bad teeth and runny stockings, trailing their grocery bags behind them. They filled me with a kind of horror. I edged out the front door, while behind me I could hear her voice rising. "—lost your mind? ... statutory rape ... why the bleedin' hell don't you get a proper job ... bleedin' Chink—"

The outdoor cold was razor-keen, salutary, shrivelling away the drowsy sense of well-being that the dope induced. I made the bus with seconds to spare; as it pulled away with me huddled in the back seat on the upper deck, I saw the pool boy sprinting for the bus-stop in bare feet that looked absurdly white and long on the grimy pavement. He was shouting into the wind, waving at the bus. As we rounded the corner, my last glimpse was of him pulling up, winded, and then he straightened and spat into the road, in disgust or frustration, I couldn't tell.

Monday was fogbound, relegating the spring sunshine of the past few days to a dim memory. The school loomed out of the fog like a marooned ship. From the classroom, the pavilion housing the pool could not be seen. I looked down at my physics textbook and none of the diagrams made sense. I excused myself.

The pool boy was packing up his things when I arrived.

"What took you so long?"

"How did you know I was going to come?"

"'Course you were."

I didn't know why I had come either except that I couldn't get the image of him running barefoot along the pavement out of my head. He had plenty of pride, and his mother's outburst must have been humiliating. I'd witnessed that humiliation and it felt as though I'd unwittingly opened some invisible door and stepped a little further into his life against my will and now I was wondering how to get myself out through that door again.

His manner was a little abrupt and he wouldn't quite look me in the eye. He fumbled in the pockets of his dungarees and produced something wrapped in waxed paper. "Here. I got this for you."

It was a silver dragonfly brooch, old-fashioned and serene and finely-wrought all at the same time. With my years of trailing my mother to the best jewellers, I knew immediately it was expensive; I wondered if the pool boy knew it. I doubted his money box could have paid for this.

"Go on."

"I don't care what your mother said. Honestly."

He said, fiercely, "It's got nothing to do with my mum, all right?"

I held it in my hand, astonished at its beauty and what it revealed about the pool boy and me. I took his hand in mine, pressed it briefly fingertip to fingertip, then streaked off across the grounds, breathless.

That night, we heard that one of the girls had lost a family heirloom, a silver dragonfly brooch conservatively estimated at several thousand pounds. A police report had been made.

I had a biscuit tin in which I kept the Chinese tidbits that my mother sent me, extravagantly, by airmail. I emptied the tin, wrapped the brooch in layers of tissue before laying it at the bottom of the tin and replaced the biscuits.

Saturday seemed an eternity away and yet when it came I put off going to the pool boy's narrow brick house. I took the bus to the town and walked through the shopping centre. I had an ice-cream. Time ticked itself away. An hour later, I boarded the 49 bus.

He opened the door promptly, too promptly. He'd been waiting for me. I tried not to think of that. His face was cloudy. "What happened to you?"

To forestall his questions, I put my arms around his neck and, surprising myself, kissed him. He wasn't expecting that; he kissed me back warily and looked up and down the street as though to see who might be watching.

"I thought you weren't coming."

"What if I hadn't?"

He shrugged. "I don't know. Go to the school and look for you."

"That wouldn't be wise."

We had not made it up to his bedroom; we were still downstairs. I looked round curiously, as though seeing it for the first time: the worn, stained furniture, the moth-eaten rug, the yellowed photographs on the side-table. His house felt different after the encounter with his mother: tight, airless, contaminated.

His tone was a little snippy: "Why not?"

"Someone lost a brooch at school. She made a police report."

He didn't blink. "Oh yeah?"

I took the brooch from the pocket of my jacket and held it up to the light. "It's lovely."

For a moment he was silent and then he broke into laughter. "Yeah. Isn't it? Moment I saw it I knew it was meant for you. *Jade.*" His hands had slipped round my waist; I slipped out of them.

"How did you find it?"

He replied easily, as I knew he would, "In the changing room. You'd be surprised what you find in the changing room."

"And you didn't think of returning it?" He looked at me as if I were mad. "Finder's keepers. You look out for yourself."

I was looking at the photographs on the chipped side-table. The pool boy as a small child, with a perfectly round face and the same unruly hair. At the beach. Having a birthday party. His mother in the background, younger, smiling, hopeful. She seemed to have no connection to the frowsty woman I had seen the other day, laden with shopping bags.

"Why do we stay in your room all the time?"

"We don't have to."

"Where would we go?" And indeed I couldn't imagine us in any other setting; the pool boy was as immutably fixed in his room as a figure in a painting.

He hazarded, frowning, "Strawberry picking?" He stood with his hands in his trouser pockets, watching me narrowly.

"*Never.*" I had once picked strawberries with my mother in a field near the school on one of her visits. We had not realised that strawberries grew on the ground in bushes. It was infernally hot as we picked and pricked our fingers and then a stormcloud loomed out of nowhere and drenched us. The strawberries were crushed by the time we brought them back to the hotel. "Well," my mother had said, shaking out her hair, "*that's* the last time I'm doing such coolie work."

In one of the photographs, a man lurked in the background at a child's birthday party. Something about the planes of his face seemed familiar. "Who's that?"

He said slowly, "My father."

A small click sounded in my head, as of something slotting into place. "He doesn't live here."

"He's dead. Or in prison. Or a millionaire in the Bahamas. I don't know. Don't really care. He walked out when I was five. How'd you know?"

"My father died when I was thirteen."

"What happened to *him?*"

"He was kidnapped. The kidnappers killed him."

My mother paid the two million dollar ransom immediately, against the wishes of my father's father and the police, who wanted to negotiate. She screamed at them that they knew nothing. A few days later, my father's body washed up in Hong Kong harbour. According to the autopsy, he had been shot minutes after being snatched. The kidnappers fled across the border to the Chinese mainland, where they could not be extradited. Six months later, all three were shot, execution-style, in the back of the head in a brothel in Guangdong province. The Hong Kong papers speculated that my mother had hired assassins to extract revenge; my mother sued the papers for libel and won.

The pool boy's attention was caught. He said, "You're pulling my leg."

"Why would I pull your leg?"

"Why? I don't know—I'm sorry."

"Don't be."

He took his cue from my tone: "That kind of thing happen much in Hong Kong?"

"It's a cottage industry."

"Sometimes you sound so old. A hundred or something. And you're just a kid."

He came up behind me and turned me round and I was too late averting my wet face. Furiously, I ran my sleeve across my eyes. What I felt was not grief; it was the facsimile of an emotion, as precisely cued as the swelling music on a movie soundtrack; I wept because it was what the script demanded. The pool boy did not know this (how could he?). He started kissing me just above the eyes, slowly, gently, as though I were gossamer and might snap and whispered my name like a mantra and I let him; I did nothing to let him know that he was mistaken about the kind of person I was. Then I told him, "I have to get back early today," and he watched me leave and said nothing. It was the first time I had left without our making love. My step quickened the further I got from his house: I don't know what I was running away from—his animal warmth and dead life that seemed like a trap or the fact that he thought he was in love with me.

A huge bouquet of roses and a pair of jade earrings wrapped in silverfoil arrived for my mother on her thirteenth wedding anniversary. They were delivered by van, just as my mother was about to leave for lunch. She received them in her best actressy fashion, arms thrown wide, her perfect, white-capped teeth drawn back in a tinkling laugh. The delivery boys made her day by recognising her and asking for her autograph.

"Darling," she said to me, "aren't they lovely?" I was on my way to piano class. "Lovely," I echoed. I looked at the flowers and wondered whether my father had knowingly chosen this particular shade of dried-blood. Probably he had simply instructed his secretary to pick something out of a catalogue. Knowing this did not make me feel better. I was jealous of my mother, jealous that my father had even troubled himself with this token gesture. The jealousy, I knew, was insanity. This was my mother. She had given birth to me. In the Chinese way of thinking, I owed her my life.

I was in no mood for piano class. I rang the teacher with some excuse and, after the chauffeur had dropped me at the piano studio, I sneaked round the corner and took the bus to the ferry terminal. I sat on a bench, hugging my arms to myself in the stiff wind and watching the Star Ferry dock again and again. It was over a week since we had returned from Bali and everything was out of joint. All I could think of was my father's touch and how I could get him to repeat it and yet continue to be his child and my mother's child at the same time. There were times I thought I was going mad just thinking about it. My father had uncorked something in me that day at the bar and it could not be bottled again. I looked at couples in the street and felt such an intensity of curiosity I could barely prevent myself from asking them outright what it felt like to kiss the beloved's lips. The girls at school talked about boys in a silly, giggly way; what they were saying seemed to have nothing to do with what had happened between my father and me and I would walk away when they started. I had a reputation for being prudish.

My mother's manner to me since the holiday was different. Too careful, too bright. The way you might deal with someone you suspected to be unhinged, or damaged. She was waiting for someone or something to snap, possibly herself. That night in Bali, my father had caught up with her as she was about to barricade herself in her hotel room. I was not there, but I could picture the scene because I had seen it so many times before: my mother hitting out at my father in a frenzy and my father catching hold of her wrists in an iron grip until she'd calmed down. Except that this time she would not have calmed down quickly, she would have screamed that if he was capable of what she suspected, she would kill him. And he would have talked her out of her fears—my father's one strength was talking—he would have pointed out the absurdity of her delusions and the harm she would do if she persisted with these accusations. My mother was nothing if not pragmatic. And she desperately wanted to believe him. When I got back from the restaurant, the door to their room was shut and everything was silent.

My mother called to say she would not be back for dinner. I ate alone, watched some television in the study and fell asleep on the sofa. When I woke, the study lamp was dazzling my eyes and I heard the clink of the decanter.

My father was saying, his voice light and amused, "I lost a deal today that would have made us twice as rich. All the man wanted was an invitation to dinner and I wouldn't give it to him because his father runs the mafia in Macau. I was prepared to take his money, but I wasn't prepared to invite him to dinner. There's something flawed in that reasoning, isn't there?"

Then he said, and he'd dropped the bantering tone, "You've been avoiding me, Jade."

I sat up. Sleep had vanished; my mind was cold, clear.

"I haven't been avoiding you."

He slung his tie on the door knob and settled down slowly in the shadows at the other end of the sofa from me. The glass in his lap glimmered.

"No," he said at last, "I've been avoiding *you*."

He was silent for so long I thought he might have fallen asleep. My knees, tucked under me, were beginning to cramp.

Then he spoke again. "What does a man do who's fallen in love with his daughter?" I saw the reflection from the glass as he lifted it and drained it. "If he were a decent man—the kind of man he'd like himself to be—he would put a bullet through his head for even thinking those thoughts. But what if he were the kind of man who's been brought up to think that the world is for his taking? A cold, selfish, arrogant bastard who's never stopped to consider the effects of his actions on other people? Who's never been told there were any limits to what he *can* want?"

His arm stretched out along the back of the sofa, still holding his glass. "Of course, this is a purely hypothetical case I'm talking about." And then he started to laugh and the laugh turned into a cough and in his coughing fit he dropped the glass onto the sheepskin rug.

My mind was a blank—a pure, petrified blank—as I reached out and slipped my hand in his. He drew me to him and then his mouth was in my hair ("I can smell the sea, you've been to the harbour today, haven't you") and at my neck and his arms were around me. It was quiet, very quiet; the ticking of the clock over the door was deafening.

An eternity can be compressed into a few seconds. I saw my mother first, a black, slender column silhouetted in the doorway; my eyes travelled upwards to the clock and my first thought was that time had hardly moved. Then I half-fell, half-tore myself from my father's arms and landed in a heap on the floor. It was undignified, farcical; in any other circumstance, my father would have laughed. In any other circumstance, he would have unfolded himself languidly to his feet and fired the spiel that he kept ready like a gun that was always cocked. But this time he seemed slow, befuddled. He spoke my mother's name and then his voice trailed off uncertainly. My mother advanced into the study, into the circle of light cast by the standing lamp, and I thought how beautiful she still was, how wasted all that beauty was. Then I heard her raspy, unnatural breathing. It was the last thing I heard, before I fled the study and locked myself in my bedroom.

The first thing my mother said, the first thing she always said whenever she came to visit me at school was, "I can't stay long."

The next minute her mobile phone rang. "*Wei?*" She broke into rapid-fire Cantonese. Her conversation lasted fifteen minutes; she was discussing the flooring in the latest office block she was developing back home. She wanted something polished, *high class*, and she reeled off the Italianate names of different kinds of granite like a pro. She was wearing a silver-grey silk trouser suit and her hair was bundled up in a neat chignon at her neck; since my father's death her beauty had developed a professional, untouchable sheen.

"Now where were we?"

"We weren't anywhere, Mother."

While she was talking, I'd been walking and my path was taking us to the pool. Then I remembered it was Monday and wanted to turn back, but my mother was already gaining on the French doors, exclaiming *lovely*

lovely the way all the parents did when they came in high summer with the trees in full bud and the sprinklers doing their watery ballet across the lawns. Except that it was a cold grey day, the sky the texture of porridge, and there was no reason for her fulsome praises apart from having to prove to herself that she was getting her money's worth. "It's closed for cleaning," I said to the air.

The pool boy was having his customary morning cigarette. He stopped when he saw my mother, but he needn't have bothered, because my mother never noticed people like him. Where she came from—where I came from—we took people like him for granted. I waited by the door and we both watched as she did a sort of sprint around the pool, admiring its watery extravagance. His eye caught mine, and I thought of the time that I had kissed him down the length of his scar and my face started to burn.

When my mother wafted back to the door, she said to me, in a dissatisfied way, "There are *dead leaves* in the pool."

It was the pool boy who answered. "I haven't finished cleaning, Mrs Wong." His tone was polite, too polite. He'd been goaded and he was aping a servant's deference for her benefit. Stop it, I wanted to tell him, my mother's not stupid.

He'd gone too far; that *Mrs Wong* was a red flag. My mother took in my burning face and her eyes focused for the first time on the pool boy in that intent, android stare of hers, the stare that meant her brain was processing a billion gigabytes of information per second. The pool boy was the one to blink first. "'Scuse me," he muttered and shambled off with his pails.

I left first, half-running up the path to the main building. My mother caught up with me, her high heels clicking like machine gun fire along the stones.

"How long has that boy been working here?"

"I don't know."

She looked at me directly. "I don't like the look of him."

"Then you should tell the principal."

I practically fell headlong into the principal's office, I was so anxious to cut short any tête-à-tête with my mother. In the clink of the translucent tea-cups they wheeled out for such occasions, I hoped my mother would forget the pool boy.

The principal and my mother discussed my future. I sat dumb; I had no role to play although the principal did turn to me once and said brightly, "And I'm told you want to be a doctor, Jade?"

"Oh yes," I said. It was what my mother wanted and ever since she had caught me with my father, my life had been devoted to doing what my mother wanted. Even if the sight of blood did make me sick. I drained the cup, while my mother and the principal discussed university rankings.

Outside, my mother said, "What's this I hear about you not wanting to swim?"

"I don't like that pool."

"I hope you're not getting morbid. I can't stand morbidity—"

Her phone rang again. I thought about the hard splat that a body makes when it gets thrown into water and displaces an equal volume of liquid. Then I saw the colour rising in my mother's cheeks as she turned away and lowered her voice. I caught the word "dearest" in Cantonese.

When she had snapped shut her phone, I asked, "Who was that?"

She took a deep breath. "I may as well tell you. I'm getting married again to—" and she named the man whose father my father had described as running the Mafia in Macau. "It'll be a quiet ceremony, don't worry, you don't have to fly back for it."

I stared at her dumbly. She broke out, "Your father's been dead three years." I flinched; we seldom mentioned my father.

"Is he moving in?"

"Well, *of course*, he'll be my husband and your stepfather. What's the matter?"

"Nothing. I'm very happy for you, Mother."

She looked at me for the first time in her life in something approaching despair. I looked round. Don't, I was praying, don't break the code by which we've lived for three years. Namely, never talk about anything between mother and daughter that you wouldn't mention in front of a dinnertable of complete strangers. It was a good code, one that had got us through the days after she'd found me with my father, when her façade of normality, worn with all the bravado of the Emperor's new clothes, was the only thing that kept us from the nuthouse.

"What really happened that night at the harbour, Jade? Did you see the men waiting for your father?"

I found my voice. "Of course not. I *told* you before." My voice was high, childishly indignant. Any prospect of breaking the code left me in a cold sweat. And in the same instant my mother's features smoothly rearranged themselves once again into the clear-eyed, clear-browed fearless look that I'd seen her use so many times in the movies to face off the invaders/ corrupt officials. I used to wonder why she felt it necessary to use that look on me, but I had long since given up wondering.

"Well," she said at last, "I have to go."

We hugged clumsily as we always did, with a palpable sense of relief that the visit was over, and I saw her to her rented Jaguar in the carpark. She went through her pre-driving ritual: quick peek in the compact to ensure that her always impeccable make-up was still impeccable, a quick dab at her hair.

She started the engine and was about to swing off when something struck her.

"Oh, by the way, I've told the principal to get rid of that pool boy. She's agreed."

"I've been thinking that we should enrol Jade in boarding school in England."

My mother let this fall, light and inconsequential as a feather, during Sunday lunch with my father's parents.

"A very good idea," my grandmother said. "It'll be easier for her to get into university in England."

My mother and grandmother seldom agreed on anything; this was a rare, noteworthy event.

My father said, "She is *not* going away to boarding school."

"Oh, come now," my grandfather interjected. "You went to boarding school."

"And I hated every minute of it. The class system. The sneering sense of superiority of the English."

"You do like to exaggerate," his father said mildly.

My father had drunk too much; the wine decanter at this elbow was almost empty. "I swore I would never let a child of mine go through what I did."

My mother said, as though she hadn't heard him, "Jade and I are going to England next week. The principal of—" and here she reeled off the names of certain of the more prominent boarding schools—"has kindly agreed to meet us."

My father looked at me with something approaching hatred. "Did you know about this?"

I said, "Yes." It was a complete surprise to me, but I hewed to the vow I'd made when I'd fled the study that night. Do whatever my mother wanted. Empty myself of all will and desire and become her vessel. Only in that way, it seemed to me, could I pretend that nothing had happened.

I had waited all night for the sound of breaking glass, my mother's rising voice, but it never came. I heard only her quick, light step as she made her way upstairs, then the click of her bedroom door. Towards dawn I fell asleep out of exhaustion and it was my mother who came to wake me for school. "You'll be late, darling." She, too, looked as though she had not slept, but her voice was steady. So that was how she'd decided to play the game: preternatural calm; eerie restraint. A shrewd move: it was more terrifying, more effective, than any glass-throwing spree. I felt no real remorse, I felt nothing; there was no room in me for anything except a sense of panic that I'd driven a knife straight into the heart of my family without intending to. (But hadn't I intended it to happen? Was thoughtlessness only an excuse? Who was the seducer and the seduced?) Complete abnegation of self, absurd and pointless though it was, seemed the only course of action.

We were not allowed to be alone together anymore, my father and I. My mother was always present now, a hovering, watchful shadow. The servants had also been warned. Not in so many words, but they had formed a habit of materialising, silent, tactful, at my father's elbow if my mother had to leave the room. Of course my father knew what was happening, but he was powerless to stop it. I think for the first time in his life he was beginning to be a little afraid of my mother.

My grandparents looked a little surprised at this byplay but did not probe further. They were habitually incurious people. My father's marriage to my mother had rocked that lethargy briefly but once they had resigned themselves to her, the lassitude had descended again. The family business was into third generation sclerosis by the time it reached my father, well past the second generation danger stage that the Chinese always predicted for wealthy families.

My mother laid her hand—the fingers slender, the nails manicured, the skin cool to the touch—on mine. "It's settled then."

'Happy?"

"Yes." I didn't know what the word meant but this was not the time to temporise. He stretched out on the seat with his head in my lap and mechanically I ran my fingers through his hair. In five minutes he was asleep. *Let's go*, I prayed, and miraculously the engine started and the near-empty bus pulled out from its bay. I shut my eyes, but my brain continued its feverish whirr. I shrugged off my coat, then pulled it back on again: I was cold yet burning up and shaking uncontrollably. This was what cold turkey must be like. I was weaning myself off three years spent in the service of my mother's will; I was weaning myself off my mother. After my father's death, I'd cleaved to her in shock. I'd said nothing when she took over the family company; I took her side against my father's parents; I allowed her to hire two Nepalese bodyguards whose thin, dark presences I did my best to outwit while they put up with my antics with resigned, smiling grace. She had every right to get married, I knew, and yet it still felt like a betrayal. Of me. Of my father. I'd thought the lesson of my father's death was that my mother and I were bound in fealty to each other, and it turned out I was wrong.

Better not to think of how I'd sneaked out of school with nothing except fifty pounds (all the hard cash I had in the world) and the brooch that the pool boy had given me. Nothing else, not even a toothbrush. Better not to think of the uproar that would result when the school discovered me gone the next morning or my mother's reaction. Better not to think at all.

I thought, the pool boy had said, *we might run away together* and when I'd asked, *where?* he'd said, *London.* I'd almost burst out laughing, at the paucity of his imagination; I'd almost asked him, *why not Shanghai? Durban? Patagonia?* Instead, I'd said, absurdly, *London's a good place to start.*

After my mother had disappeared, I'd run back to the pool, no longer caring whether anyone saw me. He had finished cleaning and was seated on one of the stone urns outside the French windows in the watery sunshine, the sleeves of his dirty white Arran jumper tugged down over his hands. We didn't say anything for a while and I thought how great it would be if I could just freeze his sculpted perfection forever in that moment in time and never have to break the silence.

I told him, unnecessarily, "My mother's gone."

He said, slowly, "You look like her."

"But I'm not her."

"She's tough. But she's had to be tough, right? Whereas *you.* You've never had to fight."

"You think you know me."

"I don't know anything about you. I'm crazy to be even talking to you. But you can't do everything by the book, can you?"

That was when he said, "I thought we might run away together."

I did try to warn him. "You can't afford London. You can't afford me."

He didn't understand. "I've got money saved. I know someone who can put us up til we find our feet. I'll get a job—"

"My mother will find us. She'll eat you for breakfast."

He laughed. "Oh yeah? What's she going to do, give me a clip on the ear?"

"She'll press charges." I heard his mother's voice: "Statutory rape. Sex with a minor. Whatever it's called."

It seemed to be filtering through; his eyes became very green, glassy, the way they did when he was intent on something. "Why are you doing this?"

"Doing what?"

He said, succinctly, "Being a bitch."

"I'm laying down the facts if I go with you."

"I know what they are, thank you very much."

I was wired; on a roll. Exhilaration pounded in my veins. If I'd wanted to, if I'd cared enough, I could have made him hate me in five minutes flat. I could have driven him away and spared him all that was to follow. But though his innocence was touching, I hadn't enough compunction for that. "The midnight bus then," I said, and he nodded, his face still cloudy and then he leant over and gave me a quick, hard kiss. *Don't love me*, I wanted to shout at him, *I don't want to be loved.* But I held my tongue.

We'd have a splendid fortnight in London, checking ourselves into a swanky hotel and living off the pool boy's dope money. Then I saw us at the end of two weeks when his money ran out, trudging back to the dingy bed and breakfast that was all he could now afford, a room not large enough to swing the proverbial cat in, the neighbours furtive and prone to being roused from bed by the police. I knew nothing about poverty and suspected I would be bad at it. The pool boy would keep promising to look for a job and in the meantime he'd stray into peddling soft drugs, the only thing he knew how to do. Unless they had pools in London that required cleaning (and I almost laughed, except that this would have scared the sole other passenger, a middle-aged lady, on the bus). In no time we would be at each other's throats. When we reached that point, I would pawn the brooch he'd stolen to give me and flee like a rat in the night. And I thought again, Shanghai. Durban. Patagonia. There would be time enough for those places. A lifetime. If my mother didn't ferret me out first. But I owed her nothing now.

I wondered if I would feel a pang when I left the pool boy. Probably not. I had betrayed my mother once and my father too, and each time the guilt and the will to expiate had run its course. I was an expert at betrayal.

Why have you let me into your life, Jade?

He knew nothing about people for whom there were no limits to wanting, who took who and what they wanted and discarded the toys when they'd outlived their usefulness or got too troublesome.

Don't ask.

On the last evening of my father's life, I gave my mother the slip and made my way down to the bar where I knew my father was certain to be. My father came back very late these days or not at all, or else he would come home and go straight out again to some party or casino that he once would have avoided like the plague. It was my mother who now seldom went out, who maintained her unflagging sentinel's vigilance in the house.

I was going away to boarding school in a month's time. My mother had arranged it, and I had acquiesced, but now as the moment drew nearer I began to panic. I was being sent into exile for an error of judgement. I was not entirely without guilt but surely the punishment was worse than the offence? I could not speak to my mother; our conversational patterns by then had evolved into a series of bright, meaningless, parrot-like exchanges. And my father avoided me; I could not hide this fact from myself.

I ran down from our house to the main road, huddled against the wind, my coat drawn tight around me. The typhoon warning to which we had woken that morning had been downgraded but the wind was still powerful enough to bend the newly-planted trees along the street close to the ground and bowl tiny pebbles through the air. At the main road, breathless from being pummelled by the wind, I got on a bus that was headed in the general direction of the harbour.

It was late, almost six, by the time I got off the bus and tried to pick my way to the street that I had seen only once. I remembered a giant black crane silhouetted like a cross against the sky, swinging bales of goods; I used it as my point of reference. The sky was grey and leaching colour even as I walked. Here the wind seemed to die down a little, defeated by the maze of warehouses. People stared at me as I passed—

there were few women in these streets—but no-one made any attempt to stop me. Then I rounded a corner and saw my father's mahogany-brown Jaguar parked with careless insolence, the front wheel up on the pavement, next to a no-parking sign. The car was empty; he'd come out without the chauffeur.

Two stocky men in worn leather jackets were loitering on the pavement next to the Jaguar, smoking and examining the sky. As I passed them, I heard one of them say to the other, in a mainland-tainted accent, "Nice car." They did not notice me. Loitering did not seem to be an uncommon activity in this area.

My father was in his usual place by the bar. The same melancholy Cantonese love song played on the jukebox. There was only one other patron, an elderly man asleep against the wall with his mouth open.

It was the bartender who saw me first and jerked his head in my direction.

"Jade," my father said. "What are you doing here?"

He had loosened his tie and rolled up the sleeves of the Italian shirt that my mother had picked out for him last Christmas. His eyes were a little bloodshot.

"I wanted to see you," I said.

He laughed, a little nervously. "My daughter," he said unnecessarily to the bartender.

"We've met." He moved further down the counter, polishing his glasses noisily and whistling through his teeth.

My father said, "How did you come?"

"I took the bus."

"This isn't a safe area, you know."

"I felt quite safe."

He wouldn't look at me; his hands fiddled with the stack of coasters on the counter. "I'll take you home. Your mother will kill me if she knows you're here." It was said with a hollow jocularity, like something he might have said months ago when the subject of my mother was still capable of being treated as a private joke between us.

"I don't want to go home. I don't want to go to boarding school."

"I tried to save you from *that*, but you were determined to be hanged, weren't you? Now it's too late."

I wanted to reach him so badly I could feel myself shaking. "Daddy."

He winced and put up his hand as though to fend off something. "Don't—" He said, his voice quite flat, "I can't give you what you want. You know that."

The song ended and we heard the disc flip over. A slight electronic whir and then the next song, equally plangent, equally theatrical. And suddenly I experienced a spurt of the irritation that my mother always felt when my father played these records at home. This was music for wallowing, for fastidious aesthetes who would have liked life to take on the smoky tints of some languorous arthouse film about love. That was my father's problem. Life was too real for him. He wasn't *real*. Like a moth—fleeting, flitting, insubstantial—he defied pinning down. My mother, though, was real. She had a reality that scorched whatever it touched.

My father toyed with life; he toyed with my mother; he was toying with me. He probably saw himself as a romantic, thwarted figure in a fantasy of illicit love. The fantasy—the torment, the irresolution, the voyeuristic thrill of the forbidden—was enough for him; he could feed off it forever. But it wasn't enough for me.

"Tell me to go away," I said.

"What?"

"Tell me to go away."

"Don't be ridiculous," he muttered. "Go and wait by the car. I'll be out in a while."

A girl emerged through the bead curtain separating the main bar from the back area. She gave a quick, knowing glance at my father as he passed; I saw her bare arm, extending all the way from slim shoulders left exposed by a halter-top, brush against his. His face, as he looked at her, was full of a shamefaced complicity. She was young, not much older than I was. She seemed oddly familiar, like the figures one comes across in dreams, and I realised, after a beat, that she looked like me. *Was* me. My doppelgänger.

I was already at the door when I saw her tie on an apron, pick up a cloth and flick it desultorily at the bar counter. The bartender picked his teeth and watched her with the same complicity I'd glimpsed in my father's face, tinged with exasperation. She yawned, and stretched her arms above her head, unselfconscious, feline. And I remembered how I had wondered why my father chose to come to this place.

The sun had sunk out of sight but night was still a hair's breadth away and the street lamps were unlit. A damp wind was blowing hard, bringing with it the swampy smell of the harbour. A far-off ship's klaxon sounded. Most of the shopfronts had closed for the night.

The two men in worn leather jackets were still smoking beside the Jaguar, though I noticed they had zipped up their fronts and that their feet were beginning to tap out an impatient rhythm on the pavement. They exuded now the coiled, waiting restlessness of pumas or some other powerful animal kept under the barest of restraints. My step quickened. One of them was casting an impatient upward glance at the sky; the other saw me and looked at me in puzzled recognition. He said something to his friend, all the while keeping an eye on me as I passed the car and rounded the corner. I kept listening for the sound of footsteps behind me but I heard nothing. I carried on walking. I knew better than to look back.

Did I foresee that, when my father stepped out of the bar, one of the men would accost him to ask for the time and that my father, with his habitual courtesy towards strangers, would say, "The time? Let me see," before noticing, too late, that the man wore his own watch? Or that my father would break into a run and that the two men would stride after him with unhurried insolence (he was tipsy and middle-aged, they were young and powerfully built) before wrestling him to the ground and shoving him into a waiting car parked across the street, just like in the movies?

Of course I couldn't have foreseen all that. Could I? Nothing in my life has been intended. I fall into things; things happen to me. All I'm guilty of, if I'm guilty of anything, is the sin of omission. It's true I wasn't thinking clearly. I kept seeing her yawn, and stretch, and yawn, and stretch, again. My father didn't need me; he had her. Did he fall in love with me because I reminded him of her, or was it the other way around? It didn't matter anymore. What a fool I was. Anger was the first unstinted emotion I'd felt in weeks and it was strangely liberating: it might have gone to my head.

It's true that I didn't warn my father about the two men. It's true I didn't turn back even when I heard my father cry, "Jade" as he fell, his shout breaking the silence of the twilight. I ran faster, my fists crammed into my mouth, my eyes stinging from the wind. I did nothing because nothing could have made any difference. I know this rationally but rationality brings meagre comfort. I tell myself that sins of omission don't kill. So why is it that, in the dreams I have of my father dead in the water, I wake knowing that they do?

Highway

"The usual?"

The usual, yes. Local coffee, strong on sweet condensed milk, served in a cracked glass on a green plastic plate, none of that designer stuff that retailed criminally for five dollars at the fancy outlets that had sprung up all over the city. All as usual, including the packet of cigarettes he'd bought that morning at a 7-Eleven and had been saving for this moment. Nothing in a long shift ever felt better than this mid-morning coffee break in a still-empty hawker centre in the middle of town.

The policeman made a show of drawing his wallet. Halim, the stallholder, said hastily, "Please. On the house."

All as usual. The ritual had begun several months ago, after the policeman had done Halim a favour by pounding the head of a loanshark who had been bothering Halim against the wall of a lonely side-lane until the loanshark had pleaded for mercy and agreed to forgive the loan. The policeman had taken no money for the favour. Halim had come to him at a low point and he had thought, *why not?* It was as simple as that. Yet, after it was done, it somehow seemed less simple. Halim had thanked him, of course, with a profuseness that bordered on obsequiousness, his eyes bright with a fear that the policeman realised, after a beat, was of *him*, he who had just done Halim the favour, and he'd almost laughed, except it was no laughing matter. So he kept coming back to Halim's stall, though he knew it would be better to stay away, because he had the irresistible, and perhaps slightly cruel, urge to test the limits of that fear.

He sat for some time, his ashtray filling up with half-smoked cigarettes. His coffee grew cold. As a traffic policeman, he'd perfected the art of sitting or standing and staring for long stretches without getting bored, waiting for the one stray vehicle or accident that could transform an otherwise dull day into an adrenaline rush. He thought of nothing in particular. He was good at that too. It was what kept him sane; that, and the always comforting possibility of suicide. It had been some weeks since he'd last sat up in bed cradling the gun he ought to have returned after his shift, his finger cocked on the trigger. The hour before sunrise always the worst, when he despaired of the night ending. In those hours of raging wakefulness, the sweetest sound was the rumble of the first rubbish trucks rounding the corner, the signal for him to tuck his gun back in his holster. Always, always, this petty, indestructible, shameful will to live. The charade of the cocked pistol its own perverse comfort.

He stubbed out his last cigarette. The last vestiges of the morning cool still lingered in the cavernous hulk of the hawker centre, the sun finding its only entry through cracks in the metal roof. He did not want to leave, to move through the dazzling rectangle of light that was the entrance into the furnace of the street. But it was time to go.

He became aware that a Chinese man at the next table was staring at him, too insistently for him to ignore. Late thirties, tall for his race, his long legs sticking out into the passageway while he stirred his coffee; he looked trim, tanned, too upscale in his red polo t-shirt and khaki pants for this place. His face wore a perplexed frown.

The policeman studied him for a moment. Memory stirred, sluggishly. A weekday morning, watching a trickle of vehicles string themselves along the dusty black ribbon of the North-South highway. Ensconced in his police car artfully concealed in a layby, he had been jolted out of his stupor by a truck with Johor plates thundering past at one hundred and thirty kilometres an hour, spewing black smoke. Behind the truck trailed a silver BMW with Singapore numberplates, just outside the speed limit.

Perhaps it was the gleam of the newly-waxed car in the morning sunshine. Perhaps it was the way Singaporeans drove, always hovering just around the speed limit with their prissy, useless regard for rules. Whatever. In this job, he didn't need an excuse. It was the arbitrariness of the whole thing that was its attraction.

He pulled the car over.

"Ah—is there a problem—"

"Passport."

Tan Kai Ming. Aged 39. A seasoned traveller, to judge from the crazy patchwork of immigration stamps. Mr Tan travelled a good deal to Malaysia on business. But there were other stamps as well: Pretoria, Sao Paolo, Prague. Where were *those*? Places he would never see. Never go. They touched him with a kind of wonder, and unexpected longing.

Mr Tan tried again in passable Malay. "Officer. I was *inside* the speed limit."

"Not according to my monitor."

"Then your monitor was wrong."

"It's never wrong."

"Oh, come on. Then why didn't it catch the truck in front of me? Why stop *me*?"

The man had been wearing sunglasses, the policeman remembered, small, fashionable, gold-rimmed ones like a movie star's. (The policeman's were black, impenetrable, like those of a thug or a Latin American dictator. The truth was he had weak eyes; strong sunlight made them water.) They looked too young on a face that hovered near middle age, and the policeman was irrationally irritated by them. That, and the aggrieved belligerence and the Singaporean assumption that you could always prevail with reason. In the policeman's experience, reason had no role to play in the forces animating mankind.

"You were speeding."

"You want a bribe."

They were speaking in English now, the transition so rapid that neither registered it. The policeman leant into the interior of the BMW, inhaling the smell of leather and air-freshener. In the backseat, he saw an array of brochures on toilet bowls and shower stands. Evidently, Mr Tan was a salesman for bathroom supplies. Again, the policeman experienced that sense of irrational irritation: what business did a bathroom salesman have driving a car like that?

"You see a policeman in this country and immediately you think he's corrupt, he's dirty, right?"

"You tell me whether I'm wrong to think that." Mr Tan began to rub his eyes behind his sunglasses. His back slumped. The policeman had the impression that defiance was not natural to him, that some last restraint had snapped that morning. Maybe his business was going badly. Maybe his wife had left him. Just as quickly as the unexpected twinge of fellow-feeling had arisen, it was stamped out.

"This is *my* highway."

"What are you talking about?"

He repeated, slowly, deliberately, so there would be no mistake, "This. Is. My. Highway. Understand?"

Mr Tan stared at him. "You're crazy."

"You want we can go down to police headquarters right now and settle this."

"What the shit!"

He paid, of course. They always did. Five hundred ringgit. Paid it in complete silence as though he'd suddenly realised the presence of a mightier force than justice or fairness or any of those shibboleths, and then he'd roared off in a cloud of dust and gravel. The policeman smacked the bills against his palm and whistled through his teeth. Money was always useful, but he was aware he didn't really need it, not today, not in this manner. No, he had taken the money simply because he could.

In the hawker centre, Mr Tan looked younger, more defenceless, without his sunglasses. The policeman could tell he was debating with himself whether it was the same policeman. What were the odds of them ending up in the same place, at this hour? A thousand to one? To discourage further speculation, the policeman turned away. He took care to finger his holster. He felt no guilt over his victims but the encounter was vaguely disturbing, like the bizarre juxtapositions that one found in bad dreams.

Outside, the bright sunlight made him blink; he donned his sunglasses hastily. The phrase, *home free*, occurred to him, though what was there to be afraid of? Mr Tan had not stirred—the policeman had not expected him to—though he had been acutely conscious of the man's stare boring into his back as he threaded his way out. Then he heard the sound of running footsteps behind him, and he turned sharply, but it was only Halim.

"I meant to tell you ... I heard something from a friend of a friend. It may be nothing, but I thought you would want to know all the same—"

The policeman listened without expression. Of course he would check out this tip, as he'd checked out all the others he'd received since Deanna's flight three years ago but he guessed that, as with all the others, this would also come to nothing. He was more preoccupied with observing the ingratiating smile that slid fitfully around Halim's mouth and seemed to have a life of its own. Halim was a blameless, hardworking man; it was the policeman who was at fault for letting him this far into his life.

He nodded, meaning, *thank you*, and turned away.

"God speed," Halim called.

He had once had ambition. He remembered it vaguely, or thought he did, but it was hard to recall its texture exactly. It was like trying to remember the sensation of pain: so searingly real at the moment of its happening, the memory of it vanished into a void once its source was removed.

He had once spent a year in college studying electrical engineering, paid for by a hardwon bursary; it was one of the rare periods in his life when things had come together in perfect riveted fashion. Then his mother fell ill with cancer.

Mother. *Ibu.* Whenever he thought of her, it was of how he'd found her the day his father had upped and left the *kampung* for good: stretched out like a pale lovely corpse on the mat, her face upturned tragically to his, a trickle of blood from her wrist staining the floor. His baby brother Anwar propped next to her in dirty diapers, one finger stuck in his mouth. The older boy was eight, too young to know that the sheer theatricality of her pose meant that she couldn't possibly be dying. He'd screamed for his grandmother, who clumped over from her house next door and slapped her daughter on the cheek. His mother sprang to her feet with a yelp.

"You can't even kill yourself properly," his grandmother snapped.

His mother said, defiantly, "I'll try again."

His grandmother snorted. "No, you won't." His grandmother was as tough and stringy as the chickens that she reared for eggs. She had seen a man decapitated during the Second World War and nothing had ever shaken her since.

His grandmother was right. His mother never tried suicide again, but all the same she'd made an indelible impression on him. He vowed to look after her, no matter what. (He would forget his father, a feckless charmer who had met his mother one morning on his deliveryman's route while she was walking to school and found himself, a bare three months later, the husband of a pregnant teenage bride. *Bapak* had been good at fishing, singing and making balloons into funny shapes to amuse his sons, but abysmal at providing for the family. Money flowed out of his pockets and he could not account for it; women flocked to him and he could not turn them away. His leaving was only a matter of time, as inevitable as the turning of the world on its axis.)

Ibu was still young (just sixteen when she gave birth to him), still pretty (he remembered sourly the men who'd competed to take her out after his father left), still not entirely devoid of hope that she would meet the right man. When he was a child, she'd seemed to him the most enchanting creature alive, with her delicate perfumes and her small refinements and airs. Nobody else's mother, he thought, was like his, and he was right. *Princess*, his grandmother used to call his mother; as he grew older, he realised it had not been meant as a term of endearment. His mother was completely unsuited to poverty and the string of low-paying jobs that she had to take to support her sons. Older, he thought her a fool. Still, she was his mother.

The government doctor that he brought her to see pronounced the illness terminal. An innate stubbornness led him to seek a consultation with a private specialist that he could ill afford. Gently, the specialist told them that treatment was expensive and that government assistance would only go so far. The specialist was quite old and trying to be kind, but it was clear he wasn't used to dealing with people like the future policeman, who wore flip-flops into the hushed, spotless office and paid for the consultation with crumpled notes fished out from various parts of his clothing.

"Let me die," his mother had begged her sons, "don't spend the money" and Anwar, a boy tender as a bruise in his emotions, had wept with her like a pair out of a soap opera. Coldly, her older son told her not to be stupid. The next day, he signed up with the police for no better reason than that the station round the corner had a large recruiting poster in the window.

His tutor urged him to reconsider. He was bright; promising; hardworking. The compliments echoed emptily in his ears. In the police, he accepted the first posting that was offered him; it happened to be in the city's traffic division. It was not what he would have chosen, but he wanted only to draw his first pay cheque as quickly as he could. Hope or ambition or whatever it was called had not entirely deserted him: he still harboured vague dreams of becoming a superintendent.

Superintendent! Later, years later, during long, dull stretches on the highway, he would think of this and laugh. Not bitterly, but in a kind of enduring wonder at his youthful innocence.

He did not think of himself as corrupt. Or not more than most, anyway. He did not take money for greed, or necessity, or because everyone was doing it—all the usual, tedious reasons, or at least, he no longer took it for those reasons. No, he took it simply because he could.

What was it the inspector had told him, the morning that he'd called the policeman into his air-conditioned sanctum? "You need flexibility in human relations. As you do in everything else."

And he'd said, too cocky for his own good, "Is this about human relations? I thought this was about law and order and justice."

He could see the car even now. A silver Lamborghini, so sleek and aerodynamic it looked like it could skim the air. He would have noticed it even if it hadn't run a red light, narrowly missing a truck; running the red light the way it did only added to its general air of insolence. The policeman gave chase, though, as the Lamborghini led him on a white-knuckled ride through the busy downtown streets, he wondered if he'd been wise to do so; his lumbering police vehicle couldn't keep pace, surely, with the gaudy bird of a car in front. Someone would get killed, probably *him*—like a charm, his thoughts had the desired, opposite effect. The Lamborghini mounted a central divider, crashed the railings and turned turtle, its wheels spinning uselessly at the sky.

The driver was not hurt, only angry. He was a *bumi* dressed in what looked even to the policeman's untrained eye like a very pricey ensemble: black sharp suit, black pointy shoes made out of some poor reptile's hide and cufflinks bright enough to blind. He cursed the policeman, his voice rising to a high-pitched scream. "Do you know who I am?" he kept saying. "Do you *know* who I am?" Unmoved, the policeman continued taking down his details. It was only when the man started jabbing him in the chest—hard, so that the policeman almost fell into the path of an oncoming car—that he snapped. He remembered pinning the man to the side of his wrecked car and wrestling on the handcuffs, breathing hard and feeling a kind of psychotic rage that made him tremble from fighting the urge to break the window of the Lamborghini with its driver's head. (And indeed he couldn't sleep that night, the vision of the man's head crashing through the glass recurring so persistently that he was almost afraid he'd done it.)

The first thing he saw in the inspector's office, apart from the fine, upright figure of the inspector himself, were the arrest sheets he'd painstakingly filled in for the Lamborghini driver. He'd guessed instantly what was afoot. The inspector did not waste his time on recruits of slightly more than a year's standing unless there were good compelling reasons. And so he'd waited out the pleasantries and the small talk, knowing that these were but distractions on the circuitous route to his subornation.

Finally, reluctantly, the inspector had tapped the arrest sheet. There was a long silence.

"You know that was the son of—" and the inspector had named a prominent businessman, who was said to be close to the finance minister.

"Really."

"Didn't you guess?"

His tone was more belligerent than he intended: "No, I don't know his family, do I?"

Oh yes, he was thinking, my heart will really bleed if the scion loses his licence, gets convicted and upsets his father's well-laid plans for him to enter politics ... He let the inspector fumble and turn red in the face and didn't help him a whit.

He said, flatly, "I can't do it."

The inspector drummed his fingers on the table. The hum of the air-conditioner was very loud—the fan-belt needed repairing—but he was perspiring freely. Idly, the policeman wondered what favour the businessman had done the inspector (helped a brother? a cousin?). The details didn't really matter; it was the nature of the payback that was always the interesting question. And now he remembered a rumour he'd heard about the inspector having once been an army officer. The rumour had it that a cache of arms had been stolen on his watch by a band of Muslim extremists. Or else he had failed to salute some general. Whatever it was, he radiated the anxiety of a man who had messed up one safe pension and did not intend to lose another. And yet he was not a bad man in his way: he was kindly, he remembered names, he let the men have time off readily if they'd worked shifts, which was more than could be said for other officers.

"Why the hell not?"

"He ran a red light. He assaulted me."

"He says he tapped you in the chest."

The policeman laughed.

The inspector said, slowly, spelling it out for a congenital idiot, "I can override your arrest, but it looks better if you withdraw it yourself. Say you made a mistake."

"I didn't."

"I know you're a good policeman. I've seen your appraisals. You're honest. That's good."

"Thank you." If his tone was ironic, the inspector failed to notice it.

"But honesty isn't enough to make it. Do you follow?"

And that was when he'd made his remark about flexibility in human relations.

The policeman had been curiously detached, his mind cold and clear. Graft didn't shock him. Graft was everywhere. Graft had reared its head his very first day on the job, when he'd booked a white Honda for parking on a double yellow line and its owner, a pretty Chinese housewife weighed down with grocery bags, had tried to buy him off with a 'gift'. He had not liked her imperious manner and so he let the ticket stay and was startled by the invective which she showered on him. He was under no illusions as to his own principles. He was honest when it was convenient to be honest. And he had a sick mother and a baby brother to support. But he wasn't yielding his virginity without a pantomime of righteous indignation, not least because he needed time to think.

Everything had its price. A week later, he named his.

The inspector had laughed. "So that's what it's about? The money?"

He'd said, smiling, though it'd felt as though someone was holding up the corners of his mouth with tweezers, "It's always about the money, isn't it?"

His mother lived another four years after the onset of the cancer. Lived through the loss of her hair, the collapse of her teeth, the shrivelling of her skin and the pain that saw her ratchet up higher and higher doses of morphine to little effect. He'd been amazed and not a little awed by her resilience, her determination to cling on to a life that so far had disappointed her at every turn. Towards the end, barely able to move, strapped down as she was by an intricate fretwork of tubes and drips, she'd asked to go home. He'd asked her if she was sure and she'd nodded her head, barely.

(Home, the leaky shack in the small *kampung* that she'd lived in all her life and that the policeman had fled with such relief. In the force, he was to meet former kampung boys like himself but, unlike them, he did not sentimentalise his rural roots or deplore the anonymity of the big city. Anonymity was what he craved. Only in the throngs clacking heedlessly along the pavements did he finally feel the pressure lift: nobody whispering that his father had deserted the family, nobody poking into the dark clouded recesses of his soul to ask why he wasn't more like his saintly fool brother. No more tripping over the chickens that wandered underfoot and fouled the ground with their droppings; no more *kampung* nights when the blackness became something physical, suffocating. In the city, total darkness was rare and he slept with the streetlights shining full into his room.)

Those last few days, she'd seemed almost serene. He drove the hundred kilometres after his shift every evening to be with her, and she'd look up dozily from her mat on the floor at his entrance. He slept in a rattan bed in the next room, alert to her every movement. One night, thinking she was asleep, he was startled to find her eyes, large in her shrunken face, fixed on him. She beckoned to him with difficulty with one finger and he brought his ear close to her mouth. Even then, he'd had difficulty making out what she was saying.

"You can be more than this."

He brought his ear away. Her lips were still moving. She thought he hadn't understood, but he had, only too well. The anger that was his faithful companion flooded his veins.

"You can be more than a policeman."

"Being a policeman," he'd told her with icy contempt, "paid for your treatment." More precisely, graft had paid for her treatment, but he wasn't about to draw these fine distinctions. "Being a policeman puts food on our table. It's what I am. It's *all* I am."

And in one of those explosions of temper that his mother was so familiar with, explosions that made her shrink back in her mat even where there was no room to recoil, he'd got on his motorcycle and driven back to his rented room in the city. In the morning, he was sorry, but it was too late. Anwar was on the phone, crying. His mother was dead.

He had stood over her grave that same day while it was being dug, eyes stinging from dry-ness. It was not the memory of his last conversation with his mother that was eating at him. It was the knowledge that he was finally free.

His freedom brought him no sense of liberation. He was like a prisoner, grown used to his windowless cell, feeling a surge of agoraphobic panic at his first glimpse of the sky outside. For weeks afterwards, he would return to his room and look round with dazed unfamiliarity. He could not remember what he was meant to be doing. He forgot to eat. He went back to his old college and walked around the hallways trying to screw up the courage to ask about re-admission procedures. A friendly student accosted him: "How can I help you?" He looked at the boy's smooth, unlined face and shook his head. The boy was only a couple of years younger but they seemed to have nothing in common.

Then he'd met Deanna. Zigzagging drunkenly across the street, causing traffic to screech to a halt and drivers to lean out of their car windows to yell at her. She wore a yellow sundress, flowing down from her armpits and stopping just above her knees. Her beatific smile never wavered.

He was waiting for her when she finally made it across.

What he noticed first were her eyes: large, feverishly pinwheeling holes punched into a tiny heart-shaped canvas of a face. He realised that she was high, not drunk. And then he saw that she wore no shoes and that her feet left bloody prints along the pavement. "Officer," she said with a giggle, before pitching forward at his feet.

Amphetamines, the emergency room doctor had said with a sigh, a truckload of them careening their way through her system and enough to send her sky-high and crazy; they would have to pump her stomach. He mentioned the latest designer drug. The policeman nodded and left, meaning to go back to the station to write up a report, but somehow he found himself shelving this. Somehow, he found himself, after his shift, walking up to the hospital and asking for the girl who had been admitted that morning. Deanna, the receptionist said, vaguely waving in the direction of the wards.

She was awake in bed and staring into space. Her feet were in bandages. When she saw him, she drew her arms across her chest; she'd recognised him even out of uniform and he felt a strange elation at the thought.

"Am I going to be charged?"

He said, with a clumsy attempt at humour, "Not unless you want to be."

She stared at him and for the first time he saw that half-smile of hers appear. "Of course not."

"Are your parents here?" She looked like a kid, eighteen at most.

"My parents?" She considered this and laughed. "My parents have disowned me. I'm not as young as you think. I'm probably older than you."

Detoxed, she looked wan and skinny and not even very pretty. Her eyes, something in the slant of which made him think she could not be fully Malay, had gone flat and unwinking like the stone eyes of a statue. Her fingers picked, obsessively, at the bandages on her feet until she saw him watching and then she flushed and tucked her hands beneath the bedclothes like a little girl and he had a sudden impulse to untuck them and hold them in his own, an impulse of such unaccustomed tenderness that, alarmed, he took himself out to the corridor and walked it up and down several times before he could bring himself to return to the ward.

He stayed until visiting hours were over and she let him. When he said goodbye, she gave no indication of having heard, but he wasn't disheartened. He came again the next day and the next. The bandages came off and he found himself staring, surreptitiously, at her bare feet as though he'd never noticed feet before and in a way he hadn't (who did except for shoe salesmen?). She never seemed surprised to see him; she never evinced any emotion. She accepted his presence with total passivity and he had to be content with that.

Then she told him she was being discharged. Told him this while sitting by the side of the bed, swinging those bare feet of hers just above the floor.

He asked if she had a place to stay. She shook her head. The words popped out of his mouth before he could recall them: she could stay with him. She looked at him and her mouth curled up in what might have been scorn or a smile: he couldn't tell. But she didn't say no.

It never struck him, until he brought her back to his room, what a rathole he was living in. The once-elegant pre-war building now crumbling and sub-divided illegally into more rooms than seemed humanly possible, the air fetid with the smells of cooking from the hawker stalls below. The room itself containing just bed, chair, table, portable TV, wardrobe, sink and a small cooking range. He thought: *this is the kind of room where a dead man can lie undiscovered for days.* But it was also cheap and anonymous and in the beginning that had been its attraction.

From the doorway, the girl said, "It's nice," and he wondered if she was being sarcastic but then she smiled at him, as though knowing he needed to be reassured, and he felt a sudden tightness in his chest that filled him with foreboding.

Every day he expected to find her gone, but she was always there when he returned after work. Sometimes watching TV, sometimes sleeping. In those days she slept with a narcoleptic's ease, and he'd stand and watch her sleeping form—curled up like a sickle, her legs bent at right angles from the knee. (He had given her the bed, while he took to the floor. "Oh ... the bed," she had said that first night, and he'd heard the quizzical note in her voice.) She seemed to sense his presence, even in her sleep: eyes flying open, she would sit bolt upright and, "Oh, it's you," would escape from her, in that ambiguous tone he could never fathom. Who did she expect, who did she want to see?

He never asked. Just as he never asked what she was doing on the street the afternoon he'd found her. She discouraged all questions, even the simplest ones, and her techniques were many and varied. She would yawn, or feign deafness, or cast him a look of infuriating blankness or, if all else failed, tell him sweetly, but with an unmistakeable mind-your-own-business belligerence, "It's all *so boring.*" Her mind, her wit, was quicker than his; often, he found himself lumbering in her wake.

At times, he was tempted to yell at her, "And who's paying for you now? Where would you be if it wasn't for my charity, my milk of human kindness, my crazy impulse back in the hospital that to this day I don't understand?" But he didn't, because he knew the answer anyway. He could glimpse a procession of shadowy men in darkened rooms, the girl on her back watching the ceiling fan whirr and waiting only for her customer to finish before she could pocket the money, roll off the bed and totter off to her dealer. And every time he thought of this he would feel his vision blurring and his fingers digging into his palm until his nails drew blood: it was not the girl he blamed but the men and he thought with loving hatred of what he would do to them if he ever laid his hands on them.

So he held back his questions because he did not want to take advantage of her like those other men and because the fact of her presence there, in his rathole room, was at times so amazing to him that all he could do was stand and watch her sleep and call himself, silently, *fool, fool, fool.*

She wore the same yellow dress for days—she must have washed it during the day and hung it out to dry while he was working and the thought of her with no clothes on and no curtains in the windows left his mouth dry—until he could bear it no longer and told her to get some clothes. He placed a wad of notes on top of the TV before he left for work and when he returned, she was wearing a new dress, one of those cheap batik things flogged to tourists, all swirling blue and white like a meteorological storm on a TV weather report. With the rest of the money, she'd bought some rice and meat and vegetables and put together a clumsy meal. "Like it?" she said slyly and he had no idea whether she was referring to the dress or the food. He shrugged, dumbly.

After that, he got into the habit of leaving her money every other day and she would pocket it calmly and never mention the arrangement between them. He was careful not to give her much, and to do a mental reckoning of whatever she bought. Food. Newspapers. Small decorative items, like cushions with North Indian beadwork and a red batik cloth to drape over the table lamp. Blue scented candles. Things he would never have chosen, but they always seemed right once they were there.

Once he asked her, "Where do you find them?" and she looked at him curiously and said that one could find these things everywhere, one just had to keep one's eyes open for them! And he heard again the laughter flare in her voice, the undertow of gentle mockery. He was not used to being teased; he felt his face turn red, and saw hers turn quizzical.

He could not tell her that her cheap knick-knacks scared him. They suggested permanence, an annexation of his territory and his emotions that seemed to be happening too fast for him to grasp. Women, with the exception of his grandmother and mother, had been fleeting in his life. Late-night fumbles with the neighbour's daughter back in the *kampung* hardly counted; nor did the prostitutes he'd visited several times in the city, always furtively and with a sense of shame so overpowering it had cancelled out whatever release he might have got from the encounters.

So he'd resigned himself to the absence of women, putting them on hold together with all the things he'd put on hold since his mother's illness, including life itself.

But now *she* was here, and all the old desire and dread and restlessness were back. He thought about her, watched her, all the time. Watched her when he thought she was not looking: during dinner, which they ate with the television on, she sitting cross-legged on her chair, the wide skirt of her dress tucked decorously in her lap, laughing at the silly jokes on screen. He observed everything about her, from the way she sat with her back perfectly straight and the way her head seemed to rest on her slender neck like a goblet perched on its glass stem. And even then, even in those early idyllic days, a splinter of ice would suddenly dart into the heat of his longing: he would think suddenly how easy it was to snap that slender neck in two, and a shiver that was very like hate, or self-hatred, would go through him.

One night she danced for him. Turned out the lights, turned up the radio on a late-night music station and danced in the rectangles of streetlight that patterned the floor. He had no idea what kind of dance it was, whether it was good or bad. He watched while her shadow skittered across the ceiling in sync with her and remembered how, even on her suicidal

[handwritten margin note: Something had been suppressed in him released by her]

trek across the road the day he'd met her, she had still managed to retain a certain precarious poise.

When she was done, she collapsed, laughing, on the bed.

"Did you like it?"

"I liked it."

The phone rang, interrupting a dreamless sleep. One look at the sky outside told him it was the brink of dawn. Who would call at this hour on a public holiday? Even as the groggy thought formulated itself, he knew the answer. Only his grandmother still got up before the cockerel's crow. He was not quick enough getting to his feet and it was Deanna who picked up the receiver.

Anwar needed a computer.

"A computer?" he repeated, wondering if he'd heard correctly.

"A computer," his grandmother said firmly. "They have computer classes in school nowadays."

His grandmother had taken in the child, but Anwar's maintenance was his responsibility, the blood money he paid for escaping from the *kampung*. His needs were endless: uniforms, books, track shoes, all the paraphernalia of a modern education that seemed to have passed the policeman by. Once he had ventured to ask whether something was really necessary and his grandmother had fixed on him her thousand yard stare, the one that led the children in the *kampung* to whisper behind her back that she was a witch. He had not asked again. Anwar was her favourite, and she was past the age of dissimulating such feelings.

A silence. He pictured his grandmother walking out in the dark to the new public payphone that the government had installed outside the provision shop, and painstakingly dialling his number from a slip of paper that she would have folded into her sarong. She refused to have a phone in her house; she distrusted phones, banks, politicians, all the appurtenances of the twentieth century. A computer! It was as startling as though she'd announced her belief in the theory of relativity.

He said, aware of Deanna's gaze hovering at his back, "I will have to see."

"That girl. Who is she?"

"A friend."

Another silence. His grandmother was famous for her silences; they were as eloquent and varied as other people's conversations.

She spoke again. "You look after your own."

He was angry now. "Don't I always?"

"You look after your own. That's all I'm saying."

"Who was that?"

"My grandmother."

She said, ready to be amused, "You have a grandmother?"

"And a brother. Yes. People do." His tone was rough, the first time he had been rough with her. Her eyes widened, but she did not flinch. She was used to this, he thought, used to violent, hurtful men; they did not faze her. "Don't you?"

Slowly, she shook her head.

"You must have someone."

"I did once. Not anymore."

"You're not self-invented. You come from somewhere. *Someone gave birth to you.*"

She said, simply, "Why are you angry?"

You look after your own. He shook his head and slammed the door on his way out.

Deanna. Not a common name, he would have thought, but the parade of wild-eyed, bold-eyed, kohl-eyed Deannas in the police files daunted him. The mugshots were not always clear and hairstyles changed but there was one file he took out and studied at length. This Deanna had grown up in the city, a woman who, if still alive, would have been several years older than he. Both parents were teachers. Her mother was Chinese. (And, fairly or not, he would thereafter attribute all her waywardness and her stubborness to this miscegenation.) Three other sisters, all with unblemished records. "Deanna" had attended a mission school, where she had shown "great promise" before "things fell apart." At sixteen, she was caught shoplifting a pair of shoes ("strappy," "slutty," "I loved them"), the last straw for the long-suffering nuns at her school,, who had put up with her truancy and smoking for years. She was expelled ("the day my life began").

A spell at a girls' home followed—not for long, because "Deanna" showed a remarkable facility for escaping. The matron of the home said that "Deanna" was a problematic case precisely because she seemed so amenable and quiet on the surface ... Her next arrest was for selling Ecstasy tablets at a rave. The arresting officer noted that "Deanna" was homeless and became aggressive when he suggested calling her parents. She said she had not seen them since she was sixteen and wanted nothing to do with them. When asked if they had abused her, "Deanna" said, "I *wish* ..." They meant well, they wanted "the best," they were boring beyond belief. She underlined *boring* with such force that the nib broke.

Asked to pen her own statement, she'd seized the opportunity deliriously; the writing sprawled off the lines and sloped precipitiously downwards as though falling off a cliff. She must, he thought, have been still high when she wrote it. ("No excuses. No justifications. No turning back. Can someone be bad through and through and enjoy being bad and bad through and through? It's an interesting question ...")

At which point he stopped reading and snapped shut the file. He didn't want to know more.

He never found her presence as intrusive as when the lights were off, when he became acutely aware of every rustle of the bedclothes, every turn of her body in the sheets. Sleep came fitfully, broken by every isolated sound of the night: a baby crying, a motorcycle revving in the street.

One night he woke with a start to find that she had slipped in beside him on the floor. She lay facing him, eyes closed, but he felt certain she was awake.

"What are you doing?"

She opened her eyes. Her fingers, cool, nerveless, traced the contours of his face. He felt a mild electric shock. He caught her hand.

"You don't have to do this." In the dead of night, his voice sounded inordinately loud. "I'm not asking for anything."

She regarded him steadily in the soupy street-light that leaked through the window. "Don't you want to touch me?"

Of course he wanted to; she was the only thing in his life that he had ever wanted with this passion of wanting that was new and frightening and made him, several times a day, pull over by the side of the road just so he could lean his head against the steering wheel and try to still the fever. He would forget over time how she looked but he never forgot how she felt in his arms, the deceptive density of her bones in that small frame of hers or the touch of her hand on the back of his neck. After making love, she would go to sleep as easily as a baby, while he lay awake for hours. Just listening to her breathe.

A vacant piece of land, the size of a football field, its red earth newly churned up, lay just beyond the monsoon drain behind his building. A faded billboard had promised for months the development of a condominium, a slice of heaven in the sky. But no building work ever commenced and he returned one day to find that a makeshift fairground had sprung up suddenly, the unmistakeable waltzy *oom-pah-pah* of fairground music penetrating all the way to his rathole room.

Deanna stood by the back window, gazing out at the fairground. A ferris wheel rotated slowly against a sky lit up by a red pulsating glow. "It's a fair," she said unnecessarily. There was a curious muted longing in her voice he'd never heard before. He said nothing, and soon she stepped away from the window to get his food.

"Oh look!" she said. "Dodgem cars!" She bent a face full of mischief on Anwar. "Shall we?" He had no choice; she pushed him into one of the cars while she lowered herself, laughing, into another. The place plunged into hell, all giant strobe winking lights and hypnotic dance music and the sound of crashing cars and whooping laughter.

It was Friday night, teenagers and courting couples were out in force, the crowds electric with an energy that could easily turn ugly without warning. In the maelstrom, Anwar waved to his brother, who did not wave back. The policeman was watching Deanna. In the bad light, her face looked distorted, cracklingly alive; he didn't recognise her.

You do your best to live your life in compartments like the double spies we all are to one extent or another, but sometimes the cross-flows cannot be controlled. Sometimes the cross-flows make the hairs at the back of your neck stand on end, such as when you walk into your room after your shift to find your lover and your kid brother seated cross-legged on the floor, playing chess on the pocket board that Anwar carried with him everywhere. Chess! Who would have imagined *she* knew anything about chess, with her barely-there dresses and semi-feral air and that slow lazy curve of her mouth that never quite made it to a full smile?

You say, "What the hell are you doing here?" And your kid brother scrambles to his feet, all the tiny chess pieces scattering to the floor, and stammers that he just thought of visiting you, he hasn't seen you in a while and he's never been to your rathole room ... Then his voice falters, because he knows what a temper you have, and the girl's eye catches yours and she's looking at you in a new, grave way that you don't like. I look after my own, you want to tell her, don't look at me like that. But the fact is you never go back to the kampung if you can help it and you're so much older than Anwar that he sometimes seems more like your son than a brother, a son you never wanted and towards whom your primary emotion is one of duty than of love. And of course you haven't invited Anwar to this rathole room because would you invite anyone to a place like this if you could help it?

But what you think about chiefly is what Deanna and Anwar have been discussing while playing chess and how all this will play back in your grandmother's house, the description of your rathole room and the girl—especially the girl—tripping artlessly off Anwar's tongue and into your grandmother's ears. Your grandmother fears her own sex with good reason. All you want to do is run Anwar out of the house as fast as you can but all you can do is concur, stonily, when Deanna, looking from one brother to the other, puts her hand on your arm and says, as though it were the most natural thing in the world, "Let's go to the fair."

So they go to the fair. He does not remember what they do: eat sweet sickly candyfloss, fire at a row of moving ducks, sit in the stomach-churning pirate ship? He's always disliked fairs and amusement arcades, loud pinging noises, accordion music and the general concept of fun. He doesn't understand fun. He doesn't understand when he's supposed to be having it. When he's not working, he's sleeping. Or holding down a second job as a security guard, anything he can find.

But Anwar and Deanna are having fun. At least, he supposes they are, because they seem to be laughing a lot and talking like co-conspirators. He hears her telling Anwar about her schooldays, when she played truant to "go to the fair"; he hears her say that she wanted to be a dancer when she was younger. She reveals more in those few hours with his brother than he's heard her divulge in weeks of living with him and a kind of pain or could it just be heat spreads across his chest. And Anwar's eyes follow her about with undisguised fascination: he's never seen anyone like her, or rather he's never met a girl who's paid him as much attention as Deanna has tonight.

He cannot believe that Anwar cannot immediately see Deanna for what she is, but then the things that Anwar knows and doesn't know never cease to stump him. Anwar can talk New Economy until the policeman's brain cells are fizzing with boredom, but he can't open a tin without cutting himself. Anwar is—touch wood—destined for the white-collar life in one of those gleaming glass towers in the city that the policeman only skirts at street level to hand out parking tickets. It is a future that Anwar's grandmother and brother have been working towards, in unspoken complicity, ever since he began to top his classes with unnerving regularity. He is their joint investment, the payoff for all the sacrifices they've made. Like a prize thoroughbred, he has to be kept in mint condition, free from any whiff of disease or sabotage. And Deanna is more than a whiff, she's a storm, a gale-force, of corruption, and it takes all the self-control he has to watch their heads bobbing together and their cars crash without leaping in to keep them forcibly apart ...

He steps away from the Dodgem car arena for a smoke. In the five minutes that he steps away, it happens.

The cars have mercifully stopped their crashing when he returns, but he sees from Anwar's face that something is not right. All the animation is gone and he is in a suspicious hurry to leave. But Deanna looks fine; she looks fine enough for two. Her hands are clasped to her shoulders and she's swaying a little to the love song blaring from the loudspeakers. A group of boys whistles at her and she doesn't appear to notice.

"Let's go," the policeman says to Anwar. He will walk his brother to the bus-stop; Deanna can find her way back. Anwar strides ahead of him, and it is the policeman who has to sprint to keep up.

"Stop." The policeman's hand falls warningly on his brother's shoulder. "*Slow down!*"

Anwar's eyes glisten with the tears he is too ashamed to shed. It comes out in a rush. After the Dodgem cars stopped, they tried looking for the policeman. Where was he? (But the question is rhetorical.) Deanna said she felt giddy. She asked him if he had pills. Or knew of anyone who wanted to buy or sell any. Anwar didn't understand at first. Was she sick? If she was sick she should see the doctor. She looked at him for a moment, took his face tenderly between her hands, and pealed with laughter. He'd never felt such a monumental fool.

"You're not angry?" That perennial cry of the child Anwar, goading the policeman beyond endurance in days past to small petty cruelties.

"No. *Go.*"

He sprints back to his room. Takes the hallway steps three at a time and kicks open the door. She sees his face and is on her feet, dancer-nimble, but there is nowhere to run. He catches her round the waist and they fall in a heap on the bed. "You leave my brother out of this," he hears himself saying, over and over again, in a voice he doesn't recognise. After a time, he realises she isn't resisting, that the face she directs at him from where she lies flat on her back on the bed is composed and remote. He falls back and covers his eyes with his hands.

She turns on her side then and he feels her hand slide experimentally across his chest. "Do you want me to go?"

His mind toys with various answers, all sensible, rational, judicious. What he says is, "No. Stay."

Madness, to be going to the beach at noon beneath a blinding white sky in the face of a hot wind that was like the breath of a fire-spewing monster and on a motorcycle that afforded no protection from the elements. But the only heat he felt was the warmth from her arms around his chest and cheek where it rested against his back. She wore no helmet, and her hair whipped against his back and his neck. "It's illegal not to wear a helmet," he'd shouted to her above the wind, and she'd called back, "Who's going to book me—you?"

She made him do things he would never have thought of doing. Going to the fair, for one (though it was not something he liked to think about, and certainly not the way he'd ransacked the room after his brother's visit, looking for the pills he was momentarily convinced she must have stashed away somewhere, while she stood by the door and watched him expressionlessly.) Bringing him to the rooftop of his building, for another, late one night when it was too hot to sleep just so they could sit at the parapet with their legs dangling over the side and only a railing separating them from the street ten floors below. She made him feel—adolescent. Tautly aware of being alive in a way he hadn't been since he was a kid, racing with the other kids across the sharp curve of the railtrack that used to run beyond the *kampung* and leaping clear just as the snout of the train engine rounded the corner.

The beach was not much of a beach,—just a strip of dirty sand bordered by a seawall and a high hedgerow shielding it from the main road. He had glimpsed it once from the top of a bus; it was always empty, not least because of the sign warning of deep water and strong currents. He had no time to call out to Deanna as she shucked off her sandals, kicking them high in the air like a child and running straight into the sea.

Then she was gone. He looked again, but the sea from where he stood looked clean of people. From where he stood, the sea looked like a great rippling sheet of gunmetal beneath the sun, so dazzling it hurt the eyes. He yelled her name and plunged in. *I can't swim.* He felt the current at once, a high-speed urgency in the water that could have knocked a child off his feet. The sand beneath his toes was trickling away in frighteningly fast rivulets; he thought, with a fear that was almost like exhilaration, that he would lose his footing and drown, here, in seawater not even seven feet deep. He steadied himself and swore.

Someone spoke his name. He swung round and saw her head bobbing just above the water, her hair hanging down in crazy rats' tails on either side of her face. He couldn't be sure, but he thought she was smiling.

"I didn't mean to scare you. Honestly."

He could have hit her. Instead, he turned his back on her and waded back to shore.

Jump.

That was what she'd whispered to him, that night on the roof, while she was leaning against his shoulder. He wondered if he'd dreamt it, but it came again, insistent, unmistakeable. Urging him on to satisfy that irrational vertiginous itch he always got to test whether he was immortal whenever he looked down from a height. *You know you want to. Jump.*

He'd jumped. In his mind, where it mattered, he jumped. Again and again.

"I heard about your mother."

His eyes flew open. The sun lay low and streaky-red in the sky. He had fallen asleep on the strip of dirty beach. She was sitting up, hugging her knees, facing the sea.

He said nothing. He'd been waiting for this. She had been watching him for days ever since Anwar's visit, weighing the sum of his parts to see whether they added up.

"Tell me," she said. "Tell me. How does a trainee policeman pay for his mother's medical bills in a private hospital?"

He said, tightly, "He manages."

"By the grace of God."

"God doesn't enter into it."

She turned to look at him then, and it was a look of complicity. "That's what I thought."

She said, "It's another world."

He thought, yes, she was right. The North-South Highway at three A.M. in the morning, silent but for the deafening buzz of insects in the plantations flanking the highway, pitch-dark except for the glow of instruments on his dashboard and the yellow snaking lights of a lone, stray car hurtling past—it was another element altogether. Elemental. One where the modern world, squawking through his car-radio at jarring intervals, seemed very far away. It was like night in the kampong again, but blacker, vaster and with the secretly comforting knowledge that he could, at any time when it felt as though the night was closing in too tight, step on the accelerator and take off.

She had wanted to know what it was like, sitting in his police car like a sentinel of the night, and he had weakly agreed to bring her along in breach of all the rules. (*Sit low*, he'd kept hissing at her while he steered his way through the city; it was only when the highway unfurled itself before him in all its black plenitude that he could breathe again.) At three am in the morning, she was unnervingly alert (yet why shouldn't she be? she slept all day), curled up in his passenger seat and running her fingers along the dashboard.

"So this is what you see. All those nights when you don't come back."

"Why do you care?"

Another car shot past on high beam, yellow lights raking the sky, rocking his police car in its layby. He looked at his speed monitoring device: one hundred and seventy. The driver was asking to be killed on a moonless night like this with a treacherous curving stretch of the highway looming up just ahead. But he let it go.

"I wanted to see," she said, "where God doesn't enter into it."

He looked away. An absurd resentment came over him that she was trying to drag him down to her level. He wanted to tell her they were not the same. *I sin for a principle. To look after my own. But you?*

The rains had stopped. The monsoon was unusually long that year, culminating in a downpour that had continued, with varying degrees of intensity, for almost three days. The drumming rhythm of the rain had seeped into his brain, playing tricks with it; one day, he walked into the

inspector's sanctum and asked for a transfer to narcotics. He did not tell
Deanna. The wet days and nights turned his room into a cocoon; they fell
asleep at night to the sound of water sluicing into the drains and clattering
like gunfire on the zinc roofs of makeshift shacks behind their building. "I
like the rain," Deanna had said, "I wish it would never stop," and he knew
what she meant, even though it made street patrols wet, hazardous work.

The rains had lifted and suddenly he felt restless, cooped up in his
rathole room. He suggested a drink at the hawker centre. "Must we?"
Deanna said, but she got up and slid into her sandals. A light wind
brought with it the smell of a freshly rainwashed city; thousands of points
of reflected street-light glistened from wet, slick pavements. Her sandals
quickly becoming soaked, she took them off and walked barefoot. Her
hand was on his shoulder. Happiness. Was that what this feeling was,
of total immersion in the moment? He'd always thought that only the
very young and the very old could be truly happy—happiness was born
of obliviousness, of truncated memories and garbled time. He turned to
Deanna, but the sensation was already gone: to think it was to lose it.

"My friend," Halim said, pumping his hand, "you take the trouble to
come here, after your shift. I'm honoured."

Who was Halim? No-one really. Just an acquaintanceship the policeman
had struck up while on his patrols. No-one that he gave any real
consideration to, not until that night, when he saw Halim's glance alight
on Deanna in grave astonishment. (Too late he remembered that Halim
was a pious man who had quoted religious texts to him in their infrequent
conversations.) And then it was as though he were seeing Deanna for the
first time too in her flimsy dress and all her barely-dampened sensuality
and he wished he could just turn on his heel and leave but it was too late
for that. The shame had entered him like a poison.

It was the shame, working its way through his blood, that made him say
to her when they were seated, though he knew it would be better not to,
"Why do you always dress like that?"

She stirred her coffee, her face assuming the thin, fox-like aspect it
always did when she sensed she was under attack. "Like what?"

"Your dress shows too much."

"Since when does it bother you?"

"It bothers me when other men look at you."

"It's not my dressing that bothers you. What bothers you is what other people think."

Knowing she was right, he could only say feebly, "If you know so much, why don't you give consideration to my feelings?"

She looked at him incredulously. "I'm not your wife."

He stood. "Let's go."

She said, with demure sarcasm, "If you wish."

They threaded their way among the packed tables. The whole world seemed to be out that night, eating, coughing, laughing, talking, clattering in a cacophony and a fug of cigarette smoke that the policeman suddenly found oppressive: he wanted only to get away.

He heard someone shout Deanna's name. He had time only to see her mouth tighten and feel her hand tugging him, urgently, towards the entrance, before he turned to find a man bearing down on them. Tall, mixed race, his white blood showing itself in the pointed, quivering nose and the light brown hair. He wore a tight fitting t-shirt and a narrow pencil moustache. He had the kind of seedy good looks that reminded the policeman of his father.

"Where's my money?" the man was demanding, in English and Malay. "Where's my money?"

"What money?" the policeman said. He could feel Deanna's hand twisting in his, trying to pull free; he only gripped harder.

"My money! That she stole! From me! To buy her pills!" After each exclamation mark, he spat on the ground. In his agitation, his sleeve tugged upwards to reveal a red tattooed heart slashed through with the word Deanna.

"You're mistaken," the policeman told him. He turned to go, but the man lunged over his shoulder to grab a fistful of Deanna's dress. She gave a muffled scream. Without thinking, the policeman whirled round and hit the man square in the face, a blow that sent him sprawling across a table, scattering food and diners in all directions. The place erupted in an uproar, people shouting and gesticulating. The policeman had a glimpse of

Halim dashing out from his stall, mouth agape, hands clutching his head in a theatrical display of consternation. And now Deanna had managed to wrest her hand away and she was gone, running, stumbling, pushing, overtaken by a pure instinct for flight.

He chased her down the street. It wasn't a long chase; she wearied quickly and didn't resist when he pulled her into an alley and pushed her against the wall.

"Who was that man?"

She looked him in the eye. "He used to be my pimp."

She must have seen something in his face because she flinched. He took his hands away from her shoulders.

He pointed out, "Your name was tattooed on his arm."

She shrugged impatiently. "So?"

"So he must have been more than your pimp."

"Maybe he liked the name Deanna. Who knows?"

He did not like her when she was defiant, when she came back with answers that were like whiplash in their speed and ferocity. To his utter surprise, he heard himself saying, "I think we should get married." And realised, even as he released his grip on her shoulders, that this was what he had been building up to ever since the night of the fair. She had him in her thrall and he resented it. Marriage would turn the tables, redress the balance of power between them. Marriage would be an act of munificence, charity, on his part. Making her his own. He looked after his own. And as his wife she would have to acknowledge his will.

She stared at him, then burst out laughing. "Don't be ridiculous."

They walked back to the room in silence. He could feel her watching his every move and for the first time since he'd met her he wished that he could be alone, just to think. He turned off the light and lay down on the mattress and made himself lie still, even as she slid in beside him. "Talk to me." "What about?" She stood then and helped herself to one of his cigarettes. He watched the lighter flare in the dark. "He means nothing to me. He's just dirt, scum." The words rolled over him like a wave. He slept, heavily.

"*Talk* to me."

"What about?"

The tables were turned; usually it was he who wanted to talk, while she fended off what she perceived as attempts to pry. He felt no inclination to talk; what was wrong with that? He had no intention of being cruel, so why was she keeping at him like a small yapping dog? Talk to me. One night, as he was falling asleep, he heard her voice, barely audible, come at him out of the dark. "We can get married. If that's what you want." There was a note of anger in her voice, but he chose to ignore it.

At night, lying beside him, she made a pillow of her body for him and he burrowed into and held her without moving. The nights were cool and after the food stalls below had closed the breeze would bring the very faint smell of frangipani from the stunted trees in the street. A childhood habit came back to him, of trying to catch the exact moment when his eyes closed and he drifted off. He never did, of course, and he would wake stiff from their sleeping entwined through the night. That should have been enough for him: Deanna, her nightly presence, her sinewy adolescent body. He should have been smart enough to know this and not tinker with it. Not hanker for permanence but to take his happiness where he could find it. But he wasn't.

There was a certain side-lane off Jalan—, which he never visited if he could help it. At the corner stood a crumbling mosque, its walls a shabby blue, where he and Deanna had been married. It did not escape the notice of the imam that Deanna seemed vague about the simplest personal details of her life. Her age, for instance. Whether she'd previously been married. The pace of the ceremony, short as it was, seemed excruciatingly slow to the policeman; he did not intend to walk out an unmarried man. No-one came to the wedding; no-one had been invited. It was a squalid, furtive ritual and they were both silent as they emerged at last into the long slanting rays of the late afternoon sun.

He had always supposed he would marry one day, but not like this. This felt like the end of something, not the beginning. He had taken his grandmother's injunction to heart and made her his own but even then he had a premonition that in doing so she would, finally, elude him. For want of something better to do, they walked to a nearby park, a handkerchief of greenery between two buildings. Deanna took off her shoes, ignoring the sign that forbade walking on the grass, while he watched from a bench.

"Well?" she called.

He echoed her, reluctantly: "Well?"

"Isn't this what you wanted?"

And he would recall, again and again, like a snippet of film that had snagged in the projector and kept replaying itself, the way she'd cocked her head and looked back at him and how the new ankle-length dress she'd bought for the day had flowed about her hips like water.

The day he married her was the day his marriage ended. Of course he'd always known it was there, the manic self-destructiveness lurking just below the surface like water never quite coming to the boil. Wasn't it what had attracted him to her in the first place, if he was honest? He knew he was himself indestructibly sane, that he came with his own inbuilt, permanently-hinged safety catch and there were times he felt imprisoned by his own sanity, the sheer impossibility of giving way to heady irresponsibility. Craziness in others, beginning with his own mother, had always held a sneaking, seductive appeal for him. But his mother's version had been a low-grade, controllable variety, amenable to another's strong will. Deanna's was not. Marriage, to her, was the final turn of the key in the prison lock and she devoted herself immediately to escape.

The cunning of the addict: it was a many-headed serpent, a hydra he could never slay. He suspected her of doping again. There was an evasiveness about her, the hint of a new secret life. Yet, try as he might, he could never catch her in the act of buying her poison, popping a pill, or even discovering where she hid them. She developed a habit of drifting in and out at all hours without explanation; when he questioned her, she would fling herself in a chair and light a cigarette with one slender leg drawn up, regarding him with the bold, unsmiling look she'd never used on him before they were married. He learnt to get up, catlike, in the middle of the night to rifle through her meagre possessions, looking for things he didn't want to find.

Nights, she would turn the radio up loud, her eyes fixed on him in what seemed like a challenge. (But a challenge to what?) "Dance with me," she'd say. Always, he said, stubbornly, "I can't dance." So she would dance alone, every small gesture or turn of her head feeling like the tightening of an invisible cord around his throat.

There were times when he wondered if his memory was playing tricks on him, that there must have been moments, days, even in the midst of the madness, when things came together with a perfect clarity of pitch. Moments when she still made love to him with that cool detachment of hers that drove him wild; moments when, watching her sleep in the streetlight, he would try to believe that things would work out. That she would settle down. Slip into normalcy. But the outlines of those moments were blurry, gauzy, and they kept getting overlaid by those other images, the ones he didn't want to remember, the ones that had a frantic, kinetic energy and that brought him roaring out of sleep in the middle of the night for months after she left, to find himself drenched in sweat and his heart racing.

"I need money."

"What for?"

"Food. Necessities." She pronounces the word as if it were an obscenity. He has stopped giving her money; he does the shopping and accounting, he even buys her clothes. He is afraid, so afraid, that she will use whatever he gives her to buy drugs. The fact that he no longer gives her money does not go unnoticed, though she is too wily to attack him directly. "I'd like to buy a little canary bird," she says. "A little yellow canary to do my bidding. I'd feed her, clothe her and put her in a cage. Wouldn't that be nice?"

His hands are round her throat. He sees from her eyes this is what she wants, there is a kind of delirium in her goading. She tilts her head. "What's stopping you?"

Her dress flowing around her hips like water. Ricewater frothing over the rim of the saucepan on the stove, slopping onto the floor of an empty room, its door ajar. He slams out of the room, hurtles down the stairs. Puddles of dirty rainwater have pooled in the potholed back lane behind his block; they glimmer with a false magicality under the night lights. Deanna treads barefoot through the puddles, with the elegance of someone making her way down a catwalk. Three giggling children and a mangy cat follow her, a band of rag-tag disciples. He shouts her name and the children imitate him: "*Deanna!*" Cuffing them round the ears, he sends them away crying. The girl stops, with unerring instinct, beneath one of the street lamps, turning her beatific smile and pinwheeling eyes on him.

Things can go wrong, he learnt, with terrifying speed, like a plane ploughing into the ground at hundreds of miles an hour and exploding in a fireball and a cloudburst of debris. And the wrongness is irreversible, the good irrecoverable. The crash site smoulders while bits of metal wink incongruously in the sun. If this were a film, he could rewind the tape, reassemble the debris and stitch back the pieces until the superstructure is gleamingly new again, but this is life. And there is no going back.

Her life was all boom and bust, highs and lows, periods of normalcy where everything was a flat staleness followed by the big blowouts that nearly killed her and sent her, meekly, back to the normalcy until the cycle began again. They could have had a sort of life together if he'd been willing to fit himself into this pattern. Accept her for what she was, but he wasn't. And she didn't want to be reformed. Saved. Made new. Led into the Light. Or whatever the hell he decided to call his overzealous bloody interference in her descent into the abyss. Or so she informed him during the long, hysterical days that mark the end of their marriage, days of screaming fights that had the neighbours banging on their walls to silence them, days of long, sullen walks around the city that resolved nothing. Days when she threatened to jump from the window if he didn't give her the money to get her dose. Days when she held a knife to her throat and when he said, "Go ahead," tried to stick it in his hand instead. Sleepless nights merged into hungover days and he began to have difficulty distinguishing his nightmares from his waking life. In his nightmares, he dreamt that she was dead. Awake, he knew that he was the one who had killed her.

One morning he woke and knew with a flat, absolute certainty, even before he'd opened his eyes, that she was gone. Her absence was something palpable, a force sucked out of the air. When he did sit up and look round, he saw that she had removed all traces of her existence as cleanly as if she'd never set foot in the place. The room was as monastic as the day he'd moved in. He hurled the plastic chair against the wall and it bounced off and landed squarely on its legs again, mocking him.

The uncompleted shopping mall lay marooned, a massive concrete outcrop, in the grassy wasteland, its unclad upper floors gaping like cavities at the sky. Cruising down the highway, he had seen it often and never given it another thought; it was just another orphan of the recession, one of many pitting the city skyline. In the distance, the rumble of traffic on the highway was just audible, like surf on a distant beach. Mounds of gravel lay in conical heaps across what would have been the carpark and a dumpster blocked the main entrance to the building.

A Sikh *jaga* sat on a rattan mattress behind the dumpster. He looked with suspicion at the policeman. "Nobody here, officer, nobody here at all."

It was late evening, the sun sinking rapidly in streaky rashes of red and yellow. In an hour, less, this place would be swallowed up by the night and be indistinguishable from it except as a faint ghostly outline rearing out of the dark to startle travellers on the highway.

It was madness to detour here on nothing more than a tip from Halim. Who would operate a vice ring in this desolation? Yet to ask the question was to acknowledge the perfect logic of it. No-one would think of it, therefore it had to be. He tried again. "I want to see the big boss. I'm not here on official business. You understand? I'm here as a customer. A *customer*."

The *jaga* still looked unconvinced. Impatiently, the policeman pulled out his wallet. "How much?"

He gained entry into a bombsite, a cathedral to destruction. Rubble littered the atrium; exposed pipes ran along the walls and clumps of wires hung from the remnants of the ceiling. It was strangely bright, the sunlight tumbling in a long straight shaft from a skylight. A couple of crows beat a hasty, cawing retreat at his entrance; he saw they had been picking at a packet of rice thrown amidst the rubble. The rice looked fresh. He picked his way towards the EXIT sign, as the *jaga* had told him to do, and knocked on a door that looked new and reinforced.

The man with the tattoo opened the door. The moustache was gone. He wore a business shirt and sharply-pressed pants, but the same seedy, underworld handsomeness was still intact. Seeing the policeman, he tried to slam shut the door but the policeman had wedged his foot in the doorway. He placed one hand on the man's chest and shoved him smartly back.

"Bloody *jaga*, he didn't tell me you were a policeman—"

"I'm not here as a policeman. OK? Relax. Sit down. Shut up."

He was in an office, rudimentary but functional. He saw a fax machine and a laptop, heard the thrum of air-conditioning. Nice, very nice. He turned back to look at the man with the tattoo, who'd collapsed in a chair and was watching him with the blank wariness that he knew so well from his own face. The man didn't recognise him. Well, why should he? The policeman was just a passing painful encounter from the past. "I'd like a girl."

"No girls here. You're mistaken."

"You don't trust me?"

"I don't trust policemen."

"I pay cash. I'll pay twice the going rate."

The man with the tattoo watched him carefully. "Why?"

"There's a girl you have I want to try." A long pause. "Her name's Deanna." Another long pause. The man said, "Let me see your identification." He took the ID and wrote down the details. His expression, as he passed it back, was still wary but also undecided; he didn't want to turn away custom. Again, the policeman fished out his wallet and counted out the notes.

Mollified, the man said, "Deanna's the best."

The policeman said, smiling, "So I've heard." For months he had dreamt of this moment: the neat hole in the centre of the forehead, the look of stupefaction under the slowly caking blood. For some reason, his fantasies of violence always had a purplish tinge, like a bruise; as the violet haze cleared, he saw the man busying himself with a set of keys, still very much alive. His hands shook a little with the effort of keeping them away from the gun at his hip.

Oblivious to his own narrow escape, the man said, "This way."

Corridors: a warren, a labyrinth of them. He lost track, while the man with the tattoo strode ahead at a fast clip, like a guerilla who didn't particularly care to linger in territory he had infiltrated.

"Stop."

He found himself gazing into a dormitory, a cattle market of dozing women. Windows whitewashed to stop prying eyes, drying lines of clothes strung across the ceiling, a smell in his nostrils of too much sleep and too much powder and perfume that yet could not quite disguise the staleness of too many female bodies in a confined space.

The girl in the last bed stumbled out at a jerk of the man's head. The policeman did not look round, but he knew she was following them into a room with a mattress on the floor and a rigged-up air-conditioning system. Again, the windows were whitewashed and the sole light came from a floorlamp,—over which a red *batik* cloth had been flung in a forlorn attempt at decoration. The policeman recognised the cloth; it had once been draped over the lamp in his room.

They were alone. She looked at him properly for the first time. Then she smiled her slow, beatific smile. "Why—it's you."

Now he had found her he felt dizzy, afflicted by a kind of vertigo as though he were looking down at both of them from a great seesawing height. He spoke slowly, in between the pounding in his brain.

"I looked for you. Everywhere. *Everywhere.*"

In the places they had gone to, in the case files, in the dead and missing persons reports, which he pored over obsessively until they began to invade his dreams, this kingdom of the lost and murdered. He'd begun to wish she were dead; he'd longed for her death with the hope that others reserved for news of life; her death would have been his release.

She came over and raised a hand to his cheek; he struck her hand away.

"You're still angry. After all this time? Of course, I forgot. You were always angry."

She'd cropped her hair, which ended now in a lank bob just below her ears. Gone too was the adolescent thinness, replaced by a strange pneumatic fullness in the face and in the thickened waist. Only the dress, the blue and white dress she had bought in her first week with him, was the same. He realised, with a kind of shock, that he would not have recognised her on the street looking like this.

"How did you find me? But you were always good at that, weren't you? I've been looking out for you. I knew you'd show. I never thought you would turn up, all those times I got into trouble, and you always did. You were so dependable."

The loquacity was new, but it was a slow, effortful loquacity: her voice drifted like a hand trailing through seaweed; her movements had a dreamy, slurry quality to them. No more pinwheeling eyes; no more methamphetamines. She'd chosen sedation instead.

She repeated, "You were so dependable."

He asked, bluntly, "Why did you leave?"

"Why did I leave?" He wanted to shake her, to douse her in cold water until she broke free of her lethargy screaming. "Because I couldn't see myself playing Mary Magdalene to your Jesus Christ for the rest of my life."

"What the hell are you talking about?" "Sorry. I forgot you didn't go to a mission school." She'd always had the knack, he remembered now, of making him feel stupid, uneducated. She was speaking again. "And you're still a policeman."

He said, with unexpected bitterness, "Yes."

After she'd gone, a kind of paralysis had set in. He'd sleepwalked through the days, while the nights brought with them their tormenting insomnia, their vivid delusions that she was there beside him where she'd always been. His transfer to narcotics was approved but he turned it down; he could no longer remember the impulse that had prompted the request. He began to volunteer for night duty to avoid his rathole room but even then there was no escape. She was in the car with him while he waited in his layby, her voice sibilant in his ear; she was with him while he cruised down the highway, headlights staking a path through the darkness.

He said, and they could both hear the anger beginning to lap at the edges of his voice, "Well, aren't you going to make love to me? I've paid for this hour."

"If you want me to."

In truth, he did not want her to, not like this; this new sluggishness repelled him. He kicked at the lamp in the corner, shattering the bulb and plunging the room into near-darkness. She stumbled backwards towards the door with a little cry. "Stop this," he heard himself saying, "*stop this.*" Though whether he meant their banter or the life she had chosen for herself, he couldn't be sure. "Listen," he said with renewed urgency. "You can come away with me."

He felt, rather than saw, her shake her head.

"Why *not?*"

"I think you'd better go."

"Tell me why."

She said, and for the first time her voice sounded almost normal, the way it used to, "This is me. This is what I am."

"Is it *him?* Do you love him?"

"I detest him. But he lets me be who I am."

"Who you are—who you are—you are not this. You only think you are."

But he could feel the futility of his words beating like the wings of a maimed bird on the air.

"I tried with you. I really did. Do you believe me? But I'm not like you. I'm not responsible. I don't want to be. It's just too much *work.*" And now he could hear the old Deanna in her voice, the one that had led him out to the highway in the middle of the night just to see where God didn't enter into it.

"I don't understand. Make me understand."

"I'm not afraid. I have nothing to be afraid of. Whereas you. You're afraid of everything. What people will think. What people will say. What's in the afterlife. I don't care. I'm free."

"You're not making sense. You're not free. You hate yourself."

"So do you."

"Yes, yes, and that's why we can help each other—" He stopped. He could feel her sliding away from him, back into her trance. It was getting hard to breathe; either there was not enough air or it was heavy with dust, but a strange kind of dust, the dust of the innards of a building collapsing slowly within itself. "Deanna." Clumsily, he moved towards her. His eyes had not adjusted well to the dark; he had not noticed her hand resting on the doorknob. With one twist of the hand, she was gone.

He stumbled after her. She was nowhere to be seen and he could not remember where the dormitory was. At the end of the corridor he could see the last of the evening light tumbling into the atrium below. He began to run towards it.

ABOUT THE AUTHOR

Since beginning her writing career at the early age of seventeen, the prolific Claire Tham has gone on to pick up several accolades, including two Commendation Awards from NBDCS and another two Golden Point Awards from the SPH-NAC Short Story Writing Competitions. One of her short stories, "Lee" (from *Fascist Rock: Stories of Rebellion*), was adapted for television on MediaCorp's *Alter Asians*.

A CHIJ, Hwa Chong Junior College alumnus, Tham graduated with a degree in law from Oxford University. Away from writing, Tham is currently a partner at a prestigious law firm in Singapore.

Besides this collection of short stories, her other works include a novel, *Skimming* (first published in 1999, reissued in 2010).

p. 265 - Aimee Mann
singing "Driving Sideways"
p 366 Rhapsody in Blue
Gershwin